Sophie Last Seen
Marlene Adelstein

Sophie Last Seen
Red Adept Publishing, LLC
104 Bugenfield Court
Garner, NC 27529
http://RedAdeptPublishing.com/

First Print Edition: November 2018

Cover Art by Streetlight Graphics

This is a work of fiction. Names, characters, places, and incidents either are the product of the author's imagination or are used fictitiously, and any resemblance to locales, events, business establishments, or actual persons—living or dead—is entirely coincidental.

For my parents, Bernard and Connie, with love.

In memory of Carol Drechsler,

inspired writer, voracious reader, and quick-witted raconteur,

but, most of all, dear friend.

Rather the flight of the bird passing and leaving no trace.
Than creatures passing, leaving tracks on the ground.
The bird goes by and forgets, which is as it should be.
The creature, no longer there, and so, perfectly useless,
Shows it was there – also perfectly useless.
Remembering betrays Nature,
Because yesterday's nature is not nature.
What's past is nothing and remembering is not seeing.
Fly, bird, fly away; teach me to disappear.

from "The Keeper of Flocks" (1911-1912)
Alberto Caeiro, Portugal

Chapter One

The feel of the smooth glass stone between her index finger and thumb could always calm Jesse Albright, especially when she felt the start of a panic attack. Like now. Setting the stone down on the dashboard, she turned to the passenger seat and said to her daughter, "We're here, Soph." She pulled into the entrance of the Countryside Mall, parked the truck, and got out.

"You know the drill, sweetie." Jesse gazed around the parking lot, her head cocked to the side like a dog listening intently. Not hearing anything in particular, she strode into the mall, heading straight for the trendy clothing store, Zone, as if she owned the place then went directly to the KidsZone section.

"May I help you?"

Jesse recognized Monica's loud, nasally voice. The dark-haired high school student took her sales job way too seriously.

"Oh, great," Jesse muttered to Sophie. "You-know-who is working today."

Monica gave her a questioning look.

"I'm just browsing," Jesse said.

"You *do* like to browse here, don't you?" Monica said sarcastically.

"Yes, I do."

The girl turned toward the checkout counter and grunted.

"Blue jay, right?" Jesse said to Sophie. "That's what you'd call her. Pushy, show-offy. A bully. Right, hon?"

Monica spun around to face Jesse. "Just who are you talking to?"

Taken aback, Jesse straightened her shoulders. "No one. No one at all."

Shaking her head, the girl mumbled, "Weirdo." Then she twirled back around and walked over to the front desk, where she conferred with her young colleagues, rudely pointing and nodding toward Jesse.

No, her daughter wasn't there. She hadn't been in years. But Jesse often spoke to her and was fairly certain Sophie heard her, somehow. She didn't care if people thought she was crazy. For Jesse, who spoke to few people anymore, it was a comfort even if Sophie never actually answered back. She moved on to the circular clothes rack where she had last seen Sophie six years ago. She'd always told her daughter that if they ever got separated, she should go back to the last place they had been together. "If you were with me in the cookie aisle, wait for me back in cookies," she would say, as if it were all a game. So Jesse kept coming back to the Zone, week after week. Just in case.

Fall V-neck sweaters in autumn shades hung where colorful cotton T-shirts had been displayed That Day. Jesse stood at the very spot, her own ground zero, still looking for Sophie or any kind of clue.

"I love this, Mommy. Can I have it?" Sophie fingered a pink top *with the image of one small red bird with a black wing. Her bird obsession had begun when she was five, after her dad bought her a simple backyard feeder. After that, she'd devoured any book on the subject and began keeping a bird-watching journal. And later, she'd started her life list, an inventory of every bird she'd ever seen.*

"Not today, honey."

"But, Maaah–aaahhhm, it's so cute."

"Don't whine, Sophie. You're not a baby." Jesse was in a foul mood. *She'd been working on a commissioned painting that wasn't going well—a large oil of the Buckley Barn over in Deerfield. The perspective*

was off, and Jesse wanted to trash it. And she had argued with Cooper that morning over something stupid. Two hours later, she couldn't even remember what had precipitated it—running out of milk? Cooper having to work late again?—but it turned into their typical fight. They'd both left mad, their unspoken issues hanging in the air, heavy and unresolved. Things had been strained between them for months—little sex, no real communication, but plenty of pent-up anger.

"But, Mom, it's the tanager from this morning. Isn't that amazing?"

Jesse looked over at her daughter. She had smallish hazel eyes and dark eyebrows that made her look serious and worried. Her black binoculars hung around her neck. She never went anywhere without them and often fell asleep with them clutched in her hand at night. Jesse sometimes imagined Sophie as a young woman walking down the aisle in her wedding gown, wearing those damn things round her neck.

The pink top Sophie held had the word tweet *below the bird in a lowercase typeface. She would have looked cute in it.*

"But, Mom, I need it."

"You need *it? I don't think so. You have lots of tops."*

And those were her last words to her daughter. Jesse bit the inside of her cheek until she tasted blood, then she shook herself out of her memory.

She turned away from the KidsZone section and caught a whiff of something. *Watermelon? Sour Patch watermelon gum. Sophie's favorite.* It seemed to come from a petite teenager exiting the dressing room, carrying an armful of clothes. Her short brown hair was chopped and shaggy, as if she'd given herself a bad haircut without a mirror.

"Any luck?" Monica asked the girl.

"I'll take this one," the girl said in a high-pitched Minnie Mouse voice that made her sound about six years old. There was something about the girl, something familiar, and it wasn't just the watermelon gum.

Jesse turned back and cruised through the store, making her usual rounds. She touched the clothes, scanned the floor, the shelves, and the racks, sliding hangers over, looking for that missing piece of the puzzle. A secret hatch in the floor where a ten-year-old girl could have fallen and disappeared. An article of clothing. A shoe. But there was nothing. As usual. It was just a store like any other.

Not bothering to check for size, Jesse grabbed a long-sleeved white top and headed for the dressing rooms. Over the years, she methodically checked each dressing room over and over. She walked past the numerous vacant ones, bending down to look under the closed door of each cubicle in case Sophie was hiding there.

She entered the last one, locked the door, and sat on the small bench. She tried to avoid looking in the full-length mirror, not wanting to see what she'd become. At forty-eight, her face was drawn and pale, her body thinner than it had ever been. But her startling white mane was the first thing people noticed and still something she couldn't get used to. Sprinkled with black, the mass of wispy strands hovered about her head like a prairie warbler's nest. Even though she had stopped painting after That Day, she still dressed like an artist in paint-splattered, patched jeans and men's oversized thrift store shirts. She hadn't cared about her appearance, put on any makeup, or had a haircut in years.

No one would be able to tell that she'd once had a happy life. A husband. A child. Work she loved. She exhaled, whispering her mantra, "Mommy, Daddy, Sophie," her eyes glistening. Memories of her old life were always seeping into her brain. Trying to keep them at bay was exhausting.

A shiny reflection bounced off the mirror, something on the floor catching the light just so. She got down on her knees and reached under the bench, and as sometimes happened two, three, and four times a day, Jesse found a lost item. It was an old Nokia flip phone. "2 Voice Messages," the screen said. It wasn't password-protected, and she played back the messages. Both were hang-ups. The numbers were from an area code she didn't recognize. She snooped around, looking for photos and texts. She found only one blurry photo of someone's feet wearing purple flip-flops. It was hard to tell if it had been taken on purpose. If the phone had received any texts, they must have been deleted. She tossed the phone into her purse to examine it later.

Exiting the dressing room, she saw that teenager again, walking out of the store with a Zone bag. The girl wore purple flip-flops. So it was her phone. The girl could have been sixteen. *The age Sophie would be now.*

Sophie had long brown hair, but that was years ago. It could be short now, like the girl's. And Jesse realized the girl had Sophie's habit of biting her lower lip, giving her the same worried expression. But the high-pitched voice wasn't Sophie's. The girl wasn't Jesse's daughter, yet something pushed her on. Jesse followed her and the sugary scent of watermelon gum into the food court, where she often observed teen girls. Over the years, she'd followed some as they texted and gabbed into their cell phones, oblivious to everything but their addictive plastic screens. Jesse often saw teens who resembled the grown-up Sophie in Jesse's imagination. But when Jesse got close, the similarities always faded away.

The girl with the choppy hair and purple flip-flops glanced behind her. Her eyes met Jesse's, then she sped up and ducked into the entrance of the Cineplex without buying a ticket.

Jesse followed the girl until she felt a firm hand on her arm, accompanied by a deep male voice. "You'll have to come with me." He was a linebacker-sized man in a navy-blue blazer with Security embroidered on the pocket.

"Oh, I'm not going to the movies. I left something in there. I'm not crashing or anything."

"I've been watching you. I've seen you loitering around here before, stalking teen girls. They got names for people like you."

"What? No, no. I'm not going to hurt anyone."

He tugged Jesse along by the arm. "Explain it to my boss."

AN HOUR LATER, SHE was still sitting alone in an airless basement office in an uncomfortable hard-backed chair. She was dying for a cigarette, but a large No Smoking sign loomed down at her from the wall. She'd had enough, gotten up, and reached for the doorknob, only to realize she was locked in.

"You gotta be kidding me." She pounded her fist on the door. "Hey! Somebody open up!"

She sat back down, extracted a cigarette from her jacket pocket, and nervously lit up. She touched her purse on her lap, feeling the book inside it, and her shoulders dropped with relief.

A couple of minutes later, she heard the sound of a key in the lock. She quickly tossed the cigarette on the floor, ground it out with her heel, and waved the air in front of her face.

The security guard who had hauled her in entered, followed by a burly guy with an air of authority and a crew cut. Burly, obviously the boss, sat at his desk, and his underling bent down and whispered in his ear, "Bird Mom," as if Jesse weren't sitting just two feet from him and couldn't hear. That was how Jesse had been referred to in the newspapers and online after That Day. The boss glanced up at Jesse, steely eyed. She knew people gossiped about her and "Bird Girl," as Sophie had come to be known.

"Listen," she said, clutching her purse to her chest, "there's been a big mistake. I did nothing wrong." She turned to the guard who had grabbed her. "What did I do? Nothing!"

His boss proceeded to lecture her, claiming to have numerous videos from the mall's security cameras, showing her following young girls. "You're lucky, Mrs. Albright. I'm going to let you off today, but I don't want to ever see you here in the Countryside Mall again." He spoke to her as if she were an insolent child, wagging his finger. "Not at the Cineplex or the food court. And definitely not the Zone. And if you do, charges will be pressed. I'm sorry for your tragedy, but I got my job to do. This is no joke. We'll be watching."

She stood, fists clenched. "What's the idea, locking me in here? I'm not some criminal, for God's sake. I'm a mother. I have rights. And I have a lawyer, who you'll be hearing from."

She raced out of there, relieved to finally be out of that hellhole. She would need to lie low for a while, and of course, they would never hear from any lawyer.

Jesse sat in the parking lot in her twilight-blue Ford Ranger, which she'd gotten when she'd traded in the Volvo wagon, her one attempt to remove any remnants of family life. She let her head rest on the steering wheel while she took deep calming breaths. She rubbed her glass stone. Lately, her thoughts and actions had felt out of control, as if some evil puppet master were pulling her strings. She took out the tattered paperback copy of *Bixby's Birder's Bible* from her purse. The book fell open to page five, where Jesse had repeatedly opened the book to reread a particular passage.

She read aloud from the first chapter. "Birding is fun because you never know what to expect, what birds you will find, or how long they will stay before flying off. Each time out is a new adventure. Some birds"—Jesse lifted her eyes from the page and recited from memory—"are elusive and particularly difficult to find."

Sophie was her elusive bird, reluctant to show herself. Jesse's own ivory-billed woodpecker. She gazed out the window and scanned the parking lot slowly, then she went in reverse. She continued to recite,

"To find birds, you must pay close attention and be patient. Stop. Wait. Watch. And most of all... listen."

She closed the book and held it to her chest. She had to keep the faith. She took one more look out the windshield, then kept her head still while she listened. Tires on pavement. Cars honking. Kids shouting and laughing. She wasn't sure what she was listening for but figured she would know it when she heard it. She slid the book back into her purse and started up the truck. She headed onto Interstate 91 then picked up Route 9 in Northampton. The drive from the mall in South Holyoke back to her home in Canaan was a good forty minutes, but it gave her time to think.

Today had not been a good day. Being called out by that snotty salesgirl. Hauled in by that guard. Humiliated by his boss. Years ago, a policeman had given her a pamphlet: *When Your Child Is Missing: A Family Survival Guide*. Jesse had read and reread it a thousand times, and for her, life had become all about survival. "Force yourself to eat and sleep. Find time for physical exercise." Those made sense. But she took one command most seriously of all: "Never stop looking."

She was exhausted physically, mentally, and emotionally. The years of not knowing had taken their toll. And the recent disastrous call from Cooper about selling the house weighed heavily on her. She didn't know how much longer she could hold on. She glanced in her rearview mirror as if she might see Sophie. "C'mon, Soph. Drop me a clue. A tiny nugget. Please, sweetie. Please."

She made her way back through Canaan with its classic New England farmhouses and stately white churches. But what had drawn her to the tiny western Massachusetts hill town in the first place was the simplicity: no big box stores or strip malls and spotty cell service. It was a sleepy community east of the Berkshires, population 1,835, where dairy, sheep, and maple sugaring farmers mingled with city transplants, like she and Cooper had been, looking for a gentler life.

It was a sweet, peaceful town, where they had good neighbors. And they'd loved living there.

She drove down the extra-wide tree-lined main street and by the town lake where she and Sophie used to swim. Well, Jesse would swim while Sophie bird-watched. She passed the quaint clapboard-covered shops and two-pump Citgo, and she saw something large in the middle of the road. A fallen tree limb perhaps. She pulled the truck over, got out, and saw it was a downed road sign. Someone, maybe drunk, must have plowed into it the previous night. It was a banged-up yellow metal No Stopping sign. Jesse saw where it used to be posted in front of the Canaan church. She looked around stealthily and, when she didn't see anyone, picked it up. It was heavier than she'd imagined, and she hauled it into the bed of her truck. Another clue from Sophie. "No stopping" meant "Keep looking."

As she slid back behind the wheel, she overheard some man she hadn't noticed near the church say, "That's public property. You can't take that."

Screw him, she thought and drove on. Up the road, she caught a glimpse of her boss and old friend, Blue Silverman, lugging a box of hardbacks in his arms. He was heading toward the Book Barn, where they worked selling, of all ridiculous things, used books.

She thought back to the conversation she'd had with him yesterday.

"Jess," Blue had said while sitting on the corner of his desk. Wearing overalls and a full graying beard, he looked every bit the old hippie his name suggested. "Star has started to work here after school on your off days."

"You mentioned she might."

"She's sixteen now. Seems more like a walking black cloud."

Jesse fiddled with some papers. "Sounds typical... from what I hear."

"Beth and I just want to get her out of her room. Learn about earning money. Responsibility. Anyway, she may overlap with you some days. You okay with that?"

What was she going to say? That she didn't want her quiet oasis of the Book Barn shattered by a sullen sixteen-year-old? That she didn't want her daughter's best friend around her? That although she used to love Star, after That Day, the sight of her was more than she could handle?

Get over yourself, she'd thought. The job got her out of her house and out of her head. "You're the boss, Blue."

She looked back over at him crossing the street. If he'd known how she'd spent her day off, or every day off, he might not be so accommodating. She flipped him a wave and drove on through town.

Chapter Two

Already a good hour late for her meeting with Gary, her realtor, Jesse pulled into the long drive on Blueberry Lane. The neighborhood was newer and more monied than where she lived in Canaan. The house was a modern design, all tall glass and sharp angles.

Jesse burst through the door and found Gary pacing in the kitchen.

He rushed up to her. "I didn't think you were coming."

"Sorry, I got held up," she said, rummaging around in her purse for another cigarette.

He was in his early forties and wore out-of-fashion large wire-rimmed glasses. With his shaggy hair that hung over his ears and wrinkly sweater, he looked like a rumpled John Denver. And although she wasn't one to advertise it, Jesse had liked John Denver in the day.

"I was worried," he said. "You're so late."

She found a cigarette, lit it nervously, and inhaled deeply.

"Are you okay?" He put both his hands on her shoulders.

She wasn't about to tell Gary about her weekly trips to the mall or her run-in with security. He knew enough of her secrets; he didn't need to know all that, too. There would be no more Zone, and she didn't know what she'd do without it. She had recently walked out on her therapist, Lila, for the third time in two years. That woman had a way of pushing Jesse's buttons. So Jesse would have to deal with it on her own.

She took another drag of her cigarette and watched as Gary distractedly rearranged the various realtors' business cards that had been left on the kitchen counter. On the card for his company, Hill Town Homes, his phone number and website were printed alongside an old photo of him wearing a droopy mustache he'd shaved off years ago. He'd never gotten around to having another photo taken. The poor guy always had good intentions but never seemed to get it together.

Jesse wandered to the picture window and gazed at the wooded yard out back. The little cabin next door, tucked away behind a stand of pine trees, had been empty all summer, and it was already closed for the oncoming winter. With its shades drawn tightly, it looked lonely and desolate, just how Jesse felt.

After Cooper moved out, Gary's wife, Carol, had begun her persistent prodding, bugging Jesse to look at houses with him. "How can you live in that house without Sophie or Cooper?" she'd asked. "The memories have to be killing you."

Jesse feared that if she moved, Sophie wouldn't know where to find her, and she still had a fantasy of coming home from work one day to find Sophie playing in her bedroom as if the nightmare had never happened. So she'd refused for years, until finally, she gave in and went to look at a listing. She was up-front with Gary and told him she had no interest in moving, not revealing the real reason.

Now Jesse turned abruptly and kissed him while backing him against the granite kitchen island. They stood that way for a minute, frantically kissing and touching.

"Looking at houses" had quickly turned into a long-standing affair. The vacant house on Blueberry Lane had been on the market for two years, and it had become one of their regular rendezvous spots.

She grabbed his arm and led him upstairs, ducking into the master bath and the enormous newly renovated marble walk-in shower. She pulled off his sweater as he unzipped her jeans and removed her shirt. She took his hands and held them over his head as she pushed her whole body against him, pressing him into the cool white marble. She craved his healing touch. The skin-to-skin contact was like a salve.

She closed her eyes. She didn't want to think about missing girls. Or the gruesome scenarios that tormented her constantly. Cold dark rooms. The scent of urine. Horrible threats. Dark attics and basements. Knives and blood. Sexual assaults. Nor did she want to keep thinking about the recent upsetting phone conversation with Cooper. Him telling her she had to put the house on the market within the month because he couldn't afford two mortgages any longer. Having to leave the safety of her cocoon. Her home. Sophie's home.

A few years after That Day, Cooper had divorced Jesse, remarried, left town, and had another child. Jesse had remained in their family home, waiting. Alone. She shut it all out and breathed in, letting herself be swept away. Northern Gannett. That was what she would be—a most spectacular gleaming white sea bird that glided and flapped in flight. She felt weightless, soaring, rising, swooping. Free.

They finished, falling against each other and the slick marble in a sweaty heap. How she wished the reprieve could last longer. *Create space for yourself. Find a place of refuge—away from the pressure of the search and the investigation, where you can be alone with your thoughts and regroup.* No matter that its advice might not have been apt after so many years, she still followed the instructions in the survival guide. The affair was her refuge. She needed it... desperately. The guide book, along with her job, had saved her. Jesse reached for her clothes, but Gary pulled her back into the shower and kissed her.

"Oh God, what do I do about you?" He grasped her hands, lacing his fingers through hers. He kissed her breasts. "You're beautiful."

She shook her head. "No, I'm not."

"You are." He played with strands of her hair.

She handed him his underwear, then she stepped into her panties and pulled her top over her head. Looking at herself in the mirror, she shuddered involuntarily. Her stomach growled as it always did after sex with him.

Gary stood behind her and put his chin into the crook of her neck. They stared at themselves in the mirror.

"We look good together, don't we?" he said.

They stood that way for a whole quiet minute. Gary was slight, small in stature, and jittery. A piping plover. Sophie had pointed one out on the beach in Wellfleet. Always on the move, it darted about in jerky, anxious movements. But Gary was a kind bird. He didn't judge her. He was there for her in his way. The winter after Cooper left, Gary had flown over to her house with a blow dryer to thaw the frozen kitchen pipes, then he'd raked snow off the roof. He was considerate, and she was grateful for that.

Cooper, on the other hand, was strong, aggressive, and masculine. Hawk. She missed him and the good days of long ago, the years before it all turned black and unraveled. She missed herself, for that matter. She'd gone from a carefree white-throated sparrow to a gangly, aggressive brown thrasher.

She looked up, and Gary turned and hugged her tightly.

"Don't be sad," he whispered. "I'm here for you."

He meant well, but his words just made her feel sadder. She smiled at him and shook her head. "Oh, Gary, we're a pair."

He slipped his hand under her shirt and caressed her breasts.

She stepped into her jeans then tried to neaten her hair, which wouldn't be neatened. It always had that wild just-had-sex look even without any sex.

The sound of a car engine coming up the driveway ended their moment. They both looked out the window and saw Peggy Collins, another realtor and the town gossip, get out of her SUV with a young couple.

"Shit." Gary frantically tugged on his clothes. He brushed his hands through his hair, adjusted his glasses, then nodded for Jesse to follow him. They headed downstairs. He turned back to Jesse and said loudly and stiffly, "Nice bathroom renovation, wouldn't you say, Ms. Albright?"

Peggy stood in the middle of the living room, her pink lipstick clashing with her dyed red hair, her arms crossed over her chest. A bright-eyed couple stood next to her and stared as Jesse and Gary came down the stairs. Jesse avoided eye contact.

"Oh, hello, Peggy," Gary said.

"Showing Mrs. Albright yet another house, eh?"

"There's always another house."

"Your sweater's on backward, Gary."

His eyes darted to the young couple momentarily. "Ah, thanks, Peggy," he stuttered, "but I always wear it like this. Have a nice day, folks." He nodded and followed Jesse out the front door. They walked over to their cars.

"Fucking Peggy. That was too close," he whispered then glanced back while slipping out of the arms of his sweater and turning it right side front. "You know this Saturday is the Pumpkin Harvest Festival thingy. Carol always organizes the party. You used to come, remember? I know you won't go, but she told me to remind you when I saw you. She knew I was showing you a house."

Jesse tilted her head. "She *really* doesn't know about us?"

He shook his head.

"Maybe I'll just have to make an appearance at this party. I haven't been to one in years."

"What? You're kidding, right? About coming." He looked at her, squinting. "I figured you'd never go. That's really not a good idea, Jess."

Jesse knew Carol. She'd been in a book club with her years ago. They'd been casual friends. She was an executive at some computer software company based in Pittsfield. A real go-getter. The opposite of Gary. Jesse had done a good job of mostly avoiding Carol, giving a quick wave and hightailing it if she saw her in town. Jesse didn't want to hurt her—she liked Carol—but it wasn't about Carol. The affair was Jesse's coping mechanism. Her key to sanity. She thought back on what Lila had said the day she had finally confessed the affair in a session. "Passive-aggressive and self-destructive. You've created your own set of rules." Jesse remembered Lila sitting there all high and mighty. She had tapped her pen rhythmically on her yellow pad. "You need to own your actions."

Looking up at Gary, Jesse shook her head. "Don't worry. I'm not going to the Harvest Fest." She walked toward her truck.

He called after her, "So, have you given this house another thought? Quality bathroom reno, huh? Great light?"

"Give it up, Gary," she said, sliding into her pickup, then drove off.

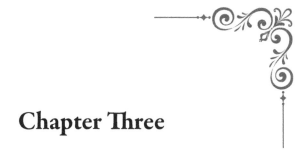

Chapter Three

While peering out the front window of the cabin, Star Silverman watched Jesse Albright drive off in her truck. She turned back to Ophelia, the new girl she'd met that day. The odd name seemed to fit the girl. She'd come into the Book Barn, trying to sell a stack of moldy books she'd probably found in the trash.

Star had started working for her dad at the shop recently, hoping to get her parents off her back about finding a job. It was easy, and mostly, she just sat around playing music or texting Ruby. There weren't many customers wanting used books. *Who even buys books anymore, let alone old smelly ones?*

So when the girl walked in looking lost, Star had felt sorry for her and given her a few bucks out of the petty cash box. Maybe it was her little-girl voice. Or her really bad haircut. Maybe Star had been kind of lonely herself lately. All her friends, except Ruby, had seemed to disappear. They didn't get her anymore. Or maybe it was the other way around. Star just wasn't very interested in them. They were all about what colleges to apply to and what they were going to major in. Star couldn't concentrate on schoolwork, and she'd done poorly on her SATs. She had other things on her mind—ugly things that crept into her brain and took work to tamp down.

"Where do you live?" Star had asked Ophelia.

"I'm just passing through. I kind of need a place to crash. Could I maybe stay with you? I could sleep on the floor, just for a night or two."

No way Star's parents would allow some stranger to sleep over. And she couldn't risk sneaking her in. But there was something about the girl. A desperation in her eyes. "I know a place," Star had said.

"What are you looking at?" Ophelia said, pulling Star back to the here and now.

Star stepped away from the window. "Nothing." But she still watched as Jesse turned out of the drive. She thought about the old days. Back when she and Sophie were BFFs. Back when Star hung out at the Albrights' house practically twenty-four, seven and Jesse was really nice to her. She had to admit it; she used to have a serious mom crush on Jesse. Star had wanted Jesse for her own mother. Jesse was totally awesome, with her messy hair and the holey jeans she wore before they were even in style. She was so unlike Star's own mother, who was just a regular mom—uncool. Jesse's paintings were big and loaded with extra-thick paint. Landscapes mostly and lots of barns. But after Sophie went missing, everything changed. Jesse's hair literally turned white, like she was some cartoon character who'd just seen a ghost. She started hoarding junk, or at least that's what everybody said. She barely left the house. It was all so confusing to Star back then. She'd tried to stay close to Jesse, who'd only pushed Star away as if she had some disease.

"Star, it's time you hung out with kids your own age," Jesse had said, sounding like a robot.

Star's mom said that Jesse was in pain. "You remind her of Sophie."

AFTER WORK, STAR DROVE Ophelia to the Stop-n-Shop in her new car. She'd gotten her license last month and inherited her dad's old Honda, which gave him an excuse to buy the latest Prius.

Ophelia picked up chips, an energy drink, and cereal. *A real health food nut. Not!*

Then they drove to Blueberry Lane, where Star had discovered the deserted cabin not far from her home. It was next door to a fancy house where Jesse and her "secret" boyfriend, Gary, met. When Star first discovered the cabin, she noticed one of the back windows was unlocked and easy to climb through. It was a cool place to hang out and spy on Jesse. There was no such thing as privacy any-more—everybody knew that—so Star didn't think she was doing anything wrong. Not much anyway.

Star climbed in the window as usual and opened the door for Ophelia, who walked in and gazed around the place. She took note of the small bedroom, couch, and kitchenette, even opening the fridge and looking inside, checking out drawers and cupboards. "Wow, Star. This place rocks."

Star couldn't tell how old Ophelia was. She could be fifteen or even seventeen. She was all covered up with a ratty red hoodie and jeans. Hardly a fashionista, but Star should talk. Lately, she could barely drag herself out of bed, let alone put on nice clothes. And her hair, which usually got her compliments because it was long and normally really shiny, had been looking dull and greasy, as if she'd stopped washing it, even though she hadn't.

"This place has been closed up for the season. No electricity or water. There are blankets, but no working shower or toilet, and the fridge is turned off, too. So you can't stay here long." She hoped no one would come snooping around and find Ophelia. Jesse and Gary always seemed preoccupied and in a hurry. Star had even crouched down close to the big house and looked in on them through a win-dow a couple of times and seen them having sex. Star wasn't sure why she was obsessed with knowing what Jesse was up to, but watching her was like binging on a real-life reality show.

As Star wandered into the bedroom and plopped onto the bed, Ophelia followed. "How old are you?" Star asked.

Ophelia glanced up at the ceiling. "Twenty-one, but I've always looked young."

No way this girl is twenty-one. "Did you run away from home?"

"I'm twenty-one. I don't live at home anymore. I graduated, like, eons ago. I have my own place."

Star didn't buy it. "Awesome. Then why are you here?"

She exhaled. "I'm taking a little break. Don't you ever feel like you need to get away from it all?"

"Duh. Like all the time, but I live with my parents." She rubbed her fingers on the quilt. It was soft, with tangerine-colored flowers. Whoever owned the cabin had good taste. "Where are you from anyway?"

Ophelia looked away, as if she didn't hear the question.

Star tried again. "Are you from around here?"

She shrugged. "Star, don't ask me so many questions."

"Sorry."

They didn't speak for a long time. Ophelia bit her fingernail. "I like your name. Star."

She rolled her eyes. "I hate it. My parents thought they were hippies when they were young and had to go and name me a stupid hippie name. It wasn't the sixties, for God's sake. Do you know how many starfish jokes I've had to live through?"

"I like it. It's pretty. Romantic."

"Whatever."

"You're lucky. This seems like a nice town, and you have nice parents who care about you."

"No offense, but how do you know? My parents are okay, but Canaan is boring as hell." Star started babbling away about leaving town, visiting her favorite cousin, Harry, at college. "He's in upstate New York. Bard College. He's going to be a filmmaker. I've visited him there. It's cool. That's where I'm going to school. I'm going to be an artist." There she was, blabbing a bunch of stuff to a total stranger. She hadn't realized how starved she was for conversation. She'd been spending a lot of time alone lately. Ruby had a new boyfriend, and Star never liked being a third wheel. Ophelia seemed kind of weird, but she was a good listener.

"Star, you're not going to tell anyone about me, are you?"

"Why would I?"

"I don't know. I just would rather you didn't."

"No problem."

"Thanks."

"Is there someone you need to call, like your parents, to tell them you're okay?"

"They're the last people I want to talk to. My dad's dead, and my mom's a heroin addict. She's hooked up with this total creep. He dopes her up at night and comes into my room."

Star tilted her head. "I thought you said you had your own place."

"Right. I do." She sat up and looked away. "I mean he used to before I moved out."

"Oh." There was definitely something off about this girl.

Ophelia looked down at the ground then back up at Star. "Did that hurt?" She nodded at Star's wrist.

A green-and-black barbed-wire tattoo encircled her left wrist like a bracelet. She'd gotten it the weekend she visited Harry, using some phony ID he'd gotten her. "It kind of stung when the guy was doing it. Now I forget it's there. Of course my mom went ballistic." And she laughed, since that was basically the reason she gotten it. She wasn't sure why messing with her mom was so much fun. It just was.

"I'm going to get one," Ophelia said. "An angel with big white wings and a sweet smiling face. On my back, right above my butt."

"Oh. Okay." *Who doesn't want a smiley angel on their back?* Star thought. *Gross.*

"I really appreciate your helping me, but I don't have money or anything to give you. Just so you know."

Star hugged her knees. "Shit, Ophelia. I'm not doing this for money. I'm just helping out a girl who needs a place to stay. It's fucking nuts out there, you know. There are lunatics and crazies and drug addicts and whackos that prey on young girls."

Ophelia zipped her sweatshirt up to her neck then flipped the hood over her head. "You're creeping me out, Star." She bit her bottom lip, reminding Star of the way Sophie looked when she was off in a Sophie trance.

"Well, it's true. I had a friend when we were ten... who just disappeared. I mean she was snatched or something, and they never found her. It's too scary to think what might have happened to her." Lately, though, that was all she could think about. She'd shoved the terrifying thoughts away, and they'd stayed tucked in a dark corner of her brain for years. But then she kept hearing scary news reports of other missing girls, the thoughts popped out, and Star couldn't put them back. She pulled a Camel out of her jacket pocket and offered it to Ophelia. She shook her head, so Star lit it for herself.

"You mean they climbed in her bedroom window and kidnapped her?"

"No, I mean she disappeared from a fucking Zone. She was even with her mother."

"Wow, I was at a Zone today. That's terrible."

Star didn't say that nobody but her mom shopped at the Zone anymore. Plus she wouldn't be caught dead in one nowadays. Just walking by the store made her start shaking.

"God, you must miss her."

"Yes. No. I don't know." She took a drag of her cigarette. "I guess."

Ophelia sat up tall. "Maybe she'll turn up one day. Wouldn't that be amazing? Like you'll be at the mall or the Olive Garden, and sud-

denly, you see her walk in. You'll have a 'holy shit!' moment, and
you'll shout out her name...what was her name?"

"Sophie."

"Yeah, you'll shout out her name, like, 'Hey, Sophie... is that
you?' And she'll stop and turn and look at you and run into your
arms, and you'll hug for like ten minutes and start crying. She'll look
all pretty and grown up. Someone will film it, and it'll go viral. Then
you'll both become famous. Maybe that will happen." Ophelia's eyes
were wide, and she smiled like she'd just unwrapped the greatest
Christmas present ever.

Star said, "You're cracked. She's dead. Her decomposed body is
lying in some ditch. Or her bones are in a Hefty bag in some hand-
dug grave after she was forced to commit vile sex acts on some per-
vert. Maybe she was tortured or buried alive, brainwashed or muti-
lated then raped and killed." Her mind went back to the three Cleveland girls who were all over the news a while ago. "Or she's alive being held by some sicko in an attic, chained to the wall, and she's had
his baby. After all these years, there's no fucking happy flowery rose-
scented ending to this story. That's the thing of it. Your mind just
wanders to all the awful but probably real possibilities. There is no
good news in this story, Ophelia. No happy ending. Wake up and
smell the rat poison."

"Jeez. That's so dark."

"Welcome to the real world, girl. It could happen to anyone. It
could've happened to me. I could've been at the Zone that day with
them. I was normally with her, like, all the time." Star couldn't help
it. She felt the need to protect the girl, to tell her the facts of life.
"You can't trust anybody. Well, I mean you can trust me. I won't hurt
you, but probably you shouldn't even trust me. Definitely don't trust
men." She checked the time on her cell phone. "Shit. I better go. Do
you think you'll be okay?"

Ophelia nodded apprehensively.

"Lock the door after I leave."

Star walked over to the window she'd climbed in and locked it. She went to each window, checked the locks, then double-checked them. She found a flashlight in a drawer. It worked, and she handed it to Ophelia. "You'll need this. The phone is disconnected. Do you have a cell?"

"I did, but I lost it."

Star thought for a minute. Life without her cell was, well... torture. But she needed to help the girl. She could always snatch her mom's iPhone for a while. She'd done it before. "Take mine for now, just in case. Don't use up my minutes on bullshit. I mean it. My parents are crazed about my minutes. Just be careful. I'll come and check on you tomorrow after school. But if I was you, I'd be thinking about a plan. You can't stay here forever."

WHEN SHE GOT HOME, Star found her mom scrubbing the kitchen countertop furiously, her dirty-blond ponytail bobbing up and down. That couldn't be good. She usually turned to cleaning when she was upset—washing the floor after a fight with Star's dad or scrubbing toilets when she was exasperated with Star. She was wearing her long Kiss the Cook apron over her too-baggy mom jeans. Star had seen photos of her mom when she was young. She'd been a dancer, and she was hot. She still had an amazing body for an old person, even if she never showed it off and refused to buy a decent pair of jeans that fit right.

"Where were you?" her mom asked, glaring at her.

"No place."

She rubbed the countertop harder. "I called you, and some girl answered. Did you lose your cell again?"

"You must have dialed wrong." *Damn. I should have told Ophelia not to pick up if Mom called.*

"How could I dial wrong, Star? I have you on memory. Who were you with?"

"God, Mom. No one. You know how lame you are with technology."

"We waited. We finally ate without you."

"I told you to start without me."

"Chicken parmesan, your favorite."

"Mom, seriously? I've told you like a million times—I'm vegan now." Star sighed loudly. Her mom had some mental block about it.

"All right, all right." She shook her head. "You're inconsiderate, Star."

Star looked up at the ceiling and mouthed, "Blah, blah, blah." She'd heard it all before. She went to the fridge and saw her mom had left a whole plate of chicken parm for her. And it did look good. And she was really hungry and not like religiously vegan, but her mom had ticked her off, so she grabbed a water instead. She knew it was stupid, but she did it anyway.

"I can make you something else. Something vegetarian."

"Vegan. There's a difference."

"Vegan," she said, like it was a dirty word.

"I'm not hungry."

"How can you not be hungry? Did you eat already?"

"Why do I have to tell you my every little move? I'm not three years old," she said, whining like she *was* three years old.

"Star, have some respect. I'm your mother." She turned to the living room and shouted, "Blue, will you please step in here? Star is being rude again."

In the living room, Star's dad lifted his head from his newspaper and glanced at them. "Star, listen to your mother," he said then went back to reading. He liked to stay out of the fray.

Looking at Star pleadingly and using a softer, calmer voice, her mom said, "Star, what is it? Why can't we have a normal conversation? I've seen you speak to other people."

In recent years, Star was either fighting with her mom over the stupidest stuff, like food or her messy room, or feeling guilty about the mean things she'd said. And the closer it got to college, the more Star said and did things to set her mom off. Star knew she was pushing her mom away. The thought of being far away from her parents in some antiseptic dorm room actually freaked her out. She loved her parents.

"Honey, I'm worried about you. You look terrible. Are you feeling okay?"

Star was so not into the conversation. She took a drink of her water. Her mom exhaled and released her shoulders, letting her anger subside.

Star could never tell her mom how she really felt or that a once-well-adjusted kid had slipped into freakdom and become a total worrier, a real loser. She was good at covering up, though. *Maybe I should think about becoming an actress,* she thought, walking into the living room to see her dad.

"Hey, sweetie." He put his paper down and looked up at her. He still insisted on getting a real newspaper instead of reading it online. Totally old school.

"Hi, Daddy." They bumped fists, their little ritual, and he smiled. Her dad was also clueless, but somehow, he didn't bug her the way her mom did.

"We missed you at dinner. You should have called when you saw you were going to be late."

"Sorry, Daddy." She gave him a kiss. That worked every time.

He pulled back and looked at her questioningly, his brow furrowed.

"What?" she said.

"You been smoking?"

Shit. Forgot to eat some Tic Tacs. "Some of my friends were smoking, and it gets in my clothes and hair and makes me reek of it. I hate it. It stinks, doesn't it?"

She wasn't sure if he bought it. "It's a terrible habit," he said. "There's lung cancer, of course. And it's really hard to quit. Not to mention cigarettes are expensive. Don't you guys care about any of that?"

"You know kids, Dad. They like to experiment and think they look cool. Didn't you ever try smoking when you were young?"

"Me? Never." He gave her a wicked smile. She knew for a fact her dad had smoked, plus he was a pothead in college and still smoked weed. When she was low, she even snuck a little from the stash in his underwear drawer. That was one thing father and daughter had in common. And she also knew that her mom used to be into it, too. *Maybe if Mom smoked pot more, she'd lighten up some.*

Parents used to be just like kids. They did exactly the same stuff—drugs, sex, and alcohol. They used to be fun and have a good time. Then they grew up and started acting like what kids did was so shocking. Star didn't understand what the big surprise was all about.

"How's work going at the shop?" he said.

"Great. It's fun." *Ha*, she thought. *Most boring lame job in town.* Ruby worked at the fitness center, where she got to use the machines, take free yoga classes, and look at hot guys. Heather worked at Fresh, the cute new clothes store. She got a big discount. Meanwhile, Star got all the free old dusty books she wanted. *Oh goodie.*

She waved to him then headed up to her room.

Chapter Four

As usual, by the time Jesse left Gary, that intense feeling of relief was gone. And when she pulled up to 421 Bug Hill Road, the reality of her life was waiting for her once again. The old farmhouse was in need of serious TLC. Its front porch sagged, and its paint, a dingy and dirty off-white, was peeling badly. The grass was overgrown, and her once-lovely cottage flower beds had been inundated with clover and poison ivy. Out back, a ramshackle barn listed to the right, looking as though it might fall down with the next storm. If one didn't know, they would assume the house was abandoned, which was mostly true.

She reached into her mailbox and pulled out a stack of bills and a piece of paper that fluttered to the ground. She picked it up, unfolded it, and saw it was a dictionary page that included the words: *retribution, retrieve, revenge, reverse, revile, revise.*

Another clue. How it'd gotten there, she didn't know. But when she thought about it, the words could pertain to her life. Sophie used to sit and read the old Webster dictionary Jesse had received as a high school graduation present from her parents. An odd thing for a kid to do, but Sophie wasn't a typical kid. She was extremely bright, intense, creative, and unpredictable. So knowledgeable and articulate about her birds, she sounded far older than her actual age. Jesse remembered when Sophie stumbled onto the word for the nesting place of birds, a *rookery,* and how enchanted she was with it, using it all the time. Jesse and Cooper had started slipping it into sentences, too. But their daughter could also be stubborn and obsessive, existing in her own Sophie world.

Jesse stood on the wraparound porch, looking out at the large front yard. Cedar trees and forsythia lined the edges, and lilac bushes and hydrangeas near the house exploded in lavender and magenta in spring and summer. She thought back to her recent conversation with Cooper and his demand for her to sell the house. She had known it would happen someday, but she still wasn't ready. The house was all she had left of her old life. Of Sophie. She had to hold on to it. She had loved the house and loved living there with her family. And besides, she wondered who would want to buy the neglected and possibly cursed house.

A slight breeze blew, rustling the leaves. For a second, she thought she saw something off in the distance. It could have been a large bird. Or... "Sophie?" she whispered.

She turned and let herself into the house. The initial sight of the living room was always a shock, as if she'd forgotten how she'd left it. She inhaled sharply. Years' worth of ephemera and objects were stacked in overflowing boxes that lined the perimeter of the room then turned into a mazelike pathway shoved next to the couch and chairs. Jesse had haphazardly labeled the boxes in black marker. *Paper* boxes held massive mounds of notes, letters, clippings, lists, and receipts. Others were marked Jewelry, Clothing, Metal, Wood, Toys, Knick-knacks, and Miscellaneous. The boxes held everything from passionate love letters to quirky shopping lists and broken eyeglasses to rusted mufflers. She collected anything and everything that people had lost or discarded. Her living room looked like a junkyard—an organized one but a junkyard nonetheless.

She'd heard people in town talking about her behind her back, mumbling about hoarding. They would glance at her with disapproving looks. She supposed they'd seen her hauling her finds into her truck or noticed the piles that had started to accumulate next to the barn, where she stored the larger items she didn't bring inside: a busted Raleigh bicycle, a store mannequin, and funny-shaped metal pieces whose purpose she couldn't begin to guess. The No Stopping sign would go there. She realized the piles made it look like the house of one of those scary hoarders on reality TV, and she even attempted watching an episode once to convince herself otherwise. Those hoarders were disgusting. Some had bugs and rodents in their homes, crawling out of their dirty stuff. That wasn't her. Her house was a bit cluttered, but each piece was important, and she was clean. She had quickly shut off the show but Googled "the difference between collecting and hoarding" to prove to herself she wasn't crazy. Collectors displayed their items proudly. Compulsive hoarders were often isolated, embarrassed by their habits, and very distressed when confronted with the prospect of discarding their items. She had shouted, "I'm not a hoarder. I'm a mother, damnit!" and slammed down the lid of her laptop.

When she was part of a real family with Cooper and Sophie, the house was a normal home. Tidy. Cozy. The scent of baking apple pie or chocolate chip cookies wafted through the place. But that was before That Day, before she began finding things. It began with Sophie's birding book, the Bixby Bible. After Sophie went missing, Jesse had found it next to Sophie's bed. That wasn't unusual since she studied it obsessively. It was the bookmark at Chapter One, "How to Find Birds," with its pink-highlighted passages that convinced Jesse her daughter was guiding her. *To find birds, you must pay close attention and be patient. Stop. Wait. Watch. And most of all... listen. Bixby's Birder's Bible* became *her* Bible, and she carried it with her everywhere.

Then she began finding scraps of paper in books at work: funny lists and letters, love notes, photos, and even money. After a while, she was also finding things outside of work. On the sidewalk, in her grocery cart, or caught in her hair after being blown by the wind.

The finds were amusing and fun to collect, and she was convinced they came to her specifically via Sophie or her spirit. Before she knew it, she had quite a stash. But soon, she began finding other objects, which she collected, as well. Single gloves. Old toasters. Costume jewelry. Lampshades. Tools. Once, she even found a prosthetic leg. They seemed to have been dropped in her path, left exclusively for her.

So she filled up her house with these clues—that was how she thought of them. She was convinced that with Bixby and Sophie as her guides, she would follow the various finds to the answer of what had happened. She had to.

She placed the dictionary page on top of the pile of her most recent finds. She hung her jacket on one of the coat hooks next to the door. Sophie's purple parka hung there by its hood, and her flowered rubber rain boots stood in the plastic boot tray below it. Jesse walked into the kitchen to get something to eat. She let her hand slide along the doorjamb of the pantry. The pencil markings climbing the wood indicated her daughter's height with the corresponding year next to it. There were marks for Jesse's and Cooper's heights as well. Proof she once had a family.

She took a small bowl from the cupboard. Sophie's favorite, it was white with blue polka dots around the outside. She lingered over it for a moment, rubbing her thumb around the rim. Her child's presence filled the house. Every dish, spoon, and plate she'd ever touched. Every chair she'd sat in. Every light switch she'd flicked on or off.

"How about some Cheerios, Soph?" Jesse poured cereal, but no milk, into the bowl and took it out to the back screened-in porch that overlooked a creek. She sat in her favorite rocker and ate the Cheerios by hand, one round oat piece at a time, the way Sophie used to every morning. Looking down at the two yellow Adirondack chairs on the lawn near the water, Jesse drifted to a memory.

"Sophie, I'm talking to you." Jesse would often have to call her a million times to come in for lunch. "Sophie." She could see the back of her daughter, not budging. "Sophie!"

"Mom, don't yell. You'll scare her away." She was, of course, peering through her binoculars.

"Who?"

"Field sparrow."

Just then, as if on cue, a bird with a white belly, pink bill, and reddish cap landed on the lip of the birdbath in the yard, pulling Jesse back to the present. The field sparrow sang a plaintive song. *"Cheep, cheep, cheep, cheep, trriiilll."* The series of clear whistled notes ended with a lovely long trill. Sophie had taught Jesse how to really watch and listen.

Numerous bird feeders hung from trees around the yard, all of them empty and swinging eerily in the wind. Glass hummingbird feeders, caged squirrel-proof ones, plastic tube feeders, ceramic domed ones, and suet socks. Sophie had kept them filled religiously. And back then, the yard had looked and sounded like a wonderful bird sanctuary. Absolutely magical. So alive with bird song, colorful feathers, and flashes of movement. Sophie would not have been happy with the sad state of her forsaken feeders.

In the days right after she'd disappeared, Canaan had been transformed into a freakshow, with police, FBI, television trucks, and news crews all bustling about. Jesse and Cooper's home had been turned into missing person central. Police scoured their house for clues. Tables were set up in the dining room, with laptops and call-in phone lines for people to report possible sightings. Maps noting locations to be searched were tacked on a large bulletin board. Friends canvassed neighborhoods, distributing flyers. Neighbors brought in pans of lasagna. Jesse had wandered the house in a daze. She had seen things like that in movies and on the news, but even in her tranquilized state back then, she'd understood it was real. It was her life. But with each passing month, as hope dwindled, fewer people came. The phone rang less. The lasagna deliveries stopped.

Six whole years later, the "case," as the FBI called her missing daughter, had gone "cold." Sophie had become one of those missing children who had fallen into a black abyss, never to be seen or heard from again. The commotion in town had died down. Morning gossip over coffee at Earl's Café had finally reverted to benign topics: talk of the new roof for the town hall or a potluck fundraiser for the church.

Jesse stood up and walked back inside the house. She grabbed a bottle of red wine and carried it upstairs, running her hand along the smooth maple banister her child had touched each day. She opened the door to Sophie's room and poked her head in, just in case. Then she closed the door and continued to her own bedroom. On her nightstand was a framed photo of Sophie standing on the wooden seat of the rope swing in the back yard, wearing a two-piece bathing suit, her binoculars hanging around her neck. The letter *S* on one lens cap and an *A* on the other were visible. She'd used blue gaffer tape to mark her initials. It was taken a week before That Day. Caught in mid-swing, Sophie held on to the rope handles, and her long brown hair flew behind her. She wasn't smiling. She rarely did in photos, and her head was tilted to the left. She was a nice-looking girl. Not one most people would call "pretty." There was a haunting quality about her. Wistful. Introspective. She had Cooper's eyes and his straight nose as well as Jesse's dark hair—when it had been dark—and pale skin. The splash of freckles came from who knew where.

Jesse poured herself a glass of wine then put on sweatpants and a T-shirt. She lit two white votive candles on an altar she'd made. Holding to her heart a little plastic figure of the saint she'd purchased off the internet for $14.95, she recited, "Saint Anthony, lead me to my daughter. I have faith in you. News about my daughter will come to me in a good way, for the good of all, with harm to none." Saint

Anthony was the patron saint of lost things and missing persons. She'd read about the ritual online, thanks to her mother, who was always emailing her information she claimed would help her find Sophie.

Even though she'd had absolutely no results, Jesse found the ritual oddly comforting. The Saint Anthony instructions said, "When the ritual is completed, eat something of the earth," and Jesse was sure that fermented grapes in liquid form qualified as earthly. And maybe, she justified, the more she drank of the earth, the closer she would be to finding Sophie. She finished one glass and poured another.

Jesse had hermited herself away, going out only when she had to, avoiding old friends, and doing her food shopping late at the all-night Stop-n-Shop. Only an occasional delivery man came to the house anymore. So when Jesse heard loud knocking at her front door, she assumed it must be somebody new. She had the UPS guy who brought her Winestogo.com deliveries trained to leave packages on her doorstep.

The knocking continued, so she blew out her candles and quietly snuck into the bathroom. She pulled the curtain aside and peered out the window to see a bright-yellow VW bug in her drive. From her vantage point, she could see only the sneaker-clad feet of a man standing at her front door. Red high-tops. He was yelling, "Hello? Hellooo?"

She let the curtain fall and stepped away from the window.

"I'll only be a moment, ma'am," the man shouted. "I just have a question for you."

"Damn." He had seen her at the window. He could be a pesky reporter. Once or twice a year, a tenacious one would appear, wanting to do a follow-up story. "Whatever happened to Sophie Albright? Six years later..." That kind of thing.

"Hello. Ms. Albright? I know you're home. Just one moment of your time. Please."

Jesse went downstairs and through the maze of boxes. This guy was persistent. If she didn't get rid of him now, he would probably come back—or worse, he would sit and wait for her to leave the house. She tiptoed to the front door, waited, and listened.

"I'm here about a young woman. A missing girl. Please open up."

Jesse's heart lurched. It wasn't Mallory, the FBI agent who had been tracking the case; she would have recognized his voice, and he always called before coming over. She hadn't seen him in two years. *Maybe they assigned a new agent to the case. Maybe there's actual news.* She sometimes wished she would get that phone call or visit from a policeman saying, "We think your daughter's been found. You have to come identify the remains." *Wouldn't it be better knowing? Would it?*

She unlocked the door and threw it open. Standing in her doorway was a tall black man casually dressed in black jeans and a white button-down shirt with a flowered necktie. And those red high-tops.

"Why didn't you say why you were here in the first place?" Jesse said.

"Didn't you hear me knocking?"

"Yes, yes." Her hand smacked the air as if waving away his words. "What information do you have? Is she alive? Have you found her?"

The wind gusted, and his tie fluttered up so she could see the label on the backside. *Zone.* It figured. She opened the door wider and let the man in.

"You know about her?" He took off his cap and placed it on a table near the door that held keys and mail and a piece of folk art—a six-inch black crow made out of metal. Jesse had bought it for Sophie at a flea market. Sophie loved it and wanted to keep it in the living room so everyone could see it. "Crows are super smart," she'd said, "and this one is good luck."

He looked at Jesse. The man's hair was cropped close to his head. His eyes were darker than his skin, which was the color of a warm teak wood. He looked young, although Jesse couldn't guess his age. He could have been in his thirties or his fifties. The expression "Black don't crack" popped into Jesse's head. She'd heard Oprah say it on TV, and it had made her laugh at the time. Oprah was right, at least about this guy. He had no wrinkles or signs of stress.

He held himself with confidence as he gazed around the living room. His smile faded as he took in all the piles of junk. His eyes seemed to rest on a bouquet of dusty plastic tulips then moved on to a small black-and-white TV, its rabbit ears askew. "Is this some kind of..." He made a gesture with his hands while he searched for the word. "Recycling center or something?"

Jesse shook her head. "No, no. Never mind that. The reason you're here. The girl. Please just tell me."

"Right, of course. I'm sorry." He put his hand out to shake hers, but she ignored it. "I'm Kentucky Marcus Barnes. A private investigator. I'm here about a young woman—"

"You said that. What about her? Get to the point."

"Her name is April Johnson. She's been missing now for three weeks. She's from Parsippany, New Jersey, and I've been hired by her family to locate her. She was—"

"What?" Jesse cut him off. "April Johnson? You mean Sophie. Sophie Albright. My daughter. What's wrong with you?"

He took a step back and held up his hands. "I think there's some misunderstanding here."

Jesse took a deep breath. "You mean you're not here about Sophie? You know nothing about Sophie? Who the hell are you?" She picked up his cap, shoved it into his gut, and pushed him toward the door. "Get out."

"Now, Miss... Ms. Albright. Wait a second, please. Please. I'm looking for a missing girl. I have reason to believe that you may have seen the very girl I'm searching for. You might be able to help. Don't you want to help?"

Jesse felt the shooting pain in her chest that came and went and placed her hand near her heart. *What kind of cruel joke is this?* She had nothing left in her to give. She sighed and shook her head. "I haven't seen anyone. I don't see people."

The detective pulled something out of the inside pocket of his jacket. He shoved it under Jesse's nose. "Now hold on. This is a photo of April. She's seventeen, and we believe that she's in this area. We think she purchased some merchandise at the Zone store at the Countryside Mall earlier today. I understand that you were there around the time that April may have been. We're looking for any clues. Do you remember seeing this girl at the Zone?"

The fucking Zone again. Jesse glanced at the photo. It looked like it was from a high school yearbook. The girl had long blond hair and a sweet smile. She wore a white turtleneck and pearls, giving her a pure, innocent look. Jesse must have gone to every house in Canaan and every neighboring town, showing Sophie's photo to strangers. She had searched downtown Boston, Times Square in New York City, and every porno joint, strip club, and sleazy bar in between looking for Sophie or the person who may have snatched her. She looked at the photo again. She'd seen lots of teen girls at the mall, including the one she'd followed earlier, but none looked like the girl in this photo.

She shook her head. "I'm sorry." And she handed the photo back to him.

"You're sure? Take your time. Do you remember seeing anyone at the store? Anything suspicious?"

"No. Sorry."

"All right. Well, I appreciate it. The family is worried sick. You can imagine. We're pretty sure she was at the mall today. She's been using a stolen credit card. It's how we've been keeping tabs on her general whereabouts. We're following any leads, no matter how far-fetched. Well, anyway. Thank you. Sorry for the misunderstanding before. Goodbye."

Jesse ushered him to the door. When he had his hand on the knob, he turned back to Jesse. "Forgive me for prying, but I can't help but wonder about your daughter. How long has she been missing? Could your daughter have known April Johnson? I know it's a long shot, but it does seem odd that—"

"You're not from around here, are you? No, my daughter couldn't have known this April."

"But if you're concerned if she's even alive—"

"Are you with the FBI or the local police or what?"

"I'm a private investigator, like I said, hired by her family."

"You're not a reporter, are you?" *What kind of detective drives a VW Bug, and a yellow one at that, and dresses in jeans and sneakers?* None that she'd ever met, and she'd met plenty.

"No, no. Like I said—"

"I'm not about to hire another detective. I have no money. I don't see the point."

"I don't need you to hire me." Then he stepped back. His mouth dropped open as if he just remembered something. "Oh, no." He shook his head and held his hands up. "I just realized... Albright. Sophie Albright. I'm so sorry. I didn't expect to be meeting..."

"Bird Mom."

"A young salesgirl told me your name, but that's all she said. I didn't put it together until just now. I'm terribly sorry."

"I'm the sorry one. I thought it was odd to lose a child. Apparently, it's not. It happens all the time. I'm sorry about this other missing girl. You have no idea how sorry I am. But I just can't help you. You'll have to leave now." She placed her hands on his chest, was surprised how solid it felt, and gave him a little shove out the door. And just that quick connection, her hands to his body for one moment even through his clothes, was startling. She closed and locked the door. Then she sank to the floor. She let her head fall into her hands.

"Mommy, Daddy, Sophie," she whispered. She closed her eyes. Another missing girl. And that hellish Zone, swallowing up innocent girls like a sinkhole. But that man, something about him, something in his eyes. She felt stupid and mad for letting herself think just maybe...

A few moments later, Jesse heard his voice coming through the door. He was speaking softly. "Listen, Ms. Albright, if you can hear me."

Jesse looked up, holding her breath as if she'd been caught doing something wrong.

"I'm very sorry for what you've gone through. I'm just going to slide a copy of that photo of April under the door, along with an article about her from the paper. My card with my number is stapled to it. You never know. Something may come to you later. Some little thought or idea. You get one of those little sparks of a memory, even just a glimmer, I want you to call me. I really would appreciate it. I'll be in the area for a while. Even if it seems downright silly to you, it won't be to me. You just call me anytime. Here it is. I'm sliding it under your door now."

And two pieces of paper appeared under the door. "Okay, Ms. Albright. I'm going to go and leave you to your day. You have a good one, and thank you for your time. I'm sorry if I disturbed you or upset you. I would never mean to do that on purpose. Well, anyway, good day."

She went upstairs to the bathroom and listened at the window. She heard him walk away, clomping on the gravel of the drive. He got into his car and drove off. Pulling back the curtain, she saw his VW turn onto the street. Jesse crawled into the bathtub fully clothed, as she sometimes did, and opened the half-empty bottle of Sophie's shampoo that she kept on the shelf in the corner. She brought it to her nose and inhaled, letting the sweet grape scent pull her back to bath time. She tucked her knees up to her chest and hung her head down. He couldn't possibly know about the little sparks, those glimmers of memory, the ones that haunted her daily.

Chapter Five

Later that night, Star changed into her comfy clothes, a sleeveless T-shirt and gray sweats, and sat in bed under her Lady Gaga poster, instant messaging Ruby. After saying all there was to say about the new cute boy in school, she signed off and began scouring the internet. First, she visited Sophie's website, which was like a fan page where people posted comments, prayers, hopeful messages, and supposed spottings. But there were always some sickos who wrote on the message board:

She deserved whatever happened to her.

I know where she is.

Come over here, and I'll show you how she likes it.

Star quickly exited that site and went over to fbi.gov/wanted/kidnap. She typed in Sophie's name, and the description of what had happened six years ago came up with two side-by-side photos, and *whamo*! She was back to that day, sitting at the dinner table, eating grilled steak and zucchini, when Cooper called her parents with the news, asking if they'd seen or heard from Sophie. The first photo was the one from Sophie's missing persons poster that had been everywhere back then. Each store, telephone pole, and lamppost in Canaan and every town in the state had one. Sophie looked like the happiest ten-year-old around—basically nothing like the real girl, the serious one who rarely smiled for the camera. The other photo was one of those computer-generated ones showing what she might look like today, at sixteen. Somebody had given her dark lipstick and a really bad haircut a la Ophelia. Short and layered, it looked more like something out of the 1980s. The whole effect was super creepy—a smiling version of a young Sophie that Star didn't exactly recognize next to an altered older version she couldn't imagine being friends with. Two strangers. Star couldn't wrap her head around it.

If she wasn't careful, Star could get sucked into the rabbit hole of the missing. There was one scary website after the next. Missingkids.com, Childfindofamerican.com, Pollyklaas.org and on and on. She imagined all the never-found missing kids floating around in some in-between universe, like virtual ghosts all tethered together, although lots of them would have already become never-found adults. She used to think it was rare for someone to disappear, but reading about so many kids made it clear, it happened all the time.

She clicked on the faces of other smiling kids, and as their profiles flashed before her eyes, she skimmed some of the disparate facts:

Missing since 1971, 1999, September 8, 2012.

Last seen in their home, exiting a Greyhound bus accompanied by a grandparent, at a Zone clothing store.

A book bag recovered, their abandoned car found, a rainbow backpack left behind.

Has a butterfly tattoo on her shoulder, a birthmark on his thigh, wearing binoculars around her neck.

Reward of $25,000 offered, needs medical attention, believed to be in imminent danger.

Last seen. Last seen. Last. Seen.

It was draining, all the sad stories. She thought about Ophelia. The girl sure had some crazy romantic ideas about life. Smiling angels with white wings. Running into Sophie at the Olive Garden. *Yeah, right.* Star just didn't want Ophelia to end up on one of these websites like Sophie. Another depressing statistic.

She stepped away from her computer, checked the locks of her windows, and turned on all the lights—the hallway and bathroom nightlights, the overhead bedroom, closet light, and desk lamp, too. She couldn't remember exactly when she'd become afraid of the dark.

She tiptoed down the hall and peered through the keyhole of her parents' bedroom, as she did each night. They were still there, sleeping. She let out a breath. She thought about asking to sleep with them in their bed like she had when she was little, before Sophie went missing, when it was just for fun. But she knew they wouldn't go for that. She'd asked once the year before, and they'd looked at each other worriedly. "You're too old for that, honey," her mother had said in a pathetic voice.

Suck it up, she'd thought. So she'd taught herself to put on a mask and pretend she was someone else, the tough girl who wasn't scared. The exact opposite of how she really felt.

For a while after Sophie disappeared, her presence was always hovering nearby, like a mild earache. But Star learned to ignore it and went about her life. She went ice skating at the new Canaan rink. Birthday parties at the lake. Piano lessons. Homework. She was a regular kid who had moved on from a tragedy. Then little by little, as the years went by, Sophie started whispering in her ear. Then the whisper became a normal voice. Then a shout. The earache wasn't so easy to ignore anymore.

It was late, and Star was getting tired and definitely didn't want to fall asleep. Ever since she'd read about what had happened to those three Cleveland girls, she'd kept having nightmares. So she made extra-strength coffee and drank lots of it, heavy on the sugar. It was all she could think of to stay awake and fend off the bad dreams. Lately, everyone had been on her case about being sleepy at school, missing classes, and failing tests. She'd been doing this nightly routine for a couple of months, and she was whipped, feeling like a total zombie. She looked like one, too. Hell, she was only sixteen and had freaking black circles under her eyes. She'd started to lose weight and was swimming in her clothes. Whenever she smelled grilled meat, what she now called "missing person food," it made her gag. She had diarrhea, so she secretly guzzled that gross pink stuff and didn't feel like eating.

The last time she remembered looking at the clock, it'd read 3:13, and she could barely keep her eyes open in spite of the fact she'd drunk about three atomic coffees. She felt a pull, like a magnetic force that took her whole body slowly under as if she were drowning, but she couldn't do anything about it. She couldn't shout, cry, or even talk. Not being in control was frightening, but it was also kind of relaxing to be taken, to finally let it all go and not fight it anymore, like a warm, heavy blanket was being tucked around her.

"Hey, Rats." It was Sophie's nickname for her—Star spelled backward. Sophie sat on Star's bed, legs dangling over the side. She still looked the way Star remembered her. A ten-year-old girl. She wore stone-washed jeans with her "Life's a Beach" T-shirt and her black clogs with orange socks, the same outfit she'd worn the day she disappeared. Her long dark hair hung loose down her back, the way she usually wore it. She was still little, hadn't grown an inch. Still had her freckles. And her binos, as usual, were hanging around her neck.

Star jumped when she saw her. "Jesus, Sophie, you scared me. What are you doing here?"

"Just visiting my BFF." Sophie hopped off the bed, walked over to the desk, and looked at photos of Star and her friends pinned to her bulletin board. There were some of Ruby and Star with their arms around each other, smiling broadly.

Sophie gazed at them and turned back to Star. "No pictures of me?"

Star shrugged.

"That sucks."

Star didn't tell her she'd put them in a cigar box under her bed with other mementoes from their times together and that they creeped her out to look at them, just like seeing Sophie did now.

"How come you haven't gotten older?" Star said.

Sophie gestured to herself. "This is what Limboland looks like."

"I heard your mom thinks she gets signs from you. Is that really you sending her stuff?"

"Wouldn't you like to know."

"You don't talk like a ten-year-old. You sound different."

"Some things make you grow up fast. Besides, this is your dream, not mine."

Am *I dreaming?* Star wondered. *Or is this really Sophie's ghost?* She'd never really thought about ghosts before. *Didn't they like show up because of unfinished business or something?*

Dream Sophie or Ghost Sophie was rifling through Star's stuff on her desk: her journal, papers and books. Then she saw a Beanie Baby, a little dog, sitting on a bookshelf, and she turned to Star. "Really? George?"

The doll had been Sophie's. A week after she'd been missing, the Albrights' house was so chaotic, strangers bustling in and out of the place, that Star had just walked into Sophie's room, ducking under the yellow police tape without anyone noticing. She could have taken anything, but the little dog had seemed to call out to her. So she'd just slid it into her pocket. Star sometimes held it in her hand in bed at night.

"I don't get you, Sophie. What do you want from me?"

Sophie nodded toward Star. "You must want to see me. You Google stalk me, like, every day."

Oh, that. "So what? What do you really want?"

"Patience, Star. Remember, birding takes patience."

"What does that mean? You're not a bird."

"Tweet, tweet. And I don't mean Twitter." She laughed. "I thought we were best friends? Blood sisters," she said and wiggled her index finger at Star.

They had done a blood pact when they were nine. Best friends forever. No matter what. They'd pricked their fingers with a safety pin. It hurt, but Star remembered they'd both laughed as they pressed their index fingers together, their blood mingling into one new shade of cherry juice.

"Maybe you should stop coming here."

Sophie looked up at the ceiling as if thinking about it. "No, I think I'll keep coming."

Suddenly, Star felt so tired, she had to prop her head up with her hands. "I need some sleep."

"Who's stopping you?"

"Maybe you should go visit your mom. Or your dad."

"I don't think so."

"Sophie..."

"What?" She had brought her binos up to her eyes and was pointing them right at Star.

"When are you going to stop coming to me?"

She pulled them down from her face and giggled. "Never."

SUDDENLY, STAR BOLTED upright in bed. She looked around the room. No one was there. Her heart was racing. Her tank top was drenched in sweat. She opened her bottom desk drawer and pulled out her little sewing kit in a clear plastic zippered pouch. The scissors that came with it were small, with orange plastic handles, and they were surprisingly sharp. Her mom had given her the kit two years ago. Star didn't sew, and she didn't intend to start, but it was filled with lots of perfect tools—rows of shiny straight pins that had small colored balls on their heads and a sharp seam ripper, too. Star had discovered a new purpose for the kit last month after a really bad visit from Sophie.

She shoved her left sleeve up past her elbow, took the scissors, and scratched a two-inch line down her forearm. Winter was coming, so she would have months to wear long sleeves and cover up. It hurt but not that much, which meant she hadn't pressed hard enough. She went over the scratch and pressed harder. The first burst was always a surprise. Not like the tiny pin prick from her blood pact with Sophie. This was dark and thick like crimson syrup. It kept coming and made her think of maple tree sap. When she was in elementary school, her class went on a field trip every March to the Norton Farm. The kids helped collect sap in metal buckets and watched the sugaring in the little wooden shacks. Star's sap ran down her arm and dripped into a pile of paper towels she kept in the same drawer as the sewing kit. She wiped off the scissor blades and used one of the points to make another deeper cut next to the first one. More syrup came, and she heard pounding in her ears. The cut hurt, but the pain was what she needed. It put Sophie in her place. It put Star in control.

"You think you can get me to stop coming by doing that?" Sophie was back.

Star just shrugged. Sophie couldn't bother her anymore.

"That's pathetic."

"Maybe so, but it works."

"Not this time. I'm still here."

She cut into a new spot on her arm near the inside of the elbow. More sap. More syrup. "I can't hear you."

Usually, it took about fifteen minutes. She could never be sure because she'd go into a sort of trance while cutting. Everything disappeared. All sounds and smells. She would slip into another place where there were no missing girls harassing her. Where she didn't have to put on an act.

When she was done, she had to press really hard with Kleenex to stop the dripping. Sometimes she licked the little drips, and it even tasted like maple syrup. Then she dabbed all the cuts with alcohol, which stung like hell. She wiped up any stray blood drops. She'd gotten good at her ritual and was pretty neat about it. She retrieved her stash of Band-Aids hidden in the back of her closet. Gazing at the ugly cut, it came to her. *Today's journal entry.*

She took out her old digital camera from her desk drawer and turned it on. It came to life with a whooshing sound as the lens slid out. She pointed it at her arm, on the fresh red line, and zoomed in close. Jagged and raw, it looked abstract, like a zigzagging road from far away. *The road to nowhere,* she thought with a chuckle. That would be the caption. She hit the button, and it flashed. She would print it out and paste it in her journal later. Next, she put on a Band-Aid, the big square kind, nice and tight. Then she dropped the syrupy Kleenex down the toilet. Star was so tired, she crawled into bed with her clothes on and fell asleep with the lights ablaze.

Chapter Six

Jesse got in bed with her iPad and a bottle of wine, and before she knew it, hours had melted away while she made the rounds of the numerous missing person sites. The horrifying, frightening truth of kidnapping, human trafficking, child pornography rings, prostitution, abuse, brainwashing, and even organ harvesting was really more than she could bear. Not being able to protect her daughter was her torture. But if she stayed away from the websites for too long, she worried she might miss a piece of news, some obscure clue about Sophie. So as painful as it was, she always went back.

She then turned to snooping on Cooper, a favorite pastime. She went to Google Street View and swiped up and down his block, looking for what exactly, she wasn't sure. She tried to enlarge the view, look in windows, and zoom into the back yard. To find clues of his new life. But she could never see more than just the outside of the house. It was a brick townhouse style on a cobblestoned street in a pricey neighborhood. She'd scoped it out on Realtor.com, too. It was worth more money than her house. She'd tried to imagine living there but couldn't. She preferred her rural, small-town Canaan. But if she were being honest, she supposed what she wanted was simply her old life back. The way things used to be, even if it wasn't perfect.

When she was sure she'd seen all she could, she picked up the phone, punched in a number, and waited. After the fourth ring, a groggy man's voice answered, "Hello, Jess."

She felt around under the covers near her feet and pulled Mr. Bear onto her lap. Sophie's dingy, stuffed polar bear was missing a black button eye. Lila Teller had called it a "transference object." Jesse didn't care what it was called. She needed to hold it in order to fall asleep.

She gulped down some wine, picturing Cooper in bed. He had always slept naked, two scrunched-up feather pillows behind his head. When she was last with him, a small patch of his chest hair had started to turn gray. She looked to the left side of the bed, Cooper's old side, and touched what had been his pillow then let her hand slide down to the empty space next to her. She ran her hand over the sheet. She couldn't recall how or when she'd told Cooper what happened That Day. She had long ago blocked that out, plus the meds she'd been given then dulled her memory. But she could remember one of the last times they made love when it was still good. From the start, they'd had a strong chemistry. Only during the last years they were together, had they seemed out of sync. She'd wondered then if it was just the normal ebb and flow of a marriage. Of passion.

But that one Sunday, it had been like old times. Sophie was off with Star, and Jesse and Cooper had the house to themselves, a rare occurrence. They kept being interrupted—a phone call and a neighbor stopping by—then the power went out in a windstorm. Jesse went with Cooper to the basement and held a flashlight while he messed with the fuse box, naked. They went back to bed, laughing about the coitus interruptus, then their bodies came together again. She wondered what had brought the heated excitement to that time. *Did I do something differently? Been sexier, somehow? Maybe we felt freer without Sophie in the house?*

"Jess, it's late," Cooper said in a whisper. "You know we get up early."

Even after so many years, hearing his voice put her at ease. When she and Cooper were together, Jesse had helped him start Country

Hikers, a touring company with excursions in the Northeast, hikes in beautiful settings and overnight stays in charming B and Bs. Cooper had led the hikes. He loved being outdoors and meeting new people. He could be charming and was knowledgeable about the area. Jesse had done the office work and kept the books until being a mom became too time-consuming. It'd been a small business, and they had struggled to stay afloat, but Jesse thought he was happy. But once he remarried, he sold the business, went back to school, and got a law degree. He wore suits every day and worked at a big law firm. The old Cooper had vanished along with Sophie. At least he could afford to pay her alimony.

Cindy, Cooper's second wife, had worked with him in the Country Hikers office after Jesse quit. She was eight years younger than him and skinny, with big boobs that Jesse was sure weren't real. She didn't like to read books, garden, have discussions, go to museums, or stay home to cook or bake, like Jesse. She couldn't sew a Halloween costume for a child. She liked to shop and work out. Period. And Jesse would be the first to admit that Cindy *was* a very good shopper. And always ready with a recommendation for a trendy vacation spot or a new restaurant.

Cooper claimed the stress and strain of their tragedy had pushed him into the affair with Cindy, but Jesse thought it might have started before Sophie disappeared. Sophie had been a demanding child who needed structure and routine. And if Jesse or Cooper failed to follow it, Sophie would fly into wild tantrums. Raising her had placed a strain on their marriage.

After Cooper and Cindy married, they moved out of the sleepy hill town to Newburyport, closer to Boston, where the shopping was better. Their son was born. Cindy stayed home and took care of Caleb, who was now four years old.

Jesse never understood how Cooper could end up with Cindy. An affair, yes, sure, that was a no-brainer. She was younger and attractive. Sexy, for sure. But marriage? A child? All Jesse could come up with was that the sex must be amazing. She used to think the sex she and Cooper had was amazing. Clearly, Jesse knew nothing about anything.

"I've been thinking about our last conversation," she said.

"That's good. Did you contact a realtor?"

"Not yet. I'll need more time. A month is crazy."

"Because of the junk? Rent a roll-off. Or hire someone to get rid of it, haul it all away."

She wasn't going to start that conversation. He never got it that Sophie was leading her. She wasn't ready to let go of the finds. Not yet. She was getting close; she felt it. *Never stop looking.*

"Not just that. The house needs work. You know that. You want to get the most money you can, right? It needs to show well. It needs a paint job. The downstairs bath is so dated. And the kitchen is a wreck. Plus, we'll need to stage the place."

Jesse felt numb, disconnected, as if she were floating in an ocean, cut off from her old life, which she watched as it drifted away, getting smaller and smaller. She'd been operating that way for such a long time. It was nearly inconceivable that the number of years that she had waited and searched for Sophie was approaching the amount of time she had actually spent with her.

"I don't know, Jess. A paint job, fine. Call Ray. He'll do it for a good price. But remodeling? No way. There's no money for that. Someone will want it the way it is. They'll fix it up themselves to their liking."

"But I need more time." She had to draw the time out for as long as possible. Then again, maybe an imposed deadline would spur her on. She could go through her finds, each clue, study Bixby some more. Stop. Wait. Watch. And most of all... listen. *But a month? No, impossible.*

She couldn't have Sophie returning to a houseful of strangers. New children sleeping in her bedroom. And the memories. *What would become of the memories?*

"Please, Cooper. Just packing up to move takes so much time. I have nowhere to go."

"All right. Two months. But that's it. I'm not kidding."

More silence. "She's there, isn't she?"

"You mean Cynthia?" He called her Cynthia, as if using the formal name made her more intelligent. Jesse still called her Cindy, what she'd gone by when she was working for Cooper, wearing too-skimpy halter tops and shorts. Jesse remembered how they used to joke that she was an East Coast Valley girl. "Of course she's here. She's my wife."

Jesse wondered if he ever thought of her. Of their life together. Before. Their early days in New York City, when they couldn't keep their hands off each other. They'd struggled financially, living in cheap East Village apartments, but life was fun and so full of possibilities. Years later, they'd stood atop East Chop Light on the Vineyard at sunset for their wedding ceremony then moved to Canaan. Bought the house. Had Sophie. Jesse could recall her infant daughter's tiny hand grasping Cooper's pinkie. *Does he ever think of any of it?*

More silence. Cooper must have covered the mouthpiece because Jesse heard muffled talking. Then he was back. "And you might as well hear it from me now. Cynthia and I are expecting."

She gasped as if someone had socked her in the gut. "Expecting what?" she said after a moment, only because she didn't know what else to say.

"A child, Jesse. Another child."

"Funny how you only wanted *one* when we were together. Yes, I distinctly remember you being adamant about that even before That Day. 'One child is enough.' Your words."

"I'm sorry, Jess. Things change. People change. We're having an-other baby. End of story."

After Sophie went missing, people were constantly giving unso-licited advice to her and Cooper. "Have another child," they would say, as if Sophie were like a lost pet and getting a new one would be the perfect distraction. But she and Cooper were barely speaking, let alone having sex... with each other anyway. And then years after Cooper left her, those same people would stick their noses into her business again. "Lots of single women are adopting these days," they said. But Jesse didn't trust herself with another living creature. Not even a goldfish.

Jesse wasn't jealous of their having a baby. She really couldn't imagine ever wanting another child. Sophie could be difficult, and life with a special child was hard enough. They came with their own set of issues. Yet after reading a book about raising "gifted" children, Jesse had come to think of Sophie that way. It best explained her reading, writing, and creative skills that were way above average. The way she could absorb, retain, then linger in her bird world for hours on end. But she also fit into the "spirited" category—kids that some experts described as normal children who were just more sensitive, perceptive, intense, persistent, and more uncomfortable with change than other kids. And that certainly described Sophie. More. More. Much more.

No, what Jesse was jealous of was Cooper not only being able to imagine having another life but actually going ahead and having one. "You don't sound too happy about it," she said.

"Of course I'm happy. But it's late and you—"

"What I want to know is how did you do it?"

"Do what, Jesse?"

"Get over Sophie."

"I've told you before. I haven't gotten over her. I'll never forget her or stop loving her. I've moved forward. And that's what you need to do. Get back to some of your old activities, things you loved to do. Gardening, sewing. How about your plein air painting?"

She used to drive out to Cummington or Shelburne Falls and plop her canvas stool down on a picturesque country road. She would take out her portable easel and paints then breathe in the air and scenery that always recharged her. Being outside in nature was always a treat. But she hadn't done that in years.

"I'm not painting. You know that."

"Well, you should get back to it. It would be good for you. Moving out of that old house will be good for you, too."

She looked down at her ringless left hand. She'd finally removed her wedding band a couple of months ago. The tan line was visible on her ring finger, barely, but still there. That, too, would soon disappear with the rest of her old life—daughter, husband, house, marriage...

"You love Caleb more, don't you? He's filling up that Sophie spot, isn't he?"

"I'm going to hang up, Jess. I'm tired of your wallowing in self-pity all these years. Have you once asked how I was doing? You're not the only one who lost a daughter. You're not the only one who's been affected by it. I can't talk to you when you're drunk. You need help."

"I'm not drunk." She could hear him breathing. "I had a little wine. One glass." Jesse lifted the almost-empty bottle. "All right. Two." She tilted her head back and let the last drops of wine slip into her throat.

She let the wine bottle drop to the floor. She'd wanted to tell him the other thing for so long. But still, she couldn't. Instead, she said, "Don't hate me." Sophie used to say that after a tantrum, as her way of apologizing. Then Jesse and Cooper had picked it up as well, and it'd become an inside family joke.

"Jess, go to sleep. We'll talk another time when you're sober." And he hung up.

It seemed inconceivable to her that a marriage could survive what she and Cooper had been through. She sank into her pillow, closing her eyes. The images that preyed upon her nightly came to her.

"But, Mom, I need it."

"You need it? I don't think so. You have lots of tops." Jesse glanced away from the T-shirt rack and saw fall school clothes on the next rack. "Oh, honey. You do need some new school clothes. How about..." She let go of Sophie's hand, still thinking about the morning's argument with Cooper.

They were just back from their summer vacation on the Cape with the Silvermans. For the past five years, they'd rented side-by-side cottages in Wellfleet, and it was always the highlight of their year. Even though she and Cooper tried to put on a good face, she hoped that Blue and Beth hadn't picked up on the tension between them.

When Jesse turned back, she didn't see her daughter. "Sophie?" She looked all around the T-shirt rack. "Sophie. Don't play. Come on." She searched under and behind it but found no sign of her. "Sophie?" Jesse walked around the whole store, her anger rising. Why does she have to pull this now? *"Sophie!" She looked in the dressing rooms. She came back to the rack where she'd last seen Sophie. Jesse dropped to her hands and knees, peering between the clothes. Her heart beat faster by the second.*

She began shouting, "Sophie? Have you seen my daughter?" to every shopper and sales clerk in the store. How long did I look away? Five seconds? Twenty? A minute? *She stood in the middle of the Zone, clutching the Tweet shirt in her hands while strangers scurried about, looking for Sophie. Employees shouted, "Code Adam!" The overwhelming panic and fear rose in her chest as the impossible became a reality—she'd lost her daughter.*

Jesse opened her eyes, trying to forget. Luckily, the wine would help her fall asleep sooner rather than later. Otherwise, she would lie awake for hours, replaying in her head the film from the Zone's security camera. In the grainy black-and-white image, Jesse and Sophie stood next to the circular rack of clothes, holding hands. Sophie reached over and pulled out a T-shirt. Jesse letting go of her hand, turning away, and walking off camera as Sophie headed in the other direction then slipped out of frame. Gone. Forever.

Just a moment, a second or two of film, but it was ingrained in her mind. The slow-motion version of the clip was replayed over and over for the police then repeatedly on the nightly news. The mother let go of her daughter's hand. It reminded Jesse of the famous clip of Patty Hearst wearing a beret, holding a machine gun. She knew how humiliated Patty must have felt.

Jesse's precious good memories of her past had been bulldozed by the horrific ones. The store should have been called Twilight Zone because after That Day, Jesse felt like she was living in another dimension. What kind of mother loses a child?

In the beginning, suicidal thoughts kept sneaking up on her. She would try to imagine going through with it—car exhaust in a garage, knife to wrist, pills—but all she could think of was botching it, leaving a bigger mess for Cooper and her mother. But really, she didn't want to die. She needed to be there if Sophie returned. When. When she returned.

She thought again of that girl from the Zone. She didn't look any more like Sophie than other girls had over the years. The girl didn't sound like Sophie, either. *Then what was it?*

She let her mind wander to some of her recent finds. That grocery list in the bushes on Main Street that included Cheerios, Sophie's cereal. A purple scrunchie—Sophie's favorite color—bubbling to the surface of her compost heap. The girl with the squeaky voice and funny haircut at the Zone chewing watermelon Sour Patch gum, Sophie's flavor.

Some birds are elusive and particularly difficult to find... To find birds, you must pay close attention and be patient. Stop. Wait. Watch. And most of all... listen... Never stop looking. She shuffled through the clues, searching for a connection, the thread of a story, until she fell asleep.

Chapter Seven

Jesse woke to the sound of a dog barking, which didn't help her hangover. She looked over at her clock. 8:28 a.m. Early for her. She sat up and pressed her palm to her forehead as the throbbing intensified. Tentatively, she got out of bed but tripped over an empty wine bottle. *Cynthia and I are expecting.* She kicked the bottle, which rolled under her nightstand next to the others. "Stupid," she mumbled to herself.

She plodded down the stairs to see what the noise was all about. Her closest neighbor didn't have a dog. *So whose could it be?* She pulled back the curtain on her front window and saw the rear end of an animal on her front porch. And she heard more barking. Slowly, she opened the door a crack, and there, sitting upright as if waiting for her, was a brown dog with floppy ears, wearing a red tartan collar. As it panted, its long pink tongue hung out of its mouth. Maybe part lab, part cocker spaniel. But all mutt.

"What do you want? Who do you belong to?" Her first thought was of the man who'd been by the day before. *Is he back with a dog?* She poked her head out farther and shouted out, "Hello? Anyone there?"

The creature's ears perked up. She looked about, but there was no sign of anybody. She was surprised she actually felt a twinge of disappointment. She shook it away and gently reached her hand down in a fist and let the dog smell and lick it. She often didn't speak to a soul for days if she didn't have to go in to work, and she didn't know how she felt about a visitor, even a non-speaking, furry one.

She filled a bowl with water and put it on the front porch. The dog lapped it up quickly. "Thirsty, huh?"

He had no tags. She wasn't about to let in some stray. That was the last thing she needed. But he gazed up at her with big, soulful eyes. And he held his tail high, wagging it furiously, then let it thump on the ground rapidly as if trying to tell her something. He was clearly very happy to see her. She couldn't help but smile.

"Hold on," she said, closing the door partway and turning to get the sample package of kibble she remembered finding last year. The dog pushed the door open with its nose and trotted in.

"Hey, wait a minute," she said, reaching to grab him, but he slid out of her grasp. He proceeded to sniff every surface then came back to Jesse and nudged her hand. "All right. All right." She petted his head then his soft coat.

She rummaged around a box of her finds and pulled out the little bags of Iams she had found left or forgotten near her truck one day at the Book Barn. She poured the contents into a bowl, added a bit of water, swooshed it around, and set it down for the dog. He gobbled it up then came over to her. She petted him a little more. He seemed sweet.

"Do you know something?" she asked him. "Can you help me?" She looked up at the ceiling. "Sophie, is it you? Did you send this guy?"

He tilted his head, which gave him a questioning look that made Jesse smile again. Sophie had nagged for a dog and convinced Cooper to campaign for one, too. Even though Jesse had grown up with an array of loveable rescue mutts and loved dogs, her hands had been full with parenting. The responsibility, undoubtedly, would have fallen to her. As much as Sophie loved animals, Jesse would have been hard-pressed to pry her away from her binoculars in order to walk a dog. But maybe Sophie was ratcheting things up with living, breathing clues. That girl at the Zone with the watermelon gum. And now the brown dog.

The phone rang. As usual, her heart leapt. *News about my daughter will come in a good way, for the good of all, with harm to none.*

After That Day, Jesse always pounced on the phone, praying to hear Sophie's voice or some news. But as time went on, there was less news and fewer friends calling to offer support. Just more wackos with phony leads or repulsive messages. So she'd started screening her calls.

After the fourth head-pounding ring, her answering machine picked up.

"Honey, it's me."

Mom. Jesse let out her breath.

"Pick up."

As much as Jesse would have liked to ignore the call, she couldn't. Her mom was one of the few people Jesse spoke to anymore. "Hi, Mom."

"Hi, dear. Are you all right?"

"I'm fine. You?"

"Oh, the usual. My tennis elbow is acting up. Silly, since I don't play tennis. But could be worse." Just like her to put a positive spin on things. "Sweetheart, I haven't seen you in ages. How about I come for a visit?"

"Maybe next month."

"It's never a good time for you."

"I'm just busy."

After That Day, her mom had come to see her often, but eventually, Jesse had put an end to the visits with a series of excuses. The unspoken fact was that Jesse didn't want to deal with her mom's disapproving looks or offers to help de-clutter her finds. At first, her mom was willing to listen and seemed to understand the meaning of the finds, but as time went on, she drifted into the same toss-it-all-away camp as Cooper.

"You're always busy."

"Let's not do this now, Mom." The dog was rooting around in one of her boxes, poking his snout deep inside, making a racket.

"All right. But you know I miss you, and you're always welcome here."

"I know." She fingered her favorite necklace, which she always wore. Cooper had given her the antique silver locket for her birthday years ago. "With Eternal Love" was inscribed inside in fancy script. Sophie had always played with it, sliding the locket back and forth on the chain around Jesse's neck. *Eternal love, right.* She had actually believed it back then. She thought about telling her mom about Cooper's house ultimatum, but she knew what her mom's response would be. She would offer to come and help pack, clean up, and toss out. No, Jesse planned on getting more time from Cooper whether he knew it or not. She could tell her mom sometime down the road. "Listen, there's news. Cooper and Cindy are having another baby."

"Really? Well, good for them."

"Good for them? God, Mom, whose side are you on?" She watched as the brown dog went upstairs, clomping up the steps slowly.

"Are we feeling a little ouchy today?" The annoying phrase was one of her mom's favorites, which had unnervingly had found its way into Jesse's speech with Sophie.

"No, I'm not ouchy. God, Mom."

"Of course not."

"I'm not."

"You need to let it go, dear. He's not in your life anymore."

"I've let it all go, Mom. There's nothing left." Jesse could hear the clickety-clack of the dog's nails on the bare wood floor upstairs. It was odd having sound come from up there. She felt as if someone were invading her privacy.

"Well then, time to create a new life. I've done it." Jesse's dad had died a few years prior, after a sudden heart attack. Her mom had started over, moving out of the family home in Skokie into a modern high-rise in downtown Chicago. Jesse always thought her parents were the luckiest people because they had such a loving marriage. But her mom had surprised her by moving on so quickly. At least that was how it looked to Jesse. Her mom had made new friends and taken classes in art history and French cooking. She seemed happy. Jesse wondered if her mom ever thought about her dad the way she still thought about Cooper. Missing the old days and the good times.

"You can start a new chapter, dear. Maybe you need to step out of your comfort zone."

Comfort zone? Do I even have a comfort zone anymore?

"What about that nice writer who's interested in you?"

Blue had nicknamed the bespectacled bowtie-wearing writer from nearby Shelburne Falls Professor Pollen after his reading of his book, *The Rise and Fall of the Honeybee*, at the Barn a few months ago. Jesse had gone out that evening only to help Blue. The guy was apparently smitten with Jesse. Blue had even been leaving silly little notes and drawings for Jesse about Pollen. *I should never have mentioned him to her.*

"We don't know if he's nice, Mom." Something crashed upstairs, startling Jesse. She stood up. "Listen, I've got this dog here. He's getting into trouble. I've got to go deal with him."

"You got a dog? That's great. I bet he's good company."

"I'll let you know. Bye, Mom. Talk to you later."

"Call me. I want to hear about the dog. Love you."

"I love you, too." She put the phone down and dashed up the stairs to see the dog next to her bed. He had knocked over her Saint Anthony altar and was crouched down, his head under his paw, looking guilty, which made her laugh. She picked up the broken plastic saint from the floor. "Hey. My Saint Anthony."

The dog's ears perked up.

"Anthony? Saint Anthony?"

He cocked his head, which made Jesse laugh again.

"Should I call you Saint Anthony?"

FOUR ASPIRIN AND THREE cups of coffee later, Jesse wandered into the dining room, dressed in old gray sweats and a white long-sleeved L.L. Bean T-shirt of Cooper's she'd never returned. Saint Anthony, her new shadow, followed her. She petted him, and he settled himself on the rug.

The long pine dining room table had become another catchall. It was covered with more piles of her finds: losing lottery tickets, black-and-white Polaroid photos from the sixties, scraps of clothing, and plastic pieces of toys. Months of stuff she'd yet to log in. She had created a database on her computer similar to the one she'd set up at Blue's, where she logged the used books. Where and when she'd found the items, what their possible connection to Sophie could be—she analyzed and tallied everything, making comparisons and suppositions.

Early on, Jesse had shown her finds to several police officers, private detectives, and Cooper. They'd all just looked at her funny and shook their heads at the crazy grief-stricken woman hoarding junk. From then on, she'd kept them to herself to figure out on her own.

Lately, though, her database had become cumbersome and was hard to keep up with. She had started to fiddle with the finds on her dining room table and had begun making visual calendar-like boards by gluing bits and pieces of the finds in squares, each square representing a day of the month. She didn't need the writing anymore. Jesse repeated patterns and themes, moving the pieces around, making arrangements. On one, small strips of stained material that could have been either blood or ketchup from a white sailor's shirt, girls' size six, that she'd found on a hiking trail lay next to one another in rows like a line of little girls, all standing tall.

She let her finger run over the pieces of fabric, up and down, one strip at a time, and suddenly, Jesse was back sitting on the couch with Sophie on her lap, taking turns reading aloud from Sophie's favorite book, *Madeline.*

When Sophie was six, she went through a three-month phase where she spoke only in made-up French with a made-up French accent and answered only to Madeline. *"Mademoiselle* Mom, pass the cereal, *s'il vous plaît."*

Star had played along with her and was relegated to being Miss Clavel, the tall headmistress who was always shouting, "Girls!"

It was cute at first, but like the other things Sophie hyper-focused on, after a while, it became exhausting. She had demanded that her parents play a role in the French charade, all the time, too. They would go along with it for a while, but both Cooper and Jesse would forget or get tired of the game, which was not Sophie's plan. Shouting and tantrums ensued. It never ended well. Around that time, kids in her class had stopped inviting Sophie to birthday parties and sleepovers. Except for Star, other kids thought she was weird and just gave up trying to relate to the girl whose face was perpetually hidden behind binoculars.

The dog lifted his head and barked at something outside, pulling Jesse out of her memory. She looked back down at August's pile of junk, which was spilling over onto September's. She got to work and pulled out a large piece of trapezoid-shaped plywood. She quickly took materials from the pile: one shoelace, corduroy fabric, a New York City subway map, old photos, rusted wire, and a grocery list that included eggs, milk, bread, and mousetraps. She began to lay out the scraps in a different way. No squares for days. No structure. She was deconstructing the finds, working quickly, thinking less. Weaving the items together. Tearing pieces by hand. Gluing them. Collaging. Then she shellacked over the piece. It was satisfying. A calming way to keep her hands busy. And it gave her a feeling of accomplishment.

She stepped back and looked at the piece she had created. It bore no resemblance to the earlier visual calendars and was certainly far removed from her chart-like database, but the result felt just as urgent. Just as important. Maybe more so. It was dark: blues and blacks with large textured shapes, with parallel strips of fabric and bits of maps here and there. It felt strong. It was evocative and, to some, might suggest a story. The process felt intuitive. Organic. It felt right. *Who needs therapy? Screw Lila.*

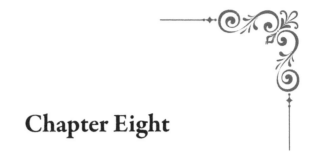

Chapter Eight

With Saint Anthony beside her in the pickup, Jesse stopped on Main Street in front of Canaan Hardware. She took a handful of flyers out of a box in the bed of her truck and walked into the shop. The owner, Bert, a gray-haired man wearing his signature red suspenders, was standing behind the counter. He was having a friendly conversation with Martha, a nurse from the elementary school. They were laughing. Jesse heard the words "cat got out" and "broken screen door" amid their chuckles. She walked up to the counter, holding one of the flyers. Last year's missing person poster was in the front window of the store, obscured by Weber grills, bags of charcoal, and birdseed. That flyer was almost identical to the new one in Jesse's hand, except the sixteen-year-old version of Sophie had a different hairstyle than last year's. A few store owners still had the poster prominently displayed, but Jesse noticed that many seemed to have grown tired of the whole affair and had taken it down.

"Hey, Bert. Hi, Martha. Sorry to interrupt. Mind if I put this new flyer in your window?"

He didn't make eye contact with Jesse. Many of the locals didn't anymore. And Martha just looked uncomfortable.

"I guess so." Bert held his hand out, and Jesse gave him one, but she had a feeling it wouldn't make it into the window. As she walked out the door, she heard them whisper, "Five years."

"No, six."

"When's she going to let it go?"

"Fucking idiots," she mumbled under her breath. They were parents. They both had children. She sucked it up and went into the other shops on the street, handing out the new flyer. Some locals were pleasant and sympathetic, wanting to chat with Jesse. But others just looked uneasy, as if they picked up Jesse's discomfort.

Back in her truck, she turned off Main onto Church Street and pulled into the parking lot of Blue's Book Barn. It was a creaky nineteenth-century barn painted an eye-catching yellow with purple trim.

Inside was homey and welcoming: reading nooks with overstuffed chairs, used books spilling off the shelves and onto the floor and side tables, and free cookies and coffee for customers. "Blue's Picks," brief synopses of recommended titles, were handwritten on index cards and thumb-tacked around the shop under his chosen books. The Barn was a quaint throwback to a time when people browsed in an actual store, lingering over print on paper, instead of frantically texting, tweeting, and downloading onto pads and pods.

Blue had made a killing with a start-up technology company during the early dot-com days and got out at the right time. That was the only reason he could afford to run a used bookstore that never made money. Jesse, on the other hand, had been a struggling artist in New York during those years, working a day job as an office assistant for a nonprofit arts organization. She'd known nothing of computers or IPOs back then. She'd lived in the top floor of a walk-up above a funeral home, using the bedroom as her painting studio since that room had the best light. She'd met Cooper at CBGB's the night Puffed Gorilla played there for the first and last time. And although the band really wasn't any good, Jesse was smitten with the lead singer, and he was taken with her beauty. Cooper bought her a drink after his set, and from then on, they were a couple.

Now Jesse went about her morning ritual, flipping over the Open sign on the double-wide door, turning on lights, and making coffee. Then she headed to her hideout, the cramped back office, and the dog followed. There were two old walnut desks, Blue's and hers, both with clunky desktop computers. A pink Post-it stuck to her monitor said, *Professor Pollen stopped in* again *asking for you. I told him you moved to Alaska, but he didn't buy it.* Blue had drawn a funny little man wearing round eyeglasses and a bowtie with little hearts circling his head. Smiling, she added it to the others he'd left before. It reminded her of when Cooper used to leave her notes around their apartment, little love poems stuck to the fridge with a magnet or sexy messages on her pillow. So sweet and unexpected.

She went back to the books. They were everywhere. Stacks on each desk waited to be catalogued, stacks on chairs waited to be shelved, and stacks in boxes on the floor waited to be put outside in front on the Free table. Jesse arranged a blanket on the floor next to her desk, and Saint Anthony circled then settled in on it.

She picked up a book from a stack to be logged in, turned it upside down, ruffled the pages, and gave it a shake. A few flattened rose petals drifted to the floor. She picked one up and brought it to her nose. Surprisingly, it still carried a faintly sweet scent. She flipped through the rest of the books and found a few more left-behind notes, which she set aside: someone's to-do list and the start of a Dear John letter. Then she began to log the books into the database.

The Barn had fewer and fewer customers since most people preferred to buy books online or download them onto their e-readers. Bound books printed on actual paper were becoming extinct. They were Jesse's pleasure, though. The smell and feel of a real book were part of her lifeblood. She would never understand ebooks, although the lack of customers actually suited her. She huddled in the back office, speaking to as few people as possible.

When she was shelving, she allowed herself to pluck random books off the shelves and skim, slipping into other worlds for a few brief moments. With minimal people contact and a flexible schedule, the job was perfect for her. And, of course, there were her finds. They were an added bonus.

Hearing the ting-a-ling of the front doorbell, Jesse leaned over in her chair to get a look at the person entering and was astonished to see that it was Star Silverman. Even though Blue had warned Jesse that Star was going to be working, seeing Star up close was a shock. Her heartbeat quickened, and her hands actually began to shake. Usually, when Star came to the Barn looking for her dad, Jesse ducked into her office to avoid any contact or slipped out for a cigarette until she saw Star leave. As the girl got older, she came less and less.

Jesse quietly went over to the Local Authors section, where she stood hidden behind the stacks, watching. Star was dressed in ripped jeans and a long-sleeved black thermal shirt, the kind that looked like long underwear. Her stringy hair, parted in the middle, hung down, obscuring much of her face. A darkness hovered about the girl.

She sat on the high stool behind the cash register, "working" at the front counter, although the word hardly applied. She busied herself texting, her thumbs flying over the tiny keypad of her cell phone, while listening to something via her earbuds. She ignored a female customer who walked in. When she finally glanced up and noticed the customer who had asked her a question, Star plucked the tiny plugs out of her ears and shuffled toward the stacks in mannish construction boots.

Star stopped at Women's Health, looking up and down the shelves. She sighed then mumbled to herself, "How are you supposed to find anything here?"

Jesse caught a strong whiff of Star's scent—stale cigarettes mingled with coffee and something else... antiseptic, like rubbing alcohol.

As Star pulled a hardcover from the shelf, Jesse noticed a greenish-black barbed-wire tattoo that went around the girl's left wrist, a drop of tattooed blood at her pulse. The sleeve of Star's shirt slid up, and Jesse also saw what, at first, she thought was another tattoo peeking out on the same arm. But on second glance, the color and texture made Jesse realize it was a dried bloody scab from a cut. The cut was about an inch long and went perpendicular to the tattoo, a few inches above it. Jesse didn't want to think about it. She'd thought she could handle it, but seeing Star made her feel sick. She was definitely not the same girl Jesse and Sophie used to bake cookies with. Star clomped to the front of the shop, handing the book to the customer. Maybe Jesse could put in her hours and not have to deal with Star. Maybe the girl would be so absorbed in her music, she would never even realize Jesse was in the back office. *But then again, maybe better to slip out and avoid her altogether.*

Just as Jesse turned to sneak out of the shop, Saint Anthony barked. Star looked up and saw them both.

"Why are you creeping around back there? Are you spying on me?"

"What? No. I was looking for something. A book." Jesse grabbed a random book off the shelf and waved it in the air.

"I thought you weren't working today," Star said.

"No, today is my regular day. I didn't know you'd be here."

"Well, I'm here."

Saint Anthony whined. Jesse looked down and petted him. "What is it, boy?" She wished he could speak. He gave a woof, loud and deep. Star got off her stool and walked over to look at him, giving Jesse a closer view of the girl. She was very pale, and it made Jesse wonder if she'd been out partying all night.

"What's that?" Star asked, nodding toward Saint Anthony.

"A dog," Jesse said.

"Duh."

"You asked." Jesse took a breath then said tentatively, "Star, are you okay? You look terrible."

"Thanks a lot." She crossed her arms over her chest. "That's all you have to say to me after all this time?"

"No. I'm glad to see you," Jesse said, but it sounded unconvincing. She'd hurt the girl by the way she'd abandoned her. But Jesse had hardly been in a position to nurture herself, let alone others, back then. "How've you been?"

"Oh, just great."

"It's just that, well, I'm concerned. Are you feeling okay?"

"You must be kidding, right? You're concerned about me? That's a laugh." Star turned away self-consciously.

Jesse wanted to put her hand on Star's forehead to feel for a fever. She should call Beth and tell her that her daughter looked sick, or maybe she was on drugs. Then Jesse heard that overriding voice in her head that said, *Don't get involved.*

"I doubt my dad would appreciate a dog in here."

"He's friendly."

"Whatever." Star walked back over to her stool and slumped into it. "By the way, you look like shit, too." Then she put her earbuds back in, tuning out the world.

Jesse headed to her office but turned back to see Star at the front counter, holding her head up with her hands as if it were the heaviest thing in the world. What was most upsetting was that it was like looking in a mirror, seeing her own pain reflected in the girl's face.

Chapter Nine

"Saint Anthony, come," Jesse shouted, her voice high-pitched and happy, as if she were talking to a child. The dog trotted over, his tail swishing about gracefully like a paintbrush. Her sleep had been surprisingly restful with him curled at the foot of her bed. It felt good to wake clear-headed and hangover free.

She rubbed the brown dog's ear between her fingers and let herself enjoy the new companionship. She smiled at him. Scratching his chin where he'd begun to go gray, she guessed he was somewhere in his middle years. Maybe five or six.

She could take him for a walk behind her house, up to the Norton meadow. He would like that. She rubbed his chest in circles and found herself thinking about that detective again. Barnes. His steadiness. His calm manner that she found both off-putting and attractive. She thought about the article he had given her and got up to retrieve it from the kitchen drawer.

She looked at the photo of April then unfolded the Xerox copy of a newspaper article from the New York Post.

Parsippany, N.J. Teen Missing Since Monday: Parsippany authorities are searching for a missing teen, April Johnson, 17, last seen leaving her home on October 5. The girl is described as five feet tall, weighing 98 pounds, with long blond hair. She was wearing blue jeans, a white top and red hoodie, and she has a distinctive high-pitched voice that many thought sounded like a little girl's.

Jesse reread the last sentence three times. She took another long look at the photo. If April had dyed and cut her hair, maybe, perhaps, she was the girl Jesse had followed from the Zone the other day. The one who'd sounded like Minnie Mouse. And there was still something else that had drawn her to that girl. A sadness. A secret.

The article went on to quote the girl's mother: *"I know April. She's not a runaway. I'm afraid for her."*

Jesse remembered saying those same words about Sophie.

A private detective hired by the family, Kentucky Marcus Barnes of Parsippany, said they are checking out all leads and have no evidence of foul play. Her family, however, fears this is a kidnapping.

A familiar pain jabbed her chest, and she pressed her hand there. She closed her eyes and took several deep breaths. When the sensation had first occurred years ago, she'd thought she was having a heart attack. She'd come to understand it was anxiety, and she'd learned to breathe into it until it subsided. If all else failed, she popped a Xanax.

She imagined calling April's parents. *"I saw your daughter. Well, maybe, possibly, I saw her. I have no idea where she is now, but if it was her, she is alive."* That was all Jesse longed for someone to say to her. *She's alive. And, oh yeah. It wasn't your fault.*

Then the scolding, guilt-inducing voice that haunted her piped up. *Who are you kidding? Gone. Missing. Vanished. Totally, one hundred percent your fault.*

JESSE DROVE TO THE Book Barn with the dog for her Saturday morning shift. After opening the place up and turning on lights, she made the coffee. Then Star entered, looking no healthier than she had the day before. The girl slunk into her seat at the front desk without making eye contact.

Jesse tried to come up with reasons to tell Blue why she would need to change her days so as not to coincide with Star's. But none of her ideas made any sense. She had nothing else going on in her life, no need to switch other than his daughter made her uncomfortable. Blue probably thought it would be good for Star—and for Jesse—to reconnect. He had been kind to give Jesse a job in the first place. There wasn't much she could do now. She had taught art at the elementary school before. It had been fun. The kids were so uninhibited, using the boldest colors, painting the most creative scenes. But there was no way she could do that anymore. And she didn't want to make waves.

Besides, she couldn't imagine Star lasting very long anyway. If Blue asked her how Star was doing, Jesse would be honest. The girl wasn't motivated. And she didn't look well.

Jesse sat down at her desk in the back office, and Saint Anthony found his new spot on the blanket. She pulled Detective Barnes's business card from her purse then fingered it while gathering courage. She dialed his number. He answered on the second ring, and she told him she might know something about the girl he was looking for.

"I'll be right over," he said and hung up without saying goodbye.

She immediately regretted calling him. It was just some circumstantial evidence, and Jesse knew from personal experience that the wrong information could set a missing person case back for weeks and haunt parents for longer. It wasn't evidence. It was a hunch.

Jesse grabbed a stubby pencil from her desk. She closed her eyes and pulled up the image of the girl with the short, choppy hair and high-pitched voice. On the back of an envelope, she penciled in a face, uneven hair, and short bangs. She erased the nose that looked too big and tried again. Better. Mouth. Thin lips. And the eyes. Something dark and intense in them. She worked quickly and added in detailed cross-hatching of the girl's hair then the shadows and shading of her shirt. She hadn't sketched in years and was rusty. The likeness wasn't perfect, but it was close. Having a pencil in her hand felt good—she'd forgotten how good. It gave her a tingly, almost high feeling.

"Good morning, Ms. Albright."

Jesse jumped. Detective Barnes was standing behind her. She hadn't heard the jangle of the front bell, and she just realized she hadn't even told him where she was.

"How did you...?" She slid the drawing under some papers.

He smiled and nodded toward the phone on her desk, a landline. "That was an easy one. I am a detective, after all." He was out of breath, and Saint Anthony was at the detective's feet, nudging his head into the man's thigh.

"Nice dog. Regal looking." Detective Barnes was wearing running shorts and sneakers and held a bottle of water and a large manila envelope. He nodded at his outfit. "Sorry about the running shorts."

Jesse couldn't help but stare at his lean, muscular body.

"I was out on my morning run and didn't want to miss you."

She caught herself staring and looked up. "Oh. Okay."

He still carried himself with that ease. Totally comfortable. Jesse found it so noticeable because she felt exactly the opposite.

"Who's the angry girl up front?" the detective asked as he removed his cap.

"That would be the boss's daughter."

"I showed her a photo of April, asked some questions. She looks close in age. Got the cold shoulder."

"Don't take it personally. I don't think she talks much to anyone. And when she does, she's sarcastic and snotty."

"She's what? About sixteen?"

Jesse nodded.

"Sarcastic and snotty sounds about right."

She pointed toward Blue's desk. "You can sit there." She chewed on the skin around her thumb. "You deal with missing children a lot?"

"Yes, but parents also hire me to follow their teens. I give reports on what they do, where they go, when and with whom. 'Teen Surveillance,' they call it. Parents who can't or don't want to keep tabs on their kids themselves. It's a sad state of affairs, if you ask me, but it's a job, and I happen to be good at it." He paused. "Now it's all about technology. Fancy digital gizmos to track your kids, GPS devices, cell phones with 'wireless chaperones'—expensive devices to monitor their whereabouts, cameras in their bedrooms. I don't know what happened to old-fashioned talking to your kids. Spying on them may tell you where they are and what they do but doesn't give you a good relationship with them." He shook his head. "Sorry. Listen to me rambling."

Jesse shrugged. "That's okay."

"It's just that this work can be hard, physically and emotionally. That's why I'm going back to school."

"Really?" A private detective with ambition. Jesse was surprised and impressed. "What are you studying?"

"Social work. I'm interested in what's going on in their heads, not what party they're going to or who they're friends with on Facebook."

Saint Anthony returned to Barnes and sniffed him. He reached into his pocket and fed the mutt a dog biscuit, which Saint Anthony chewed loudly, dropping crumbs all over the floor.

"You'd be surprised how many dogs you run into that need pacifying in this line of work. I'd carry a steak with me if I could."

She noticed his hands. They were smooth with nicely trimmed nails. She looked down at her fingernails, which were ragged from biting them.

"So you remembered something?"

"It's probably nothing, but the girl I saw had a high-pitched voice. You know, like a little girl. I remember thinking that when I heard her. It was hard to say how old she was. Maybe sixteen. Maybe nineteen. Don't know. She had short brown hair. And it was a bad haircut. All chopped up. Uneven."

"Like she might have cut it herself."

"That's what I thought. Unless it's some new hairstyle. I don't know what's in style anymore."

"What was she wearing?"

Jesse thought back. "A red hoodie and jeans. Purple flip-flops. That's about it. But when I studied the photo you gave me, I thought that maybe it could be the same girl from the Zone. She had similar features." She wasn't about to go into the other things nagging at her. The way she bit her lower lip. The watermelon gum. That she felt the girl was some connection to Sophie. Like one of her finds. Maybe if he located this girl, she would somehow open a door to Sophie. *Pay close attention and be patient. Stop. Wait. Watch. And most of all... listen.*

Barnes opened his envelope and took out a folder. He laid out five more color photos of April on Jesse's desk. "Take a look."

Jesse had gone through the same process for the police. Sophie had worn her binoculars around her neck in her last school picture. Jesse remembered being mad that no one had told her to remove them. And there were no reshoots. But now Jesse cherished that picture. It was the real Sophie.

She had looked like most of the children in the missing person photos, like she was the happiest kid on the block. She was far from that, though. When she was good, she was enchanting, but her other side overshadowed those times. At first, Jesse and Cooper worried they were terrible parents, not firm enough. But Sophie's mood swings became more intense, lasted longer, and were far more dramatic than most kids'. The tiniest thing could set her off into wild tantrums. The scratchy feel of a sweater or sock. A move to the dining room for dinner. The word *no*. She would scream and cry, kick and swirl, destroying whatever was in her wake until her initial desire was forgotten. She would finally land on the floor of her closet, either of her own will or after being taken there by Cooper.

"I can't feel myself," she would repeat over and over while rocking herself into a calm state.

But birds were her balm, and occasionally, if they caught it in time, Jesse and Cooper could cajole her back from the darkness using a bird sighting or sound.

"Sweetie, look there, a pileated," Jesse would say, pointing out the window. "Pecking a hole in our oak tree. Did you see? His head is huge." Or "Listen, Soph. *Fee bee, fee bee.* A black-capped chickadee. So sweet." And they would prod their daughter to peer through her binoculars.

Jesse wished Sophie was with her, even with all her darkness and difficulty. But it was too late for Sophie. All these years later, Jesse was looking at photos of another missing girl. She pushed the photos away.

"Ms. Albright, I hate to put you through this. You're a brave woman."

She looked at him, shook her head. "That's the last thing I am." She wanted to scream at the detective for being so calm and understanding. Maybe that was his technique for working people, getting them to reveal stuff the way Sophie could work a bird and get it to come out from hiding.

She picked up a photo of April, studied it, then gathered them all together. She knew she should probably give him the cell phone she'd found in the dressing room, but it was her clue. She needed a cigarette. Wanting the conversation to be over and the man out of her office, she held out the photos.

"That's all you remember?" he asked as he took them.

"That's it."

"Well, thank you for your time." He looked right into her eyes.

She glanced away then slid her drawing out and handed it to him. "I don't know why I did this. It's what I could remember."

He took the paper from her and looked at it. "You're an artist."

"Not anymore."

"This is very good." He studied the drawing. "You *are* an artist. This does resemble April. I thank you for doing this. You've been a big help."

"I sincerely doubt it."

Barnes stood up to leave. Jesse had gone back to her computer, turning her back to him once again, but she could hear him breathing, standing near the doorway. After a moment, she turned to him. "Yes, Detective?"

She'd seen that look before. She didn't need his sympathy. Getting up, she walked to the door and gestured with her arm, pointing the way out.

"Call me Tuck, please. Short for Kentucky. Everyone does." He extended his hand to shake hers.

She just nodded and pointed again.

He put his hand down. "Goodbye, Ms. Albright."

"I'LL TELL MY DAD SOME cop was in here asking questions."

Jesse swung around in her seat to see Star standing in the office doorway. Jesse was surprised to see Star in her space, invading what had become her private cocoon. The girl's presence felt intrusive.

"Is this something about Sophie? Are they going to arrest you for murder?" Star asked.

"What? Are you insane? It has nothing to do with Sophie. Do you honestly think I'm a murderer?"

Star tilted her head and shrugged. "I don't know. I guess not."

"What about you? He was asking you questions, too. I guess I'll have to tell your dad that."

"No you don't."

"Star, what's going on? Do you know something?" The girl was acting peculiar and evasive, although it had been so long since she'd spent time with Star, Jesse wasn't sure. *Maybe this is normal teen behavior.*

"He was asking me about a girl. Who was he talking about?" Star said.

"Some missing girl."

"What's with our town and missing girls?"

"I know it's crazy. She might be a runaway," Jesse said.

"A runaway? How does he know?"

"You're asking a lot of questions. Do you know something?" In the old days, Star would never have lied to Jesse. *But that was then.*

Meanwhile, the dog wandered over to Star and poked his snout into her crotch.

"Jeez. What's with him?"

"Nothing. He's gentle. He won't bite."

"I am so not into canines." She pushed him away. "All sniffy and needy."

Jesse bit her tongue. She wanted to say, "Sounds like you," but she patted her thigh. "Come here, boy." And the dog ambled over.

"I bet that cop's into you." Star let out a little laugh. "Way cuter than"—she made air quotes—"your realtor."

Jesse sat up straighter, surprised to hear Star refer to Gary. She'd assumed no one noticed her, that she'd become invisible. The way she'd felt.

Star walked over to Blue's desk and sat in his chair. Leaning back, she put her feet up on the desk, pulled a cigarette out of her back pocket, and lit it.

Jesse glared at her. "You know there's no smoking in here. You don't want to burn down your dad's business, do you?"

She took a long drag and blew an obviously well-practiced smoke ring in Jesse's direction. "I could care less."

"You really want to reek of cigarettes? You think boys will like that?"

Star laughed. "Hasn't seemed to cramp your style."

"Put it out before your dad comes in."

She dropped the cigarette on the floor and stubbed it out with her boot heel. A whole minute went by while only the sound of the furnace rumbling in the basement could be heard.

"How do you stand it?" Star asked.

"What?"

"This... so-called job. It's so dumb."

"I like quiet, and I like books."

Star scrunched up her nose and made a face. "Bo-ring," she sang.

"You used to like books."

"Yeah, right."

"You said you were going to live in Paris one day, like Madeline, from the book. You and Sophie."

"I wouldn't—"

"You were tall Miss Clavel. Sophie always got to be Madeline. Don't you remember?"

Star opened her mouth as if to disagree but then she stopped, her mouth agape. Jesse imagined her childhood memories were coming crashing back to her. Star seemed to shake it off. "Why do you do that?" Star asked.

"Do what?"

"Go to the mall. Hang out at the Zone? Like every week practically."

"I don't hang out there."

"I've seen you."

Jesse went back to her computer and started clicking away.

"And I've seen you stalking kids at my school, too. It's totally creepy."

It was true. A few times a month, Jesse went to what would have been Sophie's school and was now Star's high school. She would park in different locations—across the street or in the back of the lot behind the school buses. Sometimes, she left her car at the Book Barn and walked there so she could hide more easily. She wore sunglasses, and she supposed she did look like she was skulking about. *Never stop looking.* Then a haughty twenty-something teacher caught Jesse standing behind a tree with a pair of binoculars and threatened to report her. From then on, she'd been extra careful.

"You're looking for her, aren't you?"

Jesse stopped typing. "Yes, Star, yes, I'm looking for her. I lost my child. She's still missing, and I still look for her." She didn't say, "And I talk to her, and she leaves me finds, but I don't know how much longer I can hold on, even though it says to never stop looking." She inhaled then exhaled a big breath. "Do you have a problem with that?"

"It's just weird. Everyone thinks so. They think you're crazy."

Jesse threw her head back and let out a hard, scary laugh. "Do you honestly think that after all that's happened, I would care what anyone thinks?"

Star lifted her shoulders.

"What's it to you anyway? What do you care what I do or don't do?"

"I don't. It's just..."

"What? It's just what?"

"Why do you stay here in Canaan? In that same house? Don't you want to forget the past? It's not like you're going to find her now. I mean, she's dead. She's got to be dead, right?"

The front bell jangled. Jesse looked at the girl, almost willing herself to see deep inside her, hoping to understand something. Then she opened her top desk drawer, pulled out a tin of Altoids, and held it out to Star.

Star paused, as if wondering if there was a catch. Jesse nodded, coaxing her on. The girl reached over and popped a few mints into her mouth.

"You never write back," Star said.

Jesse stared at her, not knowing what Star meant.

Star nodded at the latest pink Post-it stuck on the corner of Jesse's desk. *Prof. Pollen stung by hundreds of killer bees. News at 11.* The doodle of Professor Pollen had glasses, a bowtie, and bug eyes. His mouth formed an O as bees swarmed around his head.

Jesse's mouth dropped open. "You wrote this? And the others, too?"

"Duh. Who did you think?"

"I... I thought it was your dad."

"My dad?" Star let out a snort. "He can't draw to save his life. You know that from when we all used to play Pictionary."

"You know this guy?" Jesse tapped her finger on the pink Post-it.

"Uh, yeah. He subbed for Mrs. Bohnen when she had that skiing accident."

"Mrs. Bohnen? She was your fifth-grade teacher, right? Sophie's teacher, too."

Star nodded. "Yup. He was going on about honey bees even back then."

For the first time, she realized how ridiculous it was to think Blue would leave her silly cartoon drawings. She felt herself blush. "Thanks, I liked them." And she nodded toward the doodle.

"Yeah, sure." Star got up. "I'm out of here." She looked down, and Saint Anthony was hovering at her feet, gazing up at her as if she were a big, juicy hamburger. "What's with him?"

"Maybe he's into you."

That made her laugh, and Jesse smiled. When Star was at the door, about to leave, Jesse called out, "Star?"

She stopped and turned back.

Jesse nodded toward the little pile of Professor Pollen drawings she'd saved. "I really did like them."

Chapter Ten

As usual, Gary was waiting for Jesse when she entered the Blue-berry Lane house, with the dog trailing behind. Gary's hair was sticking up funny, and his shirt was a wrinkled mess. She was surprised his wife would let him out of the house like that. But it didn't matter—he was a friendly face, and Jesse was glad to see him.

"Hi," she said, smiling.

"Hi. Who's this?" He bent down to pet Saint Anthony.

Jesse undid the leash, and the dog wandered and sniffed. He eventually made his way over to a rug, where he circled then lay down, curled up all small.

"I found him."

"Is he housebroken?"

"Yes, Gary. Don't worry—he won't pee in your listing."

"Hey, poochie." He rubbed Saint Anthony behind his ear. "Wish I could have a dog."

"What's the matter? Mommy won't let you?"

"Never mind. Come on." He took her hand and escorted her into the den toward the back of the house. There was a rustic stone fireplace and a couch, the lone piece of furniture in the room. As if on autopilot, they moved to the scratchy, corduroy sofa and proceeded to undress. Her mind pinged and bounced about like a pinball. *Missing Persons. DNA. Scarlet tanager. Sophie. Mom, mom, mom. Star. More Sophie. More.* All these thoughts were like blown-down tree limbs, remnants one might trip over after a terrible thunderstorm.

Gary kissed her, and the feel of his warm body pulled her out of the darkness. But it was that unruffled detective who came into her head next. *What was his first name? A southern state. Something long. Tennessee or Alabama?*

She pictured his flowered Zone necktie flapping with the breeze. His lean, muscular legs in those running shorts. The sad look he gave her before leaving the Book Barn.

The dog barked once, breaking the spell of her escape. She felt oddly guilty, as if he disapproved of the affair.

"Hey, where were you?" Gary said when they were finished.

"I'm right here." She suddenly felt chilled and pulled an afghan off the back of the couch to cover herself.

"Jess, we have to talk." He fumbled around with the pile of clothes, looking for something.

That can't be good. She lit a cigarette. He had tried to end the affair once last year. Jesse wasn't sure why—an uncharacteristic pang of guilt, she'd assumed—but they had slipped back into it after taking two weeks off.

"Carol and I are having, well, getting a baby. We're adopting. From Vietnam. There's a baby, and we're going to go there to get it. As soon as we get the call. A girl."

"What?" She sat up straight. "I didn't even know you wanted a baby."

"Well, yeah. Why would you? We don't exactly talk much."

She suddenly felt like desperate Mrs. Robinson from *The Graduate.*

"We've been trying for a while to have our own baby, and it seems we can't."

She looked at him, shaking her head in disbelief. "You've been trying to get pregnant?"

He nodded.

"And you've been carrying on with me all this time? That's sick, Gary. Even I'm not that sick."

He tilted his head questioningly. "That would really have changed things with us? C'mon, Jess. Be honest."

She glared at him. He was right, of course. She was no better than him. But hearing the truth, thrown in her face, made her feel nauseated. She shoved away the afghan, stubbed out her cigarette in a saucer, and began grabbing for her clothes.

"Maybe it's run its course. Maybe *we've* run our course..." He didn't look at her. He was still messing with the clothes pile and finally extracted his underwear, white stretched-out Jockey briefs that looked like a little boy's. She'd never noticed those before.

"You wait until after we have sex to say this? Real classy, Gary." To Jesse, the affair had become a habit, like her smoking. She knew it was bad, but she couldn't stop. She didn't want to.

"I'm sorry. It's not like I want to stop. It's that I think we have to. For real this time." He put his arms around her awkwardly while she held her clothes to her chest. "I'll miss you so much. It's all I have to look forward to."

She pushed him away. "Jesus, Gary. Me, too, and there's something really wrong with that. As screwed up as I am, at least I know that."

He stepped toward her, placed his hands gently on her shoulders, then slid her hair behind each ear the way Sophie used to when she sat on Jesse's lap. The small gesture startled her. She blinked back a tear as he kissed her on the mouth, and she didn't resist. The pile in her arms dropped to the floor. She let herself melt into him.

"Will you be sad if we stop seeing each other?" he whispered.

"Oh, Gary," she said with a catch in her throat, "I'm always sad, and it has nothing to do with you. Haven't you figured that out yet?" She sighed. "You said you'd be there for me."

"I am. I will be. As friends."

"Oh God. I don't need a friend. That's not what this was about."

"C'mon, Jess. Everyone needs a friend." It sounded like he meant "Everyone needs a friend... *especially you.*"

Jesse stared into his eyes, looking for what, she didn't know. She shook her head. She felt so lonely. Her stomach growled. "I can't believe you're doing this to me now. Of all times."

Who should I be, Soph? "Osprey" came to her. *Yes, let me be an osprey. Strong and independent. Let me swoop on out of here.*

He took her in his arms and held her tightly. It felt safe there. She closed her eyes. She wanted to go to sleep and block out the world.

"I can't leave her. I thought I could, but I just can't. We have a history. And now with the baby coming..."

Jesse opened her eyes. She didn't say, "I don't want you to leave her." She would never want that. Jesse only worried about what she would do with her time. Where she would go. What she would do to numb the pain. She knew she couldn't keep drinking so much. She didn't want to hurt someone else, and that was where she was headed. She couldn't go to the Zone anymore. Thank God she'd found Saint Anthony. In a gesture of desperation, she grabbed Gary's ass, pulled him closer, and kissed him hard and deep. That kind of breathless kiss always made him beg for more.

"You make me feel so good," Gary whispered. For a moment, she thought she'd brought him back, reeled him in like a fish on a line. "But that was the last time, Jess. I've got to try to salvage my marriage. You understand. It's the right thing to do."

"The right thing? Since when have you—we—done the right thing?" She pushed him away and began to dress. "You'll be sorry, Gary. Don't come crawling back to me like last time," she spat out, even though she prayed he would. She grabbed her bag and the dog then fled.

THE NEXT DAY, JESSE skulked into Earl's with Saint Anthony and tried to fade into the regular breakfast crowd, head tucked tightly to her chest, eyes facing the floor. She wore an oversized green army cap. Its long flaps covered her ears, and the whole thing practically obscured her face. She scanned the room quickly and saw familiar faces, locals she used to be friendly with. Mac Junior and Avery Fletcher, both men who'd been farming all their lives. Jesse used to buy organic eggs and honey from them. And Maggie Leonard, who owned the yarn shop where Jesse used to take knitting lessons. They all looked away from Jesse when their eyes connected with hers. And she was pretty sure she heard a woman say, "Bird Mom," in a low voice.

She turned and noticed a customer at the front table near the window reading the *Canaan Gazette*. When he set his paper down, Jesse was surprised to see it was Detective Barnes. For a second, she felt embarrassed, as if he knew her thoughts of him while she was with Gary. *What's he doing here? Following me?* But other than the 7-Eleven on the outskirts of town, Earl's was really the only place to get a decent cup of coffee.

"Hey, boy. Good to see you," Barnes said, and the dog went up to him, his tail aflutter. Barnes stroked the dog's head then looked up and smiled at Jesse. "Ms. Albright. Nice to see you, too." He was dressed in his running gear again.

"Still here?"

"Just got here. Finished my morning run. I was reading how 'Yogurt Is Coming to Whatley Farms' right here in Canaan. Exciting, huh?" he said with a smile.

"I'll take the local news over the doom and gloom of *The New York Times* any day."

"I can understand why. Can I buy you a cup of coffee?"

"Oh, I have to be going." But she didn't move.

Barnes got up. "Let me get you a cup."

When she didn't protest, he walked over to the self-service counter and picked up a ceramic mug with *Earl's* printed on the side. She slid into the seat across from his and unbuttoned her jacket. She looked around and noticed the place had been decked out in an autumn motif, with colorful squashes, cornstalks, and a scarecrow displayed in the window next to their table. It had been years since she sat down for coffee and a long chat the way she used to with her friend Beth Silverman or with Gary's wife, Carol, after book club.

Barnes came back and placed her coffee in front of her. He pulled a dog biscuit from his pocket and set it on the table. He slid back into the booth. "Strong and black, right?"

She looked at him questioningly, wondering if he was asking about her taste in men.

He shrugged. "I noticed your coffee cup at the Book Barn." He nodded toward the dog. "Hey, what's his name anyway?"

"Saint Anthony."

"Ahh. The patron saint of lost things."

She raised her eyebrows. "That's right." She pulled her cap off and shook her head, freeing her unruly hair.

"Hi there, Saint Anthony. You're a good boy, aren't you?" He rubbed the dog's butt, which the dog loved, wriggling and pointing his snout skyward.

Jesse tapped her thigh, had the dog lie down at her feet, then fed him his biscuit. He was turning out to be a good-natured, easy dog. If he'd been a child, he would have been perfect. She looked up and saw the detective watching her. She glanced down at her outfit and saw she was wearing one of her laundry mistakes—a long-sleeved red top with a generous sprinkling of white bleach dots on it. She used to sew a lot of her own clothes, using soft, colorful cotton fabrics with appliqués and cutouts with different fabrics underneath and interesting hand-sewn stitches. She'd had her own arty style. Before. The white spots on the red shirt had eaten through the fabric, leaving tiny round holes that made Jesse think of flesh-eating protozoa. She shook her head, thinking how far she'd sunk.

She tried to make small talk. "You run a lot?"

He nodded. "Rain or shine. You have any routines? Things you have to do?"

Too many. She gave a little shrug, not about to reveal her demons, then fidgeted in her seat. "When I said 'still here' before, I meant you're still here, in Canaan."

He laughed, setting his cup down. "You trying to get rid of me?"

"No, I just..."

"I've been looking for April Johnson for over three weeks now from New Jersey to upstate New York over to western Massachusetts and now to your hill town here. This girl's been on the move, and I'm getting close. I can feel it." He shook his head. "I know it sounds crazy, but I usually get an odd sensation when I'm near one of my missing people, a rumbly feeling here"—he tapped his chest—"and a dull headache."

"I get that feeling most days." *Hungover,* she didn't say. *Depressed.* "Haven't found any missing people." She turned away for a moment. Then she let out a deep breath and looked back at Barnes. She'd met and talked to lots of detectives over the years. From the local police department. From other towns and cities. Ones she'd hired on her own. Barnes seemed different, though. Sensitive. More thoughtful. Jesse wondered what his story was. She suspected he had his own secrets, but she wasn't about to get sucked into anyone else's heartache.

"Anyway," Barnes continued, "the proprietor of the Rolling Hills Motel where I'm staying told me, 'If you want to know what's going on, poke your head in Earl's, and you'll be caught up in no time.' So here I am for my morning gossip."

"You'll hardly hear anything very interesting at Earl's. A newborn calf or the library getting the latest Barbara Kingsolver is enough to keep most folks going all winter. Canaan's a quiet hill town except for the annual Harvest Fest. That's when it gets transformed. The whole town goes cuckoo for pumpkins." She tipped her head toward the window. Outside, men were standing on tall ladders, hanging a Harvest Festival banner. Others were pounding and lifting long pieces of wood, erecting a set of bleachers in the town square. A hay wagon was loaded with pumpkins—big, fat, perfectly round ones, small hand-sized ones, and all shapes and sizes in between.

"People come from all over for it. It's huge. You can't swing a cat without hitting a damn pumpkin. Pumpkin carving, pumpkin pie, pumpkin soup, pumpkin ice cream. Then it ends with this big party. This year, it's at Earl's. It's corny and stupid, but some people think it's fun."

"Some people?"

She shrugged and looked away. She realized how much she missed her friends and the feeling of community. The simple joys of small-town life. How strangers came together to help people in need. She reached into her purse and held out a cell phone to Barnes.

He looked at it then at her. "Why are you giving me a cell phone, Ms. Albright?" He took the phone from her. "I'm good at finding people, figuring mysteries out, but I can't read minds."

"The other day, I saw April, or whoever that girl with the high voice was, come out of the dressing room, like I told you." She waited for him to nod her on before she continued. "I went in after her to try something on and found it. There's a photo in here of some girl's feet in purple flip-flops like the ones she wore."

He tilted his head questioningly. "You didn't want to share it with me before?"

She began to nervously shred a paper napkin, ripping it into little bits and dropping them into a pile in front of her. "No."

"And why was that?"

"I distrust cops."

"I'm not a cop."

"Close enough."

"What made you change your mind?"

There was a long silence while she thought how to answer. She didn't mean to be secretive. On one hand, she honestly didn't want any parent to go through what she had, but on the other, she couldn't help herself. Since it might have been a clue from Sophie, that took precedence.

Barnes scrolled through the cell phone, looking at the numbers logged in. "Mostly Florida and Chicago area codes. April is from New Jersey, but you never know. With the internet, Facebook, kids communicate with people from all over the world. Thank you. I'll check this out. Could be a lead."

Maybe Barnes would be able to connect the phone and April to Sophie. She sipped her coffee. She opened her mouth to say something, but the door flew open, and Gary burst in, all jittery with nervous energy. She'd run into him in public before, and they'd had no problem acting appropriately friendly yet distant. But seeing him the day after he'd dumped her was unnerving. Her heart picked up speed. The affair had been a rudder, and without it, she felt adrift.

He waved at Jill behind the counter, a petite woman in her thirties who always wore a smile, one of the owners of Earl's.

"Hey, Jilly, how you doing?" His head bobbed. "Any of those mixed-berry scones today?"

"Hey, Gary. I saved you one," Jill said. "Where you been?"

Jesse sank down in her seat. She grabbed her purse and began to inch her body toward the edge of the bench. Time to make her exit.

Barnes glanced at Gary then at the obviously uncomfortable Jesse. He leaned in closer to her and lowered his voice. "You all right?"

"Yeah, yeah." But she didn't take her eyes off Gary, whose back was to her. She began shredding another napkin into even tinier bits. A good-sized white paper mound had formed in front of her.

"I appreciate your bringing this to me," Barnes said, nodding toward the cell phone.

"I figured I'd run into you somewhere." Her eyes stayed on Gary as she spoke. "Otherwise, I'd have called you. Your card... that you gave me." She put her hat on, tugging it so low, it almost covered her eyes.

Just then, Gary turned around from the counter and saw Jesse. He opened his mouth to speak, stopped himself when he noticed Barnes, shot him a questioning look, then turned back around.

"You know him?" Barnes said.

"You live in this town, you know everyone." Maybe she had been deceiving herself, just as Lila had said. She *wasn't* invisible. It was the very opposite. If Star knew about her and Gary, then everybody probably did. *What an idiot.*

After paying for his coffee and scone, Gary left, obviously avoiding her on his way out.

Jesse continued shredding then blurted out, "You ever do stupid things, Detective?"

"Me?" He pointed to himself with a grin. "Never."

"Yeah, well, you observe people. What has to happen for someone to learn a lesson?"

"Just what kind of lesson do you mean, Ms. Albright? And what kind of someone?"

"Someone like me, I guess."

"Someone like you seems to be"—he pushed her hat back on her head so he could see her eyes—"maybe someone who's been hurt badly, maybe been through more than anyone should. Someone who's carried around a lot of guilt and anger. Someone who maybe should let it go, be kind to herself."

Jesse blinked a few times, sitting up straight. "Maybe someone has picked up a thing or two in their college psychology classes, I'd say."

"Indeed, but mostly, the someone I just described could have been me a couple years ago. Was me."

I knew he had some *story*. Maybe he cheated on his wife or was an abusive husband. He was smooth. Too cool. Something smoldered behind that handsome face. The dog sat up and gave a small whine, stretching his head back, looking at Jesse longingly.

Simultaneously, they both reached down to pet him, grazing each other's hands instead of the dog.

"Oh, sorry," she said, pulling away.

"Sorry," he said.

But with that little touch, she felt a spark so charged, she nearly gasped. She wondered if he could have felt it, too. He mumbled something about the dog and went back to sipping his coffee.

Finally, he cleared his throat. "Well, from my experience, I'd say people have to be good and ready to make changes, learn lessons. Sometimes that takes time. A lot of time."

She watched through the window as Gary got into his green Saturn and sped off, the car sputtering and coughing as it went. It had needed a new muffler for the last six months and probably would for the next six, at least. *Typical Gary*. But she was the last person to judge him. She reached into her purse and extracted a cigarette, which she shakily lit. She inhaled and let out a long wisp of smoke.

Barnes raised his eyebrows and whispered, "Ah, no smoking."

"Oh. Yeah. Right." She dropped the cigarette in her coffee, and it sizzled.

"Ms. Albright, come with me to the party."

She looked up directly into the detective's eyes for the first time. "Pardon me?"

"Your Harvest Festival. Real big around here, right?"

She shook her head. "Why would you want to take me?"

"Why not? I could do a little investigating. You could introduce me to some of the locals. They might have seen April. Plus, some people think it's fun."

She paused while considering if she could actually go. She had just been thinking about this man. But her racing heart advised otherwise. "I don't think so, Detective."

He cocked his head, looking her square in the eyes as if trying to get inside her head.

She let out a sigh. "Thanks for asking, but I don't go out." She went to scratch her nose, and her sleeve brushed against her mound of napkin bits, scattering them across the table. Without waiting for his response, she got up and headed for the exit, the dog by her side.

She turned back and saw him reach across the table, sweep her pile of napkin bits into his hand, and dump them into his empty coffee cup. He made one more sweep of the table, clearing any last bits. *A neat freak,* she thought.

"Hey," he shouted as she reached the door, "when are you going to call me Tuck?"

Chapter Eleven

"How's it going?" Blue said as he entered the back office. Jesse was logging books into the database, but she was finding it hard to concentrate. That damn detective. The thought of him, the way he looked at her with his piercing, knowing eyes, kept breaking her concentration. She was glad Blue showed up to drag her back to reality. He was wearing a worn MIT T-shirt and carried a large box stuffed with books. His eyes, a startling cool aqua, twinkled. Since growing a beard several years ago, he resembled a slightly sophisticated Jerry Garcia.

"It's going," Jesse said.

Blue placed the box on a table, and Saint Anthony came up to him, wagging and panting. "Hey, I heard about this guy. Nice boy," he said, patting the dog's head. Blue leaned his husky, teddy-bear-like frame against a file cabinet facing Jesse. "Went to a big yard sale yesterday. They were practically giving away some treasures." He lifted a leather-bound book from the box. "A Thoreau." He dug around and pulled out two more dusty hardbacks. "Dickinson and Barrett Browning."

"That's great," Jesse said. She could understand Blue's passion.

"Any calls?" Blue asked.

"Nope." There rarely were. Another perk of the job.

He touched her shoulder. "You okay? You seem distracted lately."

She laughed. "Just lately?"

"Well." He smiled. "Maybe more than usual. You know, if you want to talk..."

She nodded, but they both knew she was not big on talk.

"You up for a casual dinner at our house? Beth's famous linguine with clam sauce. She'd love to see you."

She shrugged. "Not yet, Blue. But thanks." Jesse wasn't sure she would ever be up for that again. They had all been such close friends once. So many dinners and bottles of wine shared. She turned back to her computer. "I better log in these books."

Jesse could hear him standing behind her, breathing. She imagined he was trying to figure out whether he should push or just give up. He exhaled. "Got to make a deposit at the bank. Back in a few."

Not long after Blue left, the front doorbell jangled. Jesse was alone in the shop, so she would have to attend to the customer. She got up and headed to the front of the store, and there, browsing through the local authors section, was Barnes. Her heart leapt. She watched him a moment while hidden behind Biography and Memoir. He seemed completely absorbed in a book.

"Ahem," she cleared her throat.

Barnes looked up at her with a smile. "Hello, again."

"May I help you, Detective?"

"Well, yes, I believe you can."

Saint Anthony came over and licked his hand.

"Hi, Brownie. How are you, boy?" He replaced the book on the shelf and walked toward her. "I'm sorry to disturb you at work, but I think you made a mistake."

"A mistake? What mistake?"

He was standing close to her, inches from her face, which she found disconcerting. She stepped back for more personal space.

"You said 'no,' but I'm thinking you might want to reconsider it. I'm pretty sure you should go."

She turned her head a bit. *This guy sure has balls.* "And how do you know that?"

"I'm good at reading people."

"Oh, you are?"

He grinned a cocky grin.

"Detective Barnes, are you flirting with me?"

He laughed. "Can't you tell?"

She smiled. It had been so long. "No, I'm not really sure."

He closed the gap between them, inching in close again. This time, he lowered his voice. "Ms. Albright, I think, perhaps, you need to step out of your comfort zone." He reached down and took her hand in his, and there it was—that spark again.

She tried to hide that her body shivered. She pulled her hand away, straightened her shoulders, and stood a bit taller. "That's funny. That's what my mother said I need to do."

"Your mother is a smart woman. You should listen to her. Say yes."

The door opened, and Blue walked in. He nodded at Barnes with a friendly hello as he headed to his office. The moment broken, she was all business again. "I've got to get back to work." She turned toward the office.

"Ms. Albright."

She stopped in her tracks, looking back at him.

"I have to say, you are a mystery. One minute, you're like a scared bird. The next, you're..." He paused, searching for the right word.

She thought he was going to say "a seductress" or "a pathological liar" or "a psychotic kook" because she did, at times, feel like all those things. She held her breath, waiting.

"An intriguing book."

She let herself smile. She plucked a book from a pile on the wheeled library cart next to her and tossed it to Barnes, who caught it easily. "Well, you like to read, don't you, detective?" And she turned and walked away.

AFTER FINISHING HER hours at the Book Barn, Jesse closed the store and rushed home. The detective was on her mind all day, as if he'd cast a spell on her. To occupy herself, she tried to catch up on her finds. She worked at the dining room table, lashing a rusty piece of coiled wire to a canvas with needle and a thick waxed thread. She glued red netting over an old photo of a woman in a graduation cap and gown. It was intriguing, the story she was telling with her finds. Her gut kept telling her they would lead to Sophie.

There was a knock at the door. Hoping it might be Barnes appearing as he had the first time, she wiped her hands on her jeans, trying to get the bits of glue off, then she went to see who was there. She peeked behind the curtain and saw Cooper. He never showed up unannounced anymore.

She flung open the door. "What are you doing here?"

"Sorry to come without calling—"

"Did something happen?"

"What? Oh, no. No news. Sorry." He paused, taking her in. "You look good, Jess."

"Yeah, right." She knew she looked like a train wreck. She brushed her hair out of her face, self-conscious about the premature gray.

He was dressed in a stylish dark-blue suit with a light-blue tie that had thin stripes of white and tan. He'd never dressed like that when they were together. It was all jeans and T-shirts, hiking boots and backpacks. She hadn't seen him in over a year, and he'd put on a few pounds. He also had less hair, and what was left was gray. But he looked good, solid and strong.

He noticed the dog, who stood next to Jesse protectively. "Who's this?"

"I found him."

"Cute."

Then it dawned on her. "You're checking up on me."

"I was nearby. Had a meeting with a client over in Pittsfield. Thought I'd stop by."

"Um-hm," she said skeptically. She caught him looking around and could tell he wasn't happy with what he saw.

"Can I come in?"

She opened the door wider and gestured inside half-heartedly. "I suppose so. But I don't want to hear it."

"Hear what?"

She gave him a squinty-eyed look.

"All right. All right. But, Jess, come on, you said you were cleaning up. Did you call Ray about painting? You were right. The place does need it."

"I left a message. He hasn't called back."

She could tell Cooper didn't buy it. He could always tell when she was lying.

"Maybe I better call him," he said.

"You don't have to. I said I'd do it."

He walked in and wandered around the room, gazing at her finds, looking from one overflowing box to the next. He lifted a tattered straw hat from one box then replaced it. He moved aside the innards of a clock, spools of thread, and a piece of bicycle chain, then he shook his head. Jesse stood aside, watching him, her arms crossed defensively over her chest.

He turned and noticed Sophie's jacket hanging on the coat hook by the door. He touched it gently. "Have you gone through her stuff yet?"

She looked away.

"Listen, Jess, I'm going to help you. This weekend. I'll come. We'll clean up. I want to help."

She just shook her head.

"Jess. Come on. Let me help you. You can't do it alone. You haven't, and you won't. Or let Blue or Beth help. They'd be happy to. Anyone. But we have to do it."

Throw away Sophie's clothes? Her collection of birds' nests? Her life list, journals, or bird-watching books? Jesse couldn't part with any of it. Didn't know if she ever could. She couldn't imagine letting the things rot and get moldy in some dank storage unit she couldn't afford, either. "Why do I have to move anyway?"

"Jess, come on. Be fair. I've warned you for years that this time would come. I can't go on paying two mortgages. I'm not made of money."

"Why did you have to buy such an expensive house?"

"Who said I bought an expensive house?"

"No one. I just know that area is expensive." She wasn't about to confess her obsession looking for digital crumbs of information about his new life.

"That's beside the point. We have separate lives now. I've moved on. Getting rid of this house will be good for you. You can't maintain it. You're rattling around in here. It's too big for one person."

She raised her voice, swatting the air angrily with her hand. "How do you know what I do? What I need? And what about my studio? I love my studio." Cooper had fixed it up himself, turning the run-down chicken coop into a wonderful light, airy painting space.

He cocked his head. "But you haven't painted in years. You've told me so. You don't go in there, you said. Are you going to start painting again?"

She didn't know. She couldn't really imagine it. But then she couldn't imagine never painting again. That was all she really knew how to do. She was firmly stuck. As stuck as a person could possibly be. She turned away from him and cupped her face in her hands, letting out a sob.

Cooper came over, put his arms around her, and gave her a hug. She nestled her head in the crook of his neck, inhaled, and remembered his scent, the feel of being in his embrace. She used to love his sweat smell after he returned from a hiking trip, metallic like pennies. Now he smelled of sweet, unfamiliar soap. New soap. New suit. New wife. New children. She didn't like it. Any of it. She had to let this man go.

And as it had many times already that day, an image of Barnes standing in the Book Barn, smiling at her, floated past her eyes. Jesse suddenly realized she had actually gone hours without thinking of Sophie. Maybe she *could* move on. Then she felt that jab in her chest. A sharp sting of guilt. She stepped out of Cooper's embrace.

"You should go. I said I'll clean it up, and I will. Thanks for offering to help, but I'd rather do it myself."

"Why be a martyr? There's no way you can do it all."

"I'm not a martyr. You give me no credit. You never did. It's just a house. I know how to clean it and make it look good. You didn't complain about how it looked when you lived here."

"Because it wasn't filled with all this crap." He picked up a dusty broken basket from one box and a dirty sock monkey missing half its head. "Jess, you have a problem. You need help. What happened to that therapist?"

She grabbed the items out of his hands. "I need a therapist? Ha! Who ran out on their marriage, abandoned his wife and child?" *Even if the child was missing.*

"What? Is that what you think?"

She didn't know what she thought anymore. She was confused and didn't need him and his new lawyerly gibberish twisting things around. She just wanted Sophie back. "Forget it, Cooper. Go home to Cindy. Did she put you up to this?"

"Of course not."

"I bet she can't wait for this house to be sold so she can go on one of her fancy shopping sprees. More clothes and maybe some plastic surgery?"

"You have some crazy ideas."

"Do I? Do I?" she shouted, shaking the deformed monkey doll at him.

"Listen, you weren't the only one affected by this tragedy. I was there, too. I was her father! I loved Sophie!" He was practically hyperventilating, his face turning an unpleasant shade of red. He opened his mouth as if to say something else, then his eyes met the pencil markings indicating Sophie's height on the pantry doorjamb. He touched the wood with his finger, and it seemed to calm him. He shook his head and turned to go. He noticed his old black leather jacket, his very favorite, tossed over a kitchen chair. "Hey, my leather jacket."

She loved it, wore it all the time. "You gave it to me."

"Well, not exactly, Jess. You kind of appropriated it."

Their eyes fixed on each other and held there. He sighed. "I'll be checking in with you soon. I'm serious, Jess."

He walked out, and she was alone again. Well, not exactly alone. Saint Anthony was at her feet, his tail whapping the floor for attention. She knelt and grabbed him, smelling the comforting doggie scent of his head. "Fucking Cooper, with his young, skinny wifey and good son." She needed a hug. Someone to be nice to her. She remembered what her mom and Barnes had said about stepping out of her comfort zone.

"Can I do it, Brownie?"

He licked her face. She went for her purse and rummaged in it, looking for Barnes's business card. Then she remembered it was stapled to that article about April. She'd put it back in the kitchen drawer, the one with all the takeout menus, rubber bands, matchbooks, and old corks from wine bottles. Real junk. She found it right away on the top layer, and she pulled his card off the article and studied it. She picked up the phone and punched in his number.

"Ms. Albright, how nice to hear from you."

She took a deep breath. "I've changed my mind. I would like to go with you to the Harvest Fest."

"I'm so glad," he said, a warmth emanating through the phone. "I was hoping you would."

Jesse touched the locket around her neck, sliding it back and forth. She let herself smile. She'd done it. *That wasn't so hard after all.*

"I'll pick you up tomorrow at seven," he said.

She hung up before she had a chance to change her mind.

JESSE FOUND THREE RESPECTABLE outfits in the depths of her closet. The long-forgotten dresses and skirts were far better than her usual ragtag recycled look. She settled on a short denim skirt, cowboy boots, black tights, and a black velvet scooped-neck shirt. Not too revealing but definitely feminine. She looked at herself in the full-length mirror.

"Not bad, right?" she said to Saint Anthony, who was lying on the floor near her.

He lifted his head and yawned. She remembered the last time she'd worn the outfit, to celebrate their seventh wedding anniversary. Cooper had gazed at her, admiring how she looked. He whispered, "Let's skip dinner," in her ear and pulled her into a hot kiss. He'd grown a goatee that summer and looked dashing. Jesse had to admit she missed feeling desired by a man. Somehow, Gary didn't count.

She turned back to the dog. "What am I doing? Should I cancel? I can still cancel."

When he didn't answer, she opened her makeup drawer and extracted a tube of mascara. She pulled out the wand, but it was nothing but a goopy, caked mess. She tossed it out. Rummaging in the bottom of the drawer, she found a lipstick that didn't look like a health hazard. She swiped on the glossy pink.

At 6:52 p.m., Jesse opened her door to see Kentucky Marcus Barnes. Of course he was punctual. He looked handsome in black jeans and a blue turtleneck, worn under the same jean jacket he'd been wearing earlier, not a crease or wrinkle in sight. And a black porkpie hat was on his head. Jesse's stomach fluttered with that nervous-to-see-someone feeling she hadn't experienced in years.

"You're right on time. Actually, you're early. I need one more minute. Hold on." She shut the door in his face, grabbed Cooper's leather jacket, and put it on. She glanced at herself one more time in a mirror. She exhaled. *You can do this.*

She opened the door again, this time with Saint Anthony panting at her feet.

"Thanks for making me wait out here on your doorstep, Ms. Albright," he said with a smile.

"Sorry about that."

"In the cold."

"The place is...." She gestured inside the house, her hand fluttering about.

Barnes grinned. "I've seen the place."

"Oh, right. The maid still hasn't shown up."

"Well, somebody looks real nice."

She glanced away. She was probably blushing. Barnes pulled out a bouquet of mums and daisies from behind his back.

"Oh." Jesse was *sure* she was blushing. "That was... Well, you didn't have to..."

"Why don't you go ahead and put them in water? I'll wait here."

"Really? You don't mind waiting? Again?"

"Waiting on you will be my pleasure. Go ahead, now." He shooed her with his hands.

Inside, she grabbed a pitcher. She put water in it, stuck the flowers in, and placed it on the kitchen table. She closed her eyes and took a few more deep breaths. After patting Saint Anthony goodbye, she shut the door and started walking ahead of Barnes toward the driveway. She looked at his yellow VW Bug, shook her head, and chuckled to herself, "Now that vehicle is downright ridiculous. *I'll* drive."

Barnes didn't protest, and they headed for her truck.

"Jeez," he said as he opened the passenger door. The inside of her pickup was nearly as cluttered as her house, filled with finds that hadn't made it inside her house. He brushed the pile of papers and junk on the passenger seat onto the floor, trying not to touch much. "How do you think with all this clutter?"

She laughed. "Too messy for you?"

"Well, yes."

"What are you? Some kind of Zen detective?"

"Clutter represents the state of one's mind. I like breathing room. I guess that may be different from your setup."

She shot him a look. "It's not my setup, Detective." She started the truck and drove off. "I know clean. I know neat. I've done them before." She took a deep breath and gripped the wheel, staring straight ahead. "Sometimes life is messy, and you have no control."

He touched her hand gently. "Ms. Albright, I'd like to understand. Really."

She concentrated on the road ahead.

They drove in silence for a few minutes, then Barnes said, "You know, there's this Native American legend I've read about. It's called 'soul keeping.' There was a father whose son died. He wasn't ready to let go of him. So he took some of his son's hair and put it into a little bundle. Then he placed it in a special tepee. That's where the child's soul was."

Jesse didn't blink or say a word. She just drove on, loosened her grip a little, and listened.

Barnes continued, "This special soul keeping was a time of contemplation. A time of atonement. And at the end of this period, when the father was ready, the soul would be released in a big happy feast. I like this story. I've told it to some of my clients whose children were missing, usually runaways who didn't want to be found. Some of them did their own soul-keeping ceremony. I think rituals are real important. Whatever it takes. Grief is a strange emotion. It makes you do crazy things."

Jesse glanced at him. "Thanks for the touching story and your armchair psychology, Mr. Social-Worker-to-Be, but I've done enough grieving for a lifetime. I'd like to relax for once and have a little fun. Let's not talk."

Barnes nodded, and they were silent for the rest of the drive through Canaan. Trees were at their autumn peak. Yellow and red leaves covered the sidewalks. The town was packed with people and cars. Jesse parked at the Book Barn, a bit out of the fray. They got out and walked over to Main Street, which had been blocked off to traffic. The shops had little white twinkly lights in their windows, along with Halloween decorations. And pumpkins were everywhere. Whole pumpkins, carved pumpkins, and pumpkins already lit with candles. The whole town glistened, pulsating with excitement. Jesse looked all around at the festivities. Even though it was hokey, she had missed the community gatherings. Sharing them with family and friends. She had always held Canaan, the little jewel of a town, close to her heart like a secret. She felt a sadness deep in her chest, the air seeping out of her. She felt homesick.

She stopped walking and turned to Barnes. "Listen, I'm sorry I snapped at you before. You know, touchy subject."

"Don't worry about it." He looked out at the crowd up ahead then back at Jesse. "Ready?"

She took a deep breath and nodded. "Ready as I'll ever be."

He reached down and gave her hand a comforting little squeeze.

Chapter Twelve

"Welcome to the 26th Annual Canaan Harvest Fest," read the banner strung across Main Street. Under a big white tent, tables were loaded with home-baked pies, fresh cider, and baskets full of apples. Kids ran shouting through a corn maze in the field across the way. And people lined up at pumpkin-carving stations, where orange chunks flew everywhere.

Jesse and Barnes walked toward a crowd where a scaffold five stories high stood in the town green. It held row upon row of jack-o'-lanterns, their funny and spooky carved faces all lit up. Below, a group was taking photos with cell phones. Barnes laughed when he saw a row of pumpkins glowing from within, each carved with a different letter. They spelled out: *Ruth marry me luv Roger.*

"What a romantic guy," he said to Jesse.

The sights, sounds, and smells brought it all back. She remembered the last time she'd been to this festival, the year before That Day. Her family had fun participating in the carving contest, going through the corn maze, the works. Although Sophie had enjoyed the festivities, spotting a great horned owl with its large ear tufts, eerie yellow irises, and stern gaze had thrilled her more. Jesse remembered the expression of wonder on Sophie's face.

"He's a melt bird," she'd told Jesse and Cooper.

"A what?" Cooper asked.

"You know," she said, "a bird who disappears into his habitat." She lowered her voice. "They're all around us." When involved in her favorite subject, Sophie could be a delight, so enthralled by her feathered friends. "Birds make me happy," she had said to Jesse once.

Jesse stopped, lingering over the memory. Staring off at a tall evergreen, she wondered if Sophie had become a melt bird, hiding in Canaan in plain sight? *Some birds are elusive and particularly difficult to find.*

"Ms. Albright? Jesse?"

Snapping out of her daze to see Barnes, she was embarrassed at being caught daydreaming.

"Shall we move on?" he said.

She nodded and walked on.

They followed the throngs of people heading for Earl's. The doors were open, and the old-timey bluegrass tune of a fiddle and mandolin wafted out into the night. Jesse looked inside the packed place, seeing many familiar faces, and her heart leapt then galloped away. *Why did I need to come to this thing, anyway?* To prove to herself that she was fine. That she could put her life back together and do normal things again. Like Cooper? To extract a bit of revenge on Gary and show him he couldn't get to her anymore?

She turned to Barnes, and he again took her hand. A wave of warmth slid through her body. She remembered why. To step out of her comfort zone. Go out on a date with a man she liked.

Jesse followed him. The place had been transformed from a cheery café to an atmospheric party space that glowed with candles and more lit pumpkins. Bunches of orange and black helium balloons were gathered on the ceiling. Matching streamers spiraled down in long curlicues. It was wall-to-wall bodies. Jesse spotted costumed guests, a few wearing masks. A vampire. A cowgirl. Charlie Chaplin. Frankenstein. Everyone was dancing, drinking, and talking above the din.

She took a deep breath to gird herself then straightened her shoulders. "Let's get a drink."

Barnes pushed his way up to the bar and turned back to Jesse. "What'll you have?"

"Beer." She realized that the rather large body huddled next to her was none other than Peggy, the nosy realtor she'd seen with Gary the other day. Jesse gave a small nod then turned away from her, imagining what rumors Peggy might already have spread about her and Gary. And Jesse had arrived with a handsome black man, somebody new for Canaanites to gossip about.

Barnes reappeared and handed her a bottle of beer. She clinked his glass with it. "Cheers." Then she saw that Gary was working behind the bar, helping Jill. Seeing him again cranked her anxiety up another notch, and she guzzled her beer.

He looked surprised and not all that happy when he spotted Jesse. He mouthed hello to her. And when he noticed she was with Barnes, Jesse was sure she saw a flicker of jealousy cross his face.

Across the room, Blue and Beth Silverman, dressed as Sonny and Cher, were talking with Carol, who wore a black cape and pointy witch hat. They spotted Jesse, smiled broadly, and waved her over. She turned to Barnes and nodded toward her old friends. Even though she really wanted to run home, she pushed her way into the crowd, and Barnes followed.

"Jess. You came. So good to see you. You look great," Beth said and hugged her, the long hair of Beth's Cher wig swishing about.

Carol was next. Her witch hat tilted at a funny angle as she hugged Jesse. "I'm so glad you came. We've missed you at book club."

Jesse managed a tight smile. Avoiding Carol had made Jesse feel as though she wasn't really hurting anyone with the affair. More denial. She had missed her friends, but seeing people from her old life was cringingly painful. They always gave her a pathetic look: tilted head and furrowed eyebrows. Then they would say something inane like "How are you doing?" with great concern. *How in God's name did they think I was doing?* She was a total wreck, barely hanging on.

It had been easier not to deal with anyone. Easier for them, too, she was sure.

Blue came up next to her, and she couldn't help but laugh at his costume. The fur vest was too small, and he looked ridiculous in his wig. The bangs covered his eyebrows. Not to mention his graying beard ruined the real Sonny's clean-shaven look. He stuck his hand out to Barnes. "I'm Blue."

"Hey, great costume," Barnes said. "The beat goes on, right?"

Jesse realized that was her cue. Introductions. She knew how to do that, but she froze.

"Call me Tuck," Barnes said, rescuing Jesse before there was any awkwardness, and he shook Blue's hand.

Jesse finished her beer. Then, like magic, a waiter walked by, carrying a tray high above his shoulder. She grabbed two glasses, took a big gulp of one, was surprised it was vodka, but finished it anyway. She was aware of conversation and laughter around her. She downed a second vodka.

She gazed about the party, feeling oddly disconnected from her body, as if observing it all from above. There were parents and teachers from Sophie's school. Kids who had been classmates. Neighbors. Nosy Peggy.

Professor Pollen was two bodies away. He smiled at her and lifted his drink in a toast. When a woman seated in a corner lifted her Sigmund Freud mask from her face, Jesse saw it was Lila, her therapist. *Well, ex-therapist...* Jesse could have sworn Lila winked at her, but maybe she'd imagined it. She gazed around. It didn't feel like a party to her, more like a bizarre dream or what she imagined an LSD trip would be like with strange-looking celebrities, friends, and acquaintances co-mingling. One of them could have followed Jesse and Sophie to the mall and snatched Sophie. She could be hidden in their basement, chained up in their attic. The town was scoured early on, nearly everyone interviewed, but some sicko could have slipped through the cracks.

Jesse heard Blue ask Barnes, "Where'd you two meet?" But she didn't hear his answer. Suddenly, she felt claustrophobic, hot and dizzy. Completely panicked. She couldn't seem to get enough air into her lungs. She rummaged in her purse and found her pill box, but it only contained some old Advils. She'd forgotten to refill it with Xanax. She must have been crazy, trying to attend a party like a normal person and without meds.

She turned to Barnes. "I'll be right back." Before he had time to respond, she pushed between the bodies, maneuvered up to the bar, got two more beers, then shoved her way out the front door. She leaned against the building, sucking in oxygen, letting her head fall back against the wall. She took a few more deep breaths. On the stoop next to her was a carved pumpkin with a wicked grin that seemed to be mocking her. She drank some of the beer and slowly started to relax a little. The vodkas and beer were starting to kick in. She was definitely feeling a buzz.

"Two-fisted, huh?" came from a familiar voice.

She looked up to see Star Silverman standing behind her. Star wore skinny jeans, a baggy shirt, and lots of dark eye makeup. She looked like a cross between a goth rocker and a raccoon. Jesse couldn't tell whether that was her nod toward a costume or her regular rebellious teen getup.

"Oh, hi," Jesse said, devoid of emotion.

Star nodded at the two bottles of beer Jesse held. "Multitasking?"

Jesse nodded then took a long swig from one. She slipped down until she was sitting on the stoop. She set one beer on the ground. "Have a seat."

Star looked down at the step, seemed to think about it for a minute, then plopped next to Jesse. "So you're here with that cop?"

Jesse shook her head.

"You're not here with him?"

"I am. Sort of. But he's not a cop."

"Whatever."

"He wanted to check it out, so I agreed to tag along. It's no big deal."

"Yeah, right." Star grinned. "You're kind of all dressed up."

"I just put on lipstick," she said defensively.

"It's okay. You look good. Pretty."

"Oh. Thanks." Jesse picked at the label on her beer, thinking she used to talk to Star all the time and have real conversations. She could do it now. "What are you up to?"

"Nothing. Waiting for my friend, Ruby. Last time I saw her, she was stalking the food table. She can't stop eating those gross mini-quiche thingies. She's, like, obsessed with them."

Jesse smiled. "Maybe they're good."

"I wouldn't know. I don't do cheese products."

"Really? Not even pizza?"

Star shook her head.

"You used to love pizza. Both you and Sophie. It was your favorite food. Remember that New Year's Eve you slept over? We watched *Sleepless in Seattle* and ordered three pizzas and ate them at midnight. Then Cooper and I let you girls have sips of our champagne."

"Well, those days are gone." Star looked away. "Besides, I'm vegan now. I don't eat pizza anymore. It makes me want to vomit in my mouth."

Jesse raised her eyebrows. "Nice." Her eyes welled up. Nothing was the same. Not one lousy thing. Not even her daughter's best friend. Not even pizza. "I still like it," Jesse said so softly, she wasn't sure Star even heard her. "I saw your parents." Jesse wanted to say, *They still eat pizza.* At least she hoped they did. "Great costumes."

Star laughed. "I don't know when they had time to dredge up those outfits. They've been super busy carving pumpkins for days. This is like the event of the century for them."

"A lot of hubbub over some big orange squashes."

"Exactly." Star abruptly extracted her cell phone from her rear jeans pocket and began texting like a maniac.

"How do you do that so fast?" Jesse tried to imagine a teen Sophie texting inane conversations. Or more likely, she would have her own bird blog. Her ringtone would be the song of a whippoorwill. Maybe she would be the star of a bird-watching reality show and have become famous. It just wasn't fair.

"Like I tell my parents all the time, my generation was born with speedy thumbs. I don't get why you guys are so obsessed with it. It's just what we do." She looked back into Earl's, craning her neck. Then spotting her friend, she waved. "There she is. I'm outta here." She turned back to the party then leaned in to Jesse. "By the way, that dorky bee guy, Professor Pollen, was looking for you. Still with the red bowtie. Boy, is he lovesick." She flashed a smile that reminded Jesse of the old Star. The sweet, good-natured kid she used to love being around.

"If you see him, tell him to buzz off," Jesse said.

"Ha. Good one." Star laughed.

"Buzz bzzz," Jesse said, giggling to herself as Star headed toward her friend, who was wearing a Kim Kardashian mask. Jesse threw back the rest of one of the beers then started the next one. She was breathing much easier. Definitely no pain. As she looked back into the party, she felt bad about deserting Barnes. She couldn't see him anywhere and was wondering where she would find him when she felt someone tapping her shoulder.

"Hey."

She turned and saw Gary standing beside her, holding a beer.

"Hey, yourself," she said.

His eyes roamed over her body, up and then down. "Wow, you look great." But he looked sad.

"I clean up nice when I try."

"I didn't think you'd come."

She shrugged. "I changed my mind." She grabbed his beer and chugged some. *How many drinks have I had?* She'd lost track. *A lot.*

"Oh. Okay. That a friend of yours?" He tossed his head toward the crowd.

She wasn't sure who he was referring to, but she nodded anyway. "Yep."

"Listen." He glanced around, probably checking where Carol was, then dropped his voice. "I'm sorry about the other day."

"No, you were right," Jesse said.

"I'm sorry about everything."

"It's okay, really." She didn't want to rehash things with Gary—not while making an attempt at moving on. She got up but nearly fell over, and Gary held her arm to steady her. Using the wall to keep herself upright, Jesse realized she was full-on drunk. *Time to find Barnes and get out of here. At least I tried. 'A for effort' and all that.*

She wobbled back inside the party. She pushed her way into the middle of the room, back into the loud, headache-inducing commotion, crushed between partygoers.

Gary was right there behind her, his hand on her shoulder. "Jess, I didn't mean for it to..."

So many people from her past were staring at her, judging her. The noise. The spinning room. And Gary was pulling her back both literally and figuratively. She felt as if she were on a moving sidewalk to nowhere, and she couldn't get off. She turned around and was suddenly in his face. "Listen, I'm just surprised you felt you had to keep the whole baby thing a secret. Was that to protect me or something?" She was getting louder, and although the party was noisy, people nearby stared at them curiously. "Did you think I couldn't handle it?" she asked, her voice at top volume, her arms flailing about. "Did you think I would care what you and Carol did? I mean—a baby, for God's sake, is the last thing in the universe I would care about. Been there, remember?"

"Jess, lower your voice, will you?"

"No, I will not lower my voice. Why is everyone always telling me what to do? You and Cooper. Everyone."

Gary tried to grab her by the arm, but she jerked away.

"Let go!" she said, showering her beer onto nearby partygoers.

"Hey," a few exclaimed.

"Sorry, sorry," Gary said.

Jesse turned back to him and shouted, "We've run our course, remember? Besides, Barnes"—she gestured into the crowd with her beer—"is very good with his hands." And she giggled.

"Huh? Him?" And he became a bobblehead swerving around, looking for Barnes. "Are you doing it with him?"

Suddenly, a little crowd surrounded them. Star was there with Ruby and Blue, and Beth came over, and Peggy was ogling them. Professor Pollen looked aghast. Even Lila was hovering, a self-satisfied expression on her face, shaking her head.

And then there was Carol, pushing her way in. "What's going on?"

Jesse felt immediately on the defensive, like the evil mother who couldn't hold on to her own daughter causing more trouble. No wonder the locals couldn't stand her.

"Nothing, nothing," Gary said. He tried to pull Carol away.

Jesse suddenly remembered why she'd stopped going out. But the beer gave her courage or jolts of stupidity. Maybe both.

"Congratulations, Carol. Gary told me your news. Oops." She put her hand up to her mouth. "Was that supposed to be a secret?"

Carol looked back and forth from Jesse to Gary and back again as if looking for some explanation. Jesse was drunk, but she still knew her bad behavior wasn't about Gary or Carol or her old friends or neighbors. It was her. Sabotaging herself. Still. Her guilt and unhappiness clutched and grabbed at her, trying to suck her back like quicksand.

Then there was Barnes, the only calming face in the crowd. He strode right up and took her by the arm—"C'mon, dear. Time to go. I've got her, thanks." He led her toward the exit along the bar side of the café, amid murmurs of "She's drunk," "Poor woman," and "What a hot mess."

Jesse turned, throwing punches into the air or at whoever or whatever was in her path. She was the center of attention, with everyone watching, pointing, and whispering. They shook their heads at the pathetic sight before them.

"Shut up!" Jesse ranted. "I'll show you a hot mess." Then she pushed whatever body was in her way, but somebody shoved back. She lost her balance and fell into the bar, hitting her forehead. She put her hand to her head as tears sprouted.

"Can I get some ice here?" Barnes asked the bartender, who quickly gave him a plastic cupful. He grabbed Jesse's elbow. "We're out of here," he said as he steered her through the crowd. "Nice meeting you," he said to no one in particular.

"You're drunk, and I'm driving," Barnes said as he took the keys from Jesse. She didn't protest. He wrapped a handful of ice in a handkerchief and placed the bundle to her forehead, which had already sprouted a bump. "Hold this."

"Barnes, I—"

"Don't speak."

She sank a little lower in her seat. They drove the whole way without a word. When they pulled into Jesse's drive, she was out of the truck before he turned off the ignition. He hopped out and followed her to the front door. She unlocked it and went inside, clearly done with him, but he followed her into the house.

Saint Anthony was there and greeted her, his tail wagging happily.

"Hi, boy," she said, bending down to pet him. She leaned in close, getting another good whiff of his comforting doggie-head smell. She kissed him. She should have gotten a dog sooner. They didn't judge and were always happy to see their people no matter how fucked up they were.

Barnes grabbed her by the elbow. "Why would you do that, Ms. Albright?"

"I don't know what you're talking about, Detective," she said, jerking her arm away.

He shook his head. "You're not going to get away with 'I don't know' this time."

She didn't respond.

He went to her freezer, took out more ice cubes, rummaged around, found a Ziploc bag, and put them inside it. "Sit," he said, and she sat on her couch. He came over and placed the ice on her forehead.

"Ouch."

"Lie back."

She leaned her head against the back of the couch and closed her eyes.

"What's wrong with you? I know you've been through a hard time, but there's no excuse for acting like that. You shouldn't be drinking. What were you after? To make that guy jealous? To get at his wife? I thought she was a friend."

"Are you done?"

"No, I'm not. What are you doing with that guy?"

"What's it to you?"

"It's a lot to me. Stupidly, I thought you wanted to come with me to this party. Instead, you get drunk, act out, cause a scene."

"You done yet?"

"No, I'm not. You're going to hurt yourself or someone else."

She looked away. "That's what Lila says. My shrink. Ex-shrink."

"Oh. That's who that was." He pulled out a business card. "Some woman named Lila handed me her card and said, 'See if you can get her to call me.'" He tossed the card on the table then looked around the room.

She saw him take in the dusty piles, the yellowed and crumpled scraps of paper, and the overflowing boxes. An old jock strap hung out of one. A Frisbee and a naked Barbie doll poked out of another. A lava lamp. A transistor radio. Rusted springs from a mattress. She never meant to have company.

"What is all this shit? Are you some kind of dealer of hot merchandise? Or just a hoarder?"

She opened her mouth to speak, but he jumped in. "Don't talk. Just keep this here so the swelling goes down." He adjusted the ice bag on her forehead then went into the kitchen and put the kettle on to boil. "You got coffee in this place?"

"Left cupboard, top shelf."

She heard him rustling around, opening cupboards and clinking silverware. She turned and saw him look at one of her early paintings, a typical Canaan landscape: a barn in a meadow fronted by a long stone fence. It was a large, richly textured oil hanging over the kitchen table. She'd done it so long ago, she barely remembered painting it. The kettle whistled, and he poured the water. He brought over two mugs and set them on the coffee table.

She pulled the ice bag off her head and looked at him. "Listen, thanks for driving me home. But you can leave now. You've done your duty."

But he sat down next to her. Why he wasn't running for the hills, she wasn't sure. She closed her eyes and put her head back against the couch, the ice back on her bump. After a few moments, melted water from her baggie started dripping down her face, and she wiped her cheek. She put the ice down and grabbed her mug. As she raised it to sip her coffee, she saw him looking at her hands. She was self-conscious about her ragged nails and cuticles. "They're ugly."

"They're not." He took her mug and set it down, then he took her hands in his. Examining them, he turned them over and let his index finger trace the veins on her right hand. "They're strong, worker woman hands. They're beautiful, like you."

"No." She slid her hands out from his and shook her head. "Pretty obvious what's been going on, I guess. Stupid me. I thought I was invisible."

He shook his head and chuckled. "How could *you* be invisible?"

"I feel invisible."

"You want to be invisible."

She nodded. "Gary's been an escape, but it's over. He ended it, and I was pissed. And hurt. And scared. I really thought I could go to the party. I *did* want to go with you. Get back to being normal." She inhaled. Her buzz was wearing off. "I was trying to... you know, go out of my comfort zone."

"Well, that's a good idea, but not when you combine it with booze. The drinking's got to stop."

She picked at her fingernail. "I'm sorry I dragged you into my mess."

He gestured to her finds. "What about all this stuff?"

"It's complicated."

"Try me."

"I haven't shown anyone. No one comes over, so no one's ever asked."

"No one?"

She shook her head. "My mom's seen some, and Cooper, my ex, has seen it. But they don't understand."

"Well I'm here, and I'm asking."

She put her mug down. "It was about five years ago when I first started finding things. After Sophie went missing. It started small. A grocery list. A note to a friend. A poem. Even money. I'd find things in the books at work. Things people left as a bookmark or a place to stash a reminder or things they just forgot. It was fun at first. A distraction. But then I started finding things wherever I went. All sorts of things. Photos, lost wallets, cameras, jewelry, love letters, hate letters, teeth, nail clippings. Weird things found in weird places in weird ways."

"Stuff is lost out there... you started paying attention and seeing it."

She shook her head. "No, that's not it."

"I've found odd things on the ground," he said. "Picked them up. Stuff is out there."

"No, no," she said, raising her voice. "You're not listening. I wasn't *looking*. They land at my feet, in my hair, dropped by a bird. They came to me like magic. And still do. They come on the back of a FedEx truck or pizza delivery car, flying out of their windows or shot out of their muffler and landing at my feet. Left in my mailbox. Down the chimney of my fireplace. All this crazy stuff. It's like some secret gnome has been sneaking around, following me, leaving bits and pieces just for me to find. Except it's not a gnome. I'm convinced, utterly and positively sure, that they are signs for me. They are clues sent exclusively to me about Sophie. By Sophie. Connections to her. I just have to put all the clues together. The answer is in here"—she gestured around the room—"somewhere."

"Answer to what?"

Her voice got louder, and she became more agitated and animated, her hands gesticulating wildly. "Whether she's alive or dead. Where her body might be found. Who took her. What I'm supposed to do. The answers. I have to log it all in and catalogue it and analyze and try to make sense of it. Because if I don't, who will?" She took a deep breath and looked at Barnes defiantly, then she jumped up, grabbed one of the overflowing cardboard boxes, and set it on the couch. She began extracting items one at a time. "Look at this, a handwritten last will and testament leaving all of Sasha's earthly possessions to Samuel, including his parrot. Sasha could mean Sophie." She set that down and moved on to the next. "An envelope containing Joe's first haircut. Brown hair, like Sophie's." She extracted curled locks of hair. She dug down deep into the box and pulled out a lined piece of yellowed notebook paper. "Listen to this." She began to read, "Dear Mom, I'm sorry I was such a burden to you. It pains me to know how I hurt you." She stopped reading and looked at Barnes. "See? Do you understand?"

"I'm trying to."

"They're signs. Clues. They find me. It's not like these were found in some garbage can. They come to me. Someone is trying to get my attention. All of this has taken over my house, my life. And things have stepped up. Finding the dog. Seeing April. And it all began with this book." She pointed to Bixby on the table. "A book Sophie read. It says what I must do: Pay attention. Wait and watch. Don't you understand? I'm close to the truth, an answer. You, of all people, should understand. You look for the missing. You know about clues." She stopped and sank into a chair. She exhaled then slowly looked up at him. "You're like the others. You don't believe me, do you?"

He opened his mouth to speak then paused as if forming his thoughts. Then he spoke slowly. "I believe you're close to something."

She smiled and nodded. *Yeah, close to snapping. Close to totally losing my mind.* She dropped her head for a minute then walked over to the front door to touch the wire crow on the little table. She pulled Sophie's purple parka close to her face and gave it a squeeze. She reached into the pockets, extracted two purple striped wool mittens, and brought them up to her nose and inhaled. She slipped her hands into them.

"When she couldn't sleep, she'd crawl into bed with us. There's nothing like a sleeping child. How angelic they look." She stopped, her eyes brimming with tears. "People gave me books about grieving, meditation CDs. They told me I had to take care of myself. They told me to take up knitting. I don't want to fucking knit. I don't want to be a spokesperson for missing kids or form a foundation. I don't want to be a politician or be on a TV show or be interviewed by Oprah or write a book. I don't want a Lifetime movie made of my child's life or mine." Her voice caught, and she paused. "I want my child back. I want Sophie! Period. I want her here, eating her Cheerios, deliberately and slowly, one at a time. I want her to babble on and on about her birds endlessly, continuously, driving me crazy. I want her to say, 'Mommy, I love you,' the way she did." Jesse could hear Sophie talking to her, the words soft and warm, wrapping around her like a flannel baby blanket. She buried her face in her hands covered in Sophie's little mittens.

Barnes stood next to her and hugged her tightly, then he rocked her back and forth, rubbing her back. "It's okay," he whispered. He brushed her hair out of her face and drew his fingers through her wild mane.

"It's been six years," she said softly. "I guess I should be over this by now, but it never ends. When I hear of some missing child found after years and years, it doesn't give me hope. It just keeps me hanging even more."

After a minute, he pulled the mittens off her and tucked them back in the pockets of the parka. "Come with me. I want to show you something." He helped her up then opened the front door, and she followed him out. He stood on her porch, looking at the sky. The moon was full and huge, hanging low. It was perfectly round and glowing extra brightly. It looked like a stage set.

"Wow," she said, standing behind him. "That's beautiful."

"Hunter's moon. It's October's full moon. So bright, it would help hunters track their prey at night."

Jesse shook her head sadly. *If only. If only.*

Barnes whispered, "Oh, Jesse, I know. I wish I could."

How does he seem to read my mind? "She's like a phantom limb. What I've read amputees feel. She was there, and now she's not. My phantom daughter. But I still feel her. All those emotions still rumble inside me. The love, the guilt, the pleasure, the sadness, the worry. I keep thinking that she's there. That I'll look in her room, and she'll be sitting on the floor of her closet, making up stories. My whole life, a phantom life. A phantom marriage with a phantom husband and phantom daughter. There but not there." A small sob escaped her lips.

Barnes pulled her into a hug, and they stood together in a tight embrace. She felt her defenses dissipating. All that anger, fear, and worry dripped down her body, from her head to her neck and through her chest. Slipping along her arms and out her fingertips. Melting down her body, her legs, and out her toes. She exhaled the most relaxed breath she'd experienced in years. She felt pounds lighter. The spot in his arms felt so comfortable and safe. She closed her eyes, smelling his neck, a wonderful earthy scent.

"When I finish this case, I'll look at Sophie's file. Maybe a fresh eye could see something."

Jesse inhaled. He was so kind. She hadn't wanted to ask for his help.

He pulled back. "Show me Sophie's room."

She blinked, about to say no. She looked at his face. Their eyes met and held there. They walked back into the house, and he followed her up the stairs.

Chapter Thirteen

After Star said goodbye to her parents, promising to text them when she got home, she and Ruby left the party. As they stepped outside of Earl's, Star pointed to the enormous shimmering moon. "Wow, look at that..." It hung so low, it looked as if it had dropped a few hundred feet in the sky. "Doesn't it look totally fake?"

"Oh, my God. Yes, but so cool. C'mon, girl. Selfie." Ruby, wearing her Kim K. mask around her neck, pulled her cell phone out of her pocket and held it in front of them, using the moon as their backdrop. She leaned close to her friend until their heads were touching.

"Smile, Star."

Star hated how she looked lately and was so not into plastering endless photos of herself online like most kids her age, but she humored Ruby and forced a fake smile.

Ruby looked at her phone. "I have to take off. Jason is lost in the corn maze."

"Yeah, right," Star said. "He just wants to make out with you in there." Jason was Ruby's boyfriend. She was normally attached to him at the lips.

Ruby smiled shyly. "Do you mind?"

Star shook her head. "I'm over this place anyway." She was actually glad Ruby was leaving. It would give her more time to be alone, which was what she preferred. But Ruby was cool. She was basically the only one who didn't think Star was a freak. She hadn't deserted Star like her other friends who wanted her to be how she was a couple years ago. Happy. Upbeat. Into clothes, gossiping, and of course, boys. But that wasn't her anymore, not since the ugly thoughts start-ed appearing. Even keeping up appearances with Ruby was hard. So having one real friend was enough.

Ruby had moved to Canaan after Sophie had been missing for a couple years, so she'd never heard stuff about Bird Girl, and she was curious, asking Star questions like "What do you think really hap-pened?" and "Who could have taken her?" Mostly, Star kept all that to herself.

Ruby was the editor of the school paper and wanted to be a writer. Star knew what was going to happen. Ruby would get into a good school, go away to college, then move away forever and become a famous blogger. With Star's crappy grades and no extracurricular shit, she would end up at a community college then have to work at the Book Barn, like Jesse, until she was eighty, when no one would even remember what a hardback book was.

Ruby said goodbye, gave Star a hug, then opened her bag to show Star a stash of squashed mini-quiches she'd taken from the food table at the party.

"Jeez, Ruby."

She laughed and put her finger to her lips. "Not for me. For Jase. He'll eat anything. See you at school."

Star watched as Ruby headed for the square, getting swallowed up by the loud, animated crowd.

Star pulled her camera out of her pocket. She liked using old-school technology and took it with her everywhere to document her life. It made her feel different in a good way. She shot some of the festivities. People with their faces painted like ghouls. Rows of lit-up jack-o'-lanterns. Close-ups from a bin of scooped-out pumpkin innards and seeds that reminded her of how she'd been feeling late-ly—all mushy, stringy, and gross.

How the town didn't burn down each year during this craziness was a mystery, but luckily, the fire department was out in full force. Her parents would be the last to leave Earl's. They always stayed to the bitter end and helped clean up like the good Canaan citizens they were. And the party was far from over.

Even though this festival was full-on lame, it made Star feel lonely. She and Sophie used to come with their families. Back then, they were kids, so it wasn't stupid to them. Only Sophie would have appreciated the lameness of the event. She wished she were there to make fun of it and their parents together. Not Sophie the creepy ghost. Sophie her old friend, the girl she missed. Star called Ophelia, and when she didn't pick up, Star left a voice message, "Hey, Opheel. What's going on? Just checking in, girl. Call me." Then she texted her, too. *Where R U?*

Instead of going home, she headed down Main and cut over to Church Street. She used her keys to enter the Book Barn. Being surrounded by all the old books felt cozy. She sat in one of the comfy chairs in the corner next to the nature section, which, of course, had been Sophie's spot. When Star's dad first opened the Book Barn, Sophie had loved to hang out and convinced her parents to buy her practically every birding book.

Without looking, Star pulled a book off a shelf. The weird thing was that of all the books it could have been—ones about trees, gardening, mammals or stars—it turned out to be *Birds of America*, one of Sophie's favorites. She flipped through it and recognized some of the birds Sophie had tried to teach her about. Grackle. Blue jay. The amazing Great Blue Heron they'd seen on the Cape that looked prehistoric when it took off in flight.

After a few minutes, she went to her dad's office in the back. She kept the lights turned low so no one would notice. Everyone was preoccupied with the festival, so it wouldn't be a problem. She turned on the computer and went to her Instagram page. Ruby had already posted a photo of her and Jason hamming it up in the corn maze. Star typed in a comment: *Eat some dairy, keep up your strength.*

She went over to Hope4themissing.org, pulled up Sophie's page, and read, once again, the description of what happened six years ago.

September 8, 2012. Sophie Albright, 10, was last seen with her mother at a Zone clothing store in the Countryside Mall in Holyoke, Massachusetts at approximately 2:25 p.m. She was shopping with her mother when she vanished from the store. Albright, who has long brown hair and green eyes, is 3'6"and weighs 60 lbs., was wearing faded denim jeans, a blue-and-green "Life's A Beach" T-shirt, orange socks, and black clogs. She also wore a pair of black binoculars around her neck. One lens cap was marked with a blue letter S, and the other lens cap has the letter A, both made from gaffer's tape. Albright has never been seen or heard from. Authorities have investigated all possible leads and do not have any suspects.

In a column on the right side, a different photo of a missing person flashed every few seconds. Eventually, Sophie's came up. A sidebar on the left showed statistics. *A child goes missing every 40 seconds in the US; over 2,100 per day.* If that wasn't completely terrifying, she didn't know what was.

She thought back to when she had shown up at Sophie's house that morning, thinking they were going to play, maybe go down to the creek to watch birds and collect rocks.

Sophie was lying on her bed, on her stomach, writing in her birding log book.

"Hey, Sophers," Star had said and flopped next to her on the bed.

"Hi, Rats."

"Who'd you see today?"

"Two cardinals. One male, one female. Three black-capped chickadees. A blue jay. Two tufted titmouse. The usual. But look what a crow left me this morning." She opened the palm of her hand to reveal a small rectangular piece of broken china from a plate or bowl. It was white with little red flowers.

Star reached for it, but Sophie quickly closed her fist. "Don't touch."

"God, Sophie. I'm not going to break it."

"Sorry. It's just that it's so special. I guess you can touch it." Crows had been leaving Sophie little items, mostly in the bird bath, for some time. Buttons. Pieces of glass or beads. Rusty screws. After years of closely observing Sophie's behavior and patterns when she fed them, they'd gotten to know her. Apparently, as Sophie told Star, crows were incredibly smart, and she'd learned there were other people around the world who were just as lucky to be left presents, too. But it was special enough that the *Canaan Gazette* had written an article on Sophie, in which she explained to the reporter that the little gifts, usually shiny objects that were small enough to fit in a crow's mouth, were the most cherished things she owned.

Sophie opened her palm again, and Star rubbed the china piece gently with her index finger. "Nice." She wasn't about to pick it up and risk upsetting Sophie. "Want to go down to the creek and play?"

"We're going to the mall to buy me sneakers. Remember? I told you yesterday. We'll get ice cream after."

Star had forgotten she'd promised Sophie she would go with her. But she didn't want to go that day. Not for the long, boring car ride just to traipse around the crowded mall. She wasn't in the mood. Sometimes, Sophie could be exhausting. Star remembered her dad telling her about "sappers," people who sap up all the energy in a room. He was referring to his Uncle Eddie, who would blab on and on with endless stories about his heroic days in the Army, but Star thought it could apply to Sophie, as well, when she was in one of her obsessive Sophie moods. Birds, birds, birds. Her way or no way.

"Uh, my mom needs me to do something. I can't go with today," Star said.

"What do you mean? You promised." Sophie sat up quickly, and the binos flung around her body, to the left and right before settling in the middle of her chest.

"I can't help it. We've got to go somewhere."

"Where?"

When Star didn't answer right away, Sophie snapped back, "Rats, you're lying. You promised."

Star knew Sophie wasn't good with change. She did best when she stuck to the schedule her mom set for her. "I'm sorry. I forgot. Don't hate me."

"What kind of best friend breaks her promise?"

"Soph, don't make such a big deal about it." She was inching her way toward the door. When Sophie was in one of her moods, Star wanted to be out of her firing range. Usually, Star didn't experience Sophie's tantrums. Mostly, Sophie was able to hold it together and flipped out when she was home alone with her parents. But Star had witnessed a few doozies, and she saw what was coming. She felt the heat rising in the room. She was at the bedroom door, about to leave, when Sophie grabbed Bixby's birding book off her nightstand. She drew her arm back and took aim. Stomping her feet, she said, "You are not my BFF anymore. You're not. You're not!" Her last words to Star.

Star ducked out and pulled the door closed behind her just as the book hit it with a loud smack. As Star took off down the steps, she heard her friend whimpering. And when she got to the kitchen, she saw Jesse and Cooper arguing about who knew what. Cooper saw Star first.

"Leaving already?" he said.

Jesse glanced at Star, her face sad and drawn.

"I've got to get home." Star dashed out the back door and didn't look back.

STAR LEANED HER ELBOW on her dad's desk, holding her head up with her hand. Sophie was super smart but could be difficult and was strict and inflexible about what she wanted. Years ago at school, Star had heard one teacher whisper to another, "Asperger's," while nodding toward Sophie. At the time, Star hadn't even known what the word meant. Sophie's parents had taken her to doctors and shrinks, trying to figure it out. Or maybe she was just gifted and temperamental as Jesse had said she was, the way some famous artists and writers were. Van Gogh. Hemingway. Virginia Woolf. Star really wasn't sure. Back then, she'd just thought of Sophie as her best friend. Sometimes she was a pain, but Sophie was always fun and different from everyone else.

Star was so tired, her whole body felt exhausted. *A nap would be so nice.* She couldn't keep her eyes open another second. Then suddenly she heard a voice behind her.

"Think, Rats, think..." It was Sophie's little girl voice.

Star swiveled around to find Sophie sitting at Jesse's desk. She was still wearing what Star had come to think of as Sophie's "gone missing" outfit.

"Kidnapping is not limited to the acts of strangers but can be committed by acquaintances, by romantic partners, and by parents who are involved in acrimonious custody disputes." Sophie seemed to be reading from a website or book on kidnapping. She sounded like a grown-up, all serious. "Rats, acquaintance kidnapping has the largest percentage of female and teenage victims."

As usual, Star was alone with Sophie's ghost. No witnesses. *Why is there never anyone around when you need them?* It was bad enough when Sophie appeared to her in her bedroom at night, but the little girl ghost was stalking her outside of her house, out in the world.

"Sophie, what do you want from me? I've heard the statistics. What am *I* supposed to do?" *I'm talking to a dead girl,* Star thought. *Have I totally lost it?* "They checked out everyone. The janitors at school. The teachers. The security guards at the Zone. Cashiers. Every freakin' person in the mall that day."

"Hey, Rats?"

"What?"

"Want to go to the mall? I hear Zone is having an awesome sale." And she let out an eerie laugh.

But when Star looked again, the girl was gone. She glanced behind her, under the desk, and back at the computer screen. Sophie's missing photo came around again.

"Shut up," Star shouted and punched the power button, but the computer had crashed and wouldn't shut down. She tapped it again and again, but Sophie's smiling young face was frozen, staring at her. With shaking hands, Star found a cigarette in her bag and lit it. Then she dug around, looking for something sharp. Nothing. She opened her dad's desk drawer, and all she came up with were dull pencils, an old wooden ruler, and scraps of paper. Nothing useful. She took another drag and stared at the cigarette in her hand. An idea came to her, and she didn't stop to think it through. She just shoved her sleeve up and stabbed the burning end of the cigarette on her arm, holding it there for a few blistering, flesh-ripping seconds.

Tears sprang to her eyes, and she shrieked, "Fuck!" Why it hurt so much more than the cutting, she didn't know. She ran to the bathroom and let cold water run over it for five minutes. When the pain subsided to a heavy throb, she grabbed her stuff and noticed that the computer screen had gone to black. She turned out the lights and hightailed it out of there. She just wanted to get home, crawl into bed, and sleep forever.

Chapter Fourteen

Jesse looked back at Barnes, and he nodded. She opened the door to Sophie's room, and what hit her first, as always, was the scent. The air was stuffy, but there was also a piney, woodsy smell. They took a step in, with Saint Anthony following. Every book, article of clothing, and piece of furniture was left as it had been That Day. The sheets of the bed were rumpled and left unmade. The top drawer of the dresser stood ajar, one white sock hanging out. Sophie's bedroom was a time capsule.

Barnes took it all in. The walls were painted with a whimsical floor-to-ceiling forest mural in all shades of nature. Different birds were hidden away like a *Where's Waldo* picture. A sheltering canopy of green fabric leaves hung over the bed.

"This is beautiful," he said. "Like being in a tree house."

Jesse reached up and touched one of the soft fabric leaves between her fingers. "When she was five, Sophie asked me to make her room like the woods. So I created this huge tree over her bed. I made the limbs out of wire and papier-mâché. I sewed these leaves out of felt and attached them." Over a hundred green leaves drooped down.

Sophie had instructed Jesse as to which birds she wanted in the mural. A large black crow with an iridescent violet patch on its head rested on a branch. With a slightly turned-up corner at the edge of its beak, it seemed to be smiling, as though it knew a secret. A blue jay was concealed behind shrubbery. A portion of a cardinal could be seen in a bird house. Jesse gestured at a large barred owl high up in a tree, its big eyes peering out from behind a cluster of oak leaves. "This guy is Mr. Nobody." And nodding over to a delicate black-capped chickadee that poked its face out of a tree hole, she said, "That's Elliot."

Barnes smiled. "Sophie named them, I take it."

"Yes. These are some of the birds she saw in our yard. They became her friends."

Bookshelves held field guides, a collection of nests, CDs of birdsongs, and the white bleached bones of a robin. Turkey feathers were stuffed in a jar like a bouquet. It looked more like the room of a teenage boy than a typical frilly girl's room.

Barnes took Jesse's hand, and they slid onto the carpeted floor, their backs against Sophie's bed. The dog circled and snuggled up at their feet.

Jesse said, "It's pathetic, but I haven't even gone through her things. I think about doing it all the time, then I just can't."

"Tell me about her."

Jesse picked up one of Sophie's field guides from the nightstand and held it to her chest. "She made up this game. She called it 'What kind of bird?' She got me and Cooper and her best friend, Star, to play. We'd have to figure out what kind of bird a person was most like. You know, by how they looked and their behavior." She smiled, remembering. "She called me a scarlet tanager. An amazingly beautiful red bird that was one of her favorites. But if she was mad at me for nagging her, I was a whippoorwill."

"Why was that?"

"Because they're big-headed and repeat their song over and over." She flipped through the field guide then set it down. "I'd come back at her and say she was a grackle. Noisy. A real nuisance. A troublemaker. Some people call it the devil bird."

"That sounds like most kids." Barnes smiled.

"Mostly I called her my little chickadee. A black-capped chickadee. Small, inquisitive. Like her. They'll eat out of your hand. They're colorful with a lovely song." Then she imitated the bird in a soft, high-pitched voice. "*Fee-bee, fee-bee.*"

Jesse gazed off for a minute then said, "Anything bird related. She was on it. But she really loved the crows."

"Crows? Really? I thought they were mean."

"They have a bad reputation, but they're actually very smart." She got up and pulled a clear plastic box down from one of the shelves. She brought it over to Barnes and sat back down next to him. She placed it gently on her lap, dusting off the lid, caressing it as if it were the most precious thing in the world. She opened the lid. It had many individual compartments, made to separate and hold lots of little things like beads or buttons. This box held numerous small objects, all different. Some were rusty; others were shiny. Metal and plastic. Glass and ceramic. A funny collection of colorful little bits.

Barnes looked up at her, waiting for an explanation.

"These are Sophie's prized possessions. Gifts left for her by her crows."

"Gifts?"

She nodded. There was an orange-colored marble in one compartment with a little white handwritten label: *Porch railing. 10:30 a.m. April 16, 2010.* A small red plastic button: *Bird bath. 3:10 p.m. July 7, 2011.* A rusty screw and nut. A green wooden bead. A piece of beach glass the color of a summer sky. A broken metal toy car. Tin foil scrunched up into a tiny ball. A chewing gum wrapper. A bent-open paper clip. And on and on.

"I know they look like tossed-away items. Junk. Like my finds. But they're not junk. They are gifts that were left for Sophie. She used to feed the crows. Peanuts mostly. Sometimes granola or pumpkin seeds. Pieces of apple. Cookie crumbs. We had a platform feeder. The crows would gather in the trees in the backyard, waiting and watch-

ing. A whole group of them. A murder, they're called, if you can believe that. Cawing up a storm. They would watch her closely, as closely as she watched them. They got to know her and her routine. Got
to trust her, I guess. Sometimes she hand-fed them. And after a couple years, when she put out food for them, maybe the next day or
so, maybe a week later or more, she'd find these little presents left
for her. Usually in the birdbath, sometimes right on the feeder. Or
the ground. At first, we thought they were dropped by accident. But
then she started watching very carefully, and we started to photo-
graph the crows in action. Cooper even set up a bird cam so we saw
them leaving the gifts."

"That's amazing. So cool."

"I know. We read books about crows. Watched documentary
films about how intelligent they are and how they've been known to
do this with people they trust." She picked up a bottle cap and turned
it over in her hand then put it back in its spot. She lifted out a yellow
Lego piece and showed Barnes. He took it in his hand and examined
it. "This went on for a couple of years. She collected the gifts, labeled
each one, made notes in her journals. Somehow, word got out, and
she was written up in the local paper." Jesse took a newspaper clip-
ping down off the bulletin board and showed Barnes. There was a
photo of Sophie holding her box filled with her tiny presents.

He read the headline aloud—"Bird Girl Gets Gifts from
Crows"—and smiled.

"The network evening news picked up the story. And then even
Charles Osgood came to interview her for his morning show. Sophie
got letters from people all over the country and England. Even Japan.
People who'd had the same experience. Everyone started calling her
Bird Girl. She became a mini celebrity for a while. It was crazy but
fun for her. The crows were still coming up until the time she disappeared. She loved those birds and especially Sheryl Crow, the one I
painted on the mural. She had an unusual shiny patch on her head."

Barnes laughed. "Really? Sheryl Crow?"

"I used to play that song 'All I Wanna Do Is Have Some Fun,' and it became our song. We sang it together a lot. In the car. At the kitchen table. Sophie loved it. We'd dance. It was silly. Anyway, Sophie was convinced that crow, Sheryl Crow, was leaving her the best gifts. Like this one." She picked up a charm, a small silver heart that looked as though it came from a bracelet. It had "Best Friend" engraved on the back.

"Those are wonderful memories," he said. "You're lucky to have them."

"I guess that's one way to look at it. Each bird I hear now brings back a different memory. When I hear the loud insistent caw of a crow, I can't help but run out to see what they're trying to tell me. Maybe some good news." She brought the little heart to her chest, smiled, then shrugged. She placed the charm back in its compartment in the box before closing the lid with a pat.

"Reminds me of some special times with Kiki."

"Kiki?"

"My daughter."

Jesse clapped her hands. "I knew you had a child. How old is she?"

He looked away, shaking his head. "She would have been twelve this December."

Jesse inhaled, a wave of shock rippling through her body. *Not her, too.* She gently placed her hand on his arm and held it there.

"She was a great kid. Happy. She was my Kikareeno. My pal." He reached into his back pocket and pulled out his wallet. He opened it, slid out a color photo, and handed it to Jesse. She stared at the photo of a slightly younger-looking Barnes with a smiling girl, their arms around each other in front of a tent.

She touched the image with her finger. "She's pretty."

"Yes, she was. I took her camping. Our private father-daughter thing. But about three years ago, she was super busy with school, music lessons, gymnastics, and suddenly, she started to drag around. She wasn't herself. She became lethargic, lost weight. We took her to the doctor. My wife and I."

She looked at him expectantly.

"Nora. My ex-wife now." He breathed in deeply. He stared off for a moment. "It was childhood leukemia. Acute lymphoblastic leukemia[1]. Once it was diagnosed, the nightmare began. What she went through..."

She shook her head. "I'm so sorry."

"If the God-awful treatment would have worked, okay, then it would have been worth the pain. But it didn't. So it wasn't. I keep thinking we shouldn't have put her through it."

"But you had to. You had to try it, right?"

"I suppose. But after, I haven't stopped second-guessing. There was a round of chemo that didn't work, then they did the stem-cell transplant. It was brutal. She had to be quarantined in the hospital. The nausea, the fevers. Eight months later, she was gone. And Nora and I didn't make it, either. It was just too much on the marriage."

Jesse nodded. "I know about that."

He shook his head. "I really fucked up. I was so stressed out. I couldn't deal with it all and my job."

"This job?"

"No. Back then, I was a cop."

"I knew it."

He nodded. "Between taking Kiki to the first round of treatments and then coping with the stem-cell transplant, the ups and downs, these intense emotions, I cracked. I started drinking. Then Kiki didn't make it. I neglected my job. I made mistakes. I just

---

1.   http://www.cancer.gov/Common/PopUps/popDefinition.aspx?id=45586&version=Patient&language=English

couldn't be a team player. I didn't care. I ended up quitting. Nora freaked. All those years toward my pension down the drain. But I couldn't think about that. There was nothing I could control anymore. I felt worthless."

It was hard to equate the calm, even-tempered man before her to the person he just described. "You were grieving. It's normal."

He nodded again. "I know that now. But everyone has to go through it in their own way." He leaned in close, looking her straight in the eyes. "You know that, right? There's no time limit on grief."

Jesse gave a tiny nod. Then he pulled away.

"Nora and I, we couldn't comfort each other. We were too angry and empty. The pain was too intense."

He could have been talking about her own fractured marriage. Her own pain. She laid her hand over his. "I'm so sorry." She'd been so immersed in her own grief, she'd never really imagined anyone else's. Not even Cooper's. "It's not fair."

"I took it out on Nora." He glanced at Jesse. "I was mean. Yelling. Sarcastic." He choked up and stumbled over the next words. "I have regrets."

"We all do."

"Nora is a good person. She didn't deserve the way I behaved." He rubbed the top of his head. "She found someone new. Months later, I moved into an apartment in Maplewood, New Jersey. I was starting all over. I got a job assisting a PI. Started by staking out cheating husbands, deadbeat dads who hadn't paid their child support, then some missing kids. After a few cases where I located a runaway teen, I started to develop a reputation. I was good and was able to use some of my old contacts. I was patient. God, am I patient. I went out on my own. I'd have preferred to sit in my office, tracking identity theft cases on the internet, but these missing kid cases were what found me. Occasionally, there's a happy ending. But mostly, it's a lot of sad stories. Sometimes lost people just don't want to be found."

Maybe it was true of Sophie. Maybe she'd run away.

He took her hand. "I'm okay now. It took a while. Day by day, you know." He took a breath. "I think I see her all the time. Young girls walking down the street."

Jesse nodded but didn't tell him of her own Sophie sightings.

"But I'm onto a new life chapter. It's my second chance. And I'm grateful for it."

A second chance. That was what she needed.

"I told you before. Now I'm going back to school. It'll take a while, but I'd like to help people."

Their eyes met. She glanced away then back to his face. "Did you... did you do anything like I did with Gary?"

"Oh, yes. I did stuff I'm not proud of." He looked away then back. "Why do you think I'm so obsessed with running now? I needed control of something. At least it's a healthy addiction." He paused then said, "Enough of this serious talk. Tell me something about yourself that no one knows."

She thought a moment then said, "I can't swallow a capsule. I have to trick myself by hiding it in some food, a piece of banana or cheese, as if I were a dog."

They both laughed.

"What about you? Tell me something."

He turned his head, thinking. Then he stood up, stared into her eyes. "I want to have some fun." He extended both his hands out to her.

She looked up at him questioningly.

"C'mon, girl," He said. "I know you want to. Sing with me."

Jesse took his hands and let him pull her up to standing. He swung her hands from side to side, and they both started singing the Sheryl Crow song and swaying to their beat. His voice was smooth and mellow. Sexy. He made up his own lyrics and sang, "Until the sun comes up over Jesse Albright's hideaway."

They sang, danced, and laughed until they fell back to the floor, exhausted. Jesse couldn't remember the last time she had laughed like that. It felt amazing. They sprawled on the carpet on their stomachs, talking long into the night. She learned he wasn't from Kentucky, as his name would suggest, but his great-great-granddad was. Barnes loved baseball and had dreamed of playing with the Yankees when he was a kid. And he liked working with his hands. He was even building a boat in his spare time. She told him about growing up in Chicago, being a daddy's girl, then later a struggling artist in New York City. Meeting Cooper. Sophie.

Finally, Jesse couldn't keep her eyes open. "I just need to rest for a few minutes," she said and lay down on Sophie's bed.

WHEN JESSE WOKE, SHE saw a small prism shining on the wall. For a minute, she didn't know where she was. Then she remembered. Sophie's room. The morning sun would catch the corner of a mirror and throw the colors all around. Sophie had called it her "morning rainbow."

Jesse was spooned with Barnes, her back tucked into his chest. He was still asleep. She snuggled in even closer then thought back to the previous night. *Oh God, the party...*

She'd made a royal fool of herself. But the time afterward had felt so intimate. The hunter's moon. That amazing hug. Talking all night. Dancing and singing together. Laughing. She got up on her elbow, turned, and looked over at Barnes's face. For the first time, she could study him without feeling self-conscious. "Best to focus on bill and face," Sophie had told her. His nose was wide but well-proportioned. His hair was short, close to his scalp, and reminded her of the texture of fleece, soft and fuzzy. It came to her. A cormorant. Gentle. Beautiful. Black and noble. She longed to reach out and touch him, but she didn't dare. She watched his chest rise and fall, his breathing soft and steady.

She quietly slipped out of bed and found Saint Anthony on the floor, curled in a ball right under Barnes's side. She reached down and rubbed his head, whispering, "Morning, sweetie."

He opened one eye lazily, groaned, and nestled tighter.

She walked up to the closet. Sophie's private place. Taped to the door was a sign: *Private. Stay out! Trespassers will be shot and stuffed.* It always made Jesse smile.

She opened the door. The large walk-in closet was filled with clothing and shoes. She separated the bottom rack, making a split in the middle, pushing bunches of clothes to both sides. The back wall was covered with a big fanciful drawing and writing in brightly colored markers. This was Jessie's favorite of Sophie's creations. Birds and people flying. Each bird was distinct and well-drawn, with its name under it. Robin. Starling. Rufous-sided towhee. And drawings of particular details: different birds' bills, wings, spotted chests, bands on necks, claws. A story written in Sophie's tiny handwriting wound around it in circles, spirals, and loops. She'd written magical stories about people with powers to fly, grant wishes, speak to birds in their own bird language, and morph into different creatures. Jesse read, *Penny rode on Harper's back. Harper was a red-winged blackbird. He could balance on a tall stem of grass on one leg then fly through the sky with Penny holding on. Penny was a regular nine-year-old girl who had shrunk down to bird size after eating brussels sprouts.*

Jesse looked to the farthest end of the closet, off to the left, down a narrow passageway perfect for a little person. Perfect for Sophie. Jesse sat on the lavender carpeted floor of the closet, just like Sophie used to, and closed the door most of the way. Jesse would often find her behind the door, hiding, talking to herself, or making up stories. With the clothes hanging down, it felt safe, like a cave. She looked up and tried to imagine exactly what Sophie had seen. Her shoes were jumbled in a messy pile. Jesse lifted out a pink sneaker, a Heely. Sophie had learned quickly how to skate fast on the one-wheeled shoe. She looked cute, zipping around in them, her binoculars bouncing on her chest. Her feet would be bigger now, maybe the same size as Jesse's. She pulled her knees to her chest, wrapping her arms around them. She turned the shoe in her hand. Fingered the lace. Spun the wheel with her index finger. "Mommy, Daddy, Sophie," she said, softer than a whisper.

"Hey." Barnes was standing outside the closet, peering in through the small opening.

"Hey yourself."

He opened the door another couple inches and poked his head inside. His shirt was wrinkled, and the bed sheets had made crease lines on his face, imprinting, Jesse imagined, a secret message on him. It made her smile. She would have liked to touch those crease lines to read his face, like a blind person.

"Can I come in?" he asked softly.

She nodded.

He opened the door just enough to slip through. He got on the floor, crawled over, and snuggled next to her. Then he pulled the door closed so only the tiniest sliver of light came through underneath, near the floor. In the dark, Jesse felt more at ease, knowing he couldn't see her.

"She liked to come in here," Jesse whispered.

"Feels safe and cozy. It's nice in here. Kiki had her own special place in our attic." Barnes picked up a small round flashlight on the floor. It was attached to a piece of elastic.

"Sophie's headlight lamp. She wore it when she hid in here. She looked like a little miner girl."

He clicked it on, but nothing happened. "Batteries must be dead."

Jesse nodded. Of course they'd be dead after six years, but it made her feel sad. Barnes pulled a little flashlight attached to a keychain out of his pocket. He turned it on and pointed the light at the wall, illuminating the writing and drawings. He gazed at the wild, meandering mural for a minute.

"Wow," he whispered. "She really was something." Then he pointed the light down toward the narrow section of the closet where her shoeboxes were stacked.

"Huh." He held the light toward the wall near the floor way in the back. "What's that?"

"What do you see?" Jesse leaned in to see that his light was highlighting a thin crack on the wall.

Barnes got on his hands and knees, shoved aside a pile of shoes and clothes, and crawled all the way to the back through the narrow space. He knocked on the wall then reached into his pants pocket.

"Boy Scouts," he said, holding up an old pocketknife. He opened the blade and stuck it in the wall into a crack. Then he jiggled it and pried open a small rectangle of wood. A small door had been cut. It had fit in the wall perfectly. He took out the piece of wood and held the light inside.

"Your plumber must have cut this. You've got some water pipes back here. A shut-off valve. Did you know?"

"Yes. We had a leak one winter. Cooper kept a lightbulb on in there. He used to check it each winter, but after that day, I doubt he ever thought to do it anymore. I certainly haven't been in there."

Barnes shined the light farther inside and rummaged around. "Sophie knew about this space."

"What do you mean? What do you see?" Her heart was suddenly off and racing.

Barnes rustled around in there then pulled something out. He replaced the door, tapped it shut with the bottom of his pocketknife, and crawled backward to the closet entrance.

He handed her a spiral notebook that had Sophie's name hand-written on the cover in the shape and colors of a rainbow. There had been a stack of notebooks that Jesse had found long ago in Sophie's room, diaries and log books, and this one looked like those. Her hands shaking, she flipped through the notebook. Like the others, it was filled with what looked like entries of a birder's journal. The first entry was dated August of 2012. Their last trip to Wellfleet.

Red in the bushes, long bill, white head, black chest with pink spots... Bright-red bands at neck. Duck-like, large body and head...

Wondering why Sophie would have hid this particular note-book, Jesse closed it, brought it to her nose, and sniffed, searching for some long-lost Sophie scent. It only smelled like a musty book, though. She would read it later when she was alone.

"I never met a child like her," Jesse said. "I know every parent thinks that about their kid. She was often in her own world. She'd sing and twirl and make up the most amazing stories or drawings. Like these." She nodded at the wall mural. "She didn't write or sound like her age, but years older. Everyone thought so. She taught me how to observe, how to watch for details, be patient. What things to look for first and record when looking at birds. It's funny how she could sit for hours watching birds, waiting, listening, because somehow, she related to them. I don't know why. Maybe she felt lonely or en-vied their freedom. Or was enchanted by their songs. Or their beau-ty. Or all of it. Whatever it was, I was in awe of that part of her."

"That's wonderful."

She shook her head. "But I didn't protect her."

"You can't always protect them. I know that."

"Things are not what they seem."

"What things?"

"Things," she snapped. "Everything."

"Jesse, what is it? Tell me." He took her by the shoulders and turned her toward him. "Tell me," he whispered firmly.

She was shaking her head back and forth. Back and forth. She couldn't stop. Holding the notebook in the air, Jesse waved it furiously. "It's a lie. It's a big, fat disgusting lie. You see this smiling girl, this happy little girl, and the town and the city and the whole country see her photo plastered in every window on Main Street, on TV, and in the papers. They think she's the perfect girl. They think we are the grieving parents of this perfect little innocent girl who was snatched away, but that's not the truth."

"What do you mean?"

"I mean the thing about Sophie..." She paused, breathing heavily.

"What? Go on..."

"The thing about Sophie... was that she wasn't really a sweet little girl... not like the impression you'd get from the picture of her that was everywhere."

"No child is *always* good."

"No. Sophie was different. She was sensitive to everything. If it was too sunny, it could freak her out. Or if a piece of clothing wasn't just right. If it was corduroy and she wanted cotton, she'd flip. Blue not purple, freak-out. Itchy not smooth, tantrum. She had trouble transitioning. She was hard to be around. Demanding. She would slip into this dark place, where we couldn't reach her. She'd go into sensory overload. She exhausted us... me. We ended up yelling at her. But stick a bird in front of her, and it was music to her. Calming. Contentment. She had these two distinct sides.

"I... we created this difficult child, and we didn't know what to do. We took her to doctors and shrinks. Numerous ones. Specialists in Boston. New York City. Tests and more tests. We spent a fortune. Even took out loans to pay for it all. Asperger's was the diagnosis from a couple doctors. Others said bipolar. One even said ADHD. Sophie displayed some symptoms from each, but then she had other behaviors that would negate them. It simply wasn't clear-cut. There was never a consensus, and it became a constant conflict for Cooper and me, trying to treat different disorders, living with uncertainty. Living with Sophie."

Barnes touched her arm, but she pulled it away.

"We tried medications, but she hated how they made her feel. I don't think they worked anyway. She wished she were normal. She couldn't control her tantrums. It was like something overtook her. She came here to her closet to rock herself into a calm state. She always felt remorseful afterward. I felt terrible for her. She mostly held it all in and only exploded around us at home. So most people thought she was different—creative, moody, obsessive—but not the full extent of who she was." She paused then went on. "Sometimes, I wished I could return her and trade her in for a good kid. I actually thought that. I actually *said* that aloud to Cooper once."

"Everyone thinks that about their kids at times."

"Or it was me, my genes. Cooper had Caleb with his second wife. And from what I hear, Caleb is normal. You know... easy."

"Jesse, the way Sophie was had nothing to do with her disappearance. Someone took her. That had nothing to do with her temperament."

"I didn't know how to handle her." She looked up at him then continued in a whisper. "Sometimes she was hard to love. There were moments I hated her. Hated myself." Her words spilled out. "To quiet her or get her to stop whining or screaming or demanding, we gave in. All the time-outs in the world never worked. We ended up giving in. That was bad—we knew it. But we didn't know what else to do. Nothing else worked. Therapist after therapist, they all disagreed." She dropped her voice even more. "I think I willed her to be taken."

She wanted to tell him the other thing. It was right there, so close to the surface. The thing she hadn't been able to tell anyone. She opened her mouth to speak, but nothing came out. He held her face in his hands. He kissed the top of her head, wiping her tears with his shirt. Then he kissed her cheek. She clutched him back, and he kissed her eyelids. They held each other for a long time. Then they found each other's mouths; they kissed long, deeply. Urgently. He tasted sweet like sugared coffee. It was so dark in the closet, she couldn't see him, but she could hear her own hard, labored breaths and Barnes's quieter shallow ones. She needed him to kiss her, to swallow her up. His hands felt strong but gentle.

The siren of a fire truck screeched. Startled, they pulled away from each other, pushing the closet door open to hear better. Another fire truck raced past. Then another. And another. Their sirens all blared. Alarms from two different fire stations went off simultaneously. A feeling of dread enveloped Jesse, and she grabbed his hand.

Chapter Fifteen

When Jesse tried to drive onto Main Street, a police barricade stopped her.

"Church Street is closed, too," Barnes said, pointing out the side window. Jesse pulled the truck onto another side street, parked, and hopped out. Barnes followed. When Jesse rounded the corner, the smell of burnt paper and wood hit her hard. Then smoke filled her nostrils. Her eyes and lungs. The heat was so intense and so strong, it literally pushed and held her in place. Crowds of people stood behind yellow police tape, looking up. Jesse followed their gazes. The Book Barn was engulfed in fire. Barnes pulled her close to him.

"Oh God!" she said.

Orange flames shot out of second-floor windows. Clouds of thick black smoke billowed up from the structure. Fire trucks surrounded the Barn. Throngs of people huddled together, gawking, their hands held over their mouths in shock. The sight was surreal.

Voices murmured: "All those pumpkins."

"I heard arson."

"Poor Blue."

With Barnes close behind, Jesse pushed her way between people. "Excuse me... I work here. Excuse me."

"Let the lady through," Barnes shouted.

Jesse inched closer to the front, feeling pulsating waves of that incredible heat. Firefighters aimed their hoses at the flames bursting through the roof.

Tears ran down Jesse's face. She thought of all the times she'd lingered over books, how all the stories had comforted her. Being surrounded by the books had given her a sense of security when she needed it most. She loved the Barn. Now it was gone, too.

Everything she loved. Gone.

"I'm sorry," Barnes whispered.

She shook her head slowly. "Everyone loved the Book Barn."

She saw Blue, Beth, and Star huddled together off to the side, just watching numbly. Blue was clutching a book to his chest. Jesse saw neighbors go up, hug them, speaking in hushed tones.

Jesse turned to Barnes. "I'll be right back." She walked over to the Silvermans and wrapped her arms around Blue, then she hugged Beth tightly. They stood in their embrace for a moment. Jesse hadn't been close to Beth in years. Hadn't talked to her or hung out since That Day. She'd given a quick hello and exchanged a few brief pleasantries when they ran into each other in town, but nothing real. Raising daughters the same age, both only children, had been a strong bond all those years ago. At that moment, memories came racing back to Jesse. Late-night calls comparing worries about the girls. The time Sophie had the measles, which Star promptly caught. When Jesse confided in Beth about her difficulties with Sophie. They would often meet for morning coffee at Earl's just to catch up, sharing laughs and tears. Then it all stopped.

"Did anyone get hurt?" Jesse asked.

"No, thank God," Beth said, her face pale and drawn.

"Oh, Jess," Blue said. "I can't believe it. I just can't believe it."

"What happened?"

"They don't know yet," Beth said. "They know it started sometime this morning. Jack Connors was working the early morning clean-up crew after the Harvest Fest. He saw smoke and called the fire department. They don't know if they can save it. They let Blue go in earlier to get the cash box, some important papers, and to try to save the computer."

Blue shook his head. "The firemen took me inside, and the heat was just overwhelming. The muck and water..." Tears sprouted from his eyes and rolled down his face. "All the books, Jess. The shelves are black. The books... ash. Everything ruined." He hugged Beth. "I grabbed one on my way out." He held up an early edition *Collected Works of Shakespeare*. He shook his head. "Why didn't I grab more? I could have taken more."

Star stood off to the side, staring at the Barn in a daze, her face red and blotchy from crying.

"I'm so sorry," Jesse said.

Beth said, choking back more tears, "Everyone's been so kind. People have been handing us money to help rebuild."

It reminded Jesse of when Sophie had gone missing, how the town had rallied. Neighbors and people she didn't even know rushed to her house; some slipped pieces of paper into her pockets, phone numbers and notes offering help. And now, here they were again, the community of Canaan, offering their unwavering support. She looked around at the crowd, all the people she knew, young and old, and saw the anguish on each and every face.

She watched Star walk across the street toward a group of teens. They reached out for her, taking her hand, pulling her to them. Gone was the snotty teen who seemed to hate her dad's store. She looked like a lost little girl.

Jesse turned back to Blue and Beth. "Let me know if there's anything I can do. Anything."

She headed back over to Barnes, and they stood mesmerized, along with most of the town, for over an hour, just staring and watching the blaze helplessly. Barnes's cell phone rang. He answered it and spoke quietly for a minute. Then he slipped the phone back in his pocket.

"There's been word on April Johnson," he said to Jesse. "I have to go, but I'll be back."

She nodded. That girl was part of the puzzle, somehow. She felt it. He took her hands in both of his and brought them to his lips. "Remember, I see you," he said softly then gently tapped his index finger on her forehead.

BY LATE AFTERNOON THE fire was finally contained. Fire Chief Michelson came out to talk to the crowd. He took his helmet off, extracted a handkerchief from his pocket, and wiped the soot and sweat that covered his face. Then he said, "The good news, folks, is that the fire is finally out."

The crowd mumbled.

He held up his hands. "Wait now, wait. Unfortunately, there's some bad news. The structure will have to come down soon."

This brought on a communal groan then more murmuring.

"The building is a hazard now. I'm very sorry."

Jesse watched as a fireman added the Book Barn sign that she had painted years ago to a small pile of saved items off to the side: the Free Books table, the antique cash register, and a handful of rescued hardbacks.

Slowly, the crowd dispersed. As Jesse walked back to the truck, a smoky haze lingered, and when she looked up, she saw tiny pieces of paper and black bits floating down from the heavens like charred snow, some landing in her hair. She extended her hand. At first, all she caught was a handful of ash, but when she opened her hand a second time, she saw crumbs of book pages, fragments of words and sentences. She looked up to the sky and whispered, "Soph?"

It was early evening, and Jesse took Saint Anthony down to the creek, where she used to love to sketch and just chill out. It was one of her favorite spots. She sat on one of the yellow Adirondack chairs facing the water, and the dog lay down beside her on the grass. She'd brought the notebook Barnes had found in Sophie's closet, along with an old sketchbook. Between the disastrous party, baring her soul to Barnes, and the devastating fire, she was wrung out. She hadn't had a chance to look through the notebook. Even though she could seriously use a drink, she needed to be clear-headed. She flipped Sophie's notebook open and saw mentions of a herring gull, a bird that scavenged along the beaches. The pages were filled with Sophie's tiny handwriting and drawings.

Herring Gull steals nest materials from other birds.

She flipped to another page.

He collects stuff for nest: garbage, plastic, fabric bits, string.

Flight pattern: takes off at 9:30 a.m. Returns at 5 p.m.

Takes a bird bath. Dumpster dives for food.

Jessie thought she'd found all the birding notebooks Sophie used to keep her life lists, notes, and sketches in. *Why would she hide this one?* It looked like the other notebooks. Then it dawned on her. Sophie knew about the water leak. She was there when the plumber had cut the hole in the wall. She knew Cooper checked it each winter. She must have put this notebook there on purpose, knowing her parents would open the little door at some point. *She* wanted *us to find it.* Sophie was leading her somewhere.

Jesse set it down and picked up the old sketchbook, one she hadn't touched in years, and pulled out a charcoal pencil from her pocket. She gazed out at the creek. She listened to the rushing water, watching a red-tailed hawk glide way up in the sky, making its high-pitched screech. She noticed a bird's nest up in a fir tree. She didn't know what kind. Sophie would have been able to identify it. Jesse always found the empty, vacated bird homes sad. All that work, and then the intricate things were blown to the ground or left abandoned in a bush. In the same way, she'd neglected her own home, which she'd once nurtured so lovingly.

She closed her eyes, and an image of Sophie looking through her binoculars, staring out at the creek, came to her. A girl whose face was obscured by a pair of goggles. A girl searching for something.

Jesse opened her eyes and scanned through the pages of her old sketchbook. The last drawings were done before That Day. Landscapes. The Wetherby barn out on Kettle Corn Road. The McIntosh farmhouse. She'd sketched them so long ago, she barely recognized her own drawings. They certainly didn't mean anything to her anymore.

She turned to a blank page, intending to sketch Sophie from memory. Using the edge of the charcoal, she marked an outline. But what started to emerge was the smiling image from the missing poster that had been implanted in her mind. The one that didn't truly resemble the real Sophie. She scratched it out, marking over it with dark, jagged lines. She turned the page to start again. She closed her eyes once more, letting whatever picture of Sophie she could conjure rise from inside her.

What came through was a memory of Sophie sitting on her lap on the couch. She remembered stroking Sophie's long dark hair, curling a piece of it behind her right ear, making a loose French braid.

"Mom, Mom, Mom, write me a story."

They had a game in which Jesse would draw letters on Sophie's back with her finger. Sophie had to guess what Jesse was writing, letter by letter. Once she got the first few letters, Jesse would begin to tell her a story, then they would switch. Sophie thought it was a game, but Jesse was glad for something that sometimes calmed her daughter.

"Make it a good one. A long one."

"Okay." She rubbed Sophie's back on top of her shirt in big soothing circles, as if cleaning a slate, then began. She drew an *M* on Sophie's back.

"M," Sophie said.

She drew an *A*, which Sophie guessed right away, then a *D*.

"Madeline," Sophie shouted.

"That's right." Jesse began the story of Madeline, going to the zoo in Paris.

Sophie was interested for a minute but grew restless. "Let me."

Jesse turned around so Sophie could draw on her back. She wrote an *E* then an *M*.

"Auntie Em from the Wizard of Oz?" Jesse guessed.

"No, no. It's Emmet. I've told you about him before."

"Tell me again."

Sophie began spouting one of her stories. "Emmet the woodpecker. He's pileated. Really big"—she demonstrated with her hands, spreading them apart wide—"and noisy."

All she needed was a little push, and like a jazz musician, Sophie was off on a riff. "He lives in a hole in a tree. He made the hole, and he lives in it with his friend, Frances, the tree frog. They make music together. Emmet pecks, and Frances croaks."

Jesse didn't dare move. She didn't want to spoil the rare peaceful moment with her daughter. Sophie wasn't good at transitioning, and any different subject or movement, any veering off the course that had been set, could be disastrous.

Then a loud slam startled them both. And Cooper appeared in the doorway, back from one of his weekend hiking trips. He looked tired, sporting three-day stubble and boots caked with mud. He dropped his backpack on the floor. "Hi there. How is everyone?"

Jesse shot him a look and blinked a few times as if trying to signal some secret code with her eyes. "Hi, honey," she said.

He'd ruined the moment, not on purpose, but ruined it just the same. It never took much. If she'd heard his car drive up, she could have forewarned Sophie, eased her into the change. Sometimes that helped.

"What's for dinner?" He glanced between Jesse and Sophie and back to Jesse.

"Not hungry," Sophie said. "What letter is this? You're not guessing, Mom."

"Sweetie," Jesse said.

"How about *pasgetti*?" Cooper said, trying to cajole Sophie. "How about a hug hello, my chickadee?" He cautiously touched her arm.

"*No.*" She shook him away angrily. She only liked to be touched when she wanted to be touched.

Jesse exchanged looks with Cooper. They knew what they were in for. *Help me,* she tried to say with her eyes. As if a switch had been tripped, Sophie was fully charged like a ball of raw electricity. From restful green to the frightening red zone in seconds flat.

"I said *no!*" she shrieked. Legs, arms, fingers, darting, jabbing, flailing, grabbing at whatever was in her path. Lamps on tables, pictures on walls, hair on parents' heads. She erupted into a full-blown tantrum. Screeching, kicking, hair flying, tears. A wild-child rage. Patty Duke playing Helen Keller.

Cooper scooped her up in one swift practiced motion, being careful to hold her tightly as he carried her upstairs to her room.

She shouted, "I hate you. I hate you. You're hurting Emmet."

Jesse knew he would put her on her bed, leave the room, and close the door behind him. They'd long ago learned that when she hit a certain point, there was no stopping her tantrums. Like a fire that had to burn out on its own, Sophie would find her way to the comfort of her dark closet and rock herself into a calmer state.

Jesse was filling a pot with water at the kitchen sink and hadn't heard Cooper come back downstairs when he said, "She's decompressing."

She jumped. "You scared me." And as she spun around to see him, the pot slipped from her hands into the sink, the water slopping out all around.

"Sorry, honey," he said.

She bent over the sink and covered her face with her hands.

He put his arms around her. "I know."

"Do you? She's been like this all weekend. I'm so stressed. What are we supposed to do?"

"I don't know." He turned her around and hugged her. "We'll get through it. It'll get better."

"How? When?" She pulled away from him. He wasn't around enough to get the full impact of Sophie's highs and lows. Jesse couldn't help but resent him for it. "It was so nice for a minute. One little minute, it was normal. She was sweet and funny. She was telling me one of her wild bird stories."

Cooper shook his head. "Maybe we should try a new medication."

"You know she hates how they make her feel. She won't swallow it."

"You don't know. A different pill may help. A different dosage."

"They never work for her. And if it is Asperger's, you know there are no meds for that," she said. "Those doctors are idiots grasping for answers, and we'll go broke bouncing from one to the other while they use our daughter as a guinea pig."

"We have to stick with the routine she needs. Learn how to deal with it."

Easy for you to say. You're never here. She'd read so many books on different techniques: look for Sophie's cues, give her the space and private time she needs, help her to use her words to express her feelings, stay in the calm green zone, and make sure she gets plenty of exercise and sleep. But Jesse just looked at Cooper and held her tongue.

She shook her head then whispered, "I like the last shrink's diagnosis."

That therapist, probably the eighth or ninth one they'd taken Sophie to, had said, "I've seen this before. Exceptionally spirited. I think she'll outgrow it."

About twenty minutes later, Jesse went upstairs. She found Sophie deep in her closet, wearing her headlight lamp, holding Mr. Bear.

"I can't help it, Mommy," she whimpered.

Jesse sat on the floor next to her. "I know, honey. I know," she said, stroking Sophie's hair. It was as if her daughter lived in a different weather pattern than everyone else, as though she were always fighting a terrible storm that was coming at her, being pelted by atmospheric disturbances.

"I wish I were normal," she moaned.

Jesse kissed the top of her head. "You feel a little ouchy?"

Sophie nodded. "Don't hate me."

Jesse smiled and hugged her. "I don't hate you, my chickadee."

"I love you, Mommy."

"I love you too, sweetie."

Sophie reached up and held the silver locket that was around Jesse's neck. She slid it on its chain back and forth, back and forth. She opened the locket and looked at the two photos, one on each half of the necklace. On the right side was a photo of Sophie with her binoculars around her neck, looking serious, taken the summer before on the Cape. The other was one of Jesse and Cooper, their arms around each other, both tanned and happy, smiling widely. Sophie closed the locket with a click and lightly touched the engraved inscription on the front. "With eternal love," she read aloud. "Forever, right?"

"Forever, right." Jesse kissed her index finger and placed it on Sophie's lips.

For Jesse, it was these moments after a tantrum when things felt most ordinary, literally a calm after the storm. *Is this the kind of moment most parents enjoy every day?* She pushed down the rumbling feeling of envy.

She picked up Sophie's well-worn copy of *Madeline* and began to read.

WHEN JESSE CAME OUT of her reverie, she looked down at her paper and saw the beginning of a drawing of Sophie. Her long hair. Her thick worried eyebrows. Her round face. But the rest of her features were not there. Jesse had drawn a blank face, as if the real Sophie were fading away.

Although Sophie's tantrums mostly took place at home, now and then, she would act out in public, and Jesse could never predict when it might happen or what would set her off. She would get "the look" from strangers that meant "You're a bad mother who can't control your child." She would say, "She can't help it" or "She has a condition." But usually, she said, "Sorry. I'm sorry" before slinking away. Jesse never knew exactly what she was sorry about. Sorry her kid had disturbed them or made a scene? Sorry she felt embarrassed? Sorry her daughter wasn't like theirs? Easy? Normal? Just plain sorry.

She turned to a new page of her sketchpad and started drawing fast. What came out this time was an image of Barnes. She remembered him precisely. The close-cropped fleecy hair. The sweet grin. A knowing glint in his dark eyes. She thought of how he'd said goodbye to her when he left the fire scene. How he had said, "Remember, I see you."

Just last night, she'd danced and laughed with him. Just this morning, they were drawn together in that intense kiss. At first, a smile formed on her lips, but then words she'd read in that survival guide came back to haunt her. *There is no such thing as "normal" life*

as you once knew it. Everything has changed and has changed forever.
And whatever the outcome, you will be dealing with this nightmare in
some way for the rest of your life.

As guilt and ambivalence swelled in her chest, she grasped her charcoal and scrawled harsh, dark lines over and over, covering up the drawing. She shoved the pad onto the ground and shot up from her chair. Walking over to the edge of the creek, she grasped her silver locket and, with one firm tug, yanked it from her neck. *For the rest of your life.*

She closed her hand into a fist. Holding the locket tightly, she swung her arm over her shoulder then let it fly out toward the creek. Saint Anthony barked and ran into the water as if it were a game. Jesse watched as the locket landed in the water with a plop. It glistened for a moment as it seemed to float away but was quickly gone from her sight.

"Forever, right," she mumbled and turned back toward the house, the dog following at her heels.

IT WAS TWO IN THE MORNING, and Jesse couldn't sleep. Thoughts of Barnes's kisses kept creeping into her brain. She slipped downstairs, thinking she would get a drink, but something pushed her on. She walked through the kitchen, where she grabbed a set of keys off a hook on the wall. Then it pushed her into the dining room, onto the screened porch, and out the back door. Outside, she looked up at the sky. It was a clear night, full of bright stars.

She walked along a bluestone path Cooper had made to the old chicken coop out back. He'd worked so hard to restore it, to make the near-crumbling structure habitable. She unlocked the door and entered her studio for the first time in years. She flipped the switch next to the door. The lights flickered on. It was stuffy, with cobwebs hanging in corners, but otherwise, the studio was as she'd left it all those years ago. Coffee cans stuffed with paintbrushes, rolls of papers, and canvases were stashed in a corner, a set of flat files in another. A film of dust coated the tabletops. But unlike the inside of her chaotic house, she could actually breathe in the studio. It was all neatly organized. In the daytime, the space was full of light shining through the bank of windows and the two skylights Cooper had installed. Jesse had loved working there. It had been the perfect space for making art.

She walked around, looking at the pieces she had been working on right before That Day. They were left untouched. One rested on an easel, and another was tacked to the wall—the Thorntons' gray listing barn and the Fitzpatricks' stone house, both in thickly painted oils. There was also work on the floor, leaning up against the wall. She let her hands glide over the pieces, touching them as if she'd never seen them before. There were local Canaan landscapes alongside an even earlier series of vast New Mexican skies and mesas from her time spent at an art colony in Taos before Sophie was born, before she and Cooper had even moved to Canaan. The paintings were bold and desolate. They brought back memories of one of her best days ever. She had gone with a group of artists from the colony to see Georgia O'Keefe's home in Abiquiu. The stark vistas and O'Keefe's warm but spare home with rows of smooth river rocks that lined the window ledges had inspired Jesse. She'd felt an ease and contentment in New Mexico: her true self. She didn't know whether it was the glistening light so ideal for painters or the clean, clear air. She'd loved it all.

She sat in an oversized upholstered chair that had been her meditating, thinking spot, pulling her knees up to her chest. The place where she would sit to mull over her work, to see if she was finished with a painting. She stared at all the pieces, taking them in. She picked up a paintbrush—one of her favorites, a Winsor and Newton hog hair—and held it. Feeling the thick wood handle stained with numerous colors, she turned it over in her hands. Looking at the canvases, she realized she didn't miss painting mountain landscapes or farmhouses and barns. She didn't know if she could ever go back to all that. Yet holding the brush in her hand felt good, like greeting an old friend.

After sitting in her chair for a long time, absorbing her old work, letting the peace and familiarity of the place sink in and surround her, she realized she had missed this part of her that she'd shut off, and this space, her sanctuary where she could let her creativity flow whether she was successful at it or not. She stood up, set the paintbrush down, turned out the light, and headed back to bed.

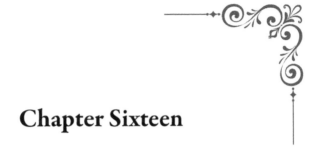

Chapter Sixteen

About three minutes before the bell, Star was standing at her locker, looking at herself in the little round mirror taped to the inside of the door. She looked like hell—pale, with ghastly dark rings under her eyes. She'd gotten no sleep last night and little the nights before that.

Someone said, "How do you spell 'No Smoking,' dorko?" And when Star looked in the mirror again, Sophie's reflection stood behind her.

Star whirled around, shouting, "Fuck you, Soph..." But it was Ruby standing there, looking totally confused. "Oh. Sorry, Rube," Star said, glancing around. "I thought you were somebody else."

Sophie had conveniently disappeared.

"Star, are you okay? You look like you saw a ghost." Ruby hugged her books to her chest. "I was texting and calling you all day yesterday. Why didn't you get back to me?"

"Hello? I was a little preoccupied."

"I know. I'm so sorry about your dad's bookstore. I went to the Barn looking for you, but I guess you'd left. It's so awful."

"Yeah, it sucks."

Their home phone hadn't stopped ringing—everyone calling to check up on them. Neighbors kept bringing food over as if someone had died. *Like tuna casserole was going to save the day.* People kept asking stupid questions.

"What'll Blue do now?"

167

"Why can't they save the Barn?"

"Will you rebuild?"

"Any books left?"

What they should have been asking was: what did Star do with that fucking cigarette? She must have flicked it away after burning herself. *But where did it land? Or did I stamp it out with my foot?* She just didn't remember. The insurance people were investigating the cause of the fire, and they were going to figure it out. Star could hear the news report: "Psychotic Self-Mutilating Teen Sets Fire to Father's Bookstore." She was so screwed. And to make things worse, Sophie had decided to show up at school, where Star had been safe from her so far.

"What's going to happen?" Ruby asked. "About the Barn, I mean."

"I don't know. Nobody knows yet. My parents are kind of in shock."

"But are they going to be okay?"

"What do you mean?"

"Like, wasn't that your dad's only job?"

"Oh. Yeah. But it was a used bookstore. Like who even buys books anymore, let alone old, moldy ones? I don't think it'll make that much of a difference. My dad made money with computers and shit years ago. I don't think we'll starve." At least, she hoped they wouldn't. She was never exactly sure what her dad had done all those years ago. He was no Steve Jobs or Mark Zuckerberg, but she knew he had been a big shot at a tech company that invented some chip or app or code or something having to do with wireless networks. And when they went public, the executives all made a bundle. It seemed funny to think her dad was a techie nerd who actually loved paper.

"Oh, good," Ruby said. "I was, you know, kind of worried for you."

All the talk about the Barn was making Star even more nervous. She noticed Ruby's new top. It was tight and pink, and Ruby loved talking clothes. "New top?"

"Yeah. The Zone."

Star paused. Not that rat trap again. "Sweet."

"They have a million different kinds. You'd look totally cute. I'll go with you." Lately, Ruby was always trying to get Star to buy new clothes and fix herself up. Put on makeup. Cut her hair. Star used to be into clothes, shopping, and all that typical teen girl stuff. But no more. She just put on whatever was handy, called little attention to herself, and covered her cuts... and that cigarette burn. Looking hot was the last thing on her mind.

Ruby was in Star's homeroom, so they headed over to Ms. Birch's classroom together. They passed Zack, who was walking with his two friends in the opposite direction. Ruby gave Star the eye and a little grin. She mouthed "MC" to her, and Star rolled her eyes. *Right. Major Crush*.

Zack nodded at the girls. "Hey, dude."

"Dude," Star said back at him.

"Sorry about the Barn. What a bummer." Then he was gone.

The night before, he had been super nice to Star, hanging out with her, watching the fire, putting his arm around her comfortingly. But right then, even her MC couldn't cheer her up. Plus she still hadn't been able to reach Ophelia on the phone. She'd kept calling last night but got no response. On top of everything else, she was worried about the strange girl, too.

They got to homeroom, and it was all abuzz with kids gossiping about the fire. It was the biggest thing to happen in Canaan since Sophie's disappearance. As the bell rang, Star put her head down on the desk and rested her eyes. The thing that kept bothering her, besides Sophie Albright, was what she had said to Jesse when she'd bitched at Star for smoking at the book store.

"Do you want to burn down your dad's business?" she had said.

"I could care less," Star had replied. But she hadn't meant it. She would never mean that. She was being a spoiled brat. She was so fucked.

Suddenly, Ms. Birch was clapping her hands to get everyone to shut up. She was babbling announcements about SATs, college applications, and recruiters coming from some expensive private college in Boston.

Ruby tapped Star on the shoulder. "Are you all right?"

She lifted her head. "I'm just tired. I didn't get any sleep last night."

Next thing she knew, Ms. Birch was standing right next to her. She was a well-meaning lady who taught English, wore long flowered skirts, and always had one braid down her back. She tilted her head then shook it sadly. She put her hand on Star's shoulder. "Star, I'm very sorry about the Book Barn. Everyone is. In fact, I want to organize a fundraiser to help rebuild." She turned to the whole class. "Who would like to be on the committee and plan an event?"

Most kids weren't even listening to her. They were tapping and swiping at their smartphones or talking to their neighbors. Star dropped her head back on the desk. It was so heavy, she couldn't keep it up. It felt good to close her eyes. She heard the commotion in the room but tuned it out and just tried to listen to her own breathing.

She hadn't told Ruby about the cigarette and burning the Barn down or about her ex-best friend's ghost. She knew Ruby suspected something was going on. She probably thought Star was into drugs. She'd asked her these serious probing questions like "Have you ever taken Adderall?" Or "Would you ever go to a shrink?" But as much as Star would have liked to confide in her about what was going on, she knew Ruby would tell her parents or some teacher, and that would suck. They would think she was crazy and send her away—Outward Bound or some reform school where they would take away her cell phone and laptop and make her life even more miserable. No, she had to deal with it on her own. The bell rang, and like robots, the kids moved on to their first-period classes.

Star's was Mr. Victor's science class. Mr. V was cute with long sideburns that he obsessively caressed. First, he stroked the right one three times, then switched over to the left side and stroked that three times. He had trendy, hipster-style black plastic eyeglasses and a gold wedding band. He always wore a button-down shirt, usually white. A different tie every day. Jeans and no jacket. He was basically nice and easy to look at.

They were discussing global warming, when somehow the topic came around to how it affected animals.

Mr. Victor said, "By the year 2050, between fifteen and thirty-seven percent of known species will be extinct."

"What does he know about extinction?"

Star turned to the voice, and there she was again, her ex-BFF stalker, sitting next to her, where Michael McDonnell, the class clown, had been a minute before. He always sat next to her, but he was gone. Star looked all around the room and didn't see him. Sophie was her ten-year-old self and looked funny sitting at that desk surrounded by sixteen-year-olds, her legs dangling but not touching the floor.

"What are you doing here?" Star whispered. "What have you done with Michael?"

"This is so boring. How do you stand it?" She brought her binos up to her eyes and focused in on Mr. V.

"Shhh." Star turned away from her and picked up her pencil. She tried to take notes on what Mr. Victor was saying, but she couldn't concentrate. She just heard disconnected words. "Greenhouse gas... extreme weather events... climate change..."

She was pressing really hard with the pencil on her notebook, staring at the dark point of the lead.

Sophie kept whispering in her ear, distracting her. "Did you think about what I told you the other day?"

Star kept shushing her, giving her the evil eye. Other kids in the class were turning to look at her funny. She slunk down in her seat, trying to disappear.

"Miss Silverman? Is there something you'd like to share with us?" Mr. Victor said. He had stopped writing on the blackboard and was looking right at her. Of course, so was the entire class.

She looked up and shook her head. "Now look what you've done," she muttered. Under her desk, she pressed the pencil point into her arm, and it broke with a snap.

"All right then," Mr. Victor said. "Shall we continue? Who can tell us some ways we can all help the environment?"

"Who can tell us about Sophie Albright? Whatever happened to her? Is she dead or alive?" Sophie wouldn't stop jabbering.

Star couldn't believe no one else heard her. The little girl ghost was like a huge mosquito buzzing in Star's ear. With each word she said, Star felt more tense.

Sophie pulled an apple out of her Hello Kitty backpack and bit into it, chewing loudly. "What about you, Star Silverman? Weren't you her best friend? Didn't you have a blood pact with her?" She jabbed her index finger at Star for emphasis. "Weren't you supposed to be with her that day at the Zone? Didn't you promise her you'd go?"

"I didn't promise," Star said more loudly than she should have. She grabbed her books and backpack and slipped out of class as Mr. V called her name and everybody turned to look at her again.

She ran down the hall and ducked into the girls' bathroom. Luckily, it was empty. She went into the last stall by the window and locked the door. She put her books on the floor, closed the lid of the toilet, and sat down. Her heart was thumping loudly, practically racing out of her chest. It was bad enough having Sophie hanging around her at night in her own bedroom. *But the Book Barn? And now school, too?*

She felt like reporting Sophie to the principal, but Mrs. Robbins would just laugh in her face. Star wondered if Jesse saw Sophie as she did. Star closed her eyes and took a few deep breaths. Finally, it was quiet. She thought that she had lost her. *Breathe. Just breathe.*

"You don't have to run away from me."

Star looked up, and there Sophie was, standing with her back against the closed door of the stall. Star felt like crying.

"I don't see you doing anything to find me. My mom may be crazy with her junk collecting, but at least she's trying in her own demented way."

"What can I do?"

"Blood sisters forever. Remember?" And she wiggled her index finger at Star.

"What does that mean?"

"You know, Star, not all secrets are meant to be kept forever. Not if it means life or death."

"What secrets? What are you talking about?"

"You're not thinking." And she tapped the side of her head with her finger.

Star needed to get rid of her once and for all. The ghost or whatever was totally creeping her out, ruining her pathetic sixteen-year-old existence. Her parents kept saying, "These are the best years of your life," and she didn't know what the hell they were talking about.

She grabbed her backpack and started rummaging around in it. She pulled out her mom's cell phone and wondered if there was anyone she could call who could help her. There was really no one. Then she had a brilliant idea. She could take Sophie's picture. She had to make somebody believe her. A photo would be proof that Sophie existed in some shape or form. She aimed the phone at the girl and pressed the button. It flashed, and Star saw yellow spots for a minute.

Sophie laughed. "I don't think so, Rats."

She turned the phone and looked at the photo she'd taken—a perfect shot of the bathroom stall door covered in graffiti. No Sophie. No person. No ghost. Just the marked-up door. *I should have known.*

Star reached into her backpack and felt around. Tic-Tacs. Hair clips. A pen. She dug deep into the bottom and pulled out a couple of pennies, lip gloss, cigs, a lighter, that note from Vicki about her crush on Jason, and paper clip. *Paper clip!* She straightened the clip so it was all the way open. One long piece of metal wire. Classes would be over soon, so she had to work fast.

"Are you crazy? A paper clip?" Sophie said. "Might as well use a cigarette again."

Star just dug right into her arm. Literally. She wasn't timid. It hurt, but the wire wasn't really sharp enough. She only managed to scrape a messy, bloody hole that hurt like hell but wasn't a real cut. The bell went off, and Sophie was still there, laughing at Star.

"Shit." She tossed the paper clip into her bag, unrolled a ton of toilet paper, and wrapped it around her arm as tightly as she could. As Star was pulling down her sleeve, two girls entered the bathroom, so she flushed the toilet and collected her stuff. Opening the stall door, she nearly bumped into Collette, a girl from her science class. She always sat in the front. Always knew the answers. A real brain.

"Star, are you okay? Did you get sick?" Colette asked.

"I didn't feel well. But I'm okay now." And she rushed out of there.

It was only nine-thirty, but she pushed out of the front doors, ran down the steps, and just as she'd expected, nobody followed or said anything. Nobody really cared about her anymore. The air was cool and crisp, and it looked all Froot Loops outside—what Sophie used to call the bright berry and lemony colors of the trees in autumn. Fall used to be Star's favorite time of year. Playing in the crunchy fallen leaves. Layering up with sweaters. Going to the Hill Town Haunted House. Now it was as if her life were one big haunted house. Her mom's cell phone rang. Carly Simon was singing "You're So Vain." *What a stupid ring tone.* Star pulled the phone out of her bag.

Star's cell number showed up on the caller ID. *Ophelia, at last. Thank God.* "Hello?"

"Star?"

"Yeah, Ophelia. Where have you been? I've called a zillion times."

"Can you come meet me at Blueberry now, please?" She sounded even more upset than Star felt.

"Are you okay? What's wrong?"

"Just come now, please."

"What is it? Did something happen?"

"I need you. I'm freaking out." And she hung up.

Star was lightheaded and kind of dizzy. But maybe going to see Ophelia, helping someone else, would get her out of her own head. She walked down the street fast, taking long strides, and she didn't look back. Maybe she could outrun the little girl ghost.

Chapter Seventeen

That morning, Jesse woke from a deep sleep to hear her cell phone vibrating on the night table. She hoped it was Barnes, even though the thought of him scared her. He had texted her last night. *I C U.*

But when she looked, she saw it was Gary calling. Jesse knew she shouldn't pick up. He'd tried to end the affair last year, and they had both agreed it was the smart thing to do, but neither had really meant it. Jesse had known he would be back. She'd known she held some kind of power over him. But this time felt different. The baby business put a whole new spin on things. The Barnes business, too. She only wished she could have been the one to end it first.

"Please," he said. "Meet me at Blueberry Lane. One more time. At ten thirty?"

She looked over at Cooper's old side of the bed, thinking of how he used to make her coffee on Sunday mornings and bring it to her in bed. He would pre-warm her cup with boiling water so it would be hot when he put in milk. "Your coffee, baby," he would say, and she'd loved the whole ritual. Then a different memory eclipsed the first—Cooper dashing out of the house one evening after a call from Cindy about "computer problems" at his office. Right then, the haze of denial lifted, and the truth and the subtext of all their fights and sniping became clear.

Cooper had been having an affair with Cindy before Sophie went missing. He had gotten Jesse to believe it was after, but it wasn't, and somewhere deep inside, she'd known all along. She and Cooper had gone to therapy, but the sessions had mostly revolved around day-to-day coping with a missing child. *But what if we'd made more time for each other? Hadn't taken each other for granted?*

She'd known deep down about his affair but had chosen to close her eyes. She wondered if Carol had done the same with Gary. She assumed so. She wished she could just tell Gary to fuck off right now.

Then her thoughts ran to Barnes—a new man who could hurt her. *Who am I kidding?* Gary was familiar and safe, and right now, she could use a dose of that.

"Jess?" Gary said.

"Ten thirty."

SHE DROVE TOO FAST down Bug Hill Road then cut over to Creamery, taking back roads, which were bumpy with deep potholes, reminders of last year's rough winter.

"Froot Loops," Jesse said to Saint Anthony when she saw the leaves at their intense peak colors. She turned to the dog, who was sitting upright in the passenger seat beside her. "Don't ask me what I'm doing. Lila saw it coming, and I didn't listen." She waited as if he would respond, then petted his head. "I wish you'd say something."

The drive to 235 Blueberry Lane normally took fifteen minutes, but for once, Jesse didn't want to be late, and she sped through town. As she passed Church Street, she got a glimpse of the remains of the Book Barn: a collapsed roof, charred posts, and beams all tilted, bent, and blackened. It was an ugly, disturbing sight. The air smelled like burnt toast, and tiny flecks of ash still dotted the air. She had an uneasy feeling and tried to calm herself with a few deep breaths. What Barnes had said the other night replayed in her head. *"I believe you're close to something."* *But what?* She felt like a stranger in her own skin.

She picked up the small glass oval stone from the plastic shelf under her radio and rubbed it between her fingers. Lila had offered it to her during a hypnotherapy session, and Jesse had picked the green stone from a dish of multi-colored ones because it made her think of summer. Grass. Basil. Mint. All things she still found pleasant.

Right at that moment she didn't know what to visualize. Part of her wanted to tell Gary off. To send him packing once and for all. She had been using him as a crutch for too long. She was clutching onto remnants of her past: the house, Gary, and even Cooper with her late-night calls to him. But if she let go and got involved with Barnes, it would just be something else for her to screw up.

During one of their last sessions, Lila had asked Jesse to keep a journal of her feelings. What she felt before a rendezvous with Gary. What she felt after. What she felt before she called Cooper late at night. What she felt after they'd hung up. But Jesse didn't want to keep track of all that. Jesse had looked at Lila and asked if numbness counted as a feeling.

Lila had been wearing a colorful skirt in a pretty Indian print and tall leather boots, very stylish. Jesse had looked down at her tattered jeans and paint-splattered shirt. She was probably a few years younger than Lila, but she looked and felt much older. She wondered if it was weird to be jealous of her therapist and if she'd have to put those feelings down in the journal, too.

"What about during the sex with Gary?" Lila asked.

"The sex?" Jesse laughed. "Sounds rather clinical."

"What would you rather I call it?"

"A drug."

"And what do you feel while you're doing this... drug?"

Jesse closed her eyes and remembered the amazing videos of a murmuration of starlings that she and Sophie would watch over and over. Sophie had read about it and taught her mother the term. The large mass of birds would fly so fast, swooping into unbelievable hairpin turns all together as if one. She looked up at Lila and said, "Like a starling. Free."

"Free... as in liberated?"

"I don't know. Free, as in I can breathe."

"And afterward?"

"Afterward, my stomach growls. I feel empty and need to eat."

"Do you think sex with Gary will bring Sophie back?"

That had never occurred to her. She shook her head. "Of course not. Sex with Gary is just a momentary blip."

"Is that what it is to him?"

As heartless as it seemed, Jesse didn't really care. She did know that the sneaking around, meeting in vacant houses, although risky, added a level of excitement. A shared secret. "Honestly, I have no idea. You'd have to ask him."

Lila was always pushing Jesse, and she'd gotten tired of being pushed.

The smoothness of her green stone helped calm her. She held it up and touched it to her face, sliding it up and down along her cheek. It felt cool. She thought again of Barnes. He was stirring up old, dormant emotions. Those little butterflies in her stomach fluttered. She put her stone back on its little shelf.

She pulled up next to the house on Blueberry. Surprisingly, Gary, who was usually early, wasn't there yet. She scratched Saint Anthony's chest and fed him a biscuit from her pocket. She thought of Barnes, who carried treats for the dogs he met on his travels. She liked that about him.

She went to the back door, but it was locked and had Gary's lock box around the door knob. She'd never been the first to arrive. She sat down on the stoop and waited. She kept checking her watch and cell phone, but he hadn't called or texted. Even though he'd never done it before, Jesse imagined him changing his mind and standing her up. Then she imagined him getting in a car accident or being pulled over for speeding. Both seemed unlikely as well. She checked her watch again and thought about him getting in a big fight with Carol right before he was to leave. Reaching over, she rubbed behind Saint Anthony's ear and waited some more.

After twenty minutes and still no Gary, Jesse heard voices coming from the cabin next door, and Saint Anthony heard them, too. He gave a few warning barks. The place had been closed up for the season, so she got up and went to investigate.

"Hello? Anyone here?" She approached the door of the cabin, which was ajar. Cautiously, she stepped inside then stopped abruptly when she saw Star Silverman sitting on the couch. "Star? What are you doing here?"

The dog trotted in, his tail wagging furiously. He sniffed the floor, the couch, and everything on his way over to the kitchenette. He shoved his snout into the garbage and snuffled around in there.

"Nothing. I'm leaving." Star jumped up quickly.

"Shouldn't you be in school?" Jesse stood in the doorway, blocking it.

Not making eye contact, Star said, "I'm on my way. Missed the bus. You know, so much commotion at home with the fire and all." It was obvious she was lying. She tried to creep around Jesse and slip out.

"Hold on there," Jesse said, putting her hand on Star's shoulder. "What are you doing here?"

"Are you, like, following me or what?"

"No, I'm not following you. I'm meeting someone next door. My realtor. I heard voices over here, and I knew it had been closed up." She glanced around the place, her eyes darting back and forth. She sniffed the air. *Is that Sour Patch Watermelon?*

Then there was a loud thump outside from around the back. They both jumped and looked at each other.

"What was that?" Jesse asked.

"I don't know."

Saint Anthony barked, poking his snout under the closed bathroom door. Jesse heard the water running.

"Who's in there?" she asked.

Star shrugged.

Jesse walked over to the bathroom, turned the knob, and went in. Star followed. The one small window was wide open. The water was running in the sink. Jesse turned off the faucet then stepped up to the window and stuck her head out. She looked down and around. Star came up behind her and looked out at the ground then off in the distance. A figure was running through the woods. Just a flash of red and a bit of blue dashing away through the trees.

"Who's that?" Jesse asked.

Star paused as if thinking about how to respond. "This girl I met at the Book Barn. Ophelia. She needed a place to stay for a little bit. I told her about Blueberry. No one was living here, so I thought it would be okay. She must have gotten spooked and jumped out the window."

"A girl? Was she wearing a red hoodie?"

Star didn't answer.

"Bad haircut?"

She swallowed then blinked.

"Watermelon gum?"

"What? Are you psychic?"

Jesse went back to the window and looked out again. She spoke in a monotone voice, "If birds suddenly fly off all at once, most likely a predator has just visited."

"What?" Star said.

Jesse turned back to Star. "I think she's the girl that detective is looking for. April Johnson. I think she's a runaway... Why didn't you tell the detective you'd met her?"

"I didn't know she was the one he was looking for. They look totally different. And she said her name was Ophelia. I thought it would be okay if she hung out here while she figured out what to do next."

"Have you been coming here? That's breaking and entering, Star. You could get in trouble for that."

"I was only trying to help her. She called me this morning while I was at school. She sounded all upset." She looked out the window again, but "Ophelia" was long gone. "Should we go after her?"

"It's too late. We'll never catch her now."

Star reached in her pocket, pulled out a cigarette, and looked at it. Shaking her head, she shoved it back. "I'm going to go now."

Jesse bent down and picked up a pink shirt off the bathroom floor. Jesse held it up—a pink T-shirt with a little bird and the word *tweet* on it. Just like the shirt Sophie had wanted at the Zone That Day. The one Jesse wouldn't buy for her. She gasped. "Where'd you get this?"

"It's not mine," Star said.

"What's it doing here?"

"I told you. I don't know. It's not mine." Star bit her fingernail nervously.

"Was it that girl's?" Jesse demanded.

"I don't know. Stop asking me so many questions."

Why would the girl leave it? Where did she get it? Jesse's head was spinning. She stared at the shirt then brought it up to her nose and caught a whiff of that sweet watermelon scent. She looked up at Star. "Do you know what's going on?"

Star shook her head, looking scared.

Jesse waved the T-shirt at her. "This is another sign. She's dropping clues, like birdseed. Leading us somewhere."

"Who is? Ophelia?"

"Ophelia. April. Sophie... I don't know. We just have to watch and listen." She stuffed the shirt into her big leather purse.

Star went into the bedroom, looking for something on the floor, under the bed. She went back into the bathroom and looked some more.

"What are you looking for?" Jesse asked.

"My backpack." Then something seemed to dawn on her. "I saw something blue bouncing as she ran off. Shit. My backpack. Ophelia's a klepto."

"Hold on a minute." Jesse pulled her cell phone out from her purse. "I'm calling Barnes. Whether the girl is April or not, he'll know what to do." When she got his voicemail, she said, "Hi. Uh. It's me. Jesse... Albright. The strangest thing just happened. I'm at 235 Blueberry Lane. Well, next door to it. There's a little cabin. There was a girl here. Star Silverman saw her. She just climbed out the window and ran off. She's gone, but I'm thinking that maybe she's your April Johnson. Red hoodie. Bad haircut. Call me." She clicked off her cell and shoved it in her pocket. She gazed around the cottage and said, "Let's get the hell out of here."

BACK AT THE BIG HOUSE, where Jesse had parked her truck, Star slid into the front seat, and the dog jumped in after her. He scrunched in, his rear end on Star's lap, and he stuck his head out the open window. He was panting with his huge tongue hanging out, drooling on Star.

"Gross," she said.

His thick tail thumped on the seat. He looked ecstatic, if a dog could be ecstatic.

"What's with him?"

"He loves to ride." Jesse scratched his ear as she started the truck and headed out. Just as she made the turn out of the driveway, Gary's pathetic Saturn appeared, racing down the road. It made a racket, coughing and sputtering, with a trail of smelly black exhaust.

He rolled down his window and shouted, "Jess. Sorry. I got held up."

She smiled at him and nodded but drove on.

"Hey wait. Wait!" he shouted.

Jesse nodded again. "Yeah right," she muttered. Sticking her arm out her window, she gave him the finger.

Star laughed.

Gary stopped his car and got out. He was standing in the middle of the road with his hands on his hips, shaking his head, looking confused.

"Isn't that your *realtor*?" Star said, putting the word in air quotes.

"Not anymore." Jesse hit the gas, and they sped off.

Chapter Eighteen

Jesse entered her house with Star following closely and tossed her keys on the side table.

"Holey-moley," Star said, as she stood in the middle of Jesse's living room, surveying the tall stacks of boxes. She walked over and picked up a couple of items: a plastic backscratcher and a utensil that might have been a potato masher. She pointed at a pair of off-white lady's panties that hung out of another box. "I've heard rumors, but I never thought it would be like... like this." Star wrinkled her nose. "Did you turn this into some kind of recycling center?"

"Of course not. I live here, remember?" Jesse pulled the Tweet shirt out of her bag. She held it out and looked at the front and back then brought it to her nose again. She placed it on top of her latest pile of finds, thinking she would examine it more closely later when she was alone.

"Yeah, but where'd you get all this...stuff?"

The dog was nudging up against Star's thigh. He licked her hand.

"Hey, cut it out," she said, wiping the back of her hand on her jeans.

Star had been quiet for the whole ride to Jesse's house. "I'll just hang out with you for a while," she had said when Jesse asked if she should take her to school or back home. The girl seemed depressed—about the fire, Jesse assumed. She knew how that felt. So she agreed to let Star come home with her for a bit.

Tossing her jacket and purse on a chair, Jesse said, "Never mind about the stuff. Just come in and sit down. Do you want something to drink?"

Ignoring her, Star wandered around, touching things. She hadn't stepped foot in Jesse's house in years, and she seemed to be taking it all in. She stood in front of Sophie's purple parka hanging on the coat rack and let her hand graze it. She got to the dining room and the mess scattered about the table—Jesse's newest batch of deconstructed finds. She stopped to look, picked one up, and studied the rectangular piece of old wood with strange items attached to it.

"Don't you use your studio out back anymore?" asked Star.

"Oh, I haven't in a while. I don't do art anymore. It's nothing," she said, taking the piece out of Star's hand. "Come on. This isn't really meant for visitors." And Jesse tugged her by the sleeve, wondering if she'd made a mistake letting the girl come over. But Star pulled her arm away and went back to examining the pieces.

"Have you sold any of these?"

Jesse shook her head.

"Why not?"

"They're not art."

"They're not?"

"No. And they're not for sale."

"Wait," Star said. "You made them, but they're not art?"

"That's right."

"Oh, I get it. You're pulling that 'What is art' business, right?" She looked at Jesse, her eyes bright. "We talked about that in class. We saw a painting that was all white, nothing else, by some guy named Robert or Berger or something."

"Rauschenberg."

"Right. And a video of a performance artist. A woman who just slept in a bed in a little room and didn't say a word. You just watched her sleep. That kind of stuff? Is it art or not? That was the question. My class got into a big argument over it. It was funny."

Jesse shook her head. "Well, that is an interesting class discussion, but it's not like that here. I didn't make this as art. This is the found stuff I've been collecting." She didn't say, *What Sophie has been sending me. I'm not a hoarder.*

"The stuff in your living room. The boxes of junk?"

"Yes. But it's not junk." She paused, deciding if she should go on, if Star would understand. She took a breath and continued. "They're clues. To Sophie. Her whereabouts." Jesse looked away then back at the finds on the table. She shuffled some of the pieces around.

Star just watched her, waiting. The silence lingered in the air. It made Jesse remember the times Lila wouldn't speak during a therapy session, waiting for the silence to make Jesse uncomfortable. And it did, so much so that she always felt compelled to spill her inner thoughts. She didn't know why. She normally reveled in silence, enjoying the peace the quiet gave her, that space between. "I don't expect you or anyone to understand since I barely do. They come to me, and they're sacred. How can I take money for these? They're about my daughter's disappearance."

Star turned over the piece in her hand and studied it. A handwritten letter. A faded black-and-white photo of a woman from the 1950s in a sundress. A piece of doll clothing. All behind screening and collaged onto wood with thick blue paint around the edges. She set it down and then looked at another piece carefully. "I don't know. I'm just a kid. I know nothing. I just think these are really cool. *I* think they're art. They remind me of the stuff we did in Wellfleet that summer we made art together. Remember? We made collages. We'd pick up stuff from the beach. Rusty cans, seashells, plastic fishing line. Junk. But it wasn't junk. You told me not to think so much. Go with my gut. It was fun. But these"—she tapped the piece with her finger—"are totally awesome. If I had money, I'd buy these and hang them on my wall. I think they're amazing."

"Well, I'm glad you like them even though they're not art."

Star rolled her eyes and exhaled. "Whatevs." She set the pieces down and wandered off.

Jesse straightened up the table, letting her fingers skim over the finds and the non-art, thinking about what Star had said, until Saint Anthony let out a muffled ruff. It sounded more like an annoyed grunt than a real bark. Then she heard a knock on the door.

Jesse opened it to see Barnes standing there, grinning. Her heart did a two-step. She couldn't help herself. The guy made her smile. Saint Anthony ambled over, sniffing Barnes's pockets.

"His Brownness. Good to see you." He patted Saint Anthony's head then pulled a dog biscuit out of his pocket. He offered it, and Saint Anthony gobbled it up.

"I went to that cabin on Blueberry Lane. Obviously, no April. You saw her there?"

Jesse filled him in on everything that had happened there then said, "I guess you didn't find her yesterday."

He shook his head.

"There was nothing I could do. She was too far away."

He reached out to touch her, but Jesse backed away stiffly. "What's the matter?" he asked. "Is something wrong?"

"No, nothing." She was such a jumble of conflicting emotions about him. She wanted him yet also felt she didn't deserve to be with him. She waved toward Star, who was back with the finds in the dining room. "Star is with me in the other room. I should probably go back to her."

"It's clear you're uncomfortable. You don't want to tell me what's wrong?"

"I don't know."

He looked at her closely and lowered his voice. "Maybe yesterday in the closet never happened."

"It did happen. You're the best thing to come my way in ages." She paused, leaving a gap of silence that felt like an eternity. Then there it was. That compulsion to speak. "I don't know why I went over there to meet him. It was stupid, I know. He pushed me."

His eyes flashed open. "You went to meet that guy, Gary? To be with him again?"

"I wanted to smooth things over with him. I made such a scene at the party. But nothing happened. He didn't show up. He was late and…"

"And what? You would have slept with him?"

"No. No… I don't know." She was a terrible liar. "We never got together."

"I thought maybe we had something here. The start of something." He looked off to the side then back at Jesse. "I don't know why, but I'm drawn to you. Maybe it was a mistake. I misread things. Maybe you just needed another detective to help you find Sophie."

"What? No. No!" Jesse had been so appreciative of his offer, but that certainly had no bearing on her attraction to him. She shook her head. "No, you didn't misread anything. It's over with him. Totally. I screwed up. But at least I saw April. Please, give me another chance."

Barnes stuffed his hands in his front pants pockets. "We barely know each other. You owe me nothing. I had just hoped…" He exhaled and scratched his head. "I better ask Star a few questions. May I go in and talk to her?"

"Yes, of course. But you're mad. I don't want you to be mad."

"I'm not mad. I'm disappointed. I've been through too much. I've got to protect myself. My heart." He nodded then walked toward Star. He'd simply dismissed her like a child.

Jesse covered her face with her hands, shook her head, thinking, *I fucked up again.*

STAR WAS SITTING ON the couch, leaning over, her elbows on her knees, her head on her fists. Jesse stood off to the side, listening to Barnes question her. It gave her a chance to see him in action.

"She made off with my backpack," Star blurted.

"How do you know?" He sat beside her on the couch.

"I saw her running, and she had something blue kind of bouncing as she ran. It had to be my backpack. I couldn't find it in Blueberry."

"Blueberry?"

"The cabin. That's what I call it. I looked all over. I'm sure she took it. I had it with me when I came in. Left it on the floor of the bedroom. I didn't mean to do anything wrong. She just seemed kind of... well, lost. If you know what I mean. She didn't seem bad. I figured she could hang out there for a day or two, get her act together, and then go home. That wouldn't hurt anyone." She lifted her head off her hands. "She didn't look like the photo of that girl you showed me. She told me her mom was a drug addict and there was this mean boyfriend who did bad stuff to her."

Barnes shook his head. "She was telling you a story. She comes from a decent family. The mom's not a drug addict. There's no boyfriend. The father is a stockbroker. They live in a nice suburban neighborhood."

"Oh." Star looked at Jesse then back at Barnes. She slouched down. "I thought maybe it wasn't all true."

"What was in your backpack?"

"All my stuff. My school books. And I had lent her my cell phone."

"That's the best news I've heard all day. Give me the number of your cell." He handed her his cell phone, and she punched in her number.

"Best news? My parents are going to kill me."

Barnes smiled. "I doubt that. Thank you. You've been very help-ful." He turned to Jesse. "I've got to go." He headed for the door.

"Wait. Please." Jesse reached out for his arm.

"I've got to find April." He grabbed the doorknob.

"Wait."

He stopped, turning back to her. "Yes, Ms. Albright?"

"Don't hate me."

He shook his head and walked out, closing the door behind him.

"Whoa," Star said. "What did you do to piss him off?"

JESSE TOOK SAINT ANTHONY for a walk to clear her head, but she couldn't stop beating herself up about her exchange with Barnes. It went so fast from their closet kisses to his abrupt depar-ture. When she returned home, she didn't see Star anywhere down-stairs, but she heard someone talking. She stopped to listen. It was coming from upstairs, but it wasn't Star's voice. It was a child's voice. A little girl's.

"Sophie," Jesse whispered and leapt up the stairs taking two at a time, Saint Anthony galloping behind her. She stood at the open door to Sophie's room, her heart thudding away, while she looked in, expecting to see her daughter.

Star was sitting on the bed under the canopy of felt leaves, her back against the pillows, her knees bent up. She held out the remote to the DVD player and small TV that sat on the bookshelf across from the bed. She was watching a video of Sophie being interviewed by Charles Osgood on *CBS News Sunday Morning*. Star pointed the remote at the TV and kept playing, rewinding, and replaying the same moment on the video.

Sophie, her binoculars around her neck, stood in their backyard, the various bird feeders hanging off trees behind her. Nearby, crows were in a tree, flapping and cawing loudly. Sophie wore a serious expression as the amiable Charles Osgood talked to her. Her brown hair hung down loosely around her face, and she wore a favorite red top. She held her plastic box of precious found items. "These are thank-you presents from the crows," she said, opening the box with all its little compartments filled with colorful bits. She picked up the tiny piece of tin foil that had been scrunched into a ball to show him.

Jesse held onto the doorframe for support. Of course it hadn't occurred to her that in reality her daughter would no longer sound like the child on the DVD. But in her mind, when memories appeared, that was who she always thought of, who she heard. She hadn't watched the video in years. She was too afraid to see it, to set off the pain again, just as she hadn't been able to go through Sophie's belongings. But seeing the image of Sophie and hearing her nine-year-old voice opened a cavern inside her chest so vast and deep, waves of emotions came pouring in.

Star sensed Jesse standing there, and she looked up, her eyes brimming with tears.

Jesse approached her. "It must be so hard for you to be in this house. In this room." She nodded toward the TV. "Watching Sophie."

Star wiped her face with the back of her hand. She shook her head no. "It is weird being here, seeing her again on that show, kind of like a dream, but that's not why I'm crying."

"Then what is it?"

At first, Star didn't answer. Then she said, "I haven't told anyone."

Jesse sat down next to Star on the bed. The DVD kept playing, and Sophie was explaining to Charles Osgood how she'd befriended the crows. "I fed them every day for months. I watched them closely, and they watched me, too. We became friends."

"Are you sure they left these things for you?" he asked.

"Of course!" she said confidently, and when he laughed, she smiled and let out a funny chortle, too, her binoculars bouncing a bit on her chest.

Jesse gently took the remote out of Star's hand and clicked the DVD player off. She looked at Star and waited. "Tell me."

Star glanced away then whispered, "It's Sophie."

"What about Sophie?"

Tears ran freely down Star's cheeks.

"What about her?" Jesse prodded.

Star stared off into space. She sniffed.

"Star, do you know something?"

Star's lower lip quivered.

Jesse took hold of her by the shoulders and pulled her closer. "Has she called you? Have you seen her?" She raised her voice. "Is she alive?"

"No." Star pulled away and shook her head, her hair flying about her face. "I don't know." She let out a huge sigh. "I don't think so."

Jesse leaned back and looked at her. "What's going on?"

"She haunts me in my bedroom at night. Once at the Book Barn. Today, she even appeared at school." Jesse stared at Star. "Maybe I'm crazy. It's freakin' weirding me out. She's trying to tell me something."

"You mean she appears to you in dreams? In nightmares? She's not real, right?"

"I guess not. She looks real. But she's still ten, and she's wearing her same outfit. The one she wore the day she went missing. Maybe it's her ghost. Or maybe it's a dream. I don't know."

Jesse swallowed hard. "Sophie never appears in my dreams. I wish she did."

"No, you don't. Trust me."

"Does she talk to you? What does she say?"

"She sounds older and mean, like she's mad at me. I drink coffee to stay awake. I thought if I don't fall asleep, then I wouldn't see her.

But now she's appearing during the day, too." She looked away then choked back more tears before sputtering, "I don't want what happened to Sophie to happen to Ophelia. Or April. Or whoever she is. That's why I had her stay at Blueberry."

Jesse had heard of bizarre things like this. People seeing ghostly images of dead loved ones. Walking in hallways at night. Appearing in windows. Curtains fluttering. *Who's to say what was real and what wasn't?*

"Have you told anyone else? Your parents?"

"Are you crazy?"

"Maybe you should."

"I'm telling *you*. They wouldn't understand. No one would."

Jesse rubbed Star's back. "Oh, sweetie. She's been on your mind, and maybe this is how you cope with it. We all have our own ways of dealing with this stuff."

"After all these years?"

"There's no time limit on grief."

Just then, something caught Star's eye. She reached over and picked up the notebook on Sophie's nightstand, the one Barnes had found in Sophie's closet. Sophie's name was handwritten in big letters in a rainbow of colored Magic Markers. "I remember this."

"You do? How do you know about it?"

"It's from our last summer in Wellfleet. I'd recognize it anywhere. She had it with her all the time."

"Barnes found it hidden behind a secret door in her closet. I was reading through it last night."

Star opened it and skimmed through the pages. Colored drawings of beaks and wings and lists of places and names of birds flipped by.

"She hid it, yet I think she wanted us to find it. What do you know about it?"

Star shook her head.

"Why would this one be special?"

"It was her last summer there. Our last summer together."

"But was it different somehow?"

Star gazed at the notebook and thought a moment. "Well, we did play What Kind of Bird a lot. And we did watch that guy on the beach a lot."

"What guy?"

"This guy. He wore flannel shirts and had a bushy beard."

Jesse thought back to that summer. She remembered arguing with Cooper a lot then trying to act nonchalant so Blue and Beth wouldn't notice their tension. She remembered Sophie and Star playing on the beach, Star sleeping over at their cottage almost every night, and how the girls would stay up late, whispering and giggling in their room. She remembered Sophie being happy on the Cape, left alone to watch her birds and play with Star. She didn't remember any guy on the beach.

"Sophie watched him like he was a bird and took notes on his behavior. She thought he was like a seagull, picking up garbage."

"I don't remember him," Jesse said, becoming more upset. "Why didn't you tell us about him?"

"I did. I told the police when they questioned me and my parents, asking about that trip. But he was all the way in Wellfleet, nowhere near the Zone in Holyoke. Nobody seemed that interested. Maybe they checked him out. I don't know. I was just a kid. Nobody told me anything."

Jesse supposed somebody could have mentioned it to her, but she was such a tranquilized zombie then she could easily have forgotten.

"Then I just put him out of my mind. It's not like I knew him. I saw him from far away. It was our private game. It was just a game. We were kids. We weren't doing anything wrong."

"Did you speak to him?" Jesse said, her voice rising an octave. "Did *she*?"

"I never did. She told me she did, but I didn't believe her. I thought it was one of her stories."

Jesse clasped her hands in fists, her voice demanding. "Star, was it a story, or was it true?"

"I don't know! It was hard to tell with Sophie. You know all those stories she made up." Star nervously bit on her thumbnail. "She said she met him and talked to him, but I didn't believe her. I just played along. It was a game. You know how she was. Sophie and her stories."

Jesse imagined Sophie making friends with a homeless stranger who was taken with her fantastical stories. He began to watch her. He asked her questions. They talked and became friendly. He learned where she lived. He turned up in Canaan to follow her to the Zone and snatched her. She could have been living with this homeless guy for the last six years. She could be alive. He was just the type of person who might have befriended Sophie.

"Acquaintance kidnapping," Jesse whispered.

"Yes. I've read about that. And Sophie's ghost has been talking about that, too."

Jesse paced the room. "This character might still be lurking around. He may know something." And just then she made a decision. "I'm taking you home, then I'm going to Wellfleet to look for him."

Star whipped around. "I'm going with you."

Jesse shook her head. "No, no. I can't take you."

"We'll get permission from my parents."

She wanted to take Star. But she could imagine the headlines: "Bird Mom kidnaps boss's daughter."

"Drive you across the state to look for a homeless man who might have kidnapped my daughter? I don't think they'd approve. I'm going to take you home first. I'm sorry."

In the truck, they didn't speak for five minutes. When they were close to her street, Star blurted out, "Listen, I have to go. You don't know anything about him. What he looks like, how he dresses, where he hung out."

"I'm sorry, Star. I just can't." She turned onto Longview Road to see it lined with cars parked on both sides. "What's going on?"

"Hello? The fire? Everyone has descended on our house. Bringing food and stuff. It's like they're paying their last respects."

Jesse pulled over about four houses away from Star's. She saw people heading into the Silvermans' house, carrying casserole dishes and flowers.

"I've seen him." Star took a deep breath. "I can take you. I have to take you."

Jesse stared at Star.

"Only I can help you find him. Find Sophie."

Jesse hesitated.

"You need me."

It was true. Jesse knew nothing of the man. The image of Sophie's mural from her closet—the trees, birds, and letters all swirling together—came back to her. *There but not there.*

She had the sensation that it really was Sophie sending her on this trip. She did need Star's help. And she had to admit that being with Star made her feel closer to Sophie. They had a better chance of finding the man or Sophie, of solving the puzzle. Plus she didn't really want to face the puzzle alone. "You'll have to call your parents. We'll need a cover story. If we tell them the truth, they won't let you go. We both know that."

Star's eyes lit up. "Leave my parents to me."

"Are you sure you're up for this? Who knows what we'll find?"

"I'm in. Definitely."

Jess put the truck in drive, made a quick U-turn, and drove on.

Chapter Nineteen

As Jesse drove east on the Mass Pike, she saw Saint Anthony, who sat in the middle, put his chin sweetly on Star's shoulder.

Star had called her parents and told them she was going to spend the night at Ruby's house. "They actually sounded relieved not to have me home."

Jesse could imagine that Blue and Beth were probably overwhelmed with insurance adjusters, pushy reporters, and neighbors offering condolences about the Book Barn.

"There were so many people hanging around, I doubt they'll miss me." Then she called Ruby to cover for her.

"I hate that you had to lie to your parents," Jesse said.

"It was the only way. Besides, they'll never know." Star turned to Jesse and grinned. "It's been a while, but I've done it before. When there have been parties I knew my parents wouldn't let me go to, Ruby's always been my go-to excuse."

Jesse prayed to Saint Anthony—the saint, not the dog—that she would make it through the trip without having a car accident and without losing Star. A long list of other disaster scenarios flashed before her, but she had to go. She just had to do it quickly and safely. She could deal with the consequences later.

Saint Anthony tilted his head up and gazed at Star.

"What's his problem? Why is he staring at me?"

Jesse glanced at him, petted his head, then turned back to the road. "Unlike us, this dog doesn't have a problem."

"What's his name, anyway?"

"Saint Anthony."

"That's a weird name for a dog."

"Excuse me, Miss Starry Night. I found this dog on my doorstep. Saint Anthony is the patron saint of lost things and missing people and happens to be a *very good* name for this dog. But you can call him Anthony if you prefer."

Star shrugged. "Whatever." She exhaled onto the window and drew her Professor Pollen doodle in the condensation with her finger.

An hour into the trip, they pulled up to a rest plaza on the Pike. Star went to the bathroom and bought snacks while Jesse walked Saint Anthony in a fenced-in doggie area. Secretly hoping for a message from Barnes, Jesse checked her cell phone, but there were no messages. She shook her head, thinking how cold he had been to her earlier. They'd only just begun to get to know each other, and she had to go and ruin things by pushing him away. Jesse wasn't sure she could mend things. She thought about sending him a text. That could be harmless. *But what would I say?* She looked up and saw Star approaching from the plaza. *No. Stay focused. Follow the clues.*

Finding the man from Sophie's journal was all that mattered—even if it might yield another dead end like all the others. She'd once driven down to New York City to meet with a famous psychic who claimed to know Sophie's whereabouts. She'd flown to Chicago and Miami when detailed sightings were called in. So many phone calls, emails, and photos exchanged over the years with strangers who said they could help. They'd all added up to a slew of nutjobs and dashed expectations. But this find felt different, as if Sophie and Bixby were taking her by the hand, telling her to pay attention to every little clue. She might actually be getting close to finding Sophie.

Star slid into the passenger seat, then Jesse and Saint Anthony got in, too.

"I was thinking," Star said. "Maybe that detective can help find Sophie. Isn't that, like, his specialty? Finding people?"

Jesse always thought the police and the private detectives hadn't done enough to find Sophie. Always too little, too late. She had to check out the lead on her own before turning it over to anyone else. Besides, she wasn't about to tell Star she'd screwed things up with Barnes. She would be lucky if he let her know about April. She could end up hearing about it on the news. "He did offer to help after he's found that girl, April."

"What'll he do with her when he finds her?"

"Get her back with her family. Get her some help with her problems."

April was part of the equation somehow. Once Barnes found her, it would become clear. The shirt. April. The gum. The homeless guy. The notebook. All pieces in the huge puzzle would add up soon.

FIVE HOURS AND A COUPLE of bathroom breaks, dog walks, and a dinner stop later, Star and Jesse were driving down Route 6, passing the Wellfleet Drive-In with its See You Next Summer billboard. Off-season Cape looked nothing like tourist-ridden high season. Pieces of plywood covered the windows of beachfront houses. End-of-summer-sale signs hung in the windows of seasonal shops. It looked gray and desolate.

They turned onto Calhoun Hollow Road then over to Ocean View Drive, heading straight for Duneside, the colony of summer bungalows the Albrights and Silvermans had been going to for five years before Sophie vanished. The side-by-side cottages they rented were a minute from the beach and tucked away in a cool, piney grove.

Jesse pulled the truck in and parked behind Ocean Breezy, the cottage she and Cooper had always booked. It was billed as "only 215 steps to the beach," which was true. Sophie and Star had counted it out. There was nothing between the cottage and the ocean but dunes and beach grass. The colony was deserted, each cabin locked up, shades drawn. Not a car in sight. Jesse remembered that the owner was a snowbird. She always closed up in early October and headed for her winter home in Florida.

They got out of the truck. Jesse rifled through her toolbox stored in the cab and pulled out a broken wire hanger and a paper clip. "These come in handy when you lock your keys in your truck, something I've been known to do." Jesse walked up to the wooden screen door to the porch, and as it always had been each summer, it was unlocked. The door squeaked as she opened it, and they both went up to the front door to the cabin. It was seven in the evening and dark, and it took Jesse a minute to find the keyhole with her wire. She inserted one end of the hanger and, using it as a tension wrench, wiggled the open paper clip in where the key would go. She jiggled it left to right.

"What if someone sees us?" Star whispered, looking over her shoulder.

"Don't worry. The caretaker probably comes early in the day to check on things when it's light." She put her ear close to the lock as she continued to work on it. "We'll be long gone by then."

"Shit. I didn't even think about a caretaker." Star bit her lip. "Maybe this was a mistake."

Jesse went back to her jiggling, and suddenly, there was a click. "*Voila.*" She swung the door open. Saint Anthony charged in. Jesse turned back to Star and whispered, "Remember, you wanted to come."

"I know. I know."

A closed-up mildewy scent hit them as soon as they entered. Jesse went to the kitchen, rummaged in a drawer, and retrieved a flashlight. The beam swept around the room, over white cotton curtains and framed seashore landscapes on the wall. The furniture had been covered with faded sheets, and the rugs had been rolled up and put away. Both families had loved the small rustic cottages with their sixties-style eat-in dinettes, cozy living rooms, and screened porches. The salt air, the lull of the tide, that fried seafood scent, the laid-back Cape atmosphere. It felt to Jesse like another lifetime.

Jesse walked into the bedroom that she and Cooper had shared and stood in the middle of the room, shining the flashlight around. It was a simple spare room with wide-planked floors that had been painted white. There were two old wooden bureaus, a rocking chair in the corner where they used to toss their clothes, and a full-sized bed with a serious sag in the middle. Jesse sat on the mattress, and it squeaked just the way it used to. She bounced a little then gazed around the room. She lay down on the bed and found herself slipping into the mattress gully, dipping back in time. She almost expected Cooper to come running in from the beach with sandy feet, his bathing suit dripping, or to hear Sophie shouting out, "Mom, Mom, Mom. A great blue heron!"

"What are you doing?"

Jesse looked up to see Star standing in the doorway.

She sat up. "Nothing. C'mon, let's check out Sophie's room." She stood then walked into the second bedroom.

There was nothing out of the ordinary. Twin beds. Nightstand. A bookshelf. She opened the door to the closet. A few wire hangers on the closet rod jangled. She looked on the high shelf near the ceiling and examined the floor. Dust bunnies. A piece of thread. A *Yankee Magazine* from 2003. She ran the flashlight over the walls and floorboards, looking for some secret little door like the one Barnes had found in Sophie's closet, but she found nothing.

She opened each drawer of the bureau, and in the second one, she found a crumpled piece of paper. She unfolded it and saw it was an ATM receipt from 2013. In the bottom drawer, she discovered a long brown hair. She picked it up and held it out. It could have been Sophie's. Fuel for her imagination. She moved on to the bookshelf. Familiar worn paperbacks were lined up there. A few new ones had been added to the same ones that had been there every summer.

Star sat on the bed that had been Sophie's, the one closest to the door, as Jesse took out each book from the shelf, scanned through the pages, and shook them upside down as she did at the Book Barn.

"What are you looking for?"

"Clues." She kept flipping pages. There had to be something else. A grocery list. A bookmark. A note with Sophie's writing. Anything. Deflated, she put the books back on the shelf. "There's nothing here."

She placed the flashlight on the nightstand—it lit the corner of the room—and sat next to Star on the bed. Saint Anthony circled and lay on the floor near them. She reached down and rubbed his head. "Hey there, sweetie. You're a good traveler. You must be tired." In moments, he was asleep, his closed eyes flickering.

Jesse leaned against the headboard with a big yawn. "Remember how you and Sophie used to stay up late, whispering and giggling?"

Star smiled. "Yeah. We'd huddle under our blankets with our flashlights. Sophie would write in her logbook about the birds she'd seen that day. Sometimes, we'd sneak into the other's bed and make plans for the next day. Then you'd come in, stand in the doorway, and whistle."

Jesse whistled the way she had back then, a clear two-note call of *"fee-bee, fee-bee"* with the second note lower.

"Black-capped chickadee," Star said.

"Right."

"And you'd say." And in unison, they said, "Lights out, chickadees." And they both laughed. Strands of Star's long blond hair fell over her eye. Jesse pushed the hair out of her face. Jesse looked at Star as if for the first time since they had left home. Her eyes were alert, her smile warm and easy. Jesse saw the sweet young girl she used to know.

"Hey, I remember this," Star said, pointing behind Jesse's head.

"What is it?"

She reached up and touched the old oak headboard, letting her index finger trace what looked like scratches. "The initials: PB. Sophie scratched this into the wood with a paper clip."

"Peanut butter?"

Star laughed. "No. It stands for Paul Bunyan. I'd forgotten all about it, but it's the name we gave to the homeless guy. He had a bushy beard, and with those flannel shirts he wore, we thought he looked like a lumberjack, like Paul Bunyan. We'd just read about him in school."

"Paul Bunyan?" Jesse reached over and touched the carved initials, as well. Yet another breadcrumb-like clue from Sophie.

"I know. It was silly. But we were just kids."

"Tell me more about what's been going on with you and Sophie."

Star took a breath and began slowly, "She keeps coming to me. It's like she's mad at me or something."

"When did this start?"

"A few months ago. I saw some show about those three girls from Cleveland. The ones missing for like ten years and found alive in that sicko's house. I think that brought Sophie on. Maybe I was thinking she could be alive like them."

Jesse had, of course, heard of that terrifying, unfathomable story. The girls had been held captive, beaten, raped, impregnated, and physically and emotionally closed off from the world. She prayed that or any version of it hadn't happened to her daughter. What could life be like for a young woman after living through something like that? Would it still be better to be alive?

Hearing about it from Star, she felt a prickly sensation in her fingers and rubbed her hands together. Maybe it was similar to the feeling Barnes had said he felt when he was near a missing person he was searching for. *I'm getting close.*

"Usually, it's at night when I fall asleep," Star continued. "She looks like she did, but she sounds different. All full of herself and angry."

It almost sounded as if Star were describing the way she'd been acting lately.

"So I try not to fall asleep because it's not fun to see her. It's creepy."

"Does she look like a ghost?"

"She just looks like her ten-year-old self. Suddenly, she's there. And then a while later, poof. She's gone. Like magic." Star put her finger to her mouth and started biting her nail. "Today, things really changed. She came to me at school for the first time. I couldn't concentrate in class with her jabbering in my ear. No one else saw her. I think I'm going crazy."

Jesse studied Star. She had matured over the years. Her face and her whole body was firmer. No baby fat. She was pretty, with fair skin and a slightly downturned mouth, but she hid under her long hair. She seemed to have taken on Sophie's creased forehead and worried eyebrows. "Introjecting," she remembered Lila called it. When someone adopted the behavior or mannerisms of someone else. Jesse noticed the nasty red cuts on Star's arm. She'd seen them that time at the Book Barn, but the small round burn mark was new.

Star tugged her sleeve down to cover up. Jesse could feel Star's defenses rise like a brick wall. She had to tread lightly and decided to ease into that subject later. They sat in silence for a moment.

Jesse roused herself. "Let's check into that motel across the way on Route 6. We have a long day ahead of us tomorrow." She gazed around the cottage loaded with memories, knowing it would be for the very last time.

ONCE THEY WERE CHECKED into the Wellfleet Motel, Jesse collapsed on one of the beds, Saint Anthony on the floor. Star took an extra-long shower, swiped the free mini shampoo and soap, and took the other bed, the one near the bathroom.

She checked out the pay-per-view TV until Jesse took the remote out of her hand, saying, "Tell me more about this Paul Bunyan character. Can you describe him for me?"

Star leaned back on the bed and closed her eyes, as if trying to conjure him up. "I haven't really thought about him for years. Not until I saw Sophie's notebook today."

"I know. Think back."

She scrunched her eyes tighter, and after a moment, she smiled as if a happy memory had washed over her. "I remember. I was with Sophie, and we were ten. We were in our bathing suits, sitting on the screened-in porch in Ocean Breezy. 'OB,' we used to call it. We sat on the glider couch, our bare feet up against the wall in front of us. Sophie had her binoculars around her neck and was peering through them, as usual." Star opened her eyes, looked up at Jesse, then continued painting a picture of her last summer with Sophie.

"Sophie had spotted something. She handed me the binos and showed me a hand, way off in the distance, lobster-red, poking out of the wild beach grass, but it wasn't moving. It looked like someone had cut off a hand and placed it there on top of the grass. After we stared at it for minutes, it finally moved, then a whole body stood up.

"We both shrieked, 'It's alive!' The sunburned hand was attached to a man. He walked around, lowered his head, and then we could tell he was peeing in the grass. We thought it was gross, but we laughed, passing the binos back and forth."

Star paused then looked up at Jesse. "He had a full gray beard. His hair was shaggy, longish, the color of wet sand. He wore T-shirts, a bunch of different ones. I heart NYC, Bruce Springsteen, Harley Davidson. Sometimes, he wore plaid flannel shirts over them even though it was summer. And dirty blue jeans held up with a piece of rope. He was skinny. He didn't look mean or anything. We figured he was homeless. He had an old red bicycle that he rode away from the beach each day. It had lots of plastic bags attached to it filled with empty soda bottles he'd collected and a fishing net hanging off the back. A couple times, we followed him on our bikes as far as we could down the bike path before we got nervous that our parents, you guys, would find out so we turned back."

Jesse was staring at her, listening hard.

"One day, we went to the beach to check out where he slept after we saw him ride off. There was a rotted wooden boat that had washed ashore. He used it to store his blankets and other stuff like a pair of eyeglasses, fishing lures, and a beach chair. It was all neat and organized. Once we left him a peanut butter sandwich and some cookies in a baggie tucked in with the blankets. Another time, we were at the flea market and saw his bike locked to a tree. We waited for him for a long time, but he never came back. There was a day we were driving with you and Cooper to town and passed him on Main Street on his bike. We giggled and pointed, but you guys didn't notice."

Star nodded to Jesse's purse. "Can I have Sophie's notebook?" She took it from Jesse and spent a little time reading several pages then flipping ahead and reading some more. Then she opened it to a random page. "'PB picks up stuff on beach for nest materials.'" She flipped to another page. "'Collects garbage, plastic, fabric bits, string.' That's self-explanatory. 'Works on his nest in the morning.' This was his routine. Every morning, he'd pee then comb his hair, then he would lay out his blankets to dry over bushes. He had a bunch of different ones. I remember a big blue one, a patchwork quilt, a dark striped one. He'd shake them out, then he'd fold and re-fold them perfectly and stash them in the old rowboat."

She flipped to another page and tapped a line. "'Flight pattern of PB: takes off at nine thirty a.m. Returns at five o'clock p.m.' He took off on his bicycle. It was loaded down with all these plastic bottles he'd collected on the beach. I guess he took them in for the deposit money."

"'Markings: black chest with red spot.'" She thought a minute. "That must have been his black Harley T-shirt with some red letters in the middle."

Jesse scrunched her eyes in confusion.

"I'm not making this stuff up. It's right here in black and white. I knew Sophie took notes on the guy, and we watched him a lot and made jokes. But she was obviously obsessed with him. He was like one of her birds. You know, like her game. Everyone was a kind of bird. You were a whippoorwill. I was a great blue heron. That Professor Pollen was a yellow-bellied sapsucker."

"Why?"

"The bird has a red throat, like his red bow tie. He had a little stutter that made us laugh, but Sophie thought it was like the *tap, tap, tap* of the sapsucker checking for sap in a tree." She closed the notebook and set it on her lap. "And Paul Bunyan was a seagull.

"I remember now she told me that his name was really Gregory, but she didn't know his last name. We still called him Paul Bunyan. She said he liked to watch birds, too. I didn't believe her."

Jesse looked straight ahead. "I never saw him, never heard about him until yesterday. I know, oblivious parent doesn't even know what her daughter is up to. Typical, right?" She took the notebook from Star and looked through it. There was Sophie's tiny writing with her small drawings in colored pencil. She'd drawn close-up images of the birds—their bodies, beaks, wings—or shown them in flight. "This book looks like all the rest of her bird journals, but she's often writing about this homeless man. Do you think it's possible? She might have spoken to him. Befriended him. She could have felt comfortable with someone different. Someone more like her, a loner. They got along, understood each other. He could have told her he'd come meet her. He could have hitchhiked to Canaan. She could have told him where we lived. He could have followed us, scoped us out. Or stolen a car." She took a breath and continued, "That's it. He drove all the way to our house, followed us to the mall. He was at the Zone that day, and she was happy to see him."

She stared off into space. "Pay close attention to outlying birds or those that behave differently." A sickly, guttural moan escaped her throat. She turned to Star, her eyes watery. "It's Bixby. It's Sophie. Leading us here. It's possible. Do you think it's possible?"

Star just looked at her apprehensively. She didn't say a word.

"Maybe he's not awful," Jesse said. "Maybe he brought her back here, and they're living somewhere. In a closed-up cabin like Ocean Breezy. Maybe he's taking care of her. It's possible, isn't it?" Her eyes grew wide. "Isn't it?" *Remain hopeful. Never give up. Never stop looking.*

"Sure, it's possible. I guess," Star said, but it sounded as though she didn't believe it at all. "But we need to know more about him. For him to come all the way to Canaan, then to go to the mall, then back here when he was homeless... I just don't know."

Jesse dropped her head to her chest.

"I have an idea," Star said. "We have to have a picture of him. Something to show people tomorrow when we look for him around town. A drawing."

Jesse nodded. "Oh, my God. Of course. You're right. I'm so out of it. I should have thought of that."

They sat on the bed with paper and pencils and worked on the drawing for close to two hours.

Star described him bit by bit, and Jesse drew. It was slow and tedious. The shape of Paul's head: squarish. The hairstyle: stringy and hippie-like. The shape and length of his nose: narrow and long. His eyes: small, brown, and close together. And Star kept looking at the drawing and telling her what was wrong, and Jesse erased it and changed it. They argued back and forth.

Finally, Star grabbed the pencil out of Jesse's hand. "This looks nothing like him. Not even close." She worked at it for another half hour, basically redoing the whole thing, and Jesse sat next to her, watching the entire time.

"Sophie told me he was a real melt bird. He just melted right into the scenery. Maybe he was. I thought he looked nice even though I was too scared to talk to him. My parents hammered it into me: don't talk to strangers."

Jesse nodded. "I thought Sophie knew that, as well."

Star studied the drawing. "If I were to see this for the first time, I'm pretty sure I'd think it was Paul Bunyan. There's that look he had on his face, something around the mouth and eyes." Jesse thought he looked as though he were carrying around a secret that he wasn't going to share with anyone. That was the way she felt about her secrets. Maybe it was how Star felt about hers, too.

Star crawled into bed with a heavy sigh, and Jesse got into hers, turning out the light. After a few minutes, Star whispered, "Jesse?"

"Yes?"

"I'm afraid."

"What are you afraid of?"

"I'm afraid of Sophie coming to me. I have nothing to keep me awake."

"Oh, sweetie. Since Sophie doesn't seem to want to see me, maybe I'll keep her away. I'll sleep with you. Don't worry." Jesse got out of her bed and crawled into Star's, sliding under the covers. Snuggling up close, Jesse curled into Star's back.

"I'm cold," Star said.

Jesse pulled up the extra blanket. "I'll keep you warm." And she moved in even closer.

After a few minutes, Star whispered, "Jesse?"

"Yes?"

"I did something bad," she said softly.

"What, honey?"

"The Barn." And even more softly, she added, "I set the Barn on fire."

Jesse sat up, took Star by the shoulders, and turned her so they were facing each other. It was dark, but they were so close, she could see Star's eyes open wide. "What are you talking about?"

"It was the night of the Harvest Fest. I left the party after you did. I didn't want to go home alone yet. I went to the Book Barn. I have a key. I made some coffee. I looked at some bird books. I was smoking a cigarette. I know I'm not supposed to smoke in there. But I did, and I don't remember what happened."

"What do you mean?"

"I don't remember where I put it out or if I even did." She described how she turned on the computer and surfed the net. And then how Sophie appeared to her, sitting in Jesse's chair. "She was talking about acquaintance kidnapping, reeling off statistics. It freaked me out. I ran out of there so fast. I burned the Book Barn down. I didn't mean to, and I'm so fucking screwed."

Jesse shook her head. "You don't know that for sure."

"They're investigating, and they'll figure it out. What else could it have been?"

"What else? There were hundreds of lit pumpkins all over town. It's a miracle there hasn't been a fire before. Sweetie, you don't know for sure."

"I've royally screwed up my life. My dad's business is gone. You don't have a job. The whole town will hate me when they find out. Everyone loved the Book Barn, and I'll be in juvey prison for years."

"I think you're overreacting. You don't know. And if they find out it was a cigarette, they won't know it's you."

"Hello? Have you heard of fingerprints? DNA? Don't you watch *NCIS*? They can figure that stuff out. I know I said I didn't care, but I didn't want to burn my dad's business down. Really." She started to cry.

Jesse hugged her. "I know. I know. Shhh, it's okay, honey. It's really, really going to be okay."

Jesse had her lie back down and pulled the covers up to her chin.

"Jesse?"

"Yes?"

"Don't tell my parents."

Chapter Twenty

After checking out of the motel the next morning, Jesse asked Star to show her where Paul Bunyan had set up camp on the beach.

"This way," Star said, leading her to the spot back near the Duneside Cottages. The morning sun was starting to burn off the thick fog as they followed a path through tall beach grass and low rosa rugosa to the ocean. Saint Anthony ran freely off-leash, galloping in and out of the shallow water.

Star turned to the right, then finally, she stopped and nodded. "This is the spot. I remember we used this telephone pole as a marker."

Jesse sat down on a big rock and gazed about. Shore birds. The tide. Seashells. Little crabs. *Listen for any movement. Stand in one spot. Gaze out with a wide view.*

Star gestured toward nearby shrubbery. "He used to throw his blankets over these bushes in the morning. And the abandoned rowboat I told you about where he stashed his stuff was around here. But that's gone."

Jesse got up and walked to where Star had pointed. She bent down, picked up a handful of sand, and let it run through her fingers. "Hey, look at this," she said, tugging at something buried in the sand. She held it up.

"An empty Snapple bottle?" Star said.

"Well, it could have been his." Jesse wiped off the bottle. "And what about this?" She kicked a broken lobster trap with ropes and other bits of plastic caught inside it.

"Jesse, it's garbage. He's gone, and all his stuff is long gone, too."

There was no sign of Paul Bunyan at all. No remnants of a person. *I must have been insane to think anything of his would be left.* She let the Snapple bottle drop to the sand and shook her head. "You're right."

She looked out at the calm ocean before her, the wide-open sky, pale blue and cloudless. A seagull with a crab dangling from its mouth swooped overhead. The goldenrod was in bloom, and the morning light was soft and yellow, perfect for landscape painting. Despite how beautiful the Cape was in the fall, Jesse wished she were back in her studio, a paintbrush in her hand, instead of sitting on a beach with a crude drawing of some homeless man who may have kidnapped her daughter.

She nodded to Star. "C'mon. Let's go."

They followed the path back and arrived at the truck. Saint Anthony gave a shake, wriggling his whole body, flinging water everywhere, and ending with a little swirl of his butt.

"Hey," Star shouted, "I already took a shower."

Jesse grabbed a towel out of her truck, rubbed the dog down, then gave him a pat on the rear. She opened the passenger door. "In you go, Brownie."

"Yuck. He smells like a wet sweater," Star said as she climbed in.

Jesse got into the driver's seat. "Let's do what we came here to do."

She pulled out onto Route 6 and headed for the center of Wellfleet. It was a sweet town, not fancy. Only a few locals were out on Main Street, making it feel more like a ghost town. She recognized many of the shops from her past visits—Hatch's Fish Market, Pickle and Puppy, and Herridge Books. She thought of the Book Barn and felt a tug of sadness.

After stopping at a diner for take-out coffee and muffins, they pulled up to the Wellfleet Methodist Church. Jesse had made a list of possible places a homeless man might frequent in town. A sandwich board sign on the sidewalk with big black letters read: Food Pantry Open Today.

Jesse looked at Star. "We're in luck. They're open." The food pantry was at the top of her list.

They parked the truck, left Saint Anthony in the front seat with the windows cracked, and followed the arrows on the sign to the church's side entrance.

Inside was a small room with a long countertop. Two women worked behind it, one older with a wrinkled face and pretty hazel eyes. The other was a young woman rocking a sleeping baby girl in a stroller. The shelves behind them were stocked with canned goods. They both had three-ring notebooks and were logging in items. Meanwhile, a lanky male customer was putting cans of food into a brown bag. He exchanged small talk with the older woman then left with his bag.

"May I help you?" the younger woman said, looking from Star to Jesse.

Jesse stepped up to the counter while Star stood back shyly.

"I don't know. Maybe." Jesse pulled out Star's drawing of Paul Bunyan. "I'm looking for this man. I don't know much about him, but he used to sleep on the beach near the Duneside Cottages, and I have a feeling he may have come to the food pantry. I was wondering if you ever saw him." She slid the drawing across the counter toward the young woman.

She looked at it quickly. "I don't think so."

The older woman came closer. "When was this?"

"Some time ago," Jesse said. "I know he was definitely in Wellfleet around six years ago."

"Six years ago. My word. That *is* a long time. Let me see that picture." She had a thick New England accent. She seemed tough, though, as if she'd survived some rough winters. She studied the drawing. "Could have been any number of young men who passed through here. Hippie types, you know? I've worked at this food pantry for fifteen years. So I've seen them all. And my memory is like a trap. Is he a relation?"

"Oh, no, no. It's a long story. But actually, I'm looking for my daughter." Jesse reached into her purse and pulled out a photo of Sophie and the missing person flyer with the computer-aged image. "We used to come to Wellfleet for vacations, and we stayed at the Duneside Cottages. My daughter spotted this homeless man, and I'm afraid she might have befriended him. He might have taken her. Or not." She let out a sigh. "I don't know. She's been missing for six years and was taken closer to our home in one of the hill towns. At this point, we're grasping at any clue."

The younger woman gasped and whispered, "Six years." Then she instinctively moved closer to her child in the stroller.

"I remember hearing about her. Bird Girl, right?" the older woman said.

Although she wanted to shout, "She has a real name!" Jesse just nodded.

"That is a sad story." The woman looked at her coworker, who was now fussing with her baby. "Melissa"—she nodded to the other woman—"only moved here recently from Florida with her baby daughter and just started at the food pantry. So she won't be any help. And I can't say I've ever seen your daughter. I'd remember. This girl has..." She paused, staring at the photo of Sophie, searching for a word. "An *intensity* about her."

Jesse and Star exchanged a glance.

The woman picked up the drawing of Paul. "This man." She tapped the drawing with her finger. "Well, he looks familiar, but as

I said, put a beard and some long hair on any of these washashores, and they all look like this." She turned to Jesse. "I'm sorry, I wish I could be of more help." She slid the papers back to Jesse then patted the back of her hand. "That's a terrible cross to bear, my dear. Just terrible. I'm very sorry."

Jesse withdrew her hand. There it was—that unsolicited vessel of sympathy from a stranger, like an unwanted gift. She'd come to hate it in the early days of the tragedy and would never get used to it. "Thank you. It was just a long shot. Good-bye." She grabbed Star by the sleeve and tugged her toward the door.

"Dear," the woman piped up. "You might want to try the Big Book meeting at eleven this morning. They meet downstairs. Those men just might know your homeless man. They look out for each other. Some of them have been coming for years and years."

"Big Book?"

"You know, AA. Give me the power..."

"Oh, right, of course."

"Good luck, dear."

There was time before the meeting, so they piled back into the truck and drove over to the Wellfleet Boatyard, the next place on Jesse's list. Star stayed put while Jesse walked up to an old wooden schooner and showed the drawing around to a few workers. The men were busy and uninterested. They gave it a cursory look.

"Who drew this? A kid?" one guy said with a snide chuckle.

"Six years ago? Are you crazy, lady?" another said then tossed it back to Jesse.

She slipped back into the driver's seat next to Saint Anthony and let out a sigh. She rubbed his soft floppy ear between her thumb and index finger.

Star pushed her hair out of her face. "Maybe we have to come back in the summer. Maybe somebody has to spend the whole summer here. You know, hang out at his spot on the beach and observe like Sophie did. You have to be super patient. You can't just blow in and expect your bird to come to you."

"I know. I know..." Jesse nodded, thinking that was what Bixby said, too. "I've waited and watched and listened for years now." She reached for her locket, forgetting she'd tossed it into the creek. Her fingers slid down her neck. She regretted having done that. She missed it. Without warning, there was a catch in her throat, and her eyes filled. "You know, I haven't had lunch with a girlfriend in years. I don't even have any girlfriends anymore. No one to call and just gossip with. I haven't read a book for pleasure or gone shopping for a pair of shoes in ages." Suddenly, tears were running down her face.

Star looked around nervously, found a crumpled napkin in the door's side compartment, and handed it to Jesse.

Jesse took it and blew her nose. "When is it time to stop waiting?" She looked at Saint Anthony, right into his big brown eyes. She leaned down to him and touched her head to his, forehead to forehead. "When is it, sweetie?" She caressed him, took a breath, and wiped her eyes on her sleeve.

Star patted Jesse on the arm. "You need a break. A little fun. Why don't you go away with Barnes? I know you like him."

Jesse nodded. Yes, Barnes. She wished he was with them. He'd know what to do. Something about him reminded her of the Dog Whisperer. Jesse used to watch his show on the National Geographic Channel even though she didn't have a dog then. He always told people to be calm and assertive for their dogs. That was Barnes. Calm. Assertive. It made her want to please him, to get him to rub her head the way he rubbed Saint Anthony's. But she'd pushed him away. She turned back to Star. "Yeah, I do like him." She knew she might not see him again. "A vacation does sound good right about now. But it's hard to turn off the brain. You know what I mean?"

They sat silently for a few minutes, just listening to Saint Anthony panting.

"I wish I could stop thinking about Sophie," Star said. "I don't mean the good things, the happy memories when we were kids. It's the bad thoughts I don't want. The creepy things that crawl into my brain and just sit there and infect it like a computer virus and make me do bad things. Then there's the stuff I'm afraid happened to her. That could have happened to me. That's the stuff I just want to delete."

Jesse thought of the cuts on Star's arms—they must be some of the bad things Star was talking about. It felt too soon to bring them up. "I know exactly what you mean. I've tried God knows what." Sex. Drugs. Alcohol. She looked at Star and thought, *We're quite a pair.* They both reached for Saint Anthony and petted him.

OUTSIDE THE CHURCH, a small group of men and women stood together, drinking coffee and smoking cigarettes. Jesse parked the truck. She and Star maneuvered their way through the crowd near the church. They entered through a side door, headed down a hallway, and found an open door. A few people were scattered about the room, sitting on folding chairs. A long table in the back held stacks of pamphlets and books: *One Day at a Time, 12 Steps and 12 Traditions, The Big Book.* They'd come to the right place. Some of the people from outside started ambling in. Jesse and Star sat in the back. A few middle-aged men came in with their paper coffee cups, giving Jesse friendly nods. Another man with a full head of silver hair, blue jeans, and a denim work shirt strode up to the front. He exchanged words with a few people, shook some hands, then called the meeting to order.

"Hi, everyone. I'm Larry, and I'm an alcoholic."

"Hi, Larry," everyone chanted in unison.

"Yoga is down the hall to the left, and Al-Anon is in the chapel. If you want one of those, nice to meet you, but you're in the wrong place. This here is your Friday-morning co-ed Big Book meeting."

Jesse glanced about nervously.

"Why don't we jump right in. Who wants to go first today?"

A few hands shot up, but Star nudged Jesse with her elbow. She gestured for Jesse to stand up and speak. "Go on," she prodded.

Jesse stood. "Hi, everyone."

"Louder," Star said.

She started again, louder this time, "Hi, everyone. I'm Jesse. I'm not an alcoholic... well," she mumbled, "I don't know. I have been drinking a lot lately."

Star stared at her and made a gesture that said, "Get on with it."

"I'm really sorry to barge into this meeting, but I don't have much time and have a very brief announcement. It's kind of important. I wonder if you might help me."

There were rumblings in the audience, and Larry stood up again. "Miss, are you here for the AA meeting? If not... no solicitations are allowed."

"No, no. Please hear me out. I'm sorry to intrude"—she started speaking really fast—"but my daughter went missing in 2012 from a shopping mall in Holyoke, Mass. She's never been found. She was ten years old at the time. We used to come here every summer, rented a cottage on the beach, and this is a drawing of a man I only recently learned my daughter may have befriended during our last visit here. He used to sleep on the beach near our place. He rode a red bike. I don't know anything about him, but it was suggested he might have come to your meetings, or maybe one of you might recognize him." She held up the drawing then passed it around the room. She pulled out the photo and Missing Person flyer. "And this is my daughter. This was what she looked like then, and here is an image of what she may look like now."

There were murmurings among the group. Someone said, "I remember that case."

Another said, "Me too."

Jesse hoped these people wouldn't bring up Bird Girl and Bird Mom. They passed around the photos and drawing. An attractive middle-aged woman in a sweatshirt stepped forward. "I don't like where this is going. What are you suggesting? Alcoholics are kidnappers? We're good people."

There was more rumbling from the crowd.

"No, no. I'm just looking for any clue as to what might have happened to my daughter. Anyone who might have seen her or might know something. I'm not accusing anyone. If you could only imagine what I've been through all these years. Not knowing where my daughter is... what happened to her."

A man toward the front of the room said, "Yep, I remember him. He came to some meetings. I think I saw him last week."

Larry nodded. "Yes, that's right. He spoke a few times. Didn't he lead a meeting or two this year?"

Finally, an older man wearing a fleece vest stood up. Tufts of fluffy white hair stuck out from under his baseball cap. He held his hands up to shush the crowd. "People, people, hold on a minute. This drawing is of Gregory Adams. The spittin' image down to his favorite Harley T-shirt. He was a buddy of mine. He did attend some meetings but not last week and not last year. There was a tragedy. Don't you all remember? It was big news. He went overboard on the fast ferry from P-town to Boston. Never did learn how to swim. His body washed ashore back in the fall of 2012. I'm sure you all heard about it."

A hush fell over the crowd, then they began chattering among themselves.

"That's right, Nate," someone said to the old man.

"He was your good friend. I remember him now," somebody else said.

The old guy spoke again. "He was the quiet type. Tended to disappear in a crowd, if you know what I mean."

Just what Sophie had told Star about him.

"He's been gone for years. Poor guy." He turned to Jesse and handed her back the drawing. "I'm sorry, miss. Don't know exactly why you're looking for Greg. He had his share of troubles to be sure, but we got along. Watched out for each other."

"You're sure it's him?" she asked, nodding toward the drawing.

"Hundred and twelve percent."

Jesse looked over at Star, who sat there wide-eyed. "Thank you," she said quietly to the man. Jesse opened her mouth to say more then decided otherwise. She nodded at Star, and the two of them walked toward the door in a daze. Jesse stopped abruptly and made an about-face. "Sir, could Gregory have left town shortly before he went missing?"

"He rode his bike to Truro a couple times a week. Hitchhiked to Provincetown once in a while. But he never went any farther unless I drove him. He didn't own a car. Didn't drive or have a license. He felt safe here. He was no pedophile, if that's what you're getting at. He'd never mess with any little girl. That, I can assure you. He was a decent man. A good friend."

Jesse said, "Do you happen to know if Gregory liked birds? You know, was he into bird-watching?"

He cocked his head to the side and squinted his eyes. "How did you know? Wouldn't pay attention to nothing but them birds. Feeding them. Watching and watching. Yapping on and on about them. Driving me friggin' crazy. Friggin' birdbrain, he was." And he gave an uncomfortable chuckle.

"Okay, thank you." She headed for the door then stopped, turning back to the old guy. "One last question. Where is this Gregory buried?"

"Out at the town cemetery. I should know. I paid for the plot."

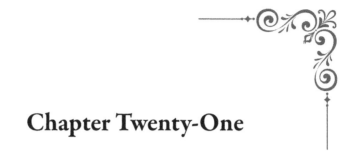

Chapter Twenty-One

Jesse walked out of the church and found Star already standing near the truck.

Star shook her head. "Well, that takes care of that. Our big clue is dead." She kicked a rock then kicked it again. "So his name was Gregory. He liked birds, and he rode a red bike, just like I said. Just like Sophie said. But he's dead." She plucked a small pinecone off a tree, crushed it in her hand, then threw it. "I'd say case closed."

Jesse planted her hands on her hips, staring at Star. "Case closed? Hardly. Don't you think it's kind of strange that the old man in the meeting didn't say how Paul Bunyan went overboard?"

"I thought he jumped."

"Well, maybe. But maybe not. And we don't know the date he died. It's still possible he came for Sophie before."

"But he didn't drive. How would he have even gotten to the mall in Holyoke, hours away?"

"I don't know. All I know is I have a daughter who's missing. And she and this Paul Bunyan character obviously met and spoke. And they both were into birds. Something is fishy."

Star shrugged her shoulders. "In the missing person business, it all seems to be pretty fishy. I think it's time we go home." She started walking toward the truck.

"Star, wait a minute. Haven't you heard there's no such thing as a coincidence? There has to be a reason. A connection between the two." She'd been thinking she was going to find him. Find Sophie.

Maybe there were more clues. Maybe Sophie was still nearby even if Paul Bunyan was gone. Jesse had been so sure the trip would lead to something. She wasn't ready to give up. Jesse inhaled. "I think we should look it up."

Star swiveled back toward Jesse. "Look what up?"

"If he went overboard and then his body was found, it would be in the local paper. Let's just confirm it, get the facts, and see if they printed a photo of Paul or Gregory. Whatever his name was. Just make sure it's the same person. Just because some old guy we never met, a total stranger from some AA meeting, is saying all this, it doesn't mean we have to believe him. Maybe he's leaving out some important detail. Maybe Paul Bunyan did know how to drive. Just because you don't have a license doesn't mean you can't drive. Maybe he stole a car or borrowed one." Jesse looked at Star, feeling determined. "You're good at finding stuff on your smartphone, right? Start Googling." And she nodded at the girl's cell phone.

They sat together under a tree outside the church. Star typed in "Gregory Adams Wellfleet" into her smartphone and pulled up a few articles from September of 2012 from the *Cape Cod Times*.

"Look at this." Star pointed to the first article on the screen. The photo of Gregory Adams looked nearly identical to their drawing. "That's him for sure. That's our Paul Bunyan." Star started reading the first headline aloud: "Authorities puzzle over passenger missing from fast ferry." She quickly skimmed the article. "A fisherman spotted a man falling or jumping off the fast ferry from Provincetown to Boston on September second. Gregory Adams was seen boarding the ferry by surveillance cameras that day, but they didn't show him disembarking. He was reported missing by friends." She looked at Jesse then back at the article. "That was days before Sophie went missing."

A later article still had no answers. The police continued their investigation, including searching the waters where the man was spotted falling in. The last article went on to say that a woman walking her dog at Race Point in Provincetown discovered a body washed ashore around 6:30 in the morning on September 6, 2012. The man's friend, Nate Acton—apparently the man they had met at the AA meeting—was interviewed and said Gregory left a note for him. According to the article, Nate said Greg was a veteran and had been depressed.

Jesse read over Star's shoulder, taking it all in.

"This confirms it," Star said. "Paul existed. His name was Gregory, and he most likely met Sophie. But then he died, probably a depressed guy who jumped to his death before Sophie went missing." Star exited the site and put the phone in her pocket.

"Back to the truck," Jesse said. "Just one more stop."

Jesse drove over to the town cemetery in South Wellfleet. The old guy had said he'd paid for the plot, but Jesse needed to be sure, to see where the last puzzle piece would lead them.

The cemetery was a small collection of uneven rows of very old gravestones bordered by tall pines. Some were tilted and leaning from years' worth of wind and harsh weather. It was quiet. No one was in sight, so they parked and wandered up and down the narrow sandy paths for fifteen minutes, reading the names on each marker. Saint Anthony happily sniffed the ground, which seemed to hold fascinating scents. Jesse began to seriously doubt they would find the grave of Gregory Adams. Most of the stones had dates from the 1800s and early 1900s. Many were crumbling, their lettering all but worn away. But a few recent ones stood in a peaceful corner under an oak tree toward the back. Saint Anthony had wandered off to that section and was rolling in the dirt next to a newer headstone.

Star walked over there then shouted to Jesse, "Hey. Look at this."

Jesse hurried over to where Star stood. "Wow..."

The inscription read: "Gregory Adams. 1950-2012. A peaceful man. Friend to all." And in the center of the stone, above the writing, was an engraving of a bird. She reached over and touched the bird with her finger, tracing its head and beak.

Star sighed. "So he was telling the truth. Here he is. Can we go home now?"

Jesse exhaled. Maybe they had come to the end of their journey. It was time to go home. Star walked toward the truck, and Jesse followed. She turned back to call Saint Anthony and saw that he'd found something in the dirt near Gregory's grave. "What's he got in his mouth?"

Star went over to the dog. She reached down and pulled the object out of his mouth. "Gross. It's all full of slobber."

"What is it?" Jesse said.

"Just a slobbery piece of plastic. It looks like a lens cap from an old camera." Star held up the round piece of black plastic.

Jesse walked over and grabbed the plastic out of Star's hand. "That's not a camera lens cap. It's too small."

"Then what is it?" Star said.

Jesse rubbed mud off one side of the cap with her thumb, revealing the letter *S* in dirt-stained blue tape. Jesse held it out in her opened palm for Star to see. Their eyes met and held. Jesse let the cap slip to the ground then shook her head fiercely, bringing her hand to her mouth.

She dropped to her knees and joined the dog, who was already onto a new scent, digging in the same spot where he'd found the binocular lens cap. She used her hands like shovels, scooping frantically, crazily, throwing the dirt behind her.

Not knowing what else to do, Jesse called Barnes the minute she found the other lens cap with the letter *A* in blue tape buried not far from where Saint Anthony had found the first. He told her to sit tight as he called the local police. Within minutes, they arrived on the scene, questioned Jesse, then began to search and dig around the same area.

She sat on a bench off to the side, still shaking, her head in her hands. Star was seated next to her, with Saint Anthony at their feet. Nearby, the sheriff and two policemen hovered over a plainclothes detective wearing latex gloves and picking through the dirt turned over by a workman with a shovel. The local reporter and a photographer both looked as anxious as Jesse felt. She had called Cooper and told him the whole story. That was when she'd lost it. In near hysterics, she'd sobbed, "Both lens caps. With Sophie's initials in blue. I found them! Buried in the dirt. She could be nearby…"

Cooper had offered to come, but knowing it was a good two-and-a-half-hour drive from where he lived, she'd said, "No. I'm leaving soon. I have to get Star home. Besides, they won't know anything for a while. And they haven't found anything else yet."

"I feel like I should be with you."

She took a deep breath. "I'll be okay. Just do one thing for me."

"Anything."

"Call Detective Jacobs in Canaan. Make sure they keep the press away from the house. I'm not up for that." He was the local police detective who'd been on Sophie's case for years.

"All right. But, Jess, call me when you get home."

The sheriff, a tall man with kind eyes, came over with a cup of coffee for Jesse and a bottle of water for Star.

"How are you holding up?" he asked Jesse.

"Okay," Jesse said then took a sip of coffee. She put her arm around Star.

The cops were milling about, speaking softly. They'd already cordoned the area off with yellow police tape.

"Ms. Albright, I think you and the young lady should head home. It's been a long day for you both. We'll be searching the entire area, and as soon as we get the go-ahead, we'll exhume Gregory Adams's grave. We're going to reopen his file, interview anyone who knew him. We'll call the minute we have news. The FBI has been contacted as well. I'm sure they'll be in touch shortly."

Jesse stood up shakily. It was totally surreal. If her life for the past six years had felt like a dream, one long horrific nightmare, what had just transpired felt even more bizarre. But unlike that day all those years ago, she didn't need to be drugged. She needed the truth. She kept moving the pieces of the puzzle around in her mind like a chess game, going over what had happened, what she'd learned about Gregory Adams.

She just wanted to turn off her cell phone, get in her truck, and get out of there. The town that had been her favorite place, so full of wonderful memories, had suddenly morphed into the set of a *Law & Order* episode.

"Do you need a ride home?" the sheriff asked.

"No. I can drive. I have to get Star back." She didn't say the girl's parents were furious with her or that they'd freaked out once they heard the shocking news. She'd called Blue, who'd also offered to come, but Jesse had assured him she was okay to drive Star home. And Barnes had checked in on her again. If he'd been mad at her before, there was no sign of that anymore. Just kindness.

Something else was niggling at her, though, what that old guy had said about Paul Bunyan at the AA meeting. *"He'd never mess with any little girl. That, I can assure you. He was a decent man... He was the quiet type. Tended to disappear in a crowd, if you know what I mean."*

A real melt bird, Jesse thought.

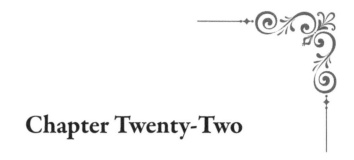

Chapter Twenty-Two

Jesse and Star barely spoke during the long ride back. Star was slouched in her seat, earbuds in place, immersed in her private universe. The trip had taken on an odd sensation for Jesse, just as time had. The years Sophie had been missing sometimes felt like a minute, sometimes an eternity. Now, she felt as if they'd been gone a week, not just one day and night. Each time her mind replayed what had happened in Wellfleet, she couldn't believe it. Still, she tried not to jump ahead, not to write a whole script without all the facts. But it seemed irrefutable.

Sophie's lens caps! Not just found but found buried—next to a dead homeless man who was into birding and had met and talked to Sophie. But he'd supposedly died before she went missing. Jesse's mind circled round and round. All she knew was that it felt like a ghostly treasure hunt, and Sophie was leading her on. *Everything has changed and has changed forever. And whatever the outcome, you will be dealing with this nightmare in some way for the rest of your life.*

She looked over at Star and saw the sleeve of her shirt had slid up. Jesse noticed, once again, the scars and the burn on her arm. The raw, jagged scab plain as day. Here was a living, breathing girl right in front of her who needed help desperately. Impulsively, Jesse pulled out one of Star's earbuds and blurted, "You have to stop this cutting."

Star glared at Jesse then quickly avoided eye contact. "What are you talking about?"

Without saying anything, she pulled Star's sleeve up and nodded at the scars.

Star yanked her arm away, tugging her sleeve back down. "How do you know about that?" she shouted. "Who told you?"

"No one. I've seen your scars. I saw them days ago at the Book Barn. I didn't know how to ask you about it. You've got to stop."

Star sank lower in her seat, fumbled with her earpiece, trying to put it back in.

Jesse grabbed the cell phone. "Do your parents know?"

"Are you crazy? They'd kill me."

Jesse placed her hand on Star's shoulder.

The girl covered her face with her hands and broke down sobbing. "I don't want to do it. But it blocks Sophie out. She scares me at night. Makes me feel like somehow it's all my fault. She's mad at me for some reason, and the cutting is the only way to get her to stop talking. I don't hear her when I do it. It hurts, but it feels good. I'm crazy—I know. Please don't tell my parents."

Jesse pulled the truck over to the side of the highway and flipped the flashers on. She pulled Star to her in a tight hug. Jesse had been so consumed with her own guilt, she hadn't noticed Star was absorbed with her own. She slowly rubbed Star's back in wide circles the way she used to comfort Sophie.

"How long have you been doing this?" Jesse whispered.

"It started after Sophie first showed up at night. I don't know... a few months ago maybe. I saw the pins and the seam ripper. I don't know why. I just did it. Now I can't stop. And now with Sophie really dead..."

"We don't know for sure yet."

"We know."

Saint Anthony nudged his head into Star's lap. She threw her arms around his neck and buried her face in his fur.

Jesse caressed her head. "Whatever happened to Sophie is *not* your fault. Not by a long shot."

"Plus the Barn. The cutting. I'm so screwed."

"I shouldn't have brought you. This was a huge mistake."

Star pulled away and wiped her eyes. "No, I wanted to come. We needed to come. It was important. It wasn't a mistake, I swear."

"All right, all right. It's going to be okay. You're not alone. I'm going to help you with this." She had no idea how she would help, but she just knew she had to try. She started the truck up, put it in gear, and got back on the road.

WITHOUT THINKING, JESSE headed toward Countryside Mall instead of continuing toward Canaan. She hadn't meant to turn there. The route was longer, really, out of the way, but she'd driven there so many times, it had become rote. She drove past familiar landmarks as if on autopilot: the Barnes and Noble on the left, the Bed Bath & Beyond across the street, the Citgo on the right corner, just as they had passed them That Day. It all came rushing back to her.

After three attempts, Jesse had finally coaxed Sophie, who was never easy to rouse, out of bed. She'd fixed her the usual, a bowl of Cheerios without milk, then done a load of laundry. She'd packed a tuna salad sandwich for Cooper.

He came into the kitchen. "I may be late tonight," he said, his back turned to Jesse as he looked for something in the pantry.

She exhaled. "Again? I barely see you anymore."

"You know it's our busy season. I've got extra trips to plan."

"You need to make time for me. For Sophie. We're a family, in case you forgot."

He shot her a look. "How could I forget with your constant nagging?"

Jesse sighed. She was a mess of conflicting emotions about her marriage—and her daughter's condition. They seemed to twist together like strands of knotted hair, making it hard to untangle and understand. Disappointment. Exhaustion. Abandonment. Guilt. They needed couples counseling, but neither of them had the energy after dragging Sophie all over the East Coast to therapists and doctors. "Whatever, Cooper."

"I can't help it. We need the money. All those doctors are expensive. What am I supposed to do?"

"Figure it out." *When did I start sounding like such a bitch?* She hated that he made her act that way.

He watched as she busied herself wiping the countertop. "Jess?"

She turned to look at him then grabbed her purse. "I've got to go. See you someday."

Sophie needed a new pair of sneakers for school. Canaan had no shoe stores, so they would have to trek to the mall—a big noisy place full of distractions. Not a place where Sophie was at ease. And if Sophie wasn't at ease, Jesse became tense, and that probably transferred back to Sophie. All the stress just bounced back and forth. There was no way around it. The mall was a challenge, and Jesse wasn't looking forward to the trip.

As they inched along the highway in heavy weekend traffic, Jessie looked in the rearview mirror. Sophie was in the backseat, absorbed in her own world, as usual, peering through her binoculars. Her long, fine brown hair, parted on the side, was blowing behind her from the open window.

"Do you know what kind of sneakers you want, hon?" Jesse asked.

Sophie, glued to her binoculars, didn't answer.

"Earth to Sophie. Sneakers?"

No answer.

"Sophie."

"I don't know. Whatever." She sat up straight and pulled the binoculars from her eyes, gazing determinedly off in the distance. She brought them back up to her face then said in a monotone, "Tufted titmouse, mourning dove, titmouse, titmouse." Suddenly, Sophie leaned forward and tapped Jesse on the head, "Whoa. Mom, Mom, Mom, pull over. I think it's a scarlet tanager. See him?"

"Not now, Sophie. I'm driving."

"But he's beautiful. You have to stop. I've never seen one. And a male." She pointed out the side window to a tree. "Please, please, please! For my life list."

"I can't stop now. Look at this traffic."

"I've waited my whole life to see a scarlet tanager!"

"You have your whole life ahead of you. There'll be other tanagers. We're shoe shopping today, not birding." Jesse knew that wasn't the way to deal with her. Not the right words.

She kicked the back of Jesse's seat. "You're a black-billed cuckoo."

"Hey. What have I told you about kicking?"

"You are an annoying cuckoo."

"Last time, I was a barn owl."

"Well, this time, you're a cuckoo. 'Cu-cu-cu-cu,' yelling at Dad. 'Cu-cu-cu-cu,' yelling at me."

Things were not going well. They were too far along to turn back for home. What would her book about handling high-spirited, gifted kids suggest? *Think, think, think.* "Sophie, I believe you are upset because you think you won't see the tanager again. I can understand that would be very frustrating."

"'Cu-cu-cu-cu.'" And she kicked Jesse's seat again. "Not stopping to look."

"I'm driving." *She can't help herself.*

Her high-pitched scream made Jesse's heart practically lurch out of her chest. She saw a flash of something in the rearview mirror—Sophie's hair flapping back and forth like a flag, whipping in a harsh wind as she angrily threw her head from side to side. Sophie had gotten hold of a map or a paper bag and was ripping it up into tiny bits, throwing it like confetti in the confines of the car, still shrieking. She was completely in the Red Zone, the place no one wanted their child to be, the place Jesse normally avoided at all costs.

Jesse maneuvered the car over to the right lane then pulled over to the side of the road, cars whizzing past her. She took a deep breath, trying to channel words she'd read in her book.

As calmly as she could, she said, "Sophie, you must stop. You can be flexible. I'm in traffic, driving, and if I'm not careful, we could get into an accident. We have to follow our plan to get sneakers, and then we can do some bird-watching. We must stick to our plan. You are enthusiastic about birds, which is great. But you are very upset, and you need to figure out what to do to calm down. A time-out would be a good idea." By then the scarlet tanager was long gone and forgotten.

A car horn snapped Jesse out of the memory. She looked around, and not surprisingly, the Countryside Mall was up ahead. *Move quietly. A sudden movement or noise, such as that made when raising your binoculars to your eyes, can scare off a bird. Move gently.* She pulled into the mall parking lot and found a spot near the cinema entrance.

"Well?" Star said.

"Well, what?"

Star sighed. "The mall?"

"I've got to show you something."

Exasperated, Star said, "We're going to the Zone, aren't we?"

Jesse unhooked her seatbelt. "Yes, as a matter of fact, we are." She just hoped that snotty salesgirl, Monica, wasn't working and that security guard was somewhere else. "C'mon. It's important. I need to show you something before I take you home." She got out, leaving Saint Anthony in the truck.

Star was sitting with her arms crossed over her chest, staring ahead.

"It will only take a moment."

Star didn't budge.

"Please, Star."

"I just want to go home."

"We will. Soon. Do this for me. Please."

Star begrudgingly climbed out of the truck. They went in the entrance between the cinema and Macy's. Once inside, they rounded the corner from the food court and walked past the Foot Locker. Jesse saw that where the Zone had been located only a week ago was a vacant storefront.

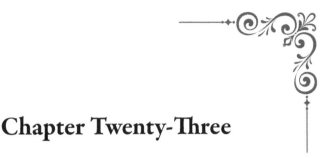

Chapter Twenty-Three

"Isn't this where the Zone is supposed to be?" Jesse stopped abruptly then turned around to see if she'd entered through the wrong door.

"I thought so..." Looking confused, too, Star went up to the metal accordion-like gate blocking off the entrance of the empty store. The sign had been taken off the front façade, but in its place were clean white spaces in the shape of the letters *Z*, *O*, *N*, and *E*. The inside had been gutted. A workman wearing a hard hat was dismantling empty shelves. Another was erecting a scaffold next to a counter with a cash register. Piles of lumber, boxes, and hangers littered the floor. In shock, Jesse and Star watched for a few minutes. Then the men said exchanged words, grabbed their lunchboxes, and headed out.

"Hey," Jesse said to the men as they slipped through the opening in the metal gate. "Isn't this where the Zone was?"

"Sure is," one of the workmen said.

"Where did it go?"

"Zone's gone."

"But why?" Jesse said.

"Got me, lady. I just work here. We're doing the reno for a Vicky's Secret."

"Victoria's Secret?"

He turned to his buddy. "Sex sells." And they both laughed.

"It was here last week. They can't just take the Zone away. Why would they do that?" Her voice sounded loud and desperate. "We *need* the Zone."

The other guy hit his buddy on the shoulder and rolled his eyes, then they both took off, snickering.

Jesse turned to Star. "How could they do that?"

Star said, "I stopped going to the Zone. I shop at Urban Outfitters. Maybe it's a sign. We aren't supposed to go there."

"Fucking Zone. It's jinxed. Since when does a store that people like just vanish for no good reason?" *Just like my daughter. Gone in the blink of an eye.* She glanced around then peeked inside. When she was sure they were alone, she put her index finger to her lips in a quiet gesture. "Follow me."

Star grabbed Jesse by the bottom of her shirt. "We're not supposed to be in there. It's gone, Jesse."

"Since when are you so cautious? I have to show you something. It's important."

"She's not in there, Jesse."

Jesse slid Star's hand off her shirt. "Obviously. Humor me. Please. I need to do this." She slipped through the gate where the workmen had exited. Star just stood outside until Jesse waved her in and mouthed, "Come on."

After a minute, she followed. Jesse led her over to the area on the left side of the now-empty room—the spot where the circular clothing rack with the colorful T-shirts had been on September 8, 2012. The last place she'd seen Sophie.

"This is where we looked at shirts," Jesse said softly. "Sophie saw a cute pink top with a little bird in the center in a square. It had the word *tweet* below it, just like the one April left behind." Jesse walked in a circle, closing her eyes, reliving those moments, her right hand outstretched, her fingers wiggling and touching imaginary shirts as if the clothing rack were still there.

"I love this, Mommy. Can I have it?"

"Sophie fingered the top. I said no. I was annoyed with her. I was always annoyed and tired and at my wits' end. And this time, I was more than annoyed. I was furious. You know how she was. She could be... you know... difficult."

Star followed behind Jesse in a circle, just listening.

"But, Mom, I need it."

"I was always giving in to her to stop the crying or shouting or embarrassing moments. It was hard to know the best way to act around her, how to handle her moods. I'd had it that day. Cooper and I had a fight that morning, said mean things to each other. He was having an affair with Cindy from his office. I knew it deep down but hadn't acknowledged it." She turned around to face Star, shaking her head. "Hell, I'm only acknowledging it now. Our unhappiness began to permeate the house. And Sophie's acting out was constant. Which came first, I'm not really sure. It was draining. She could be so hard to be around."

"You do need school clothes, though. How about..."

"I remember glancing away from Sophie, wondering if my marriage was even going to make it to the start of school. I remember worrying how I would handle it all by myself if we got divorced. Dealing with Sophie on my own—that scared me. We'd just returned from Wellfleet with your family, the one thing we all looked forward to each summer. Sophie was at peace there. She didn't want to act up in front of your family and somehow kept it under wraps there. It had been tough between Cooper and me. I don't know how obvious it was, the strain."

Star nodded, her eyebrows raised. "It was obvious."

"It was? Huh. Well, between that and the monstrous tantrum she'd pulled in the car on the way to the mall, I was a wreck. She'd calmed down by the time we got to the parking lot. Sometimes, she acted remorseful about her outbursts. Sometimes not. That day, it was as if nothing had happened. Getting all that crap out of her system must have felt good. I, on the other hand, felt like I had absorbed it all. It was awful. Anyway, we were coming to the mall for new shoes but got sidetracked. She'd pulled me into the Zone. She saw that top she liked and was nagging me to buy it."

"I love this, Mommy. Can I have it? But, Maaah-aaahhhm, it's so cute."

"I don't know why, but it just pushed me over the edge. 'Why can't you be normal?' I spat. It just flew out of my mouth. I knew right away what an awful thing that was to say. I saw her flinch. Who says that to their daughter, someone who already worries about being normal? It just came out. I didn't mean it." She let out a breath.

Star stared at Jesse. "People always say things they don't mean. I do it all the time. Like that day at the Book Barn. You asked me if I wanted to burn the place down, and I said I didn't care. I didn't mean it. It just came out. The same as you."

Jesse shook her head. "No. It's different. You don't say things like that to your daughter. Mean, hurtful things. Not to a little girl. Not to someone you love. Anyway, I let go of her hand. Right then. I said that awful thing, then I let go of her hand. You've seen that part on the news, I'm sure. I was tired, irritated. I wandered out of the KidsZone section and into the regular adult section of the store over there." She tossed her head off to the right and pointed in that direction. "I saw a rack of skirts and plucked one down, thinking maybe I needed to dress more feminine and sexy for Cooper. I didn't look at size or color. I just grabbed one. I glanced at Sophie, who was still admiring the top she liked. I took the skirt and went into the dressing room. Alone." Jesse looked for a reaction from Star, who seemed mesmerized by the story.

"Wait a minute. You left her there alone? I don't remember that part," Star said.

"That's because I never told anyone that part before."

"But you weren't gone long, right? Did she come looking for you?"

"Come. I'll show you." Jesse grabbed her hand and turned to go toward the back of the store.

"That's all right," Star said, pulling her hand away. She started walking toward the exit. "I want to go home."

"No. You have to see. You have to see it wasn't *your* fault. It could never, ever, *ever* have been your fault, Star. This cutting business. I know you blame yourself. But you shouldn't. Follow me." And she headed off toward the dressing rooms in the back of the store. Star looked around and followed reluctantly.

"I went to the very last dressing room. I could have gone to the first one. It was empty, in fact. But no, I had to take more time, be away longer, have more quiet time to myself. I went in here." And she entered the same dressing room she had gone in the last time she was at the Zone, where she'd found the cell phone. "Go ahead, sit down."

Star sat on the little bench next to the full-length mirror. She looked scared, her lower lip quivering.

"I hung up the skirt right there." Jesse turned and gazed in close at her reflection in the mirror. She brushed her hands through her wild hair. She turned back to Star. "You asked if I was gone long. Once I got in this dressing room, I sat on the little bench right where you are now. I needed to breathe. To be alone. I looked into this very mirror, and then I started hyper-ventilating. I realized it was stupid to leave Sophie alone. I left the skirt hanging and dashed back. I was gone for maybe two minutes. Probably closer to one or one and a half. I've timed it. I went back out to that T-shirt rack. I looked all around for Sophie, but I didn't see her. She'd vanished."

"Why didn't you tell anyone about coming in here?"

"A mother letting go of her young daughter's hand and losing her in a store in a big shopping mall far from home? That was bad enough, wasn't it? But to admit to saying something horrible to her and then abandoning her? Turning my back. Leaving her vulnerable and alone." She shook her head. "I tried a few times. But I could never say it. Remarkably, no one saw me come in or out of the dressing room. And the surveillance camera only caught me letting go of her hand out there. The one above the dressing room entrance was conveniently broken that day."

Star stood up. She was breathing hard. "Either way, it's not really your fault. A few seconds. You're not supposed to be tied to a ten-year-old constantly."

"That's kind of you, Star. But the evidence is damning, wouldn't you say?"

Star's mouth dropped open. Her hand flew up to cover it. "Oh, my God. That's your big secret, isn't it? The thing you've been carrying around with you for all these years? The thing that's made you kind of crazy. Collecting junk. Acting mean and weird. Dropping people you were friends with. Dropping *me* for all those years."

Jesse shook her head.

"You said something you didn't mean. It flew out of your mouth. You let go of her hand. You came in here for a moment's peace."

Jesse continued shaking her head, but her whole body was trembling.

"You were mad at Sophie because she was uncontrollable."

"I said, 'Why can't you be normal?' What mother says that to their child? I was unable to control her. Wasn't that my job? But I was unable to control my own emotions. Unable to change Sophie or my own behavior. Unable to know what to do." Jesse crumpled to her knees. She leaned all the way over, until her head was touching the floor.

"She was difficult. You didn't know how to deal with her."

Jessie's whole body rocked up and down. "Yes," she cried. "Yes, yes!" she wailed, and gut-wrenching cries escaped from deep within her.

Star backed against the wall, watching wide-eyed and afraid as Jesse keened. After a moment, she crouched down, tentatively put her arms around Jesse. Together, they rocked back and forth.

"You were a good mother," Star whispered. "You loved her. She loved you. No one is perfect. You're human."

Jesse inhaled sharply. "If I was holding onto her hand, they couldn't have taken her. That's a fact."

"But you can't hold onto someone twenty-four, seven. You can't be tied to them every moment of every day. You said it was like two minutes. One minute. That's not a crime."

Jesse lifted her head and looked at Star. "It is a crime. A crime of bad, irresponsible parenting. I didn't deserve to be a parent, so someone took her away."

"It's just not realistic to think you have to guard us kids every moment. That you *can* guard us every moment. Someone can take a child when they're sleeping. You don't guard a child when she's asleep." Star had slipped on an adult skin, speaking wise words, trying to comfort Jesse as a parent might.

"But Sophie wasn't asleep. I made a terrible mistake."

"You're not a bad person. Sophie was hard to deal with. She could have driven anyone away for a lot longer than a few minutes. Look at me. I was supposed to be with her that day."

Jesse glanced up and saw herself and Star in the mirror. The harsh dressing room light reflected her own face, blotched and mottled, like a frightened child's. Jesse's breath caught in her throat. "Oh, sweetie, you want me to forgive myself, but what about you? It's really nowhere near *your* fault. Where did you get that?"

Star sat back on her heels, looking at the ground. "Sophie called me the night before and asked me to come. I said I would. 'Promise?' she'd said, and I did. But that morning at your house, she was acting up. And I just didn't want to go. Sometimes, I didn't feel like being with her. Sometimes, she was fun, and it made me feel special to be

with her, to be chosen by her. But other times, I wasn't in the mood
for her. She could be so demanding and took all the attention. She
could sap the energy out of you. I just wanted it to be... easier, you
know?"

Oh, how I know. Jesse nodded.

"You know how she was if you broke a promise. It made her
crazy."

Jesse certainly had experienced Sophie's wrath. She'd broken a
few promises of her own before realizing that she had to be extra
careful with her words.

"But if I had gone, they could have taken me, not Sophie. Or I
could have protected her like I did sometimes at school."

Jesse grabbed Star by the shoulders and looked directly into her
eyes. "Oh, Star. I was the one who ruined everything. I was never
mad at you. I just couldn't face you or anyone. You were so wonderful
to be around. Your best friend is gone because of me. Not you. She'd
forgotten about your promise. She never even mentioned that."

"Really?"

"Really. I don't know why you see her and I can't. I want to see
her. I want to talk to her." She looked in the mirror again and rubbed
her eyes. "Sophie was a difficult child, but I loved her. I really did.
She was special. I had a hard time, but I loved her."

"I know. Everyone knows that." Star stood up and offered her
hands to Jesse. She pulled her up to standing.

Jesse wiped her face again. They hugged tightly. And just like the
time with Barnes and the hunter's moon, she felt something strange.
A shift, a feeling of space releasing in her own body. She pressed
her nose into the girl's neck, searching for her own daughter's scent,
holding on to this child as tightly as she possibly could. Then she felt
a fluttering of her heart, like the rapid beating of a hummingbird's
wings. As though a message were being sent to her.

Star pulled away. "Can we go home now?"

THEY ARRIVED AT STAR'S house, and Jesse put the truck into park. She turned to Star and said, "Don't freak out, but I'm going to have to tell your parents about the cutting."

Star shook her head violently. "What? No way. You promised."

How ironic that Star was pulling a Sophie. "I never promised. Sweetie, we need to get you some help. They aren't going to put you in jail. They love you. Your parents need to know so they can help you."

"Everyone will find out. I'm already a freak at school. I'll stop. I swear. I can do it."

"I think you need to talk to someone about your feelings. You shouldn't have to deal with this alone." Jesse reached out to touch her, but Star pulled away.

"If you tell them, I'll tell about the Zone and the missing two minutes. Do you want the world to know about that?"

Jesse shook her head. "You do what you have to do."

"I'll tell them you took me to Wellfleet against my will."

"At this point, it doesn't matter. It's time I came clean. I'll make sure you get to a good therapist who'll help you deal with your problem, maybe some special program. I really care about you."

"After I helped you find out what happened to Paul Bunyan. To Sophie. After I told you it wasn't your fault. I thought I could count on you. Well, I was lying." She sat up taller and shouted, "It *was* your fault. All of it. Sophie is dead, and it's your fault. Her haunting me. My cutting. Your fault, your fault, your fault. Live with that." She opened her door and jumped out of the car.

"Star, wait."

Star turned back to Jesse and spat out, "I hate you!" She slammed the door just as Blue came out of the house. Crying, she ran into her father's arms, and he grabbed her into a big hug. Jesse saw them exchange a few words, then Star dashed into the house.

Blue stared after Star for a moment then walked over to Jesse. He looked tired. "Jess, are you okay? I can't believe what you told us over the phone. Do they know anything more in Wellfleet?"

"Not yet."

"Beth is furious that you took Star without our permission."

"I know. I'm sorry. It wasn't the best decision."

He nodded off toward the house. "What was that all about?"

This was exactly what Jesse hadn't wanted to happen. Star freaking out on her. She considered not telling Blue and Beth about the cutting and trying to handle it on her own. Then she ran through the possible fallout of that. *Who am I kidding?* She wasn't qualified in the least. She needed to tell Blue, even if it meant Star would never speak to her again. Ideally, one day, she would get over it.

Jesse nodded and took a deep breath. "She's really upset with me."

"Welcome to our world. What happened?"

Jesse tried to gather her thoughts. *Where to begin?* "Listen, Blue, get Beth. It's important. We need to talk."

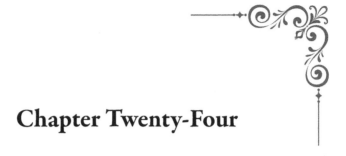

Chapter Twenty-Four

Back in her truck, Jesse sped through town as if she could outrun her problems. On the brink of maybe finding Sophie and finally learning what had happened to her, she'd been forced to sit there, listening to Beth yell at her as if she were a child. *Screw it. I did my part.* Jesse thought she should have felt relieved to be away from another dysfunctional family, but she didn't.

The conversation with Blue and Beth hadn't gone well, to say the least. They were understandably upset that she'd taken Star all the way to Wellfleet to look for a possible kidnapper without their permission. When Jesse finally got the chance to discuss Star's cutting, Blue and Beth had seemed in denial, at least initially.

"Soph, why do I feel like shit?" Jesse reached for her locket, forgetting once again that it was gone.

As she approached town, Jesse turned onto Church Street and drove by the Book Barn. All that remained was a cordoned-off pile of charred wood. While she was away, they had pulled down whatever was standing. She stopped the truck to look at the sad sight. It made her think about her lack of control over her life. Things just came and went. Endings were thrust upon her. Sophie's disappearance. Her marriage. The Book Barn.

She'd never been able to let things go easily, but maybe that was what she needed to do. Just let go. Barnes had said he'd been given a second chance and was so grateful for it. Maybe the time had come for hers—she just needed to find it then grab onto it somehow.

The image of her claustrophobic house filled with years' worth of other people's junk crept into her thoughts. But all the stuff no longer felt like clues or signs. It was simply a huge mess of overwhelming garbage. Jesse just wanted to crawl into her bed, yank the covers over her head, sleep for a month, and wake up to a clean house.

She plucked the green stone from the shelf below her dashboard. The stone that had gotten her through more than a few panic attacks. She turned the stone over and over, and slowly, the garbage littering her mind and home fell away. She envisioned the garbage breaking into jagged digital bits like a computer game, falling to the ground, and evaporating to nothingness.

She kept rubbing the little stone between her fingers, and suddenly, the smoothness made her think of the river rocks lined up on Georgia O'Keefe's window ledge at her house in New Mexico. A clean, sparse, spacious place where one could breathe. Jesse had had such a golden time in Taos. She thought it was funny how her mind could make crazy leaps from the heavy melancholy of her missing daughter to remembering those soul-nurturing days in New Mexico. She was connecting the dots. The trip to Wellfleet was bringing things into focus for her at last. She felt ready to take the next step, no matter what outcome. Her second chance. Her eyes watered. She let out a big breath, nodded a final farewell to the Barn, and drove on.

Just as she feared, when she pulled into her driveway, a news crew was waiting for her outside their van. *So much for getting help from Detective Jacobs.*

Jesse parked the truck, put on her stone face, and pushed her way through the small group.

"Did they find Sophie?"

"We heard the murderer was apprehended."

"Can you tell us what you found?"

She swatted at the camera that was shoved in her face and dashed into the house with Saint Anthony. She went around the house, making sure all the shades and curtains were drawn and all the doors locked, then turned her attention to the dog.

"Hungry, boy?" she asked, and he followed her into the kitchen. With the circuslike atmosphere swirling around her in Wellfleet and the one at home, she was grateful she had him to care for—a warm, loving creature who needed her. She bent down and hugged him. "What a good boy you are, Brownie."

She went to the pantry, scooped his kibble into a bowl, stirred in some water, and set it down for him. He gobbled it up. Suddenly dying of thirst, Jesse ran the water at the sink until it was really cold. She filled a tall glass and drank it all down in a few gulps. Then she filled it again and drank a second glassful, then a third, as if she could flush away everything. The shocking sight of Sophie's lens caps. The angry shouts from Star. The accusations spoken at the Silvermans'. All the dark thoughts pressing against her brain. She closed her eyes and shook her head. Out of breath, she set the glass down on the counter and went upstairs to Sophie's room, the dog at her heels.

She took down the plastic box with the little gifts from the crows. She sat on the bed and picked up the tiny pieces one by one, turning them over in her fingers. She lingered over memories of Sophie and her beloved birds. But they were quickly eclipsed by newer frightening thoughts.

"Soph, I found the lens caps to your binoculars." She looked upward, her eyes brimming over. "Dear God, I don't know what to pray for. Please don't let her have suffered." Tears slipped down her face. She kissed the last piece, an oblong red button, then replaced it in its slot. She closed the lid and put the box back up on the shelf.

Back downstairs, Jesse scanned the living room, thought again of Georgia O'Keefe's spare house. "This is crazy, Soph. I've been out of my mind. Fuck this." And she grabbed a box of trash bags and walked over to one stack of boxes labeled *Miscellaneous*. She pulled out a red Keds tennis shoe, child's size seven, and shoved it into the garbage bag. She plucked a single plastic doll's arm from the box, along with a broken candle and a page from a girl's diary, and tossed them all in. The little jolt in her chest—a ripple, a small buoyancy—felt good. She reached for more finds. A broken harmonica. A break-up letter written on the back of an air sickness bag. A yellowed set of dentures. More and more.

When she had filled three trash bags, it felt like a logjam inside her had loosened. There was movement. It was an unfamiliar feeling, outside her comfort zone. *But maybe this is a good thing. Maybe this is what Mom was talking about when she said it's time to start a new life.*

She gazed around the room again. She'd barely made a dent, but it was a start. She saw the pink T-shirt she'd found in the Blueberry cabin and picked it up off a pile of finds where she'd tossed it just yesterday. She shook it out and held it up.

"What?" she said aloud, and Saint Anthony turned his head, his ears perked up. "It can't be," she said, and the dog came ambling over. The shirt was pink and did have an image of a bird. It did say "tweet," but it was that damn Twitter bird logo, not the red tanager Sophie had seen and wanted. And the writing was in a different font. Jesse checked the label. It was a large—not Sophie's size—and it wasn't even from the Zone.

Deflated, she said, "It's not the shirt." She could have sworn she'd seen the very same shirt Sophie had wanted. She was sure of it. She'd thought the girl would lead her somewhere. She'd had a feeling about her. So many feelings. Her worried look. That watermelon gum. Jesse's hands fell to her lap. She exhaled then stuffed the shirt into one of the trash bags.

As she pulled the ties to close the bag, the story that Barnes was trying to tell her the night of the Harvest Fest suddenly came to her.

Some Native American tale about grief and how one tribe dealt with it. She had pooh-poohed it then, she was so angry and unwilling to listen. She wished she could remember the details. Something about ritual. If she ever saw him again, she would ask him to tell her the story once more. She picked up a small dirty stuffed animal from one of the boxes—a tiger with a long bendable tail. She turned it over in her hand. She realized now that she had created her own ritual. A wild, crazy, convoluted ritual trying to make sense of the senseless.

LATER, WHEN JESSE CRAWLED into bed totally exhausted from the last two days, Saint Anthony curled next to her on Cooper's side, snoring like an old man. Jesse shook her head and smiled. She picked up the phone and dialed Cooper's number.

"Jess, hi. Are you okay? Any more news?"

"No. Not yet. Cooper, it was so bizarre finding the caps to Sophie's binoculars." She had felt a tingling in her fingers as if the plastic pieces were alive, speaking to her. And when she had to hand them over to the policeman, she felt as though her heart were being wrenched from her body. She'd brought them to her nose, searching for some remnant of a Sophie smell, but only a musky, earthy scent remained.

"It's unbelievable," he said.

Talking to Cooper was still a comfort. No one else could understand all the feelings. "They're going to find her," Jesse whispered. "We have to prepare ourselves."

"We can't be sure. We've been disappointed numerous times before."

"No, I feel it. It's different this time. This is the biggest real clue that's been found. She's been leading me there with her journal. I'm sure of it." She paused, then continued, "Did you ever see a man who slept on the beach near our cottage that summer?"

There was a long patch of silence. Jesse could hear him breathing.

"Come to think of it, yeah. I do remember a guy. Long hair. Rode a red bike loaded with plastic bottles. Seemed harmless." The dates didn't add up, and his friend had said he was harmless, too. *But why were the lens caps to Sophie's binoculars right next to his grave?*

She couldn't believe Cooper had seen Paul Bunyan and never mentioned him to her. "Apparently, he was into birds, too."

"We have to wait. All we can do now is wait."

She realized what she really needed to tell him was the other thing—her secret about the missing two minutes at the Zone and the mean thing she said to Sophie. She opened her mouth to speak, but nothing came out. Finally, she said, "Did you know the Zone is gone?"

"The Zone? That Zone?"

"Yes, *that* Zone. They took it away. Putting up a Victoria's Secret in its place."

He lowered his voice. "It's for the best, Jesse."

"I guess," she said quietly. She felt a swirl of combating emotions. Longing. Regret. Hope. Sadness. She petted Saint Anthony and let her fingers slide over his forehead then down his snout. "Remember how happy Sophie was each time the crows left her a little gift?"

"Yes. It was amazing how they left her those sparkly little presents."

After a moment, Jesse said, "I've started to clean up. I've got bags of my finds to toss out. I'm doing it."

"Good for you, Jess. My offer to help still stands."

"Thanks, but I'm good." Just then Saint Anthony breathed out peacefully and let out a loud snore.

"Who's that?" Cooper said.

She looked over to the snoring hound and smiled. *Let him think it's a man.* "That's Anthony."

"Who's Anthony?"

It gave her a glimmer of satisfaction to think that maybe, possibly, her ex-husband felt a smidgen of jealousy. Just then, she heard Cooper's son, Caleb, calling him in the background. "Listen, I better let you go," she said. She had never been the first to get off the phone with him.

She hung up then slid Saint Anthony's heavy sleeping body over a few inches, and he didn't even stir. She pulled the covers up to her chin, reached over, and turned out the light.

AT THREE IN THE MORNING, Jesse was still wide awake, abuzz from her trip. She slipped quietly out of bed so as not to wake Saint Anthony. She put on a sweatshirt and headed downstairs. Stopping at her dining room table, still cluttered with her deconstructed finds, she looked at the pieces she'd crafted using the found bits. The vibrant shades and sharp, angled shapes were so different from her old, drab barn paintings. The many textures of the collaged materials were enticing. Interesting. This new stuff was, she realized, art, after all. Just as Star had said. It felt wide open. While she was making them, time didn't exist. Nothing else mattered.

Jesse grabbed an armful of her finds off the table. Rusty nails. Scraps of dirty fabric. Old photographs. Shopping lists. She took them out to her studio. She turned on the lights, switched on the heat, and spread the objects out on her long table. Without thinking, she just started working intuitively, cutting up pieces, collaging others, and painting on top. Time dissolved. She applied thick gobs of paint in pulsating reds, bits of ash, and collaged pieces of burnt book pages. Words and letters floated down from a sky, peeking through a hole in the canvas, and one elusive bird flew out of a window. She melted beeswax in an old crock pot, and when it was hot, she painted the wax over the entire canvas. When it dried, she buffed it with a soft rag until the piece had a muted, mysterious, opaque look.

By dawn, she'd begun three new canvases. She transformed the frightening scenes in her mind into abstract images heavy with emotions, each with a lone bird soaring out of the picture. She was exhausted yet vibrating with ideas she couldn't wait to try out later. She hadn't felt so invigorated in years. It reminded her of when she was in college, so fresh and naïve, and full of ideas just spilling out of her. She finally dragged herself back into the house.

As she lay in bed, all she could think about was her new work. She smiled, and tears came to her eyes. She felt like an artist again.

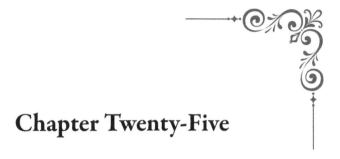

Chapter Twenty-Five

After Jesse dropped her off at home, Star hung out in her bedroom, staring at her Lady Gaga poster. She looked super cool with cat-eye makeup. Gaga would have accepted Star the way she was without squealing on her. Star had gone out of her way, lying to her parents, sitting scrunched next to that drooling dog in the truck for hours in search of Paul Bunyan. So maybe he'd been dead for years, but Sophie had been there. At least her lens caps were. Star had listened as Jesse revealed her big secret in the Zone dressing room and even talked her down from the crazy-lady ledge. But when Star spilled her own guts, Jesse snitched her out to her parents.

When Jesse was in the kitchen talking to her parents, it dawned on Star to use her old trick. Eavesdropping 101. In the old days when she was just a kid, she used to secretly listen in on her parents' "discussions"—also known as huge fights about money—after she'd supposedly gone to bed.

So she opened the heat vent and could pretty much hear everything that was being said downstairs. First, her mom was yelling at Jesse for taking her on a dangerous mission to look for a killer without their permission. Star had never heard her mom so pissed before. As usual, Star's dad, always the peacemaker, tried to calm everyone down.

"She was drunk at the Harvest Fest," Mom said. "Maybe she was drunk when she took Star. Who knows what to believe?"

After the whole trip got rehashed, Star's mom finally calmed down, then Jesse snitched Star out about the cutting.

"But that's not possible. We would have noticed," Mom said.

Yeah, right.

Then Jesse told them about Star's nighttime visits from Sophie and drinking coffee to stay awake.

I'm dead meat, Star thought.

Then Jesse, the traitor, said, "I'm sorry. Star needs help. That's why I'm here."

She left after Star's parents practically threw her out. Then they came upstairs. They didn't know how to deal with Star. At first, they were shouting at her locked door, "Star, open up."

Then her dad said, "You're grounded for a week."

But her mom shouted, "A month. Three months."

After minutes of total silence, Star heard them whispering to each other. They must have decided to change their tactic, because next, her dad was saying softly, "Honey, let's discuss things quietly. We all make mistakes."

Star still didn't say a word.

Then her mom sounded so sad, as though she were crying. "Honey, I know you haven't been yourself lately. Please talk to us."

Dad said, "I'm sorry we yelled. We'll try to understand."

Finally, Star opened the door. It was another couple of hours of them asking a million questions about the trip and the cutting and the Sophie ghost. Star barely answered, but she finally agreed to see a shrink just to shut them up. Then her parents went to bed.

All was quiet, and Star snuck downstairs for mint Milanos. She was about to make some coffee when she saw that, thanks to Jesse, her mom's Starbucks had been removed. Star was out of her personal stash, so she was in for a long night.

Now all I need is for the fire inspector's report to come back. And then the shrink's. She could see it all. She would be outed on Instagram and YouTube. Everywhere. "The teen cigarette-smoking arson-ist." Put that together with "the teen self-mutilator," and she would be famous but with a ruined life forever.

Shit.

She and Jesse had taken a really cool trip to the Cape, reconnect-ing like old times and hanging out at OB. Then she had to confide in psycho Jesse about everything. *What was I thinking? What a moron.*

With no coffee to keep her awake and the thought of everyone at her school and beyond finding out her secrets, she went for her sewing kit. Something that put her in control. She'd stashed it in her closet behind her clothes and shoes as if that would make it harder for her to get to. She opened the closet door and—

"Hi, Rats." Sophie stood in the closet, moving her hand from side to side in a little wave. She was wearing the same outfit, but her binos were missing both lens caps.

"Jesus, Sophie. You scared the crap out of me."

"Sorry. I thought it was time to come out of the closet." She gig-gled like she'd made the biggest joke ever.

Star had thought—well, she'd hoped—that finding Sophie's lens caps would mean finding *her.* Then Sophie's ghost wouldn't visit her anymore. *Wrong again.* "Sophie, I'm tired. Let's not do this tonight."

"Do what?" She stepped out of the closet.

"You know."

"I'm on *your* side. My mom ratted you out. Not me. You weren't careful enough. She *did* see the cuts on your arm, like she said."

"Yeah, I know. But she didn't have to tell my parents. I was plan-ning on stopping."

"Like when?"

"Like now."

"Really?" Sophie pointed to the sewing kit on the floor of the closet. The scissors with the orange handle. The pins with the round colorful heads.

Star had to take a deep breath to calm herself. *Now she's invading my thoughts, too?*

"Were you looking for this?" Sophie asked, nodding at the sewing kit.

"No. I told you. I'm stopping."

"What makes you think you can?"

"I can stop anytime. Just like I can get you to stop coming. It's all mind over matter." She said it, although she didn't really believe it.

"Why would I stop visiting you? It's fun."

"Fun for you. Not me. I didn't do anything wrong when you were taken or left or whatever."

"You broke your promise. You know I hate that."

"I was just a kid. I'm sorry I didn't go with you that day."

"What about me? What did I do to get stuck like this?" She pointed at her little-girl body.

Tears filled Star's eyes. "Nothing. Not a goddamn thing."

"That's right. It's not fair!" Sophie shouted and stamped her foot like the ten-year-old she was.

Star got a sick feeling in her stomach. She hoped she wouldn't throw up. It was all so confusing. Where was the real Sophie? She covered her ears with her hands and started humming. She didn't want to hear Sophie buzzing in her ears anymore. She took a deep breath and grabbed the sewing kit. She unzipped it and took out the scissors. Holding them, turning them over and over, she just looked at the scissors. She rubbed her thumb over the pointy part.

"What's the matter? I thought you said you were quitting?"

Star shoved the whole kit away and turned back to Sophie. "Paul Bunyan is dead. He jumped off the fast ferry from P-town. Or was pushed or something. His body washed ashore. What do you think that means?"

Sophie shrugged. "It means he's dead. There's no secret meaning. He was unhappy. Haven't you ever wanted to just turn everything off?"

Not until you started haunting me. "We went to find him. We thought he took you. We were so sure. You were watching him and taking notes like he was one of your birds. We thought you were leaving us a secret message."

"All you had to do was ask me. I'd have told you. Paul Bunyan wouldn't hurt a fly. He wouldn't hurt me. Or anybody."

"Then who would?"

"Follow the bird seed. You'll figure it out."

"I don't want to. Sophie, you have to stop coming. I can't help you. You have to leave me the fuck alone."

"What happened to you being my BFF? Our blood pact? Sisters forever?"

"We are. I mean, I was. People grow up. Things change. Life goes on."

"For some of us."

"I'm sorry I broke my promise. I'm sorry for whatever happened to you. I really am. I miss you, Bird Girl, but it's time to say goodbye."

Without a word, and very matter-of-factly, Sophie climbed on top of the desk, yanked open the window, and crawled toward it.

"What are you doing?" Star shouted.

But the girl moved quickly and was climbing out the window. Star rushed over and saw Sophie thrust one leg out, followed by her head, body, then the other leg. Star grabbed for her and caught her by the foot, but she couldn't hold on. Sophie slipped away. It was too late.

Star stuck her head out the window and felt the shock of the cool air hit her face. "Sophie!"

Sophie, her arms outstretched like a bird's wings, her bright-orange socks peeking out at the ankle from her black clogs, was swooping up and over the Johnsons' roof next door. Then she was gliding off into the sky. Sophie was flying away. Star didn't blink, afraid to lose sight of her. The girl was getting smaller and smaller. Soon, all Star saw was a tiny dot. She squinted, then the dot was gone. Sophie Albright, her ten-year-old best friend, had flown off into the night sky and disappeared.

Chapter Twenty-Six

The next morning, Barnes was at her door. Jesse stepped back and opened it wider. She hadn't expected to see him again. But he'd been so kind to her yesterday on the phone, when she'd needed him most. She poked her head out, looking for the media.

"They're gone. There's a cop at the end of your drive keeping the press away."

"Thank goodness," she said.

Saint Anthony trotted over to him, his tail wagging quick and high. He did a snazzy little side step back and forth. Jesse thought of it as a happy jig and wanted to do the same.

"Hi there, my friend." He petted the dog, feeding him a biscuit. "Good to see you, boy." He bent down and scratched the dog, who reciprocated with licks to Barnes's face. Barnes looked at Jesse and seemed to be taking her all in with his eyes. "How are you?"

"I'm okay. Hanging in there."

"I thought I'd come to see you. Have you heard from the Wellfleet police today?"

"I called this morning. Nothing new yet. And you?"

"I found April Johnson yesterday," he said. "The GPS on Star's phone led me to her in Springfield."

"That's great. Is she okay?" Jesse was trying to act normal, but her hands kept moving about, touching her hair and her collar. He aroused so many feelings in her. He wasn't being cold, the way he'd acted the other day after she pushed him away, which made her more jittery.

"Yes. I think she was tired of running. She's back home with her parents. They have plenty of issues to work out. But she's home safe."

"I'm so glad." And she really was. But she was also stricken with a deep feeling of envy.

"Your tip and Star's cell phone helped." And he held up the blue backpack. "Maybe you can see that she gets this. All her stuff is still in it."

"Oh." Jesse glanced away then back up at him. "Probably you should just drop it off at her house. I'm persona non grata with her right now." Jesse pushed the door open wider. "Why don't you come in?"

He stepped inside, looked left into the living room then looked right. "Something's different."

She gestured to the few filled trash bags tied up and leaning near the door. "I've started to declutter. Just the beginning." She stood looking at him, awkwardly searching for pockets she didn't have. She crossed her arms over her chest and uncrossed them. "Come, let's go outside."

He followed her out back to the screened-in porch. She sat in her old wicker. Barnes took the larger teak rocker, the one Cooper used to sit in.

Barnes gazed at the view of the yard that sloped down to the creek. "It's nice out here."

Maples and elms shaded the left side of the porch. Dappled shadows from their leaves filtered through the screens. The light in the early morning was always soft and gentle, Jesse's favorite time of day.

"It reminds me of being in a tree house," she said.

A gaggle of Canada geese flew into view, landing smoothly on the creek in V formation. They veered off into pairs, except for one goose swimming by itself.

"It makes me sad to see a loner like that one," Jesse said.

The other geese began honking noisily as if they were having a spirited discussion.

"So..." She took a deep breath. "About Star." And she proceeded to tell him everything. Paul Bunyan. Sophie's notebook notations. Star's ghostly visits from Sophie. The cutting.

He leaned in, listening attentively. She talked a little more and paused. Then she said, "I told her parents about the cutting. About going to the Cape. Now Star hates me. I mean absolutely hates me. I'm a walking Judas. And her parents aren't too thrilled with me, either."

"I'm so sorry."

"I should have asked to bring her with, but they'd have said no, of course. It was a rash, stupid decision, but she was actually a huge help. So I don't regret it. But now she feels like I betrayed her. I don't think I had a choice. I had to tell about the cutting."

"You did what you *had* to do. She'll need time to heal. Her parents, too."

"There's more." She paused, looking at the ground as if the words she searched for were written there. "That day back at the Zone with Sophie. I didn't tell the whole story. I left something out." The words came spilling out as she replayed the whole scene again. "By the time I came to my senses, she was gone. Two minutes or less. Gone." She looked up at him.

He took her hand. "You've carried that around for a very long time. That must have been a huge burden. I'm sorry you've had to live with that."

"But that's not the point," she shouted, snatching her hand away. "It's what I did. I'm the one who disappeared. I wanted to be free of her."

Barnes grabbed her by the shoulders and turned her to him. He brought his face in close and spoke slowly and softly. "You can't blame yourself for someone else's criminal act. Blaming yourself is another way of holding on to Sophie. Like your finds. Your drinking. Your acting out. It's about control. I know about this. I've seen it before. I've done it. You think that if you were in control, it wouldn't have happened. But you're not in control of the universe. Things happen. Bad things. Little boys and girls get cancer and die. Children get snatched. They disappear into thin air. We have no control. Someone I respect once told me 'Sometimes life is messy, and you have no control.'"

Jesse cocked her head. "Did I say that?"

He nodded. "Yes, you did." He took her hands in his and squeezed them. "It wasn't your fault. You must believe this. You must."

Tears ran down her face. "I want to believe that. I do. But I'm not sure that I can. She's been leading me with her notebook, with Bixby. I think they're going to find her."

Barnes nodded. "They might, but still it wasn't your fault. You can believe. Just let it sink in."

He was the second person she'd revealed her secrets to, and he, like Star, didn't seem shocked. Maybe, like Star had said, she had been a good mother, mostly. He stood and helped her up.

She wiped her nose on her sleeve. "But wait a minute. Why are you here? After the other day. The way I acted. I didn't think I'd ever see you again."

He looked deep in her eyes and took her hands in his again. He shook his head. "I couldn't stay away."

"I'm glad. I wanted to see you again."

He leaned in and kissed her on the mouth slowly and gently. She pulled back and looked into his eyes, searching for an answer. Then she threw her arms around his neck and kissed him again, harder. They kissed for a long time then held on to each other tightly. When they pulled away, Jesse said, "That first time I met you, when you came here to the house, I touched your chest." She gently placed her hand on his chest. "I pushed you away. I felt something. A jolt."

He nodded. "I felt it, too."

"It scared me. You scare me."

He placed his hands on hers, fingers spread out, palm to palm. His hands were bigger, his fingers peeking above hers. "Don't be scared."

They pressed their hands together, and she felt warmth radiating through them.

"You told me you were building a boat." She ran her fingers along his long slender ones, tracing each one as he watched. "What kind of boat?"

"A wooden canoe. I love to feel the smooth wood under my fingers." He demonstrated by gliding his hands ever so lightly under the sleeve of her shirt, touching her soft skin.

She felt vulnerable, as though she wanted to cover her skin but, for the first time in a long time, surprisingly powerful and sexy, too. The rich mocha color of his skin next to the pale creaminess of hers was beautiful, and she imagined the two colors swirling together to make a brand-new shade. She thought she must paint it later. She leaned in, took a deep breath, and closed her eyes. She gave his neck a gentle lick. The taste was both sweet and a little salty.

He drew his fingers through her hair, pulling her to him. He whispered in her ear, "You need to be touched."

It was true. "Do *you* need to be touched?" she whispered.

"I need to touch you." He ran his hand under her shirt.

She felt his fingers on her stomach, and his touch made her shudder. He started to unbutton her shirt and slipped it off her shoulders.

"I'm a mess. Is this a mistake?"

"Do you want this?"

She looked down, then up again, right into his eyes. "Yes. Oh, yes."

"Then it's not a mistake."

She took Barnes's hand and led him back into the house, up the stairs, and into her bedroom. He looked around, and she noticed him studying her little shrine next to her bed. Her candle, photo, and plastic saint.

"It's my shrine to Saint Anthony. The saint, not the dog."

He picked up the plastic figure and turned it over in his hand. He rubbed the crack where it had been glued together after Saint Anthony had knocked it over.

She lit the candle, and the room glowed.

"To us both finding what we're looking for." He tipped the plastic saint toward her. Then he placed it back in its shrine.

She smiled. "Maybe we already have."

Standing next to the bed, their bodies were drawn together like magnets. They kissed for a long time, frantically, breathlessly. Their tongues mingled, exploring.

They heard the click-clack of nails on wood and pulled apart to see Saint Anthony ambling in. He picked a shoe up off the floor and trotted around the room with it in his mouth.

"I do believe he's jealous," Jesse said.

He circled, nestling into a throw rug, and finally settled on the floor with two thuds—the shoe then the dog's body hitting the floor. Barnes and Jesse followed suit, their bodies falling onto the bed, their arms and legs entwined. First, they laughed, then they were quiet as clothes came off. Just the rustling of sheets. The gentle moans of two lovers. The soft light from the candle flickered on the ceiling above the bed. The dog gave a contented groan.

JESSE WOKE AND SAW the start of an early-morning pink sky outside her window. They'd spent the whole day and night in bed, making love, talking, and taking breaks to bring food back with them. They fed each other pieces of cheese, apple, and chocolate, but they continuously set it aside because they couldn't stop touching. They needed to be close.

She picked a shirt up off the floor, slipped it on, and looked over at the sleeping Tuck. He did look like *Tuck* and not *Barnes* anymore. She smiled. She glanced at the photo of Sophie on the nightstand—the one of her standing on a swing in her bathing suit, a serious expression on her face. Jesse looked back at Tuck. He stirred then opened his eyes.

"Good morning," she said.

He grinned. "Morning."

"Remember that story you were trying to get me to listen to the night of the Harvest Fest? The Native American tale. I thought of it the other night, but I couldn't remember the details."

He nodded and sat up on his elbows. "Soul keeping. It's a sacred ritual. It helps parents deal with the loss of a child. They cut bits of hair from the child and put it in a bundle with other prized items. It's where the soul of the child will be kept for as long as they need to grieve. They give it to a soul bundle keeper. A family member or other volunteer. Someone they trust. A holy man, who will hold onto it until the soul can be freed. During this period, it's a time of contemplation. A time of atonement. The parents are not to fight or argue. They're to always keep their child in their minds."

Jesse listened, spellbound.

Tuck continued, "At the end of this period, when the parents feel ready, the soul of their child is released in a big happy feast." Tuck leaned Mr. Bear against the pillow with a pat. "It helps the healing process for those left behind. It makes a lot of sense. Some other tribes practice mourning by painting their faces black. Others cut their hair short. Still others cut their arms and legs."

Jesse turned to Tuck, her eyes wide. "They cut themselves?"

"That's right. As an expression of their grief."

Her head was spinning. As usual, Tuck's words were comforting. She thought of him as her own sage, her personal holy man, guiding her through a maze of confusion she'd created. Calm, assertive. And he was patient, letting her come to the truth in her own time.

"Think I'll take a shower," he said and got out of bed.

"Okay. Meet you in the kitchen for breakfast when you're done." She patted his chest and headed for the stairway.

Thinking she'd heard a noise, she stopped at the door to Sophie's bedroom. She opened the door and stood for a minute, taking it all in, looking about. Everything was the same, but she entered and picked up Sophie's Wellfleet birding journal from her nightstand. Jesse sat on the bed and flipped through it once again. She stopped on a page where Sophie had drawn a bird with a red crown and a red patch at its throat. It was labeled "yellow-bellied sapsucker." Sophie's name for Professor Pollen. In her small handwriting in blue ink, Sophie had written: *He keeps singing the same song, tapping away noisily.* Then it looked as though maybe she had copied something from a guide book: *The drumming is a love-song in the mating season. In the fall they turn quiet and reserved.*

Jesse closed the book and placed it on her lap. She sat for a moment then reopened it to the first page to look for a date. Sophie had started the journal in the spring before their Wellfleet trip. Her last months of fifth grade. The same year Star had said Professor Pollen was their substitute teacher. Jesse thought back to the first time she'd met the guy, but she couldn't even remember his real name. He'd written his first book years ago. Blue had a reading series at the Book Barn, and Professor Pollen had given a little talk and read from his book. He had a little stutter that wasn't there when he read but appeared when he spoke off the cuff.

Jesse was in the audience, and he'd introduced himself. He was wearing his signature red bowtie and round wire-rimmed glasses. He'd shaken her hand. She remembered him holding it a moment longer than necessary, which made her a tiny bit uncomfortable. He'd said, "Nice to meet you. I'm a big fan."

She recalled thinking it was an odd thing to say. *She* hadn't written a book. How could he be a fan of hers? At the time, she'd put it off to his being socially awkward. When she saw him years later, at the reading for his honeybee book, he did seem overly smiley for a man she didn't really know. But he'd been too shy to actually come up and speak to her.

She flipped through the notebook, searching for what, she wasn't really sure. Another mention of the sapsucker, perhaps. Then she halted abruptly when she reread the words Sophie had written in her last entry of the Wellfleet trip. *Herring Gull and Screaming Cowbird in a fight on the beach. Friggin' bird brain! Friggin' bird brain!*

Nate, at the AA meeting in Wellfleet, had called his friend, Paul Bunyan, a birdbrain. *Could he have been involved?* She was seeing clues wherever she read. Professor Pollen. Nate. Jesse's stomach dropped, and a wave of nausea rose up. Her head was spinning. "What are you telling me, Sophie?" She slapped the book shut, took it with her, and headed downstairs.

JESSE WAS PREPARING scrambled eggs when Tuck walked into the kitchen, smelling all soapy fresh.

"Hey, something smells good." He came up from behind and kissed her neck.

"I was going to say the same thing. Hope you're hungry." She placed the eggs on the table and gestured for him to sit.

He sat and spooned eggs onto his plate. He picked up his fork and dug in. Jesse sat down but just stared into space.

"What's the matter?" he asked, putting his fork down.

She looked at him then placed her palm on Sophie's notebook, which she'd placed on the kitchen table. "This might be crazy, but I have this feeling. This awful feeling." She proceeded to tell him about the clues she found in Sophie's logbook. "Maybe one of them slipped through the cracks. Maybe the police didn't know about Professor Pollen subbing at the school and didn't question him. Or maybe that old guy had been stalking the girls on the beach. Maybe Sophie's logbooks are leading us." She looked directly into his eyes. "Is it crazy?"

"No. Of course not. Nothing is crazy. Nate lives in Wellfleet?"

She nodded.

"And this Pollen character, he lives nearby?"

"Not in Canaan but maybe nearby in Shelburne Falls or Ashfield. At the reading, they called him a local author."

"Do you know his real name?"

"I forget. Hold on." She pulled out her smartphone and Googled the honeybee book. "Here it is. Richard Lightcraft."

"Let me make some calls. Then I'll go pay your Detective Jacobs a visit. May I take this notebook with?"

"Of course." She put pieces of paper as bookmarks at the Sapsucker and Cowbird notations. "Thank you so much."

Tuck finished his breakfast and said, "I better get going." He walked to the front door. "I'll see you soon and call if I learn anything."

She held up her finger. "Wait one minute. I'll be right back." She dashed back up to Sophie's room and took down one of Sophie's bird nests from the shelf. A perfect little cup made with twigs and grasses, it was lined with soft white cattail down. So delicate. Sophie had labeled it: American Goldfinch. A small, pale-blue egg sat in the middle. Jesse found an empty shoebox in the closet and placed the nest in the box.

Next, she went downstairs and retrieved the Bixby book from her purse. She let the book fall open to Chapter One. She touched the pages, closed the book, and placed it in the box, underneath the nest. She put the lid on then brought the box up to her lips, kissed it, and whispered, "I love you, Sophie."

She went back to Tuck, who was waiting for her at the front door. She held the shoebox out to him. "I want you to be my soul bundle keeper."

Tuck tilted his head. "Are you sure?"

She nodded. "I'm very sure."

"I'd be honored." He took the box from her and brought it to his heart.

"You're my holy man, Tuck."

He smiled. "You said my name!" He gave her a kiss on the lips then tapped the box gently. "I'll keep it safe until you're ready for it."

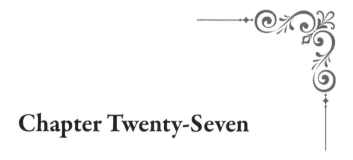

Chapter Twenty-Seven

Over six months had passed since Jesse's trip to Wellfleet with Star. Six months since Tuck had met with Detective Jacobs and since the FBI reignited Sophie's case. When the authorities exhumed Gregory's body, they found nothing suspicious. Next, they'd scoured Nate's home and found nothing there, either, but the old man had admitted to finding Sophie's lens caps on the beach after her family had already gone home. He was the one who'd buried them near his friend's grave. He knew Sophie and Greg talked about birds, so in his mind, he was just doing a good deed, thinking the caps being buried near Gregory's grave would somehow be a comfort to his old friend.

Meanwhile, back in Canaan, the local police descended on Richard Lightcraft's home and had more luck. Photos of Sophie and Jesse were pinned to a bulletin board. Handwritten notes of a very disturbed man who seemed to have concocted a fantasy about himself and the Bird Girl. Photos of the outside of Jesse and Cooper's house and Sophie's elementary school. The written rants of an obsessed, brilliant, but crazed man. Sophie's fingerprints and DNA in a dark, dirty attic. A cot chained to an old radiator. Splotches of dried blood on the floor, the wall, and the sheet on the cot.

Had Lightcraft killed Sophie when she tried to escape? Had a fight ensued? He'd needed to silence her? Lightcraft wouldn't speak to the police, so they had begun building the case against him based on evidence at the scene. Finally, the police had made the brutal discovery of a child's bones buried in Lightcraft's backyard behind his shed. Sophie's remains and her binoculars.

Lightcraft was charged with kidnapping and first-degree murder. He sat in prison without bail while both sides prepared for the trial. He was quickly labeled online with both the monikers Professor Pollen and Sapsucker after news of Sophie's birding notebook spread. Jesse and the whole community felt a collective sense of relief, yet an unpleasant pall lingered over Canaan after the gruesome details emerged. Jesse allowed herself to finally grieve. She took lots of walks with Saint Anthony and cried until there were no more tears. At least she could stop looking.

Another surge of the media descended on Canaan with the discovery of Sophie's remains, but it lasted for only a brief spell. Life in the sleepy town slowly returned to the way it had been before that day, at least for most people.

At first, after the blowup with the Silvermans, Jesse hadn't heard a word from them. When the news about Sophie hit, she did get condolence cards from Blue and Beth but then no further word. Jesse couldn't bear the silence. She'd left them messages to no avail, hoping maybe they would get over it eventually.

Over several weeks, she'd thrown out printouts of the database she had created to log her finds. She'd flipped through a few and studied the chart. It'd looked almost foreign to her. A desperate attempt to make sense of the senseless. Tuck's words had replayed in her head. "*You're not in control of the universe. Things happen. Bad things. It wasn't your fault.*" And he had reminded her of what she'd said, "*Sometimes life is messy, and you have no control.*" She kept repeating these words to herself.

Finally, she knew what had happened to Sophie, at least some of the horrific truth, but was the knowing better than the not knowing? It wasn't closure. That would never really come, but one thread of the story had an end. It was time to move on.

She had tossed away pages and pages then picked up where she'd left off throwing out her finds. She'd set aside anything useable to donate to Goodwill and saved a box of interesting pieces for her artwork. The process was like weeding a garden, a task she used to find satisfying, one where she always saw progress. Once she began to think of her finds as weeds, she was able to pull them from the overgrown garden of her living room and see, once again, the floor, the couch, and the tabletops. She could breathe.

She thought back to her first sweet night with Tuck. They'd seen each other many times since then, plus calls at night, emails, and texts. She looked forward to seeing him and felt more clearheaded than she had in years. She had a good feeling about him. That hollow, empty sensation in her stomach was gone, and Jesse realized what was different. She had dared to let herself feel happy.

JESSE WOKE TO THE LOVELY sound of *fee bee, fee bee,* the clear two-note whistle of the black-capped chickadee. She got out of bed and looked out her bedroom window toward the back yard. The sun streamed in. Buds were on the trees. Crocuses poked through the dirt. And sure enough, a chickadee sat on one of the empty feeders, pecking at the hole. It had been a long winter, and as usual, Jesse hadn't fed the birds.

"Soph, you're right. I've been neglectful." She threw on some clothes, took Saint Anthony, and headed in the truck over to the Canaan hardware store. She bought the largest bag of wild bird seed they had. Bert, the owner, seemed sincerely happy to see Jesse and even helped her put the bag into the bed of her truck.

Back home, she filled each of Sophie's bird feeders then sat on the screened porch, waiting. Within minutes, a chickadee was back, followed by an aggressive blue jay and a cardinal, its deep red a wonderful surprise. They sang and chattered as they nibbled.

"Okay, Soph. I get it."

During the purging, she'd decided it really was time to make a change. She'd called a realtor, one of Gary's competitors, and finally placed the house on the market. It had taken some time, but she finally got a good offer. Cooper was thrilled. Just the other day the realtor called to tell her that the closing had been scheduled. It was really going to happen. Jesse had looked at some houses and apartments for herself. She'd considered renting a cute cottage in town, but something had stopped her. Tuck kept suggesting she move closer to him in New Jersey, but that didn't feel right, either. She had no idea where she was going to go and no clue as to where she wanted to live, but Jesse was confident she would figure it out.

Saint Anthony behind her, Jesse roamed from room to room, looking at the house as if she were the new homeowner. The old Formica countertop in the kitchen she'd always wanted to upgrade to soapstone. The wood floors that could use sanding and polishing. She looked out the window at the unstable barn and unkempt gardens. Selling the house of the Bird Girl hadn't been easy, especially with the recent shocking revelations so fresh. But the truth was the house needed a new owner, someone to care for it as she and Cooper had when they'd first bought it. Someone to bring it back to life. The young couple who was buying it had a toddler and another child on the way. They reminded Jesse of herself and Cooper back when they'd first come to Canaan, so young and full of dreams.

She shook her head then glanced at the kitchen chair where she'd draped her favorite black leather jacket, Cooper's old jacket that she had taken over.

"C'mon, boy," she said to Saint Anthony. "Let's go for a ride." She grabbed the jacket and her purse then headed outside to her truck.

About two and a half hours later, after driving east on Route 2, she was in seaside Newburyport, with its classic brick buildings and cobblestone streets. Jesse made a right onto an upscale residential side street.

"Fancy," she said to Saint Anthony, who sat in the passenger seat.

Jesse let him stick his head out his window, and the fresh air rushed in. With his ears flying back in the breeze and his mouth open, he looked as though he were smiling.

"This is it," she said as she noted the number on a mailbox near the curb and pulled into the driveway of a three-story gabled townhouse, so different from her country farmhouse.

She parked her truck behind an SUV.

"Hey, stranger," someone called out.

She saw Cooper coming out the front door to greet her. Wearing jeans and a long-sleeved white cotton T-shirt, he didn't fit in the picture. The city, although charming and vibrant, was certainly nothing like rural Canaan, where he used to say he wanted to live forever.

"Hey yourself." She had called ahead, not wanting to drop in unannounced and have to hang out with Cindy if Cooper wasn't home.

She hadn't seen him since he'd stopped by her house months ago, pushing her to get rid of her finds and put the house on the market. With all that had transpired regarding Sophie's case, there'd been many phone calls but no real reason to see each other. She'd run through the dialogue in her head a hundred times on the drive over, but seeing him in the flesh made her anxious.

Cooper walked up to her and gave her a big hug. "So good to see you. Come on in."

"Oh, that's okay."

He stopped and looked back at her. "You don't want to come in?"

"Actually, I came to..." She paused, unable to say what she really wanted to. She reached into the driver's side window and took out his black leather jacket. "Return your jacket. I've been cleaning stuff out, and it surfaced."

"All the way for that? I thought you loved this jacket," he said with a furrowed brow. "I gave it to you."

"Well, not exactly. It's yours, so here you go." She held it out to him.

He took it from her cautiously. "Oh. Okay. Thanks." He saw Saint Anthony's head sticking out the passenger window of the truck and walked over to pat him on the head. "Hi, boy."

Jesse opened the door, and Saint Anthony came bounding out. He peed on a bush then proceeded to sniff around the yard. Jesse stuck her hands in the front pockets of her jeans. "So I guess I'll be moving."

"Have you found a place in town?"

"No. I mean moving... out of Canaan." She didn't know why she said it. She hadn't known it to be true. It just came out.

"Really? Where are you moving to?"

When she opened her mouth again, the word "Taos" popped out. She just then realized that memories of her time at that artist colony there had been creeping into her thoughts lately. Taos was loaded with like-minded people. Artists and writers. Scenery to inspire forever. That wonderful light. *Why didn't I think of it sooner?*

"Wow. That's far away."

She nodded. "It is." New Mexico was about as far as she could go by car. She didn't know a soul there—a prerequisite, she suddenly recognized, for a new home.

"It is beautiful," he said. "I remember you loved it there. I think a change will be really good for you."

"I think so, too. It may actually be a relief. Starting fresh. I can be myself instead of the mother of some tragedy. I probably should have left long ago." Her new relationship with Tuck complicated things, but for now, she needed to do this for herself. It seemed imperative to get away from the house. From Canaan. From Cooper. From her past. She and Tuck would work it out somehow.

They stood in silence for a few moments. Then she said, "I want to apologize for my behavior... for calling you late at night all those times and being so out of it."

"You don't have to apologize."

That was not what she'd wanted to say at all. Not what she'd practiced on the drive over.

He looked at the ground then at the house and back at Jesse. "I wish things could have been different."

A little boy came out and ran up to Cooper, grabbing him around the legs and peeking at Jesse shyly. He resembled Cooper, with his lopsided smile and the same close-together eyes.

"Hey, Caleb. Say hello to Jesse." He caressed Caleb's head, and Jesse felt a prick of sadness.

"Hello."

"Hi," she said and gave a wave. Saint Anthony trotted up to him and sniffed his legs.

Caleb laughed and patted him on the back. "Nice doggie."

Cindy came out, holding an infant swaddled in a blanket. Jesse had heard that they'd had their baby. Cindy looked great. Sexy and happy. And already skinny. *Probably back at the gym the day after giving birth.*

Cindy stood next to Cooper, placing one hand around his waist proprietarily. "Hi, Jesse. How are you?" She turned back to Cooper and looked at him as if sharing a private joke.

Jesse felt a tiny "that's my baby you're holding" jab, but it quickly passed, then she felt a sense of calmness.

"This is Emily," Cooper said, kissing the baby's tiny fingers.

Jesse smiled. "Congratulations. She's lovely." Really, though, with her nearly bald head and scrunched-up face, she looked more like a wrinkly cabbage. The baby started to fuss then let out a loud wail.

"She's got a great set of lungs," Cooper said.

Cindy saw the leather jacket in his hand. "What's that?"

"Jess returned my old jacket. I used to practically live in this."

Cindy wrinkled her nose at it distastefully. "You don't have to hang out here in the cold. Come on in. I could put some snacks out." She rocked Emily, trying to quiet her down.

"Snacks. Yes," Caleb shouted and pumped his fist in the air. He was cute. Looked like he would be a fun kid, someone for Cooper to play with, teach things to.

Jesse shook her head. "Thanks, but I have to be going. This was just a drive-by. A quick hello."

"I've got to get Caleb ready for a playdate and put her down for a nap," Cindy said. "Bye, Jesse. Nice to see you."

Jesse lifted her hand in a little wave. She watched Caleb follow his mom back in the house then turned back to Cooper. "You have a nice family." She paused. "Are you sorry we had Sophie?"

"Are you kidding me? As difficult as she was, I never regretted having her. I think of her every day. I've never known anyone with a spirit like hers." He glanced to the house then back at Jesse, lowering his voice. "I do miss you, you know?"

Jesse opened her eyes wide. "Really? What do you miss about me?"

"I don't know. We had a lot of fun together. I miss how I was with you. I feel like a piece of me is gone."

To Jesse, it sounded like he missed himself, how he was then, not necessarily Jesse. "That was another lifetime ago. Our youth," she said.

He nodded, gazing off in the distance. "Yeah, I miss our youth. When you're in it, you don't realize how good it is. How easy."

She wondered if he was having a mid-life crisis and if he would ever cheat on Cindy. She thought about their youth. She didn't miss it now as she had before. Everything that had happened to her lately had shaken things up. Paul Bunyan, April, Saint Anthony, Tuck, her time with Star—it had all loosened up a space in her head and heart, making room for more than just Sophie's memory. She did think about her early days with Cooper. She missed the laughter. But she also realized she'd romanticized their relationship. All the years after Sophie went missing, they'd never really told each other how they were feeling.

"Well, I guess I better be going. I just wanted to see you again. You know, in a normal, calm way. Hello, goodbye. Have a nice life. That kind of thing."

He nodded. "Well, then. I'd say mission accomplished."

Jesse pulled the keys out of her purse, opened the truck door, then stopped. She couldn't leave yet. She turned back to him abruptly. "There's something else." She launched into her story. Her secrets. What she'd told Star and Tuck. What she'd been wanting to tell him for years. The missing minutes. The harsh words to Sophie. Blaming herself. She glanced nervously at him when she was done talking. "Well?"

"I don't know what to say. I wish you'd told me sooner. But does it really matter anymore?"

And then she remembered what he'd said that day he'd stopped by unannounced. "*You weren't the only one affected by this tragedy. I was there. I was her father. I loved Sophie.*"

She had been hoarding the grief as if Sophie's disappearance had affected only her. But it hadn't. He had been there through it all, too. He'd also changed her diapers, gotten up in the middle of the night when Sophie was sick, put up with her tantrums, and trudged with them to numerous doctors. He'd built bird houses for Sophie, read and sang to her, and made her laugh. He loved her. They'd been a family.

"I'm sorry I never really acknowledged your suffering, either. I was too stuck in my own. You were a really good father. She loved you deeply."

Cooper tilted his head in thought. He smiled. "Well, thank you for saying that. I didn't know if you ever got how much I was hurting, too."

"I do now. I get it."

Cooper walked up to her. "Listen. I know I'll see you at the closing, but after that, I want you to stay in touch. I mean it. Let me know when you get settled. I don't even care if you call late at night. I'd like to hear from you, that you're okay and everything."

"Cindy won't like that."

He tilted his head and grinned in agreement.

"You can call, too," Jesse said.

"Okay. I will." He gave her a hug, and they held it for a moment. It felt familiar and nice until the sensation of loss washed over her. But it wasn't about not having Cooper anymore. It was that the thing that would have bound them forever, even in divorce, was gone. There was no reason to stay in touch. She let out a huge breath.

"Bye, Jess."

"Bye, Cooper." She opened the door to the truck. Saint Anthony hopped in, then Jesse followed. She drove a few feet down the drive then stopped. She put it in park and turned off the ignition.

Cooper was still standing near the house, watching. When she didn't restart the truck, he walked over. "Everything okay?"

She looked out the open driver's window and said flatly, "One more thing. I know you were fucking Cindy before Sophie disappeared. I was your wife, and you betrayed me and lied to me. It didn't happen after Sophie went missing, like you said. It was before, and I knew that. I've known it for some time, and you owe me a big fucking apology. You hurt me."

He opened his mouth, but no words came out at first. Then he whispered, "Don't hate me."

She reached out the window, snatched the jacket out of his hands, and tossed it into the front seat of the truck.

As she drove off, she watched him in the rearview mirror, her past standing immobilized as she lurched unsteadily into her future.

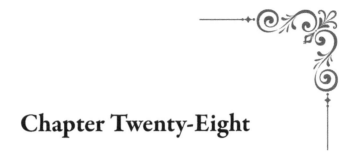

Chapter Twenty-Eight

"So, Star, have you thought about what we discussed last time?" Star was sitting in her therapist's office for one of her weekly sessions. After Jesse told her parents about her cutting business, Star's parents flipped out. *Leave it to them to find a therapist named Pebble.* But actually, the woman wasn't so bad. She had the clichéd long gray hair, kind of like Jesse's, and wore earth-mother flowy skirts and tops. Star had come to like the woman and even looked forward to her sessions inside Pebble's tasteful home in the comfort of the darkened, cozy office with lots of antique furniture, soft overstuffed pillows, and abstract metal sculptures.

When she first met Pebble, Star didn't say a word. She just sat there for the first four sessions, with her mouth clamped shut, clutching a pillow and listening to the silence. Star had tried to blank her mind out and just concentrate on the sound of the waves from the noise machine in the hallway. She didn't know how people meditated and emptied their minds of all thoughts. When Star tried to think of nothing, all she could do was think of every little thing she didn't want to think of. Sophie. Jesse. The Barn. Books. Fire. Ophelia. Paul Bunyan. Professor Pollen. Sophie. Jesse. The Barn. Books. And on and on.

Finally, Pebble got her to talk. Turned out, it wasn't the end of the world. She didn't think Star was a freak. Or if she did, she was used to freaks and acted like the cutting wasn't a big deal. Pebble was okay. Star talked about Sophie and how when she'd first gone missing, her disappearance invaded Star's house. Her school. The whole town. And not knowing what happened freaked everybody out. Not just Star. It had felt as though all of Canaan were sick. She imagined it was the same in towns where school shootings had happened.

Star guessed she had held in a lot of her emotions at the time. The bad feelings had kind of built up inside her. When Sophie's bones were found, Star was glad she was seeing Pebble because Star actually knew the killer. She had been in his class. Talked to him. Been inches away from him. Joked with Sophie about him. After the grisly details emerged, the thought that she had been so close to such a sicko kept Star up at night, her lights ablaze. She definitely needed someone to help get her through that period.

"Hello? Star? Are you there?"

Blinking, Star snapped out of her daydream and looked over at Pebble. "I'm here."

"Did you think about what we talked about last time? How you might honor Sophie's memory in some way? It could be small and personal, something you do privately." Pebble looked at Star with a kind, accepting gaze. She spoke in a calm, soft voice. "You don't have to tell anyone about it. Rituals of all sorts can be very healing."

Star had liked that idea. "I don't know yet. It has to be just right."

"No need to rush it. You'll know the right thing when you think of it."

In her heart, Star knew it would probably involve another trip to Wellfleet. Maybe a private little ceremony on the beach.

"You know people have all different ways of grieving. There's no right way. No wrong way."

"Like creating imaginary ghosts or cutting themselves?" Star said.

"Absolutely. If feelings of loss are debilitating and don't improve after time passes, it's called *complicated grief*. A fine writer named

C.S. Lewis once said that grief is a muddled process, one with no logic and no timetable. I think that's true."

Star's feelings did seem complicated and muddled with lots of strands to sort out. And as if reading Star's mind, Pebble said, "Keep writing in your journal. It's a great way to get it all out and untangle some of the confusing threads."

Star had taken Pebble's advice and had been writing in her journal. She found it did actually help, like telling secrets to a trusted friend. Sometimes she talked to Sophie and told her what she was thinking. Pebble said that was fine, too. Still, Pebble didn't blow sunshine up her ass like the school counselors, and Star appreciated that. *But, Pebble? What a stupid name.*

"And any urges these days?" Pebble said.

Star gave a smirk. "I don't suppose you mean sexual urges."

Pebble smiled and shook her head. "Your sewing kit."

It had taken a while, but Star had stopped her cutting. Sometimes she still felt a little shitty about herself or sad about Sophie, but she didn't feel like she wanted to cut anymore. That felt so gross. *How did I ever even do that?* She felt as if some creature from another planet had taken over her brain during that period.

"I threw away the sewing kit so I wouldn't be tempted."

"Good for you!"

For a while, Star had tried to locate Ophelia or April, whoever she was. She'd thought she found her on Facebook, but after Star tried to friend her, the girl's account suddenly disappeared. Star's parents and Pebble said it was best to let her go, that April needed time to heal. Star thought the adults were probably afraid April could be a bad influence. Star just hoped April was okay. Maybe she got her angel tattoo and all was right with the world. Maybe not.

"My parents told me that the insurance people said the Book Barn fire was caused by some faulty wiring in the basement. How lucky is that?" Star said.

Pebble's eyebrows scrunched together. "Lucky? How so?"

"Not that the Barn burned down but that it wasn't my fault after all."

"Oh, I guess you could say that is lucky."

"And I've quit smoking, like seriously quit. I mean I don't think I'll ever light up again in my life. So at least one good thing came out of the fire."

Pebble smiled then glanced at the clock on her side table. "Our time is up. Listen, you're doing great. It's an ongoing process. You should be proud of the work we've done. What *you've* done. I'll see you next week, and keep thinking about a ritual for Sophie."

Star turned on her cell phone as she exited Pebble's house. Jesse had texted. Again. Over the months, Jesse had called and left like a zillion voice messages and texts. Star had needed her own time to chill out, though. Maybe Jesse felt bad about ratting Star out. Even though she sort of understood why Jesse had done it, Star was still pissed.

Star got in her car and decided to read the text later. As she made the short drive home down Main Street, which with the twinkly lights on in the shop windows always gave her a warm feeling, she thought back to the last time she'd seen Sophie, when she'd flown out of Star's window. It had been quiet without her since that last visit. On the one hand, Star almost wanted to see Sophie again, even the ten-year-old ghost. On the other hand, she really didn't, since seeing her was always so upsetting. Jesse had said she never saw Sophie, and maybe that was worse. Star didn't know.

She pulled into her driveway and looked at Jesse's text. *Let's talk. Please.*

The For Sale sign that had been on Jesse's lawn for months now had a Sold banner across it. Just like that. It was unbelievable.

Star and her parents were driving by Jesse's the other day, and there it was. Rumors about Jesse were flying around town. Like she was leaving to join an Ashram in Upstate New York or she was about to run off to Paris with Barnes. All Star knew was that her childhood best friend had disappeared, and her mother was about to fly away, too.

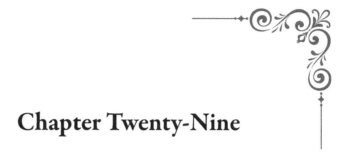

Chapter Twenty-Nine

Jesse stepped into Sophie's bedroom. Saint Anthony followed closely. Only the bed remained. She had even taken down the canopy of fabric leaves. Jesse gazed around the empty room. The door to the vacant closet was open, and she walked over and looked inside at the fanciful mural on the inside wall. A tiny bit of Sophie remained, and that felt right. The new owners might paint over the mural, but maybe not. In any case, Jesse could do nothing about it.

She sat down on the lavender carpet with her back against the bed. The dog lay down next to her, placing his head on Jesse's thigh. She caressed his snout and ears then looked up toward the ceiling. "Sophie, honey. I have to leave here. We had to sell the house. They're a nice family who bought it. You'd like them. They have a little girl. Her name's Lucy. She'll get this room. I know she'll love it. And they're expecting another child." She paused then continued, stumbling over her words, her voice thick with emotion. "I have to move on. I may not talk to you as much." A tear ran down her cheek. "Not as much as I have, but I'll always think of you. I'll always love you."

She turned back to Saint Anthony. "I had a daughter. She was difficult. She was wonderful. She loved birds. She was taken, brutally murdered. I'll never see her again. How am I going to live with that?"

His ears perked up. He lifted his head and turned to her. She petted his head then waited as if he might respond. Tears ran down her face. She rubbed Saint Anthony's ear and said, "I'll have to. I'll just have to." She kissed him on the top of his head and whispered, "It's time."

Jesse took a deep breath, pulled herself together, and headed downstairs. She sat at her kitchen table and called Tuck at his apartment in New Jersey.

"It's me," she said when he answered.

"I'm glad you called. I've been thinking about you. How's the packing going?"

"Almost done. It's weird to be in this house. So empty. It echoes." The closing was in less than a week. The movers were coming in a few days. Jesse had found a casita online to rent in Taos. She was driving out there with Saint Anthony, traveling light, putting much of her stuff in storage.

"I bet. Are you excited?"

"I am. But nervous, too."

"That's understandable."

"You'll come visit, right?" When she'd told him about moving to Taos, Tuck was quiet at first but then supportive. He'd said he understood that she had to go away. No matter what, he wanted to keep seeing her, even if it would be long distance. Maybe the move would be temporary. She thought of their last few times together, and she got a fluttery, light-headed feeling. They had an intense chemistry in bed and out. They could talk for hours. She wanted to continue to get to know him.

"Of course I'll visit," he said. "As soon as you're settled. Or before. Whenever you want me."

"I want you. In fact, I need you to come here. Soon."

He laughed. "Somebody misses me already?"

She laughed, too. "Well, yes, but it's not that exactly. It's something else. I'm ready for the soul bundle."

"Ahhh. Your soul bundle keeper at your service. You're ready to release it?"

"I am."

"That's big. Are you sure? There's no rush, you know."

"I'm sure. It's time."

"How about this weekend?"

"Perfect." It would give her a few days to prepare. She'd put a no-tice up at Earl's about a big soul-keeping potluck in the backyard. She planned to fill the bird feeders one last time. Anyone who had known Sophie could come. She'd call the Silvermans. Maybe they would be ready to see her. They would celebrate Sophie's life.

They were both quiet. She pictured Tuck sitting on his couch. She heard him breathing and wished he was sitting beside her, hold-ing her hand. "Tuck, I want to thank you"—her voice wavered a bit—"for keeping it safe. For everything."

"I wish I was there to hug you. You're doing the right thing. See you soon."

THE NEXT MORNING, JESSE stood on the porch and looked out at the creek, the trees, and the two yellow Adirondack chairs down near the water. The feeders swayed in the cool, swift breeze. She heard *fee-bee* then saw the bird swoop from the nearby oak over to a limb of a tree closer to the water. The simple call kept coming, as if the bird were waiting for a response. *Fee-bee, fee-bee.* As if the chickadee was trying to tell her something. *Fee-bee, fee-bee.* Come closer. Come closer.

She walked down the hill, and Saint Anthony ran ahead. She sat in one of the yellow chairs, and Saint Anthony lay at her feet. Jesse looked out at the view she loved. She would miss it.

Just then Jesse heard someone shout out, "Hey."

She turned back to the house and saw Star Silverman walking down the hill toward her. She looked different from the last time Jesse had seen her—so pale and angry, shouting "I hate you!" before running off. Now she seemed calm. But something else. Peaceful. More grown up. She walked tall and confidently. She had a healthy color to her face.

"I saw you sitting down here. I got your messages. Your texts. And emails," Star said.

"I didn't hear back, so I kept trying."

"I wasn't ready to answer."

"I understand," Jesse said.

"But I guess I am now. I figured I'd just come over. I hope that's okay."

"Of course."

Saint Anthony went up to her and sniffed. Star reached down and patted his head. "Hey, Anthony."

Star glanced about then said, "It's weird to be here."

"I know. Have a seat."

Star sat down. "What are you doing down here?"

"I don't know. I was out on the porch, and the view always reminds me of Sophie. And then I heard a black-capped chickadee."

"Fee-bee," Star said in a sing-song voice.

Jesse smiled. "The chairs called out to me. I'm glad you came. I don't like sitting here alone."

"You've got him." And she nodded at Saint Anthony, who had plopped down at Jesse's feet again and was staring at the water.

"Yes. He's great company, but he never answers me back."

Star opened her mouth to speak, closed it, then tried again. "I didn't know what to say to you when I heard about Sophie. So I did nothing. I couldn't believe it, and I could believe it all at the same time."

"It's okay. I know. It was shocking and so tragic. It's all like this endless dream." They sat for a moment. Then Jesse continued, "I was sad for so long. I'm not sure what I am now." She took a deep breath then said, "This weekend, there's going to be a celebration, a big happy feast for Sophie. I hope you'll come."

Star just listened.

Jesse couldn't help staring at her. She wasn't wearing dark, torn clothes or goth makeup. She had on skinny jeans with a cute blue vest and a multi-colored scarf draped around her neck. Her hair, straight and shiny, hung down her back.

"Star, you look really good."

"Yeah, right."

"I mean it. How are you?"

"Fine."

"I mean really."

"I'm fine. Really."

"You're mad at me."

Star looked off in the distance across the creek then back toward Jess. "Yeah, I'm pissed... You ratted me out."

"I'm sorry I hurt you and your parents. You, your friendship, meant so much to me. And after what we went through together in Wellfleet. I know you think I betrayed you, but I couldn't keep that secret. I'm sorry. I told them only because I love you."

Star shook her head, looking away. "It's not that exactly."

"It's not?"

"I guess I get why you told them."

"Then what?"

"You're moving away?" There was a catch in her throat, and she blinked back tears.

Jesse nodded.

"Just like that? Without telling anyone? We hear about it through the grapevine. See the sold sign out front."

Jesse turned to her. She reached out to touch her hand. "I made a lot of mistakes. It's time I move forward. I'm not sure how long I'll be away. I just know I need to do this now. But I'd like you in my life."

"I don't know."

"Maybe we can start over."

"I don't know," Star repeated.

"Don't shut me out. I've punished myself for so long. You've punished yourself. Think it over. Don't say no."

Star bit her lip then flipped her hair off her shoulder. "Pebble said maybe I need to tell you how I'm feeling."

"Pebble?"

"This therapist I'm seeing." She gave a little smile and rolled her eyes. "I know. What a stupid name. But she's okay. She's got me thinking about a lot of stuff. She's actually kind of cool. She helped me to stop the cutting. I'm sorry I said I hated you that day. I didn't mean it. I was really mad at you for telling my parents. Even though I understand why you did. It got me into therapy. But when I heard you were moving... I don't know. It felt like you were mad at us. At my parents and me. They don't—we don't hate you." She exhaled a big breath.

"I know, sweetie. My leaving has nothing to do with you or your parents."

"It's like you came back into our lives—my life—after being gone for so long, and now you're taking off."

"It's something I need to do for myself. To heal. I love you and still want you in my life. Really."

Star gave a little tilt of her head. Gazing off into the distance, she looked unsure. They watched two geese flapping their wings and honking noisily. But then a crow flew nearby, cawing. A moment later, there were two then three, and soon a murder of crows appeared like in the movie *The Birds*, descending upon the maple tree off to the left of their chairs. Their large black bodies filled the tree, all of them cawing frantically.

"What the...?" Jesse said as she sat up tall.

They were flapping, fluttering, and swooping. Their chatter made a terrible, loud racket. Jesse hadn't seen so many crows all together since Sophie used to observe and feed them. But the birds seemed different. Jesse imagined they were angry with her.

"What's going on?" Star said.

Saint Anthony stood up and barked at the tree. Then one crow with an iridescent purple patch on its head swooped down close to them. They both ducked and shouted, "Hey!" The bird had something shiny in its mouth. As the bird swooped, it dropped the glinting, shimmering object into the white cement birdbath close to the water's edge. Then it flew off high into the sky before returning to the maple tree with the other crows. Jesse and Star ran to the birdbath. Star reached in and picked up the object—a small, rectangular piece of metal. She turned it over in her hand.

"A locket." She rubbed dirt off the silver and read an inscription that was engraved on it in fancy script: *With eternal love.*

"What? No." Jesse grabbed it out of Star's hand. "My locket!" Stunned, she looked back toward the maple tree, at the crows.

"Really? It's yours?"

"Yes. It's mine."

"Where'd they get it?"

"I kind of lost it."

"You think the crows left that especially for you? The way they left Sophie all those things?"

"Yes." Jesse had saved Sophie's plastic container with the compartments. The one that held all the small gifts the crows had left her. Her most cherished things in the world. Jesse loved them, too, but mostly how the crows befriended her daughter. She had thought about using some of the objects in new artwork. "I recognized that crow. She had an unusual shiny purple spot on its head." Sheryl Crow.

"I saw that, too," Star said.

"I had tossed my locket into the creek months ago. I was angry and upset. Trying to get rid of the past. My mistakes. My grief. But then I was sorry I'd done it. Sophie used to love this locket. She'd play with it while it was around my neck, sliding it back and forth on its chain. I can't believe they returned it to me." She looked at it in her hand then pressed the tiny clasp at the top of it. The locket opened. The two photos were still inside. The serious photo of Sophie taken on the Cape and the one of Jesse and Cooper, smiling with their arms around each other. Both were a little wrinkled and damp but still recognizable. Jesse shook her head in disbelief. She drew her finger over the engraved letters then held the locket to her chest.

"It's amazing," Star said. "It's like they were watching out for you."

"Or someone was."

Jesse stood at the creek's edge, gazing at the water, still stunned at the gift bestowed upon her. She kept looking back up to the tree full of crows. Their chattering and cawing had quieted down to a dull rumble.

Jesse turned the locket over in her hand a few times. Somehow, when the crows left their gifts for Sophie, it seemed right. She'd gained their trust. She couldn't believe the crazy occurrence now and that she was able to share it with Star. Then a single crow shouted from the tree *caw, caw, caw*, over and over as if coaxing her on.

Jesse held the locket out toward Star. "I want you to have this."

"What? No. It's yours. It's special."

"It is special, but I really want you to have it. The crows could have left it for me any time, but they didn't. They waited until you were here with me. I was meant to get it back, but you're meant to have it now. It's from me to you. It's from Sophie to you. You have to accept it. With eternal love." *Forever, right.*

"But you missed it. You said you were sorry you threw it away."

"I was. But now it's important to me that you have it. Please take it. I *really* want you to have it."

Star took the locket out of Jesse's hand and opened it. She looked at the photos then clicked it shut, touching the inscription. "Really?"

Jesse nodded.

Then, one by one, the crows left the tree, flying up and away until just one lone crow remained, its large eyes watching them from a low branch. Jesse and Star stood together, looking out at the sky long after the crows had flown off. The one remaining crow opened its beak and let out a loud, sharp *caw, caw*, then it swooped down and out. They watched until it was gone. Jesse put her arm around Star's waist and tugged her in closer. Star leaned her head against Jesse's shoulder and put her arm around Jesse's waist. No one would have guessed that only moments ago, the backyard was a complete frenzy of noise as the tree exploded with big, loud, chattering crows. If she hadn't known any better, Jesse would have said it was a sign.

Dear Reader,

We hope you enjoyed *Sophie Last Seen*, by Marlene Adelstein. Please consider leaving a review on your favorite book site.

Visit our website (https://RedAdeptPublishing.com) to subscribe to the Red Adept Publishing Newsletter to be notified of future releases.

Acknowledgements

My deepest thanks and appreciation goes to Rachel Gallagher, a comrade in the writer's life whose enduring support and razor-sharp comments on many drafts of this book were invaluable, and to my priceless writers' group: Pat Anderson, Barbara Bash, and Susan Krawitz, who were always there for me whether I was writing or not. They patiently read more drafts than I care to remember and gave fabulous notes plus gentle coaxing and prodding. Not to mention that they also plied me each month with writerly nourishment—both edible and intellectual.

The following people read the book at different stages and provided me with sensitive, insightful critiques: Cheri Magid, Hadley Rierson, Carol Drechsler, Nancy Green Madia, Roz Weisberg, Shira Levin, Alison and Mike Gaylin, Carol McKelvey, Alice Peck, and Nancy Star. Benee Knauer's editorial notes were so helpful. Gratitude goes to Angela Rinaldi for her enduring support and keen notes. Thanks to Peter Golden for his ongoing interest and good advice. And for his years of heartfelt encouragement, thanks to Tom Mark. Java and Honey, my two devoted chocolate labs, were both inspiration for Saint Anthony and invaluable companions through thick and thin.

Special thanks to Yaddo, The Vermont Studio Center, The MacNamara Foundation—thank you, Maureen Barrett—where portions of this book were written during amazing, productive residencies.

A huge thank you to Lynn McNamee at Red Adept Publishing for taking on *Sophie Last Seen*; Jessica Anderegg and Stefanie Spangler Buswell, my editors at RAP, for their incisive, thorough notes that helped make this a better book; Erica Lucke Dean, for her mentorship; and the whole cheering section of Adept authors.

About the Author

After 23 years in New York City, working as a film development executive for top Hollywood producers, Marlene Adelstein began earning her living as a freelance editor working on novels and memoirs.

When she's not reading other people's manuscripts or writing her own, Marlene can be found walking local trails with her dog. She is partial to chocolate labs and in particular hers, a good-natured girl named Honey, who is never more than a few feet behind her. Comfortable and energized in a big city but preferring to make her home in a small town filled with other writers and artists, Marlene lives in the beautiful Hudson Valley where she loves to listen to the noise of the birds.

Read more at www.marleneadelstein.com.

About the Publisher

Dear Reader,

We hope you enjoyed this book. Please consider leaving a review on your favorite book site.

Visit https://RedAdeptPublishing.com to see our entire catalogue.

Don't forget to subscribe to our monthly newsletter to be notified of future releases and special sales.

CPSIA information can be obtained
at www.ICGtesting.com
Printed in the USA
FFHW021248230519
52630658-58122FF

9 781948 051187